THE NOVELS AND TALES OF
HENRY JAMES

New York Edition

VOLUME V

THE PRINCESS CASAMASSIMA

a.c

CASAMASSIMA

VOLUME I

HENRY JAMES

NEW YORK

CHARLES SCRIBNER'S SONS

V. 1

PREFACE

THE simplest account of the origin of "The Princess Casa-massima" is, I think, that this fiction proceeded quite directly, during the first year of a long residence in London, from the habit and the interest of walking the streets. I walked a great deal — for exercise, for amusement, for acquisition, and above all I always walked home at the evening's end, when the evening had been spent elsewhere, as happened more often than not; and as to do this was to receive many impressions, so the impressions worked and sought an issue, so the book after a time was born. It is a fact that, as I look back, the attentive exploration of London, the assault directly made by the great city upon an imagination quick to react, fully explains a large part of it. There is a minor element that refers itself to another source, of which I shall presently speak; but the prime idea was unmistakeably the ripe round fruit of perambulation. One walked of course with one's eyes greatly open, and I hasten to declare that such a practice, carried on for a long time and over a considerable space, positively provokes, all round, a mystic solicitation, the urgent appeal, on the part of everything, to be interpreted and, so far as may be, reproduced. " Subjects " and situations, character and history, the tragedy and comedy of life, are things of which the common air, in such conditions, seems pungently to taste ; and to a mind curious, before the human scene, of meanings and revelations the great grey Babylon easily becomes, on its face, a garden bristling with an immense illustrative flora. Possible stories, presentable figures, rise from the thick jungle as the observer moves, fluttering up like startled game, and before he knows it indeed he has fairly to guard himself against the brush of importunate wings. He goes on as with his head in a cloud of humming presences — especially during the younger, the

PREFACE

initiatory time, the fresh, the sharply-apprehensive months
or years, more or less numerous. We use our material up,
we use up even the thick tribute of the London streets — if
perception and attention but sufficiently light our steps. But
I think of them as lasting, for myself, quite sufficiently long;
I think of them as even still — dreadfully changed for the
worse in respect to any romantic idea as I find them — breaking out on occasion into eloquence, throwing out deep notes
from their vast vague murmur.

There was a moment at any rate when they offered me no
image more vivid than that of some individual sensitive
nature or fine mind, some small obscure intelligent creature
whose education should have been almost wholly derived
from them, capable of profiting by all the civilisation, all
the accumulations to which they testify, yet condemned to
see these things only from outside — in mere quickened
consideration, mere wistfulness and envy and despair. It
seemed to me I had only to imagine such a spirit intent
enough and troubled enough, and to place it in presence of
the comings and goings, the great gregarious company, of the
more fortunate than himself — all on the scale on which
London could show them — to get possession of an interesting theme. I arrived so at the history of little Hyacinth
Robinson — he sprang up for me out of the London pavement. To find his possible adventure interesting I had
only to conceive his watching the same public show, the
same innumerable appearances, I had watched myself, and
of his watching very much as I had watched; save indeed
for one little difference. This difference would be that so
far as all the swarming facts should speak of freedom and
ease, knowledge and power, money, opportunity and satiety,
he should be able to revolve round them but at the most
respectful of distances and with every door of approach
shut in his face. For one's self, all conveniently, there
had been doors that opened — opened into light and warmth
and cheer, into good and charming relations; and if the
place as a whole lay heavy on one's consciousness there
was yet always for relief this implication of one's own lucky

vi

PREFACE

share of the freedom and ease, lucky acquaintance with the number of lurking springs at light pressure of which particular vistas would begin to recede, great lighted, furnished, peopled galleries, sending forth gusts of agreeable sound.

That main happy sense of the picture was always there and that retreat from the general grimness never forbidden; whereby one's own relation to the mere formidable mass and weight of things was eased off and adjusted. One learned from an early period what it might be to know London in such a way as that — an immense and interesting discipline, an education on terms mostly convenient and delightful. But what would be the effect of the other way, of having so many precious things perpetually in one's eyes, yet of missing them all for any closer knowledge, and of the confinement of closer knowledge entirely to matters with which a connexion, however intimate, couldn't possibly pass for a privilege? Truly, of course, there are London mysteries (dense categories of dark arcana) for every spectator, and it's in a degree an exclusion and a state of weakness to be without experience of the meaner conditions, the lower manners and types, the general sordid struggle, the weight of the burden of labour, the ignorance, the misery and the vice. With such matters as those my tormented young man would have had contact — they would have formed, fundamentally, from the first, his natural and immediate London. But the reward of a romantic curiosity would be the question of what the total assault, that of the world of his work-a-day life and the world of his divination and his envy together, would have made of him, and what in especial he would have made of them. As tormented, I say, I thought of him, and that would be the point — if one could only see him feel enough to be interesting without his feeling so much as not to be natural.

This in fact I have ever found rather terribly the point — that the figures in any picture, the agents in any drama, are interesting only in proportion as they feel their respective situations; since the consciousness, on their part, of the complication exhibited forms for us their link of connex-

vii

ion with it. But there are degrees of feeling — the muffled, the faint, the just sufficient, the barely intelligent, as we may say; and the acute, the intense, the complete, in a word — the power to be finely aware and richly responsible. It is those moved in this latter fashion who "get most" out of all that happens to them and who in so doing enable us, as readers of their record, as participators by a fond attention, also to get most. Their being finely aware — as Hamlet and Lear, say, are finely aware — *makes* absolutely the intensity of their adventure, gives the maximum of sense to what befalls them. We care, our curiosity and our sympathy care, comparatively little for what happens to the stupid, the coarse and the blind; care for it, and for the effects of it, at the most as helping to precipitate what happens to the more deeply wondering, to the really sentient. Hamlet and Lear are surrounded, amid their complications, by the stupid and the blind, who minister in all sorts of ways to their recorded fate. Persons of markedly limited sense would, on such a principle as that, play a part in the career of my tormented youth; but he would n't be of markedly limited sense himself — he would note as many things and vibrate to as many occasions as I might venture to make him.

There would n't moreover simply be the question of his suffering — of which we might soon get enough; there would be the question of what, all beset and all perceptive, he should thus adventurously do, thus dream and hazard and attempt. The interest of the attitude and the act would be the actor's imagination and vision of them, together with the nature and degree of their felt return upon him. So the intelligent creature would be required and so some picture of his intelligence involved. The picture of an intelligence appears for the most part, it is true, a dead weight for the reader of the English novel to carry, this reader having so often the wondrous property of caring for the displayed tangle of human relations without caring for its intelligibility. The teller of a story is primarily, none the less, the listener to it, the reader of it, too; and, having

PREFACE

needed thus to make it out, distinctly, on the crabbed page
of life, to disengage it from the rude human character and
the more or less gothic text in which it has been packed
away, the very essence of his affair has been the *imputing*
of intelligence. The basis of his attention has been that such
and such an imbroglio has got started — on the page of life
— because of something that some one has felt and more
or less understood.

I recognise at the same time, and in planning "The
Princess Casamassima" felt it highly important to recognise,
the danger of filling too full any supposed and above all
any obviously limited vessel of consciousness. If persons
either tragically or comically embroiled with life allow us
the comic or tragic value of their embroilment in proportion as their struggle is a measured and directed one, it is
strangely true, none the less, that beyond a certain point
they are spoiled for us by this carrying of a due light.
They may carry too much of it for our credence, for our
compassion, for our derision. They may be shown as knowing too much and feeling too much — not certainly for their
remaining remarkable, but for their remaining "natural"
and typical, for their having the needful communities
with our own precious liability to fall into traps and be
bewildered. It seems probable that if we were never bewildered there would never be a story to tell about us; we
should partake of the superior nature of the all-knowing
immortals whose annals are dreadfully dull so long as flurried
humans are not, for the positive relief of bored Olympians,
mixed up with them. Therefore it is that the wary reader
for the most part warns the novelist against making his
characters too *interpretative* of the muddle of fate, or in
other words too divinely, too priggishly clever. "Give us
plenty of bewilderment," this monitor seems to say, "so
long as there is plenty of slashing out in the bewilderment
too. But don't, we beseech you, give us too much intelligence; for intelligence — well, *endangers;* endangers not
perhaps the slasher himself, but the very slashing, the subject-matter of any self-respecting story. It opens up too

ix

many considerations, possibilities, issues; it *may* lead the slasher into dreary realms where slashing somehow fails and falls to the ground."

That is well reasoned on the part of the reader, who can in spite of it never have an idea — or his earnest discriminations would come to him less easily — of the extreme difficulty, for the painter of the human mixture, of reproducing that mixture aright. " Give us in the persons represented, the subjects of the bewilderment (that bewilderment without which there would be no question of an issue or of the fact of suspense, prime implications in any story) as much experience as possible, but keep down the terms in which you report that experience, because we only understand the very simplest " : such in effect are the words in which the novelist constantly hears himself addressed, such the plea made him by the would-be victims of his spell on behalf of that sovereign principle the economy of interest, a principle as to which their instinct is justly strong. He listens anxiously to the charge — nothing can exceed his own solicitude for an economy of interest; but feels himself all in presence of an abyss of ambiguities, the mutual accommodations in which the reader wholly leaves to him. Experience, as I see it, is our apprehension and our measure of what happens to us as social creatures — any intelligent report of which has to be based on that apprehension. The picture of the exposed and entangled state is what is required, and there are certainly always plenty of grounds for keeping down the complexities of a picture. A picture it still has to be, however, and by that condition has to deal effectually with its subject, so that the simple device of more and more keeping down may well not see us quite to our end or even quite to our middle. One suggested way of keeping down, for instance, is not to attribute feeling, or feelings, to persons who would n't in all probability have had any to speak of. The less space, within the frame of the picture, their feelings take up the more space is left for their doings — a fact that may at first seem to make for a refinement of economy.

All of which is charming — yet would be infinitely more

PREFACE

so if here at once ambiguity did n't yawn; the unreality of
the sharp distinction, where the interest of observation is at
stake, between doing and feeling. In the immediate field
of life, for action, for application, for getting through a job,
nothing may so much matter perhaps as the descent of
a suspended weight on this, that or the other spot, with all
its subjective concomitants quite secondary and irrelevant.
But the affair of the painter is not the immediate, it is the
reflected field of life, the realm not of application, but of
appreciation — a truth that makes our measure of effect
altogether different. My report of people's experience —
my report as a " story-teller " — is essentially my appreciation of it, and there is no " interest " for me in what my
hero, my heroine or any one else does save through that
admirable process. As soon as I begin to appreciate simplification is imperilled: the sharply distinguished parts of
any adventure, any case of endurance and performance,
melt together as an appeal. I then see their " doing," that
of the persons just mentioned, as, immensely, their feeling,
their feeling as their doing; since I can have none of the
conveyed sense and taste of their situation without becoming
intimate with them. I can't be intimate without that sense
and taste, and I can't appreciate save by intimacy, any more
than I can report save by a projected light. Intimacy with
a man's specific behaviour, with his given case, is desperately certain to make us see it as a whole — in which event
arbitrary limitations of our vision lose whatever beauty they
may on occasion have pretended to. What a man thinks
and what he feels are the history and the character of what
he does; on all of which things the logic of intensity rests.
Without intensity where is vividness, and without vividness
where is presentability? If I have called the most general
state of one's most exposed and assaulted figures the state
of bewilderment — the condition for instance on which
Thackeray so much insists in the interest of *his* exhibited
careers, the condition of a humble heart, a bowed head, a
patient wonder, a suspended judgement, before the " awful
will " and the mysterious decrees of Providence — so it is

xi

PREFACE

rather witless to talk of merely getting rid of that displayed mode of reaction, one of the oft-encountered, one of the highly recommended, categories of feeling.

The whole thing comes to depend thus on the *quality* of bewilderment characteristic of one's creature, the quality involved in the given case or supplied by one's data. There are doubtless many such qualities, ranging from vague and crepuscular to sharpest and most critical; and we have but to imagine one of these latter to see how easily — from the moment it gets its head at all — it may insist on playing a part. There we have then at once a case of feeling, of ever so many possible feelings, stretched across the scene like an attached thread on which the pearls of interest are strung. There are threads shorter and less tense, and I am far from implying that the minor, the coarser and less fruitful forms and degrees of moral reaction, as we may conveniently call it, may not yield lively results. They have their subordinate, comparative, illustrative human value — that appeal of the witless which is often so penetrating. Verily even, I think, no "story" is possible without its fools — as most of the fine painters of life, Shakespeare, Cervantes and Balzac, Fielding, Scott, Thackeray, Dickens, George Meredith, George Eliot, Jane Austen, have abundantly felt. At the same time I confess I never see the *leading* interest of any human hazard but in a consciousness (on the part of the moved and moving creature) subject to fine intensification and wide enlargement. It is as mirrored in that consciousness that the gross fools, the headlong fools, the fatal fools play their part for us — they have much less to show us in themselves. The troubled life mostly at the centre of our subject — whatever our subject, for the artistic hour, happens to be — embraces them and deals with them for its amusement and its anguish : they are apt largely indeed, on a near view, to be all the cause of its trouble. This means, exactly, that the person capable of feeling in the given case more than another of what is to be felt for it, and so serving in the highest degree to *record* it dramatically and objectively, is the only sort of person on whom we can count not to betray, to cheapen or, as we say, give away, the value and beauty of the thing. By so much as the affair matters *for* some such individual, by so much do we get the best there is of it, and by so much as it falls within the scope of a denser and duller, a more vulgar and more shallow capacity, do we get a picture dim and meagre.

The great chroniclers have clearly always been aware of this; they have at least always either placed a mind of some sort — in the sense of a reflecting and colouring medium — in possession of the general adventure (when the latter has not been purely epic, as with Scott, say, as with old Dumas and with Zola); or else paid signally, as to the interest created, for their failure to do so. We may note moreover in passing that this failure is in almost no case intentional or part of a plan, but has sprung from their limited curiosity, their short conception of the particular sensibility projected. Edgar of Ravenswood for instance, visited by the tragic tempest of "The Bride of Lammermoor," has a black cloak and hat and feathers more than he has a mind; just as Hamlet, while equally sabled and draped and plumed, while at least equally romantic, has yet a mind still more than he has a costume. The situation represented is that Ravenswood loves Lucy Ashton through dire difficulty and danger, and that she in the same way loves him; but the relation so created between them is by this neglect of the " feeling " question never shown us as primarily taking place. It is shown only in its secondary, its confused and disfigured aspects — where, however, luckily, it is presented with great romantic good faith. The thing has nevertheless paid for its deviation, as I say, by a sacrifice of intensity; the centre of the subject is empty and the development pushed off, all round, toward the frame — which is, so to speak, beautifully rich and curious. But I mention that relation to each other of the appearances in a particular work only as a striking negative case; there are in the connexion I have glanced at plenty of striking positive ones. It is very true that Fielding's hero in " Tom Jones " is but as " finely," that is but as intimately, bewildered as a young man of great health and spirits may be when he hasn't a grain of imagination: the point to be made is, at all events, that his sense of bewilderment obtains altogether on the comic, never on the tragic plane. He has so much "life" that it amounts, for the effect of comedy and application of satire, almost to his having a mind, that is to his having reactions and a full consciousness; besides which his author — *he* handsomely possessed of a mind — has such an amplitude of reflexion for him and round him that we see him through the mellow air of Fielding's fine old moralism, fine old humour and fine old style, which somehow really enlarge, make every one and every thing important.

All of which furthers my remarking how much I have been interested, on reading " The Princess Casamassima " over, to recognise my sense, sharp from far back, that clearness and concreteness constantly depend, for any pictorial whole, on some *concentrated* individual notation of them. That notation goes forward here in the mind of little Hyacinth, immensely quickened by the fact of its so mattering to his very life what he does make of things : which passion of intelligence is, as I have already hinted, precisely his highest value for our curiosity and our sympathy. Yet if his highest it is not at all his only one, since the truth for " a young man in a book " by no means entirely resides in his being either exquisitely sensitive or shiningly clever. It resides in some such measure of these things as may consort with the fine measure of other things too — with that of the other faces of his situation and character. If he's too sensitive and too clever for *them*, if he knows more than is likely or natural — for *him* — it's as if he weren't at all, as if he were false and impossible. Extreme and attaching always the difficulty of fixing at a hundred points the place where one's impelled *bonhomme* may feel enough and " know" enough — or be in the way of learning enough — for his maximum dramatic value without feeling and knowing too much for his minimum verisimilitude, his proper fusion with the fable. This is the charming, the tormenting, the eternal little matter *to be made right*, in all the weaving of silver threads and tapping on golden nails; and I should take perhaps too fantastic a comfort — I mean were not the comforts of the artist just of the raw essence of fantasy — in any glimpse of such achieved rightnesses, whether in my own work or that of others. In no work whatever, doubtless, are they the felicities the most frequent; but they have so inherent a price that even the traceable attempt at them, wherever met, sheds, I think, a fine influence about.

I have for example a weakness of sympathy with that constant effort of George Eliot's which plays through Adam Bede and Felix Holt and Tito Melema, through Daniel Deronda and through Lydgate in " Middlemarch," through Maggie Tulliver, through Romola, through Dorothea Brooke and Gwendolen Harleth; the effort to show their adventures and their history — the author's subject-matter all — as determined by their feelings and the nature of their minds. Their emotions, their stirred intelligence, their moral consciousness, become thus, by sufficiently charmed perusal, our own very adventure. The creator of Deronda and of Romola is charged, I know, with having on occasion — as in dealing with those very celebrities themselves — left the figure, the concrete man and woman, too abstract by reason of the quantity of soul employed; but such mischances, where imagination and humour still keep them company, often have an interest that is wanting to agitations of the mere surface or to those that may be only taken for granted. I should even like to give myself the pleasure of retracing from one of my own productions to another the play of a like instinctive disposition, of catching in the fact, at one point after another, from " Roderick Hudson" to " The Golden Bowl," that provision for interest which consists in placing advantageously, placing right in the middle of the light, the most polished of possible mirrors of the subject. Rowland Mallet, in " Roderick Hudson," is exactly such a mirror, not a bit autobiographic or formally " first person " though he be, and I might exemplify the case through a long list, through the nature of such a "mind" even as the all-objective Newman in " The American," through the thickly-peopled imagination of Isabel Archer in "The Portrait of a Lady" (her imagination positively the deepest depth of her imbroglio) down to such unmistakeable examples as that of Merton Densher in "The Wings of the Dove," that of Lambert Strether in "The Ambassadors" (*he* a mirror verily of miraculous silver and quite pre-eminent, I think, for the connexion) and that of the Prince in the first half and that of the Princess in the second half of "The Golden Bowl." I should note the extent to which these persons are, so far as their other passions permit, intense *perceivers*, all, of their respective predicaments, and I should go on from them to fifty other examples; even to the divided Vanderbank of "The Awkward Age," the extreme pinch of whose romance is the vivacity in him, to his positive sorrow and loss, of the state of being aware; even to scanted Fleda Vetch in "The Spoils of Poynton," through whose own delicate vision of everything so little of the human value of her situation is wasted for us; even to the small recording governess confronted with the horrors of "The Turn of the Screw" and to the innocent child patching together all ineffectually those of "What Maisie Knew"; even in short, since I may name so few cases, to the disaffected guardian of an overgrown legend in "The Birthplace," to the luckless fine artist of "The Next Time," trying to despoil himself, for a "hit" and bread and butter, of his fatal fineness, to blunt the tips of his intellectual fingers, and to the hapless butler Brooksmith, ruined by good talk, disqualified for common domestic service by the beautiful growth of his habit of quiet attention, his faculty of appreciation. But though this demonstration of a rooted vice — since a vice it would appear mainly accounted — might yield amusement, the examples referred to must await their turn.

I had had for a long time well before me, at any rate, my small obscure but ardent observer of the "London world," saw him roam and wonder and yearn, saw all the unanswered questions and baffled passions that might ferment in him — once he should be made both sufficiently thoughtful and sufficiently " disinherited "; but this image, however interesting, was of course not by itself a progression, an action, did n't by itself make a drama. I got my action however — failing which one has nothing — under the prompt sense that the state of feeling I was concerned with might develop and beget another state, might return at a given moment, and with the greatest vivacity, on itself. To see this was really to feel one's subject swim into one's ken, especially after a certain other ingenious connexion had been made for it. I find myself again recalling, and with the possible " fun " of it reviving too, how I recognised, as revealed and prescribed, the particular complexion, profession and other conditions of my little presumptuous adventurer, with his combination of intrinsic fineness and fortuitous adversity, his small cluster of " dingy " London associations and the swelling spirit in him which was to be the field of his strange experience. Accessible through his imagination, as I have hinted, to a thousand provocations and intimations, he would become most acquainted with destiny in the form of a lively inward revolution. His being jealous of all the ease of life of which he tastes so little, and, bitten, under this exasperation, with an aggressive, vindictive, destructive social faith, his turning to " treasons, stratagems and spoils " might be as vivid a picture as one chose, but would move to pity and terror only by the aid of some deeper complication, some imposed and formidable issue.

The complication most interesting then would be that he should fall in love with the beauty of the world, actual order and all, at the moment of his most feeling and most hating the famous " iniquity of its social arrangements "; so that his position as an irreconcileable pledged enemy to it, thus rendered false by something more personal than his opinions and his vows, becomes the sharpest of his torments. To make it a torment that really matters, however, he must have got practically involved, specifically committed to the stand he has, under the pressure of more knowledge, found impossible ; out of which has come for him the deep dilemma of the disillusioned and repentant conspirator. He has

PREFACE

thrown himself into the more than " shady " underworld of militant socialism, he has undertaken to play a part — a part that with the drop of his exasperation and the growth, simply expressed, of his taste, is out of all tune with his passion, at any cost, for life itself, the life, whatever it be, that surrounds him. Dabbling deeply in revolutionary politics of a hole-and-corner sort, he would be " in " up to his neck, and with that precarious part of him particularly involved, so that his tergiversation is the climax of his adventure. What was essential with this was that he should have a social — not less than a socialist — connexion, find a door somehow open to him into the appeased and civilised state, into that warmer glow of things he is precisely to help to undermine. To look for this necessary connexion was for me to meet it suddenly in the form of that extremely *disponible* figure of Christina Light whom I had ten years before found left on my hands at the conclusion of " Roderick Hudson." She had for so long, in the vague limbo of those ghosts we have conjured but not exorcised, been looking for a situation, awaiting a niche and a function.

I shall not pretend to trace the steps and stages by which the imputability of a future to that young woman — which was like the act of clothing her chilled and patient nakedness — had for its prime effect to plant her *in* my little bookbinder's path. Nothing would doubtless beckon us on further, with a large leisure, than such a chance to study the obscure law under which certain of a novelist's characters, more or less honourably buried, revive for him by a force or a whim of their own and " walk " round his house of art like haunting ghosts, feeling for the old doors they knew, fumbling at stiff latches and pressing their pale faces, in the outer dark, to lighted windows. I mistrust them, I confess, in general; my sense of a really expressed character is that it shall have originally so tasted of the ordeal of service as to feel no disposition to yield again to the strain. Why should the Princess of the climax of " Roderick Hudson " still have made her desire felt, unless in fact to testify that she had not been — for what she was — completely recorded ?

xviii

PREFACE

To continue in evidence, that had struck me from far back
as her natural passion; in evidence at any price, not consenting to be laid away with folded hands in the pasteboard
tomb, the doll's box, to which we usually relegate the spent
puppet after the fashion of a recumbent worthy on the slab
of a sepulchral monument. I was to see this, after all, in
the event, as the fruit of a restless vanity : Christina had felt
herself, known herself, striking, in the earlier connexion,
and could n't resign herself not to strike again. Her pressure then was not to be resisted — sharply as the question
might come up of why she should pretend to strike just
there. I shall not attempt to answer it with reasons (one can
never tell everything); it was enough that I could recognise
her claim to have travelled far — far from where I had last
left her : that, one felt, was in character — that was what
she naturally *would* have done. Her prime note had been
an aversion to the *banal*, and nothing could be of an effect
less *banal*, I judged, than her intervention in the life of a
dingy little London bookbinder whose sensibility, whose
flow of opinions on " public questions " in especial, should
have been poisoned at the source.

She would be world-weary — that was another of her
notes; and the extravagance of her attitude in these new
relations would have its root and its apparent logic in her
need to feel freshly about something or other — it might
scarce matter what. She can, or she believes she can, feel
freshly about the " people " and their wrongs and their
sorrows and their perpetual smothered ferment ; for these
things are furthest removed from those others among which
she has hitherto tried to make her life. That was to a cer-
tainty where I was to have looked for her — quite *off* and
away (once granted the wisdom of listening to her anew
at all) : therefore Hyacinth's encounter with her could pass
for natural, and it was fortunately to be noted that she was
to serve for his experience in quite another and a more
" leading " sense than any in which he was to serve for
hers. I confess I was not averse — such are the possible
weaknesses of the artist in face of high difficulties — to

xix

PREFACE

feeling that if his appearance of consistency were obtained
I might at least try to remain comparatively at my ease
about hers. I may add moreover that the resuscitation of
Christina (and, on the minor scale, of the Prince and of
Madame Grandoni) put in a strong light for me the whole
question, for the romancer, of "going on with a character":
as Balzac first of all systematically went on, as Thackeray,
as Trollope, as Zola all more or less ingeniously went on.
I was to find no small savour in the reflexions so precipi-
tated; though I may treat myself here only to this remark
about them — that the revivalist impulse on the fond
writer's part strikes me as one thing, a charmingly conceivable thing, but the effect of a free indulgence in it (effect,
that is, on the nerves of the reader) as, for twenty rather
ineffable reasons, quite another.

I remember at any rate feeling myself all in possession
of little Hyacinth's consistency, as I have called it, down at
Dover during certain weeks that were none too remotely
precedent to the autumn of 1885 and the appearance, in
the "Atlantic Monthly" again, of the first chapters of the
story. There were certain sunny, breezy balconied rooms at
the quieter end of the Esplanade of that cheerful castle-
crested little town — now infinitely perturbed by gigantic
"harbour works," but then only faded and over-soldiered
and all pleasantly and humbly submissive to the law that
snubs in due course the presumption of flourishing resorts
— to which I had already more than once had recourse in
hours of quickened industry and which, though much else
has been swept away, still archaically exist. To have lately
noted this again from the old benched and asphalted walk by
the sea, the twinkling Channel beyond which on occasion
the opposite coast of France used to gleam as an incident
of the charming tendency of the whole prospect (immediate
picture and fond design alike) amusingly to *shine*, was somehow to taste afresh, and with a certain surprise, the odd
quality of that original confidence that the parts of my plan
would somehow hang together. I may wonder at my confidence now — given the extreme, the very particular truth

and " authority " required at so many points; but to wonder is to live back gratefully into the finer reasons of things,
with all the detail of harsh application and friction (that
there must have been) quite happily blurred and dim. The
finest of reasons — I mean for the sublime confidence I
speak of — was that I felt in full *personal* possession of my
matter; this really seemed the fruit of direct experience.
My scheme called for the suggested nearness (to all our
apparently ordered life) of some sinister anarchic underworld,
heaving in its pain, its power and its hate; a presentation
not of sharp particulars, but of loose appearances, vague
motions and sounds and symptoms, just perceptible presences and general looming possibilities. To have adopted
the scheme was to have had to meet the question of one's
" notes," over the whole ground, the question of what, in
such directions, one had " gone into " and how far one had
gone; and to have answered that question — to one's own
satisfaction at least — was truly to see one's way.

My notes then, on the much-mixed world of my hero's
both overt and covert consciousness, were exactly my gathered impressions and stirred perceptions, the deposit in my
working imagination of all my visual and all my constructive
sense of London. The very plan of my book had in fact
directly confronted me with the rich principle of the Note,
and was to do much to clear up, once for all, my practical
view of it. If one was to undertake to tell tales and to
report with truth on the human scene, it could be but
because " notes " had been from the cradle the ineluctable
consequence of one's greatest inward energy : to take them
was as natural as to look, to think, to feel, to recognise, to
remember, as to perform any act of understanding. The
play of the energy had been continuous and could n't change ;
what changed was only the objects and situations pressing
the spring of it. Notes had been in other words the things
one could n't *not* take, and the prime result of all fresh
experience was to remind one of that. I have endeavoured
to characterise the peremptory fashion in which my fresh experience of London — the London of the habitual observer,

the preoccupied painter, the pedestrian prowler — reminded me ; an admonition that represented, I think, the sum of my investigations. I recall pulling no wires, knocking at no closed doors, applying for no " authentic " information ; but I recall also on the other hand the practice of never missing an opportunity to add a drop, however small, to the bucket of my impressions or to renew my sense of being able to dip into it. To haunt the great city and by this habit to penetrate it, imaginatively, in as many places as possible — *that* was to be informed, *that* was to pull wires, *that* was to open doors, *that* positively was to groan at times under the weight of one's accumulations.

Face to face with the idea of Hyacinth's subterraneous politics and occult affiliations, I recollect perfectly feeling, in short, that I might well be ashamed if, with my advant- ages — and there was n't a street, a corner, an hour, of London that was not an advantage — I should n't be able to piece together a proper semblance of those things, as indeed a proper semblance of all the odd parts of his life. There was always of course the chance that the propriety might be challenged — challenged by readers of a know- ledge greater than mine. Yet knowledge, after all, of what? My vision of the aspects I more or less fortunately rendered *was*, exactly, my knowledge. If I made my appearances live, what was this but the utmost one could do with them ? Let me at the same time not deny that, in answer to probable ironic reflexions on the full licence for sketchi- ness and vagueness and dimness taken indeed by my picture, I had to bethink myself in advance of a defence of my " artistic position." Should n't I find it in the happy con- tention that the value I wished most to render and the effect I wished most to produce were precisely those of our not knowing, of society's not knowing, but only guessing and suspecting and trying to ignore, what " goes on " irre- concileably, subversively, beneath the vast smug surface ? I could n't deal with that positive quantity for itself — my subject had another too exacting side ; but I might perhaps show the social ear as on occasion applied to the ground,

PREFACE

or catch some gust of the hot breath that I had at many an hour seemed to see escape and hover. What it all came back to was, no doubt, something like *this* wisdom — that if you have n't, for fiction, the root of the matter in you, have n't the sense of life and the penetrating imagination, you are a fool in the very presence of the revealed and assured; but that if you *are* so armed you are not really helpless, not without your resource, even before mysteries abysmal.

HENRY JAMES.

THE PRINCESS CASAMASSIMA

VOLUME I

BOOK FIRST

THE PRINCESS CASAMASSIMA

I

"Oh yes, I dare say I can find the child, if you would like to see him," Miss Pynsent said; she had a fluttered wish to assent to every suggestion made by her visitor, whom she regarded as a high and rather terrible personage. To look for the little boy she came out of her small parlour, which she had been ashamed to exhibit in so untidy a state, with paper "patterns" lying about on the furniture and snippings of stuff scattered over the carpet — she came out of this somewhat stuffy sanctuary, dedicated at once to social intercourse and to the ingenious art to which her life had been devoted, and, opening the house-door, turned her eyes up and down the little street. It would presently be tea-time, and she knew that at that solemn hour Hyacinth narrowed the circle of his wanderings. She was anxious and impatient and in a fever of excitement and complacency, not wanting to keep Mrs. Bowerbank waiting, though she sat there, heavily and consideringly, as if she meant to stay; and wondering not a little whether the object of her quest would have a dirty face. Mrs. Bowerbank had intimated so definitely that she thought it remarkable on Miss Pynsent's part to have taken care of him gratuitously for so many years, that the humble dressmaker, whose

3

imagination took flights about every one but herself and who had never been conscious of an exemplary benevolence, suddenly aspired to appear, throughout, as devoted to the child as she had struck her large, grave guest as being, and felt how much she should like him to come in fresh and frank and looking as pretty as he sometimes did. Miss Pynsent, who blinked confusedly as she surveyed the outer prospect, was very much flushed, partly with the agitation of what Mrs. Bowerbank had told her and partly because, when she offered that lady a drop of refreshment at the end of so long an expedition, she had said she could n't think of touching anything unless Miss Pynsent would keep her company. The "cheffoneer," as Amanda was always careful to call it, yielded up a small bottle which, formerly containing eau-de-cologne, now exhibited half a pint of a rich gold-coloured liquid. Miss Pynsent was very delicate; she lived on tea and watercress and kept the little bottle in the cheffoneer only for great emergencies. She did n't like hot brandy and water with a lump or two of sugar, but she partook of half a tumbler on the present occasion, which was of a highly exceptional kind. At this time of day the boy was often planted in front of the little sweet-shop on the other side of the street, an establishment where periodical literature, as well as tough toffy and hard lollipops, was dispensed and where song-books and pictorial sheets were attractively exhibited in the small-paned dirty window. He used to stand there for half an hour at a time and spell out the first page of the romances in the *Family Herald* and the

London Journal, where he particularly admired the obligatory illustration in which the noble characters (they were always of the highest birth) were presented to the carnal eye. When he had a penny he spent only a fraction of it on stale sugar-candy; for the remaining halfpenny he always bought a ballad with a vivid woodcut at the top. Now, however, he was not at his post of contemplation, nor was he visible anywhere to Miss Pynsent's impatient glance.

"Millicent 'Enning, tell me quickly, have you seen my child?" These words were addressed by Miss Pynsent to a little girl who sat on the doorstep of the adjacent house nursing a dingy doll and whose extraordinary luxuriance of dark brown hair was surmounted by a torn straw hat.

The child looked up from her dandling and patting and, after a stare of which the blankness was visibly overdone, replied: "Law no, Miss Pynsent, I never see him."

"Are n't you always messing about with him, you naughty little girl?" the dressmaker returned with sharpness. "Is n't he round the corner, playing marbles or — or some jumping game?" Miss Pynsent went on, trying to be suggestive.

"I assure *you* he never plays nothing," said Millicent Henning with a mature manner which she bore out by adding: "And I don't know why I should be called naughty, neither."

"Well, if you want to be called good please go find him and tell him there's a lady come here on purpose to see him this very instant." Miss Pynsent waited a moment to see if her injunction would be obeyed, but she got no satisfaction beyond another gaze of deliberation, which made her feel that the child's perversity was as great as the beauty, somewhat soiled and dimmed, of her insolent little face. She turned back into the house with an exclamation of despair, and as soon as she had disappeared Millicent Henning sprang erect and began to race down the street in the direction of another, which crossed it. I take no unfair advantage of the innocence of childhood in saying that the motive of this young lady's flight was not a desire to be agreeable to Miss Pynsent, but an extreme curiosity on the subject of the visitor who wanted to see Hyacinth Robinson. She wished to participate, if only in imagination, in the interview that might take place, and she was moved also by a quick revival of friendly feeling for the boy, from whom she had parted only half an hour before with considerable asperity. She was not a very clinging little creature, and there was no one in her own domestic circle to whom she was much attached; but she liked to kiss Hyacinth when he did n't push her away and tell her she was hateful. It was in this action and epithet he had indulged half an hour ago; but she had reflected rapidly (while she made play with Miss Pynsent) that it was the worst he had ever done. Millicent Henning was only eight years of age, but she knew there was worse in the world than that.

Mrs. Bowerbank, in a leisurely, roundabout way, wandered off to her sister, Mrs. Chipperfield, whom she had come into that part of the world to see, and the whole history of the dropsical tendencies of whose

6

husband, an undertaker with a business that had been a blessing because you could always count on it, she unfolded to Miss Pynsent between the sips of a second glass. She was a high-shouldered, towering woman, and suggested squareness as well as a pervasion of the upper air, so that Amanda reflected that she must be very difficult to fit, and had a sinking at the idea of the number of pins she would take. Her sister had nine children and she herself had seven, the eldest of whom she left in charge of the others when she went to her service. She was on duty at the prison only during the day; she had to be there at seven in the morning, but she got her evenings at home, quite regular and comfortable. Miss Pynsent thought it wonderful she could talk of comfort in such a life as that, but could easily imagine she should be glad to get away at night, for at that time the place must be much more terrible.

"And are n't you frightened of them — ever ?" she enquired, looking up at her visitor with her little heated face.

Mrs. Bowerbank, who was very slow, considered her so long before replying that she felt herself to be, to an alarming degree, in the eye of the law; for who could be more closely connected with the administration of justice than a female turnkey, especially so big and majestic a one ? "I expect they're more frightened of me," she declared at last; and it was an idea into which Miss Pynsent could easily enter.

"And at night I suppose they rave quite awful," the little dressmaker suggested, feeling vaguely that prisons and madhouses came very much to the same.

"Well, if they do we hush 'em up," Mrs. Bower-bank remarked rather portentously; while Miss Pynsent fidgeted to the door again, without results, to see if the child had become visible. She observed to her guest that she could n't call it anything but contrary that he should n't turn up when he knew so well, most days in the week, when his tea was ready. To which Mrs. Bowerbank rejoined, fixing her companion again with the steady orb of justice: "And do he have his tea that way by himself, like a real little gentleman?"

"Well, I try to give it to him tidy-like, at a suitable hour," said Miss Pynsent guiltily. "And there might be some who would say that, for the matter of that, he *is* a real little gentleman," she added with an effort at mitigation which, as she immediately became conscious, only involved her more deeply.

"There are people silly enough to say anything. If it's your parents that settle your station the child has n't much to be thankful for," Mrs. Bowerbank went on in the manner of a woman accustomed to looking facts in the face.

Miss Pynsent was very timid, but she adored the aristocracy, and there were elements in the boy's life which she was not prepared to sacrifice even to a person who represented such a possibility of grating bolts and clanking chains. "I suppose we ought n't to forget that his father was very high," she suggested appealingly and with a tight clasp of her hands in her lap.

"His father? Who knows who *he* was? He does n't set up for having a father, does he?"

"But, surely, was n't it proved that Lord Frederick — ?"

"My dear woman, nothing was proved except that she stabbed his lordship in the back with a very long knife, that he died of the blow, and that she got the full sentence. What does such a piece as that know about fathers? The less said about the poor child's ancestors the better!"

This view of the case caused Miss Pynsent fairly to gasp, for it pushed over with a touch a tall fond fantastic structure that she had been piling up for years. Even as she heard it crash around her she could n't forbear the attempt to save at least some of the material. "Really — really," she panted, "she never had to do with any one but the nobility!"

Mrs. Bowerbank surveyed her hostess with an expressionless eye. "My dear young lady, what does a respectable little body like you, that sits all day with her needle and scissors, know about the doings of a wicked low foreigner of the sort that carries a knife? I was there when she came in and I know to what she had sunk. Her conversation was choice, I assure you."

"Oh, it's very dreadful, and of course I know nothing in particular," Miss Pynsent quavered. "But she was n't low when I worked at the same place with her, and she often told me she would do nothing for any one that was n't at the very top."

"She might have talked to you of something that would have done you both more good," Mrs. Bowerbank remarked, while the dressmaker felt rebuked in the past as well as in the present. "At the very top, —

poor thing! Well, she's at the very bottom now. If she was n't low when she worked, it's a pity she did n't stick to her work; and as for pride of birth, that's an article I recommend your young friend to leave to others. You had better believe what I say, because I'm a woman of the world."

Indeed she was, as Miss Pynsent felt, to whom all this was very terrible, letting in the cold light of the penal system on a dear, dim little theory. She had cared for the child because maternity was in her nature and this was the only manner in which fortune had put it in her path to become a mother. She had had herself as few belongings as the desolate baby, and it had seemed to her he would add to her importance in the little world of Lomax Place (if she kept it a secret how she came by him) quite in the proportion in which she should contribute to his maintenance. Her own isolation went out to his, and in the course of time their associated solitude was peopled by the dressmaker's romantic mind with a hundred consoling evocations. The boy proved neither a dunce nor a reprobate; but what endeared him to her most was her conviction that he belonged, "by the left hand," as she had read in a novel, to a proud and ancient race, the list of whose representatives and the record of whose alliances she had once (when she took home some work and was made to wait, alone, in a lady's boudoir) had the opportunity of reading in a fat red book, eagerly and tremblingly consulted. She bent her head before Mrs. Bowerbank's overwhelming logic, but she felt in her heart that she should n't give the child up for mere words she could n't answer —

10

of course she could n't answer them — that she believed in him still, and that she recognised as distinctly as she revered the quality of her betters. To believe in Hyacinth, for Miss Pynsent, was to believe that he *was* the son of the extremely immoral Lord Frederick. She had from his earliest age made him feel that there was a grandeur in his past, and as Mrs. Bowerbank would be sure not to approve of such aberrations she prayed she might not be questioned on that part of the business. It was not that when it was necessary the little dressmaker had any scruple about using the arts of prevarication; she was a kind and innocent creature, but she told fibs as freely as she applied trimmings. She had, however, not yet been questioned by an emissary of the law, and her heart beat faster when Mrs. Bowerbank said to her in deep tones, with an effect of abruptness: "And pray, Miss Pynsent, does the innocent child know it ?"

"Know about Lord Frederick ?" Miss Pynsent palpitated.

"Bother Lord Frederick! Know about his mother."

"Oh, I can't say that. I 've never told him."

"But has any one else told him ?"

To this enquiry Miss Pynsent's answer was more prompt and more proud; it was with an agreeable sense of having conducted herself with extraordinary wisdom and propriety that she replied: "How could any one know ? I 've never breathed it to a creature!"

Mrs. Bowerbank gave utterance to no commendation; she only put down her empty glass and wiped her large mouth with much thoroughness and judgement. Then she said, as if it were as cheerful an idea as, in the premises, she was capable of expressing: "Ah, well, there'll be plenty later on to give him all information!"

"I pray God he may live and die without knowing it!" Miss Pynsent cried with intensity.

Her companion gazed at her with a kind of professional patience. "You don't keep your ideas together. How can he go to her then, if he's never to know?"

"Oh, did you mean she'd tell him?" Miss Pynsent plaintively gasped.

"Tell him! He won't need to be told, once she gets hold of him and gives him — what she mentioned to me."

"What she mentioned — ?" Miss Pynsent repeated, open-eyed.

"The kiss her lips have been famished for all these years."

"Ah, poor desolate woman!" the little dressmaker murmured while her pity gushed up again. "Of course he'll see she's fond of him," she pursued simply. Then she added with an inspiration more brilliant: "We might tell him she's his aunt!"

"You may tell him she's his grandmother if you like. But it's all in the family."

"Yes, on that side," said Miss Pynsent musingly and irrepressibly. "And will she speak that fluent French?" she enquired as from a full mind. "In that case he won't understand."

"Oh, a child will understand its own mother, whatever she speaks," Mrs. Bowerbank returned, declining to administer a superficial comfort. But she subjoined, opening the door for escape from a prospect which bristled with dangers: "Of course it's just according to your own idea. You need n't bring the child at all unless you like. There's many a one that would n't. There's no compulsion."

"And would nothing be done to me if I did n't?" poor Miss Pynsent asked, unable to rid herself of the impression that it was somehow the arm of the law that was stretched out to touch her.

"The only thing that could happen to you would be that *he* might throw it up against you later," the lady from the prison observed with a gloomy breadth of view.

"Yes indeed, if he were to know that I had kept him back."

"Oh, he'd be sure to know, one of these days. We see a great deal of that — the way things come out," said Mrs. Bowerbank, whose outlook appeared to abound in cheerless contingencies. "You must remember that it's her dying wish and that you may have it on your conscience."

"That's a thing I *never* could abide!" the little dressmaker exclaimed with great emphasis and a visible shiver; after which she picked up various scattered remnants of muslin and cut paper and began to roll them together with a desperate and mechanical haste. "It's quite awful, to know what to do — if you're very sure she *is* dying."

"Do you mean she's shamming? We've plenty of that — but we know how to treat 'em."

"Lord, I suppose so," murmured Miss Pynsent; while her visitor went on to say that the unfortunate person on whose behalf she had undertaken this solemn pilgrimage might live a week and might live a fortnight, but if she lived a month would violate (as Mrs. Bowerbank might express herself) every established law of nature, being reduced to skin and bone and with nothing left of her but the main desire to see her child.

"If you're afraid of her talking, it isn't much she'd be able to say. And we shouldn't allow you more than about eight minutes," Mrs. Bowerbank pursued in a tone that seemed to refer itself to an iron discipline.

"I'm sure I shouldn't want more; that would be enough to last me many a year," said Miss Pynsent accommodatingly. And then she added with another illumination: "Don't you think he might throw it up against me that I *did* take him? People might tell him about her in later years; but if he hadn't seen her he wouldn't be obliged to believe them."

Mrs. Bowerbank considered this a moment as if it were rather an intricate argument, and then answered quite in the spirit of her official pessimism. "There's one thing you may be sure of: whatever you decide to do, as soon as ever he grows up he'll make you wish you had done the opposite." Mrs. Bowerbank called it oppo*site*.

"Oh dear then, I'm glad it will be a long time."

"It will be ever so long, if once he gets it into his head! At any rate you must do as you think best. Only if you come you mustn't come when it's all over."

"It's too impossible to decide."

14

"It is indeed," said Mrs. Bowerbank with superior consistency. And she seemed more placidly grim than ever when she remarked, gathering up her loosened shawl, that she was much obliged to Miss Pynsent for her civility and had been quite freshened up: her visit had so completely deprived her hostess of that sort of calm. Miss Pynsent gave the fullest expression to her perplexity in the supreme exclamation:

"If you could only wait and see the child I'm sure it would help you to judge!"

"My dear woman, I don't want to judge — it's none of our business!" Mrs. Bowerbank exclaimed; and she had no sooner uttered the words than the door of the room creaked open and a small boy stood there gazing at her. Her eyes rested on him a moment, and then, most unexpectedly, she gave an inconsequent cry. "Is that the child? Oh, Lord o' mercy, don't take *him!*"

"Now *ain't* he shrinking and sensitive?" demanded Miss Pynsent, who had pounced upon him and, holding him an instant at arm's length, appealed eagerly to her visitor. "Ain't he delicate and high-bred, and would n't he be thrown into a state?" Delicate as he might be the little dressmaker shook him smartly for his naughtiness in being out of the way when he was wanted, and brought him to the big square-faced, deep-voiced lady who took up, as it were, all that side of the room. But Mrs. Bowerbank laid no hand upon him; she only dropped her gaze from a tremendous height, and her forbearance seemed a tribute to that fragility of constitution on which Miss Pynsent desired to insist, just as her continued gravity was an implication that this scrupulous woman might well not know what to do. "Speak to the lady nicely and tell her you're very sorry to have kept her waiting."

The child hesitated while he repaid with interest Mrs. Bowerbank's inspection, and then he said with a cool, conscious indifference which Miss Pynsent instantly recognised as his aristocratic manner: "I don't think she can have been in a very great hurry."

There was irony in the words, for it is a remarkable fact that even at the age of ten Hyacinth Robinson was ironic; but the subject of his allusion, who was not nimble withal, appeared not to interpret it; so that she met it only by remarking over his head to Miss Pynsent: "It's the very face of her again — only for the complexion!"

"Of *her*? But what do you say to Lord Frederick?"

"I *have* seen lords that was n't so dainty!"

Miss Pynsent had seen very few lords, but she entered with a passionate thrill into this generalisation; controlling herself, however, for she remembered the child was tremendously sharp, sufficiently to declare in an edifying tone that he would look more like what he ought to if his face were a little cleaner.

"It was probably Millicent Henning dirtied my face when she kissed me," the boy announced with slow gravity, looking all the while at Mrs. Bowerbank. He exhibited not a symptom of shyness.

"Millicent 'Enning's a very bad little girl; she'll come to no good," said Miss Pynsent with familiar decision and also, considering the young lady in question had been her effective messenger, with marked ingratitude.

Against this qualification the child instantly protested. "Why is she bad? I don't think she's bad; I like her awfully." It came over him that he had too hastily shifted to her shoulders the responsibility of his unseemly appearance, and he wished to make up to her for this betrayal. He dimly felt that nothing but that particular accusation could have pushed him to it, for he hated people with too few fair interspaces, too many smutches and streaks. Millicent Henning generally had two or three of these at least, which she borrowed from her doll, into whom she was always rubbing her nose and whose dinginess was contagious. It was quite inevitable she should have left her mark under his own nose when she claimed her reward for coming to tell him about the lady who wanted him.

Miss Pynsent held the boy against her knee, trying to present him so that Mrs. Bowerbank should agree with her about his having the air of race. He was exceedingly diminutive, even for his years, and though his appearance was not so sickly as to excite remark, it seemed written in his attenuated little person that he would never be either tall or positively hard. His dark blue eyes were separated by a wide interval, which increased the fairness and sweetness of his face, and his abundant curly hair, which grew thick and long, had the golden brownness predestined to elicit exclamations of delight from ladies when they take the inventory of a child. His features were formed and distributed; his head was set on a slim, straight neck; his expression, grave and clear, showed a quick perception as well as a great credulity; and he was altogether, in his tender fineness, an interesting, an appealing little person.

"Yes, he's one that would be sure to remember," said Mrs. Bowerbank, mentally contrasting him with the undeveloped members of her own brood, who had never been retentive of anything but the halfpence which they occasionally contrived to filch from her. Her eyes descended to the details of his dress: the careful mending of his short breeches and his long, coloured stockings, which she was in a position to appreciate, as well as the knot of bright ribbon which the dressmaker had passed into his collar, slightly crumpled by Miss Henning's embrace. Of course Miss Pynsent had only one to look after, but her visitor was obliged to recognise that she had the highest standard in respect to buttons. "And you *do* turn him out so it's a pleasure," she went on, noting the ingenious patches in the child's shoes, which, to her mind, were repaired for all the world like those of a little nobleman.

"I'm sure you're very civil," said Miss Pynsent, in a state of severe exaltation. "There's never a needle but mine has come near him. That's exactly what I think: the impression would go so deep."

"Do you want to see me only to look at me?" Hyacinth enquired with a candour which, though unstudied, had again much satiric force.

"I'm sure it's very kind of the lady to notice you at all!" cried his protectress, giving him an ineffectual jerk. "You're no bigger than a flea; there are many that would n't know you from one, and not one of them 'performing' ones either."

"You'll find he's big enough, I expect, when he begins to go," Mrs. Bowerbank remarked tranquilly; and she added that now she saw how he was done for she could n't but feel the other side was to be considered. In her effort to be discreet by reason of his being present (and so precociously attentive) she became slightly enigmatical; but Miss Pynsent gathered her meaning, which was that it was very true the child would take everything in and keep it, yet that at the same time it was precisely his being so attractive that made it a kind of sin not to gratify the poor woman, who, if she knew what he looked like to-day, would n't forgive the person who had stepped into her place for not producing him. "Certainly, in her position, I should go off easier if I had seen them curls," Mrs. Bowerbank declared with a flight of maternal imagination which brought her to her feet; while Miss Pynsent felt she was leaving her dreadfully ploughed up and without any really fertilising seed sown. The little dressmaker packed the child upstairs to tidy himself for his tea, and as she accompanied her visitor to the door pleaded that if the latter would have a little more patience she would think a day or two longer what was best and write when she should have decided. Mrs. Bowerbank continued to move in a realm superior to poor Miss Pynsent's vacillations and timidities, and her detachment gave her hostess a high idea of her respectability; but the way was a little smoothed when, after Amanda had moaned once more, on the threshold, helplessly and irrelevantly, "Ain't it a pity she's so bad?" the ponderous lady from the prison rejoined in those tones which seemed meant to resound through corridors of stone: "I assure you there's a many that's ever so much worse!"

II

Miss Pynsent, when she found herself alone, felt she was really quite upside down; for this lurid crisis had never entered into her calculations: the very nature of the case had seemed to preclude it. All she had known or had wished to know was that in one of the dreadful establishments constructed for such purposes her quondam comrade was serving out the sentence that had been substituted for the other (the unspeakable horror) almost when the halter was already round her neck. As there had been no question of *that* concession's being stretched any further, poor Florentine had seemed only a little more dead than other people, having no decent tombstone to mark the place where she lay. Miss Pynsent had therefore never thought of her dying again; she had had no idea to what prison she was committed on removal from Newgate (she had wished to keep her mind a blank about the matter in the interest of the child), and it could n't occur to her that out of such silence and darkness a second voice would reach her, especially a voice she should really have to listen to. Miss Pynsent would have said, before Mrs. Bowerbank's visit, that she had no account to render to any one; that she had taken up the child (who might have starved in the gutter) out of charity, and had brought him on, poor and precarious though her own subsistence, without a penny's help from another source;

that the mother had forfeited every right and title; and that this had been understood between them — if anything in so dreadful an hour could have been said to be understood — when she had gone to see her at Newgate (that terrible episode, nine years before, still overshadowed all Miss Pynsent's other memories): had gone to see her because Florentine had sent for her (a name, face and address coming up out of the still recent but sharply separated past of their working-girl years) as the one friend to whom she could appeal with some chance of a pitying answer. The effect of violent emotion with Miss Pynsent was not to make her sit with idle hands or fidget about to no purpose; under its influence, on the contrary, she threw herself into little jobs as a fugitive takes to by-paths, and clipped and cut and stitched and basted as if to run a race with hysterics. And while her hands, her scissors, her needle flew an infinite succession of fantastic possibilities trotted through her confused little head: she had a furious imagination, and the act of reflexion, in her mind, was always a panorama of figures and scenes. She had had her picture of the future, painted in rather rosy hues, hung up before her now for a good many years; but it struck her that Mrs. Bowerbank's heavy hand had suddenly punched a hole in the canvas. It must be added, however, that if Amanda's thoughts were apt to be bewildering visions they sometimes led her to make up her mind, and on this particular September evening she arrived at a momentous decision. What she made up her mind to was to take advice, and in pursuance of this view she rushed downstairs and, jerking Hyacinth

away from his simple but unfinished repast, packed
him across the street to tell Mr. Vetch (if he had not
yet started for the theatre) that she begged he would
come in to see her when he came home that night, as
she had something very particular indeed to say to
him. It did n't matter if he should be very late, he
could come in at any hour — he would see her light
in the window — and he would do her no end of
good. Miss Pynsent knew it was no use for her to go
to bed; she felt as if she should never close her eyes
again. Mr. Vetch was her most distinguished friend;
she had an immense appreciation of his cleverness
and knowledge of the world, as well as of the purity
of his taste in matters of conduct and opinion; and
she had already consulted him about Hyacinth's education. The boy needed no urging to go on such an
errand, for he too had his ideas about the little fiddler,
the second violin in the orchestra of the Bloomsbury
Theatre. Mr. Vetch had on a great occasion, within
the year, obtained for the pair an order for two seats
at a pantomime, and to Hyacinth the impression of
that ecstatic evening had consecrated him, placed him
for ever in the golden glow of the footlights. There
were things in life of which, even at the age of ten, it
was a conviction of the boy's that it would be his fate
never to see enough, and one of these was the wonder-
world illuminated by those playhouse lamps. But
there would be chances perhaps if one did n't lose
sight of Mr. Vetch: he might open the door again —
he was a privileged, magical mortal who went to the
play every night.

He came in to see Miss Pynsent about midnight;

as soon as she heard the lame tinkle of the bell she went to the door and let him in. He was an original, in the fullest sense of the word: a lonely, disappointed, embittered, cynical little man, whose musical organisation had been sterile, who had the nerves and sensibilities of a gentleman, yet whose fate had condemned him for the last ten years to play a fiddle at a second-rate establishment for a few shillings a week. He had ideas of his own about everything, and they were not always very improving. For Amanda Pynsent he represented art, literature (the literature of the play-bill) and philosophy, so that she always felt about him as if he belonged to a higher social sphere, though his earnings were hardly greater than her own and he occupied a single back room in a house where she had never seen a window washed. He had for her the glamour of reduced gentility and fallen fortunes; she was conscious that he spoke a different language (though she could n't have said in what, unless in more wicked words as well as more grand ones, the difference consisted) from the other members of her humble, almost suburban circle; and the shape of his hands was distinctly aristocratic. (Miss Pynsent, as I have intimated, was immensely preoccupied with that element in life.) Mr. Vetch displeased her only by one of the aspects of his character — his blasphemous republican, radical views and the licentious manner in which he expressed himself about the nobility. On that ground he worried her extremely, though he never seemed to her so probably well-connected, like Hyacinth himself, as when he horrified her most. These dreadful theories (expressed so

brilliantly that really they might have been dangerous if Miss Pynsent had not been so grounded in the
Christian faith and known thereby her own place so
well) constituted no presumption against his refined
origin; they were explained rather to a certain extent
by a just resentment at finding himself excluded
from his proper position. Mr. Vetch was short, fat
and bald, though he was not much older than Miss
Pynsent, who was not much older than some people
who called themselves forty-five; he always went to
the theatre in evening dress, with a flower in his
buttonhole, and wore a glass in one eye. He looked
placid and genial and as if he would fidget at the
most about the "get up" of his linen; you would have
thought him finical but superficial, and never have
suspected that he was a revolutionist, or even an at
all bold critic of life. Sometimes when he could get
away from the theatre early enough he went with
a pianist, a friend of his, to play dance-music at small
parties; and after such expeditions he was particularly cynical and startling; he indulged in diatribes
against the British middle-class, its Philistinism, its
absurdity, its snobbery. He seldom had much conversation with Miss Pynsent without telling her that
she had the intellectual outlook of a caterpillar; but
this was his privilege after a friendship now of seven
years' standing, which had begun (the year after he
came to live in Lomax Place) with her going over to
nurse him on learning from the milk-woman that
he was alone at number 17 — laid up there with an
attack of gastritis. He always compared her to an
insect or a bird, and she did n't mind, because she

knew he liked her, and she herself liked all winged creatures. How indeed could she complain after hearing him call the Queen a superannuated form and the Archbishop of Canterbury a grotesque superstition?

He laid his violin-case on the table, which was covered with a confusion of fashion-plates and pincushions, and glanced toward the fire where a kettle was gently hissing. Miss Pynsent, who had put it on half an hour before, read his glance and reflected with complacency that Mrs. Bowerbank had not absolutely drained the little bottle in the cheffoneer. She placed it on the table again, this time with a single glass, and told her visitor that, as a great exception, he might light his pipe. In fact she always made the exception, and he always replied to the gracious speech by enquiring whether she supposed the greengrocers' wives, the butchers' daughters, for whom she worked had fine enough noses to smell in the garments she sent home the fumes of his tobacco. He knew her "connexion" was confined to small shopkeepers, but she did n't wish others to know it and would have liked them to believe it important the poor little stuffs she made up (into very queer fashions I am afraid) should not surprise the feminine nostril. But it had always been impossible to impose on Mr. Vetch; he guessed the truth, the treacherous untrimmed truth, about everything in a moment. She was sure he would do so now in regard to this solemn question that had come up for Hyacinth; he would see that, though agreeably flurried at finding herself whirled in the last eddies of a case that had been so celebrated in its day, her secret wish was to shirk her duty — if

it *was* a duty; to keep the child from ever knowing
his mother's unmentionable history, the shame that
attached to his origin, the opportunity she had had
of letting him see the wretched woman before it
was too late. She knew Mr. Vetch would read her
troubled thoughts, but she hoped he would say they
were natural and just: she reflected that as he took an
interest in Hyacinth he would n't desire him to be
subjected to a mortification that might rankle for ever
and perhaps even crush him to the earth. She related
Mrs. Bowerbank's visit while he sat on the sofa in the
very place where that majestic woman had reposed
and puffed his smoke-wreaths into the dusky little
room. He knew the story of the child's birth, had
known it years before, so that she had no startling
revelation to make. He was not in the least agitated
to hear of Florentine's approaching end in prison and
of her having managed to get a message conveyed to
Amanda; he thought this so much in the usual course
that he said to Miss Pynsent: "Did you expect her to
live on there for ever, working out her terrible sentence, just to spare you the annoyance of a dilemma,
to save you a reminder of her miserable existence,
which you have preferred to forget?" That was just
the sort of question Mr. Vetch was sure to ask, and he
enquired further of his dismayed hostess if she were
sure her friend's message (he called the unhappy
creature her friend) had come to her in the regular
way. The warders surely had no authority to introduce visitors to their captives, and was it a question
of her going off to the prison on the sole authority of
Mrs. Bowerbank? The little dressmaker explained

that this lady had merely come to sound her: Florentine had begged so hard. She had been in Mrs.
Bowerbank's ward before her removal to the infirmary, where she now lay ebbing away, and she had
communicated her desire to the Catholic chaplain,
who had undertaken that some satisfaction — of
enquiry, at least — should be given her. He had
thought it best to ascertain first whether the person
in charge of the child would be willing to bring him,
such a course being perfectly optional, and he had
had some talk with Mrs. Bowerbank on the subject,
in which it was agreed between them that if she
would approach Miss Pynsent and explain to her the
situation, leaving her to do what she thought best, he
would answer for it that the consent of the governor
of the prison should be given to the interview. Miss
Pynsent had lived for fourteen years in Lomax Place,
and Florentine had never forgotten that this was her
address at the time she came to her at Newgate
(before her dreadful sentence had been commuted)
and promised, in an outgush of pity for one whom
she had known in the days of her honesty and brightness, that she would save the child, rescue it from the
workhouse and the streets, keep it from the fate that
had swallowed up the mother. Mrs. Bowerbank had
had a half-holiday, and she also rejoiced in a sister
living in the north of London, to whom she had been
for some time intending a visit; so that after her
domestic duty had been performed it had been possible for her to drop in on Miss Pynsent in an in-
formal, natural way and put the case before her. It
would be just as she might be disposed to view it.

She was to think it over a day or two, but not long, because the woman was so ill, and then write to Mrs. Bowerbank at the prison. If she should consent Mrs. Bowerbank would tell the chaplain, and the chaplain would obtain the order from the governor and send it to Lomax Place; after which Amanda would immediately set out with her unconscious victim. But should she — *must* she — consent? That was the terrible, the heart-shaking question, with which Miss Pynsent's unaided wisdom had been unable to grapple.

"After all, he is n't hers any more — he's mine, mine only and mine always. I should like to know if all I've done for him does n't make him so!" It was in this manner that Amanda Pynsent delivered herself while she plied her needle faster than ever in a piece of stuff that was pinned to her knee.

Mr. Vetch watched her a while, blowing silently at his pipe, his head thrown back on the high, stiff, old-fashioned sofa and his little legs crossed under him like a Turk's. "It's true you've done a good deal for him. You're a good little woman, my dear Pinnie, after all." He said "after all" because that was a part of his tone. In reality he had never had a moment's doubt that she was the best little woman in the north of London.

"I've done what I could, and I don't put myself forward above others. Only it does make a difference when you come to look at it — about taking him off to see another woman. And *such* another woman — and in such a place! I think it's hardly right to take an innocent child."

29

"I don't know about that; there are people who would tell you it would do him good. If he did n't like the place as a child he'd take more care to keep out of it later."

"Lord, Mr. Vetch, how can you think? And him such a perfect little gentleman!" Miss Pynsent cried.

"Is it you that have made him one?" the fiddler asked. "It does n't run in the family, you'd say."

"Family? what do you know about that?" she returned quickly, catching at her dearest, her only hobby.

"Yes indeed, what does any one know? what did she know herself?" And then Miss Pynsent's visitor added irrelevantly: "Why should you have taken him on your back? Why did you want to be so extra good? No one else thinks it necessary."

"I did n't want to be extra good. That is I do want to, of course, in a general way: but that was n't the reason then. You see I had nothing of my own — I had nothing in the world but my thimble."

"That would have seemed to most people a reason for not adopting a prostitute's bastard."

"Well, I went to see him at the place where he was (just where she had left him, with the woman of the house) and I saw what kind of a shop *that* was, and felt it a shame an unspotted child should grow up in such a place." Miss Pynsent defended herself as earnestly as if her inconsistency had been of a criminal cast. "And he would n't have grown up neither. *They* would n't have troubled themselves long with a helpless baby. *They* 'd have played some bad trick on him, if it was only to send him to the workhouse.

Besides, I always was fond of tiny creatures and I've been fond of this one," she went on, speaking as if with a consciousness, on her own part, of almost heroic proportions. "He was in my way the first two or three years, and it was a good deal of a pull to look after the business and him together. But now he's like the business — he seems to go of himself."

"Oh, if he flourishes as the business flourishes you can just enjoy your peace of mind," said the fiddler, still with his manner of making a small dry joke of everything.

"That's all very well, but it doesn't close my eyes to that poor woman lying there and moaning just for the touch of his little 'and before she passes away. Mrs. Bowerbank says she believes I'll bring him."

"Who believes? Mrs. Bowerbank?"

"I wonder if there's anything in life holy enough for you to take it seriously," Miss Pynsent rejoined, snapping off a thread with temper. "The day you stop laughing I should like to be there."

"So long as you're there I shall never stop. What is it you want me to advise you? to take the child, or to leave the mother to wail herself away?"

"I want you to tell me if he'll curse me when he grows older."

"That depends on what you do. However, he'll probably curse you in either case."

"You don't believe that, because you like him, you love him," said Amanda with acuteness.

"Precisely; and he'll curse me too. He'll curse every one. Much good will our love do us! He won't be happy."

31

"I don't know how you think I bring him up," the little dressmaker remarked with dignity.

"You don't bring him up at all. He brings you up."

"That's what you've always said; but you don't know. If you mean that he does as he likes, then he ought to be happy. It ain't kind of you to say he won't be," Miss Pynsent added reproachfully.

"I'd say anything you like if what I say would help the matter. He's a thin-skinned, morbid, mooning, introspective little beggar, with a good deal of imagination and not much perseverance, who'll expect a good deal more of life than he'll find in it. That's why he won't be happy."

Miss Pynsent listened to this description of her *protégé* with an appearance of criticising it mentally; but in reality she did n't know what "introspective" meant and did n't like to ask. "He's the cleverest person I know except yourself," she said in a moment; for Mr. Vetch's words had been in the key of what she thought most remarkable in him. What that was she would have been unable to say.

"Thank you very much for putting me first," the fiddler returned after a series of puffs. "The youngster's interesting; one sees he has a mind and even a soul, and in that respect he's — I won't say unique, but peculiar. I shall watch with curiosity to see what he grows into. But I shall always be glad that I'm a selfish brute of a decent bachelor — that I never invested in that class of goods."

"Well, you *are* comforting. You'd spoil him more than I do," said Amanda.

"Possibly, but it would be in a different way. I would n't tell him every three minutes that his father was a duke."

"A duke I never mentioned!" the little dressmaker cried with eagerness. "I never specified any rank nor said a word about any one in particular. I never so much as insinuated the name of his lordship. But I may have said that if the truth was to be found out he might be proved to be connected — in the way of cousinship, or something of the kind — with the highest in the land. I should have thought myself wanting if I had n't given him a glimpse of that. But there's one thing I've always added — that the truth never *is* found out."

"You're still more comforting than I!" Mr. Vetch exclaimed. He continued to watch her with his charitable, round-faced smile, and then he said: "You won't do what I say; so what's the use of my telling you?"

"I assure you I will, if you say you believe it's the only right."

"Do I often say anything so asinine? Right — right? what have you to do with that? If you want the only right you're very particular."

"Please then what am I to go by?" the dressmaker asked bewildered.

"You're to go by this, by what will take the youngster down."

"Take him down, my poor little pet?"

"Your poor little pet thinks himself the flower of creation. I don't say there's any harm in that: a fine, blooming, odoriferous conceit is a natural appendage

33

of youth and intelligence. I don't say there's any
great harm in it, but if you want a guide as to how
you're to treat the boy, that's as good a guide as any
other."

"You want me to arrange the interview then?"

"I don't want you to do anything but give me
another *leetle* swig — thanks. I just say this: that
I think it's a great gain, early in life, to know the
worst; then we don't live in a rank fools' paradise.
I did that till I was nearly forty; then I woke up and
found I was in Lomax Place." Whenever Mr. Vetch
said anything that could be construed as a reference
to a former position that had had elements of distinction Miss Pynsent observed a respectful, a tasteful
silence and that is why she did n't challenge him
now, though she wanted very much to say that Hyacinth was no more "presumptious" (that was the
term she would have used) than he had reason to be,
with his genteel appearance and his acknowledged
powers; and that as for thinking himself a "flower"
of any kind he knew but too well that he lived in
a small black-faced house miles away from any good
family, rented by a poor little woman who took
lodgers and who, as they were of such a class that
they were not always to be depended upon to settle
her weekly account, had a strain to make two ends
meet, for all the sign between her windows —

MISS AMANDA PYNSENT
Modes et Robes

DRESSMAKING IN ALL ITS BRANCHES: COURT-
DRESSES: MANTLES AND FASHIONABLE BONNETS

Singularly enough, her companion, before she had permitted herself to interpose, took up her own thought (in one of its parts) and remarked that perhaps she would say of the child that he was, so far as his actual circumstances were concerned, low enough down in the world without one's wanting him to be any lower. "But by the time he's twenty he'll persuade himself that Lomax Place was a bad dream, that your lodgers and your dressmaking were as imaginary as they are vulgar, and that when an old friend came to see you late at night it was not your amiable practice to make him a glass of brandy and water. He'll teach himself to forget all this: he'll have a way."

"Do you mean he'll forget *me*, he'll deny me?" cried Miss Pynsent, stopping the movement of her needle short off for the first time.

"As the person designated in that attractive blazonry on the outside of your house decidedly he will; and me, equally, as a bald-headed, pot-bellied fiddler who regarded you as the most perfect lady of his acquaintance. I don't mean he'll disown you and pretend he never knew you: I don't think he'll ever be such an odious little cad as that; he probably won't be a sneak, and he strikes me as having some affection and possibly even some gratitude, in him. But his imagination (which will always give him his cue about everything) shall subject you to some extraordinary metamorphosis. He'll dress you up."

"He'll dress me up?" Amanda ejaculated, quite ceasing to follow the train of Mr. Vetch's demonstration. "Do you mean he'll have the property — that his relations will take him up?"

"My dear, delightful, idiotic Pinnie, I'm speaking in a figurative manner. I don't pretend to say what his precise position will be when we're relegated; but I'm sure relegation will be our fate. Therefore don't stuff him with any more false notions and fine illusions than are necessary to keep him alive; he'll be sure to pick up enough on the way. On the contrary, give him a good stiff dose of the truth at the start."

"Deary me, of course you see much further into it than I could ever do," Pinnie murmured as she threaded a needle.

Mr. Vetch paused a minute, but apparently not out of deference to this amiable interruption. He went on suddenly with a ring of feeling in his voice. "Let him know, because it will be useful to him later, the state of the account between society and himself; he can then conduct himself accordingly. If he's the illegitimate child of a French impropriety who murdered one of her numerous lovers, don't shuffle out of sight so important a fact. I regard that as a most valuable origin."

"Lord, Mr. Vetch, how you *can* talk!" cried Miss Pynsent with her ever-fresh faculty of vain protest. "I don't know what one would think, to hear you."

"Surely, my dear lady, and for this reason: that those are the people with whom society has to count. It hasn't with you and me." Miss Pynsent gave a sigh which might have meant either that she was well aware of that or that Mr. Vetch had a terrible way of enlarging a subject, especially when it was already

too big for her; and her philosophic visitor went on:
"Poor little devil, let him see her, take him straight."

"And if later, when he's twenty, he says to me that
if I had n't meddled in it he need never have known,
need never have had that shame, pray what am I to
say to him then? That's what I can't get out of my
head."

"You can say to him that a young man who's
sorry for having gone to his mother when, in her last
hours, she lay crying for him on a pallet in a penitentiary, deserves more than the sharpest pang he can
possibly feel." And the little fiddler, getting up, went
over to the fireplace and shook out the ashes of his
pipe.

"Well, I'm sure it's natural he should feel badly,"
said Miss Pynsent, folding up her work with the same
desperate quickness that had animated her through
the evening.

"I have n't the least objection to his feeling badly;
that's not the worst thing in the world! If a few
more people felt badly, in this sodden, stolid, stupid
race of ours, the world would wake up to an idea or
two and we should see the beginning of the dance.
It's the dull acceptance, the absence of reflexion,
the impenetrable density." Here Mr. Vetch stopped
short; his hostess stood before him with eyes of entreaty, with clasped hands.

"Now, Anastasius Vetch, don't go off into them
dreadful wild theories!" she cried, always ungram-
matical when she was strongly moved. "You always
fly away over the house-tops. I thought you liked
him better — the dear little unfortunate."

37

Anastasius Vetch had pocketed his pipe; he put on his hat with the freedom of old acquaintance and of Lomax Place, and took up his small coffin-like fiddle-case. "My good Pinnie, I don't think you understand a word I say. It's no use talking — do as you like!"

"Well, I must say I don't think it was worth your coming in at midnight only to tell me that. I don't like anything — I hate the whole dreadful business!"

He bent over, for all his figure, to kiss her hand with the flourish of a troubadour and as he had seen people do on the stage. "My dear friend, we've different ideas, and I never shall succeed in driving mine into your head. It's because I *am* fond of him, poor little devil; but you'll never understand that. I want him to know everything, and especially the worst — the very worst, as I've said. If I were in his position I should n't thank you for trying to make a fool of me."

"A fool of you? — as if I thought of anything but his 'appiness!" Amanda Pynsent exclaimed. She stood looking at him but following her own reflexions; she had given up the attempt to enter into his whims. She remembered what she had noticed in other occurrences, that his reasons were always more extraordinary than his behaviour itself. If you only considered his life you would n't have thought him so immoral. "Very likely I think too much of that," she added. "She wants him and cries for him; that's what keeps coming back to me." She took up her lamp to light Mr. Vetch to the door (for the dim luminary in the passage had long since been extin-

38

guished) and before he left the house he turned suddenly, stopping short and with his composed face taking a strange expression from the quizzical glimmer of his little round eyes.

"What does it matter after all, and why do you worry? What difference can it make what happens — on either side — to such low people?"

III

MRS. BOWERBANK had let her know she would meet her almost at the threshold of the dreadful place; and this thought had sustained Miss Pynsent in her long and devious journey, performed partly on foot, partly in a succession of omnibuses. She had had ideas about a cab, but she decided to reserve the cab for the return, as then, very likely, she should be so prostrate with emotion, so overpoweringly affected, that it would be a comfort to escape from observation. She had no confidence that if once she passed the door of the prison she should ever be restored to liberty and her customers; it seemed to her an adventure as dangerous as it was dismal, and she was immensely touched by the clear-faced eagerness of the child at her side, who strained forward as brightly as he had done on another occasion, still celebrated in Miss Pynsent's industrious annals, a certain sultry Saturday in August when she had taken him to the Tower. It had been a terrible question with her, once she had made up her mind, what she should tell him about the nature of their errand. She determined to tell him as little as possible, to say only that she was going to see a poor woman who was in prison on account of a crime committed many years before, and who had sent for her and caused her to be told at the same time that if there was any child she could see — as children (if they were good) were bright and cheering —

it would make her very happy that such a little visitor should come as well. It was very difficult, with Hyacinth, to make reservations or mysteries; he wanted to know everything about everything and he projected the fierce light of his questions on Miss Pynsent's incarcerated friend. She had to admit that she had been her friend (since where else was the obligation to go to see her?) but she spoke of the acquaintance as if it were of the slightest (it had survived in the memory of the prisoner only because every one else — the world was so very severe! — had turned away from her) and she congratulated herself on a happy inspiration when she represented the crime for which such a penalty had been exacted as the theft of a gold watch in a moment of cruel want. The woman had had a wicked husband who maltreated and deserted her; she had been very poor, almost starving, dreadfully pressed. Hyacinth listened to her history with absorbed attention and then said:

"And had n't she any children — had n't she a little boy?"

This enquiry seemed to Miss Pynsent an omen of future embarrassments, but she met it as bravely as she could, replying that she believed the wretched victim of the law had had (once upon a time) a very small baby, but was afraid she had completely lost sight of it. He must know they did n't allow babies in prisons. To this Hyacinth rejoined that of course they would allow him, because of his size. Miss Pynsent fortified herself with the memory of her other pilgrimage, the visit to Newgate upwards of ten years before; she had escaped from *that* ordeal and had even had the comfort of knowing that in its fruits the interview had been beneficent. The responsibility, however, was much greater now, and, after all, it was not on her own account she faltered and feared, but on that of the tender sensibility over which the shadow of the house of shame might cast itself.

They made the last part of their approach on foot, having got themselves deposited as near as possible to the river and keeping beside it (according to advice elicited by Miss Pynsent, on the way, in a dozen confidential interviews with policemen, conductors of omnibuses and small shopkeepers) till they came to a big dark-towered building which they would know as soon as they looked at it. They knew it in fact soon enough when they saw it lift its dusky mass from the bank of the Thames, lying there and sprawling over the whole neighbourhood with brown, bare, windowless walls, ugly, truncated pinnacles and a character unspeakably sad and stern. It looked very sinister and wicked, to Miss Pynsent's eyes, and she wondered why a prison should have such an evil air if it was erected in the interest of justice and order — a builded protest, precisely, against vice and villainy. This particular penitentiary struck her as about as bad and wrong as those who were in it; it threw a blight on the face of day, making the river seem foul and poisonous and the opposite bank, with a protrusion of long-necked chimneys, unsightly gasometers and deposits of rubbish, wear the aspect of a region at whose expense the jail had been populated. She looked up at the dull, closed gates, tightening her grasp of Hyacinth's small hand; and if it was hard to believe anything so barred and blind and deaf would relax itself to let her in, there was a dreadful premonitory sinking of the heart attached to the idea of its taking the same trouble to let her out. As she hung back, murmuring vague ejaculations, at the very goal of her journey, an incident occurred which fanned all her scruples and reluctances into life again. The child suddenly jerked away his hand and, placing it behind him in the clutch of the other, said to her respectfully but resolutely, while he planted himself at a considerable distance:

"I don't like this place."

"Neither do I like it, my darling," cried the dressmaker pitifully. "Oh, if you knew how little!"

"Then we'll go away. I won't go in."

She would have embraced this proposition with alacrity if it had not become very vivid to her while she stood there, in the midst of her shrinking, that behind those sullen walls the mother who bore him was even then counting the minutes. She was alive in that huge dark tomb, and Miss Pynsent could feel that they had already entered into relation with her. They were near her and she was aware; in a few minutes she would taste the cup of the only mercy (except the reprieve from hanging) she had known since her fall. A few, a very few minutes would do it, and it seemed to our pilgrim that if she should fail of her charity now the watches of the night in Lomax Place would be haunted with remorse — perhaps even with something worse. There was something inside that waited and listened, something that would

43

burst, with an awful sound, a shriek or a curse, were she to lead the boy away. She looked into his pale face, perfectly conscious it would be vain for her to take the tone of command; besides, that would have seemed to her shocking. She had another inspiration, and she said to him in a manner in which she had had occasion to speak before:

"The reason why we've come is only to be kind. If we're kind we shan't mind its being disagreeable."

"Why should we be so kind if she's a bad woman?" Hyacinth demanded. "She must be very low; I don't want to know her."

"Hush, hush," groaned poor Amanda, edging toward him with clasped hands. "She's not bad now; it has all been washed away — it has been expiated."

"What's 'expiated'?" asked the child while she almost kneeled down in the dust to catch him to her bosom.

"It's when you've suffered terribly — suffered so much that it has made you good again."

"Has *she* suffered very much?"

"For years and years. And now she's dying. It proves she's very good now — that she should want to see us."

"Do you mean because *we* are good?" Hyacinth went on, probing the matter in a way that made his companion quiver and gazing away from her, very seriously, across the river, at the dreary waste of Battersea.

"We shall be good if we're compassionate, if we make an effort," said the dressmaker, seeming to look up at him rather than down.

44

"But if she's dying? I don't want to see any one die."

Miss Pynsent was bewildered, but her desperation helped. "If we go to her perhaps she won't. Maybe we shall save her."

He transferred his remarkable little eyes — eyes which always appeared to her to belong to a person older and stronger than herself — to her face; and then he put to her: "Why should I save such a creature if I don't like her?"

"If she likes you, that will be enough."

At this Miss Pynsent began to see that he was moved. "Will she like me very much?"

"More, much more, than any one — ever."

"More than you, now?"

"Oh," said Amanda quickly, "I mean more than she likes any one."

Hyacinth had slipped his hands into the pockets of his scanty knickerbockers and, with his legs slightly apart, looked from his companion back to the immense dreary jail. A great deal, to her sense, depended on that moment. "Oh well," he said at last, "I'll just step in."

"Deary, deary!" the dressmaker murmured to herself as they crossed the bare semicircle which separated the gateway from the unfrequented street. She exerted herself to pull the bell, which seemed to her terribly big and stiff, and while she waited again for the consequences of this effort the boy broke out abruptly:

"How can she like me so much if she has never seen me?"

Miss Pynsent wished the gate would open before an answer to this question should become imperative, but the people within were a long time arriving, and their delay gave Hyacinth an opportunity to repeat it. So she replied, seizing the first pretext that came into her head: "It's because the little baby she had of old was also named Hyacinth."

"That's a rummy reason," the boy murmured, still staring across at the Battersea shore.

A moment later they found themselves in a vast interior dimness, while a grinding of keys and bolts went on behind them. Hereupon Miss Pynsent gave herself up to an overruling providence, and she remembered afterwards no circumstance of what happened to her till the great person of Mrs. Bowerbank loomed up in the narrowness of a strange, dark corridor. She had only had meanwhile a confused impression of being surrounded with high black walls, whose inner face was more dreadful than the other, the one that overlooked the river; of passing through grey, stony courts, in some of which dreadful figures, scarcely female, in hideous brown misfitting uniforms and perfect frights of hoods, were marching round in a circle; of squeezing up steep unlighted staircases at the heels of a woman who had taken possession of her at the first stage and who made incomprehensible remarks to other women, of lumpish aspect, as she saw them erect themselves, suddenly and spectrally, with dowdy untied bonnets, in uncanny corners and recesses of the draughty labyrinth. If the place had seemed cruel to the poor little dressmaker outside, it may be trusted not to have struck her as an abode of

mercy while she pursued her tortuous way into the
circular shafts of cells where she had an opportunity
of looking at captives through grated peepholes and
of edging past others who had temporarily been
turned into the corridors — silent women, with fixed
eyes, who flattened themselves against the stone walls
at the brush of the visitor's dress and whom Miss
Pynsent was afraid to glance at. She never had felt
so immured, so made sure of; there were walls within
walls and galleries on top of galleries; even the daylight lost its colour and you could n't imagine what
o'clock it was. Mrs. Bowerbank appeared to have
failed her, and that made her feel worse; a panic
seized her, as she went, in regard to the child. On
him too the horror of the scene would have fallen,
and she had a sickening prevision that he would have
convulsions after they got home. It was a most im-
proper place to have brought him to, no matter who
had sent for him and no matter who was dying. The
stillness would terrify him, she was sure — the peni-
tential dumbness of the clustered or isolated women.
She clasped his hand more tightly and felt him keep
close to her without speaking a word. At last in an
open doorway darkened by her ample person Mrs.
Bowerbank revealed herself, and Miss Pynsent thought
it subsequently a sign of her place and power that she
should not condescend to apologise for not having
appeared till that moment, or to explain why she had
not met the bewildered pilgrims near the principal
entrance according to her promise. Miss Pynsent
could n't embrace the state of mind of people who
did n't apologise, though she vaguely envied and

admired it, she herself spending much of her time in making excuses for obnoxious acts she had not committed. Mrs. Bowerbank, however, was not arrogant, she was only massive and muscular; and after she had taken her timorous friends in tow the dressmaker was able to comfort herself with the reflexion that even so masterful a woman could n't inflict anything gratuitously disagreeable on a person who had made her visit in Lomax Place pass off so pleasantly.

It was on the outskirts of the infirmary she had been hovering, and it was into certain dismal chambers dedicated to sick criminals she presently ushered her guests. These chambers were naked and grated, like all the rest of the place, and caused Miss Pynsent to say to herself that it must be a blessing to be ill in such a hole, because you could n't possibly pick up again, whereby your case was simple. Such simplification, nevertheless, had for the moment been offered to very few of Florentine's fellow-sufferers, for only three of the small stiff beds were occupied — occupied by white-faced women in tight, sordid caps, on whom, in the stale ugly room, the sallow light itself seemed to rest without pity. Mrs. Bowerbank discreetly paid no attention whatever to Hyacinth; she only said to Miss Pynsent with her hoarse distinctness: "You'll find her very low; she would n't have waited another day." And she guided them, through a still further door, to the smallest room of all, where there were but three beds placed in a row. Miss Pynsent's frightened eyes rather faltered than enquired, but she became aware that a woman was lying on the middle bed and that her face was turned toward the door. Mrs. Bowerbank led the way straight up to her and, giving a businesslike pat to her pillow, signed invitation and encouragement to the visitors, who clung together not far within the threshold. Their conductress reminded them that very few minutes were allowed them and that they had better not dawdle them away; whereupon, as the boy still hung back, the little dressmaker advanced alone, looking at the sick woman with what courage she could muster. It seemed to her she was approaching a perfect stranger, so completely had nine years of prison transformed Florentine. She felt it immediately to have been a mercy she had n't told Hyacinth she was pretty (as she used to be) since there was no beauty left in the hollow bloodless mask that presented itself without a movement. She *had* told him the poor woman was good, but she did n't look so, nor evidently was he struck with it as he returned her gaze across the interval he declined to traverse, though kept at the same time from retreating by this appeal of her strange, fixed eyes, the only part of all her wasted person in which was still any appearance of life. She looked unnatural to Amanda Pynsent, and terribly old; a speechless, motionless creature, dazed and stupid, whereas Florentine Vivier, in the obliterated past, had been her idea of personal as distinguished from social brilliancy. Above all she seemed disfigured and ugly, cruelly misrepresented by her coarse cap and short rough hair. Amanda, as she stood beside her, thought with a degree of scared elation that Hyacinth would never guess that a person in whom there was so little trace of smartness, or of cleverness of any kind, was his mother, which would

49

be quite another matter. At the very most it might occur to him, as Mrs. Bowerbank had suggested, that she was his grandmother. Mrs. Bowerbank seated herself on the further bed with folded hands, a monumental timekeeper, and remarked, in the manner of one speaking from a sense of duty, that the poor thing would n't get much good of the child unless he showed more confidence. This observation was evidently lost on the boy; he was too intensely absorbed in watching the prisoner. A chair had been placed near her pillow, and Miss Pynsent sat down without her appearing to notice it. In a moment, however, she lifted her hand a little, pushing it out from under the coverlet, and the dressmaker laid her own hand softly on it. This gesture elicited no response, but after a little, still gazing at the boy, Florentine murmured in words no one present was in a position to understand —

"*Dieu de Dieu, qu'il est donc beau!*"

"She won't speak nothing but French since she has been so bad — you can't get a natural word out of her," Mrs. Bowerbank said.

"It used to be so pretty when she spoke her odd English — and so very amusing," Miss Pynsent ventured to mention with a feeble attempt to brighten up the scene. "I suppose she has forgotten it all."

"She may well have forgotten it — she never gave her tongue much exercise. There was little enough trouble to keep *her* from chattering," Mrs. Bowerbank rejoined, giving a twitch to the prisoner's counterpane. Miss Pynsent settled it a little on the other side and considered, in the same train, that this separation of language was indeed a mercy; for how could it ever come into her small companion's head that he was the offspring of a person who could n't so much as say good-morning to him? She felt at the same time that the scene might have been somewhat less painful if they had been able to communicate with the object of their compassion. As it was they had too much the air of having been brought together simply to look at each other, and there was a grue-some awkwardness in that, considering the delicacy of Florentine's position. Not indeed that she looked much at her old comrade; it was as if she were con-scious of Miss Pynsent's being there and would have been glad to thank her for it — glad even to examine her for her own sake and see what change for her too the horrible years had brought, yet felt, more than this, how she had but the thinnest pulse of energy left and how not a moment that could still be of use to her was too much to take in her child. She took him in with all the glazed entreaty of her eyes, quite giving up his substituted guardian, who evidently would have to take her gratitude for granted. Hyacinth, on his side, after some moments of embarrassing silence — there was nothing audible but Mrs. Bowerbank's breathing — had satisfied himself, and he turned about to look for a place of patience while Miss Pyn-sent should finish her business, which as yet made so little show. He appeared to wish not to leave the room altogether, as that would be the confession of a broken spirit, but to take some attitude that should express his complete disapproval of the unpleasant situation. He was not in sympathy, and he could not have made it more clear than by the way he presently went and placed himself on a low stool in a corner near the door by which they had entered.

"*Est-il possible, mon Dieu, qu'il soit gentil comme ça?*" his mother moaned just above her breath.

"We're very glad you should have cared — that they look after you so well," said Miss Pynsent confusedly and at random; feeling first that Hyacinth's coldness was perhaps excessive and his scepticism too marked, and then that allusions to the way the poor woman was looked after were not exactly happy. These did n't matter, however, for she evidently heard nothing, giving no sign of interest even when Mrs. Bowerbank, in a tone between a desire to make the interview more lively and an idea of showing she knew how to treat the young, referred herself to the little boy.

"Is there nothing the little gentleman would like to say, now, to the unfortunate? Has n't he any pleasant remark to make to her about his coming so far to see her when she's so sunk? It is n't often that children are shown over the place (as the little man has been) and there's many that'd think themselves lucky if they could see what he has seen."

"*Mon pauvre joujou, mon pauvre chéri,*" the prisoner went on in her tender, tragic whisper.

"He only wants to be very good; he always sits that way at home," said Miss Pynsent, alarmed at Mrs. Bowerbank's address and hoping there would n't be a scene.

"He might have stayed at home then — with this wretched person taking on so over him," Mrs. Bowerbank remarked with some sternness. She plainly felt the occasion threaten to be wanting in brilliancy, and wished to intimate that though she was to be trusted for discipline she thought they were all getting off too easily.

"I came because Pinnie brought me," Hyacinth spoke up from his low perch. "I thought at first it would be pleasant. But it ain't pleasant — I don't like prisons." And he placed his little feet on the crosspiece of the stool as if to touch the institution at as few points as possible.

The woman in bed continued her strange, almost whining plaint. "*Il ne veut pas s'approcher, il a honte de moi.*"

"There's a many who begin like that!" laughed Mrs. Bowerbank, irritated by the boy's contempt for one of Her Majesty's finest establishments.

Hyacinth's little white face exhibited no confusion; he only turned it to the prisoner again, and Miss Pynsent felt that some extraordinary dumb exchange of meanings was taking place between them. "She used to be so elegant; she *was* a fine woman," she observed gently and helplessly.

"*Il a honte de moi — il a honte, Dieu le pardonne!*" Florentine Vivier went on, never moving her eyes.

"She's asking for something, in her language. I used to know a few words," said Miss Pynsent, stroking down the bed very nervously.

"Who is that woman? what does she want?" Hyacinth broke out again, his small, clear voice ringing over the dreary room.

"She wants you to come near her, she wants to kiss

you, sir," said Mrs. Bowerbank, as if it were more than he deserved.

"I won't kiss her; Pinnie says she stole a watch!" the child answered with resolution.

"Oh, you dreadful — how could you ever?" cried Pinnie, blushing all over and starting out of her chair.

It was partly Amanda's agitation perhaps, which by the jolt it administered gave an impulse to the sick woman, and partly the penetrating and expressive tone in which Hyacinth announced his repugnance: at any rate Florentine, in the most unexpected and violent manner, jerked herself up from her pillow and, with dilated eyes and protesting hands, shrieked out, "*Ah quelle infamie!* I never stole a watch, I never stole anything — anything! *Ah par exemple!*" Then she fell back sobbing with the passion that had given her a moment's strength.

"I'm sure you need n't put more on her than she has by rights," said Mrs. Bowerbank with dignity to the dressmaker, and laid a large red hand on the patient to keep her in her place.

"Mercy, more? I thought it so much less!" cried Miss Pynsent, convulsed with confusion and jerking herself in a wild tremor from the mother to the child, as if she wished to fling herself on the one for contrition and the other for revenge.

"*Il a honte de moi — il a honte de moi!*" Florentine repeated in the misery of her sobs. "*Dieu de bonté, quelle horreur!*"

Miss Pynsent dropped on her knees beside the bed and, trying to possess herself of the unfortunate's hand again, protested with an almost equal passion (she felt that her nerves had been screwed up to the snapping-point, and now they were all in shreds) that she had n't meant what she had told the child, that he had n't understood, that Florentine herself had n't understood, that she had only said she had been accused and meant that no one had ever believed it. The Frenchwoman paid no attention to her whatever, and Amanda buried her face and her embarrassment in the side of the hard little prison-bed, while, above the sound of their common lamentation, she heard the judicial tones of Mrs. Bowerbank.

"The child's delicate — you might well say! I'm disappointed in the effect — I was in hopes you'd hearten her up. The doctor'll be down on *me* of course for putting her in such a state, so we'll just pass out again."

"I'm very sorry I made you cry. And you must pardon Pinnie — I asked her so many questions."

These words came from close beside the prostrate dressmaker, who, lifting herself quickly, found the little boy had advanced to her elbow and was taking a nearer view of the mysterious captive. They produced on the latter an effect even more powerful than his misguided speech of a moment before; for she found strength partly to raise herself in her bed again and to hold out her arms to him with the same thrilling sobs. She was talking still, but had become quite inarticulate, and Miss Pynsent had but a glimpse of her white ravaged face and the hollows of its eyes and the rude crop of her hair. Amanda caught the child with an eagerness almost as great as Florentine's and, drawing him to the head of the bed, pushed him into his mother's arms. "Kiss her — kiss her well, and we'll go home!" she whispered desperately while they closed about him and the poor dishonoured head pressed itself against his young cheek. It was a terrible, irresistible embrace, to which Hyacinth submitted with instant patience. Mrs. Bowerbank had tried at first to keep her sad charge from rising, evidently wishing to abbreviate the scene; then as the child was enfolded she accepted the situation and gave judicious support from behind, with an eye to clearing the room as soon as this effort should have spent itself. She propped up her patient with a vigorous arm; Miss Pynsent rose from her knees and turned away, and there was a minute's stillness during which the boy accommodated himself as he might to his strange ordeal. What thoughts were begotten at that moment in his wondering little mind his protectress was destined to learn at another time. Before she had faced round to the bed again she was swept out of the room by Mrs. Bowerbank, who had lowered the prisoner, exhausted and with closed eyes, to her pillow and given Hyacinth a businesslike little push which sent him on in advance. Miss Pynsent went home in a cab — she was so shaken; though she reflected very nervously, getting into it, on the opportunities it would give Hyacinth for the exercise of inquisitorial rights. To her surprise, however, he completely neglected them; he sat looking out of the window in silence till they re-entered Lomax Place.

IV

"WELL, you'll have to guess my name before I'll tell you," the girl said with a free laugh, pushing her way into the narrow hall and leaning against the tattered wall-paper which, representing blocks of marble with bevelled edges, in streaks and speckles of black and grey, had not been renewed for years and came back to her out of the past. As Miss Pynsent closed the door, seeing her visitor so resolute, the light filtered in from the street through the narrow dusty glass above, and then the very smell and sense of the place returned to Millicent: the impression of a musty dimness with a small steep staircase at the end, covered with the very strip of oilcloth she could recognise and made a little less dark by a window in the turn (you could see it from the hall) where you might almost bump your head against the house behind. Nothing was changed but Miss Pynsent and of course the girl herself. She had noticed outside how the sign between the windows had not even been touched up; there was still the same preposterous announcement of "fashionable bonnets" — as if the poor little dressmaker had the slightest acquaintance with that style of head-dress, of which Miss Henning's own knowledge was now so complete. She could see this artist was looking at her hat, a wonderful composition of flowers and ribbons; her eyes had travelled up and down Millicent's whole person, but they rested in fas-

57

cination on that grandest ornament. The girl had forgotten how small the dressmaker was; she barely came up to her shoulder. She had lost her hair and wore a cap which Millicent noticed in return, wondering if it were a specimen of what she thought the fashion. Miss Pynsent stared up at her as if she had been six feet high; but she was used to that sort of surprised admiration, being perfectly conscious she was a magnificent young woman.

"Won't you take me into your shop?" she asked. "I don't want to order anything; I only want to enquire after your 'ealth. Is n't this rather an awkward place to talk?" She made her way further in without waiting for permission, seeing that her startled hostess had not yet guessed.

"The show-room's on the right hand," said Miss Pynsent with her professional manner, which was intended evidently to mark a difference. She spoke as if on the other side, where the horizon was bounded by the partition of the next house, there were labyrinths of apartments. Passing in after her guest she found the young lady already spread out upon the sofa, the everlasting sofa in the right-hand corner as you faced the window, a piece of furniture covered with a tight shrunken shroud of strange yellow stuff, the tinge of which revealed years of washing, and surmounted by a coloured print of Rebekah at the Well, balancing, in the opposite quarter, against a portrait of the Empress of the French taken from an illustrated newspaper and framed and glazed in the manner of 1853. Millicent looked about, asking herself what Miss Pynsent had to show and acting perfectly the part of the most brilliant figure the place had ever contained. The old implements were there on the table: the pincushions and needle-books, the pink measuring-tape with which, as children, she and Hyacinth used to take each other's height; and the same collection of fashion-plates (she could see in a minute) crumpled, sallow and fly-blown. The little dressmaker bristled, as she used to do, with needles and pins stuck all over the front of her dress — they might almost have figured the stiff sparse fur of a sick animal; but there were no rustling fabrics tossed in heaps over the room — nothing but the skirt of a shabby dress (it might have been her own) which she was evidently repairing and had flung upon the table when she came to the door. Miss Henning speedily arrived at the conclusion that her old friend's business had not increased, and felt some safe luxurious scorn of a person who knew so little what was to be got out of London. It was Millicent's belief that she herself was already perfectly acquainted with the resources of the capital.

"Now tell me, how's old Hyacinth? I should like so much to see him," she remarked while she extended a pair of large protrusive feet and supported herself on the sofa by her hands.

"Old Hyacinth?" Miss Pynsent repeated with majestic blankness and as if she had never heard of such a person. She felt the girl to be cruelly, scathingly well dressed and could n't imagine who she was nor with what design she might have presented herself.

"Perhaps you call him Mr. Robinson to-day —

you always wanted him to hold himself so high. But to his face at any rate I'll call him as I used to: you just see if I don't!"

"Bless my soul, you must be the awful little 'Enning!" Miss Pynsent exclaimed, planted before her and going now into every detail.

"Well, I'm glad you've made up your mind. I thought you'd know me directly and I dare say I *was* awful. But I ain't so bad now, hey?" the young woman went on with confidence. "I had a call to make in this part, and it came into my 'ead to look you up. I don't like to lose sight of old friends."

"I never knew you — you've improved as I could n't have believed," Miss Pynsent returned with a candour justified by her age and her consciousness of respectability.

"Well, *you* have n't changed; you were always calling me something horrid."

"I dare say it does n't matter to you now, does it?" said the dressmaker, seating herself but quite unable to take up her work, blank as she was before the greatness of her visitor.

"Oh, I'm all right now," Miss Henning declared with the air of one who had nothing to fear from human judgements.

"You were a pretty child — I never said the contrary to that; but I had no idea you'd turn out like this. You're too tall for a woman," Miss Pynsent added, much divided between an old prejudice and a new appreciation.

"Well, I enjoy beautiful 'ealth," said the young lady; "every one thinks I'm at least twenty-two."

She spoke with a certain artless pride in her bigness and her bloom and as if, to show her development, she would have taken off her jacket or let you feel her upper arm. She was certainly handsome, with a shining, bold, good-natured eye, a fine, free, physiognomic oval, an abundance of brown hair and a smile that fairly flaunted the whiteness of her teeth. Her head was set on a fair strong neck and her robust young figure was rich in feminine curves. Her gloves, covering her wrists insufficiently, showed the redness of those parts in the interstices of the numerous silver bracelets that encircled them, and Miss Pynsent made the observation that her hands were not more delicate than her feet. She was not graceful, and even the little dressmaker, whose preference for distinguished forms never deserted her, indulged in the mental reflexion that she was common, despite her magnificence; but there was something about her indescribably fresh, successful and satisfying. She was to her blunt, expanded finger-tips a daughter of London, of the crowded streets and bustling traffic of the great city; she had drawn her health and strength from its dingy courts and foggy thoroughfares and peopled its parks and squares and crescents with her ambitions; it had entered into her blood and her bone, the sound of her voice and the carriage of her head; she understood it by instinct and loved it with passion; she represented its immense vulgarities and curiosities, its brutality and its knowingness, its good-nature and its impudence, and might have figured, in an allegorical procession, as a kind of glorified townswoman, a nymph of the wilderness of Middlesex, a flower of the clustered parishes, the genius of urban civilisation, the muse of cockneyism. The restrictions under which Miss Pynsent regarded her would have cost the dressmaker some fewer scruples if she had guessed the impression she herself made on Millicent, and how the whole place seemed to that prosperous young lady to smell of poverty and failure. Her childish image of its mistress had shown her as neat, fine, superior, with round loops of hair fastened on the temples by combs and associations of brilliancy arising from the constant manipulation of precious stuffs — tissues at least that Millicent regarded with envy. But the little woman before her was bald and white and pinched; she looked shrunken and sickly and insufficiently nourished; her small eyes were sharp and suspicious and her hideous cap did n't disguise the way everything had gone. Miss Henning thanked her stars, as she had often done before, that she had n't been obliged to get *her* living by drudging over needlework year after year in that undiscoverable street, in a dismal little room where nothing had been changed for ages; the absence of change had such an exasperating effect upon her vigorous young nature. She reflected with complacency on her good fortune in being attached to a more exciting, a more dramatic department of the great drapery interest, and noticed that though it was already November there was no fire in the neatly-kept grate beneath the chimney-piece, on which a design, partly architectural, partly botanical, executed in the hair of Miss Pynsent's parents, was flanked by a pair of vases, under glass, containing muslin flowers.

If she thought that lady's eyes suspicious it must be confessed that her hostess felt much on her guard in presence of so unexpected and undesired a reminder of one of the least honourable episodes in the annals of Lomax Place. Miss Pynsent esteemed people in proportion to their success in constituting a family circle — in cases, that is, when the materials were under their hand. This success, among the various members of the house of Henning, had been of the scantiest, and the domestic broils in the establishment adjacent to her own, the vicissitudes of which she was able to follow, as she sat near her window at work, by simply inclining an ear to the thin partition behind her — these scenes, rendering the crash of crockery and the imprecations of the wounded frequently and peculiarly audible, had long been the scandal of a humble but harmonious neighbourhood. Mr. Henning was supposed to fill a place of confidence in a brush factory, while his wife, at home, occupied herself with the washing and mending of a considerable brood, mainly of sons. But economy and sobriety and indeed a virtue more important still had never presided at their councils. The freedom and frequency of Mrs. Henning's relations with a stove-polisher off the Euston Road were at least not a secret to a person who lived next door and looked up from her work so often that it was a wonder it was always finished so quickly. The little Hennings, unwashed and unchidden, spent most of their time either in pushing each other into the gutter or in running to the public-house at the corner for a pennyworth of gin, and the borrowing propensities of their elders were a theme for exclamation. There was no object of personal or domestic use which Mrs. Henning had not at one time or another endeavoured to elicit from the dressmaker; beginning with a mattress, on an occasion when she was about to take to her bed for a considerable period, and ending with a flannel petticoat and a pewter teapot. Lomax Place had eventually, from its over-peeping windows and doorways, been present at the seizure, by a long-suffering landlord, of the chattels of this interesting race and at the ejectment of the whole insolvent group, who departed in a straggling, jeering, unabashed, cynical manner, carrying with them but little of the sympathy of the street. Millicent, whose childish intimacy with Hyacinth Robinson Miss Pynsent had always viewed with vague anxiety — she thought the girl a nasty little thing and was afraid she would teach the innocent orphan low ways — Millicent, with her luxuriant tresses, her precocious beauty, her staring, mocking manner on the doorstep, was at this time twelve years of age. She vanished with her vanishing companions; Lomax Place saw them double the cape, that is turn the corner, and returned to its occupations with a conviction that they would make shipwreck on the outer reefs. But neither spar nor splinter floated back to their former haunts, and they were engulfed altogether in the fathomless deeps of the town. Miss Pynsent drew a long breath; it was her judgement that none of them would come to any good whatever, and Millicent least of all.

When therefore this young lady reappeared with all the signs of accomplished survival she could n't fail to ask herself whether, under a specious seeming, the phenomenon did n't simply represent the triumph of vice. She was alarmed, but she would have given her silver thimble to know the girl's history, and between her shock and her curiosity she passed an uncomfortable half-hour. She felt the familiar mysterious creature to be playing with her; revenging herself for former animadversions, for having been snubbed and miscalled by a prying little spinster who could now make no figure beside her. If it was not the triumph of vice it was at least the triumph of impertinence, as well as of youth, health and a greater acquaintance with the art of dress than Miss Pynsent could boast, for all her ridiculous signboards. She perceived, or she believed she perceived, that Millicent wanted to scare her, to make her think she had come after Hyacinth, that she wished to get hold of him and somehow mislead and tempt him. I should be sorry to impute to Miss Henning any motive more complicated than the desire to amuse herself, of a Saturday afternoon, by a ramble her vigorous legs had no occasion to deprecate; but it must be confessed that with her shrewd guess of this estimate of her as a ravening wolf and of her early playmate as an unspotted lamb she laughed out, in Miss Pynsent's anxious face, irrelevantly and good-humouredly and without deigning to explain. But what indeed had she come for if she had n't come for Hyacinth? It was not for the love of the dressmaker's pretty ways. She remembered the boy and some of their tender passages, and in the wantonness of her full-blown freedom — her attachment also to any tolerable pretext for wander-

65

ing through the streets of London and gazing into
shop-windows — had said to herself she might dedi-
cate an afternoon to the pleasures of memory, might
revisit the scenes of her childhood. She considered
that her childhood had ended with the departure
of her family from Lomax Place. If the tenants of
that scarce-dissimulated slum had never learned what
their banished fellows were to go through she herself had at least retained a deep impression of those
horrible intermediate years. The family, as a family, had gone downhill, to the very bottom; and in
her humbler moments Millicent sometimes wondered
what lucky star had checked her own descent and
indeed enabled her to mount the slope again. In her
humbler moments, I say, for as a general thing she
was provided with an explanation of any good fortune that might befall her. What was more natural than that a girl should achieve miracles when
she was at once so handsome and so clever? Millicent thought with compassion of the young persons
whom a niggardly fate had endowed with only one
of these advantages. She was good-natured, but she
had no idea of gratifying Miss Pynsent's curiosity:
it seemed to her quite a sufficient kindness to stim-
ulate it.

She told the dressmaker she had a high position at
a great haberdasher's in the neighbourhood of Buckingham Palace; she was in the department for jackets
and mantles; she put on all these articles to show
them off to the customers, and on her person they
appeared to such advantage that nothing she took up
ever failed to go off. Miss Pynsent could imagine

from this how highly her services were prized. She had had a splendid offer from another establishment, an immense one in Oxford Street, and was just thinking if she should accept it. "We have to be beautifully dressed, but I don't care, because I like to look nice," she remarked to her hostess, who at the end of half an hour, very grave behind the clumsy glasses she had been obliged to wear of late years, seemed still not to know what to make of her. On the subject of her parents, of her history during the interval that was to be accounted for, the girl was large and vague, and Miss Pynsent saw that the domestic circle had not even a shadow of sanctity for her. She stood on her own feet — stood very firm. Her staying so long, her remaining over the half-hour, proved she had come for Hyacinth, since poor Amanda gave her as little information as was decent, told her nothing that would encourage or attract. She simply mentioned that Mr. Robinson (she was careful to speak of him in that manner) had given his attention to bookbinding and had served an apprenticeship in a house where they turned out the best work of that kind that was to be found in London.

"A bookbindery? Laws!" said Miss Henning. "Do you mean they get them up for the shops? Well, I always thought he would have something to do with books." Then she added: "But I did n't think he would ever follow a trade."

"A trade?" cried Miss Pynsent. "You should hear Mr. Robinson speak of it. He considers it too lovely, quite one of the fine arts."

Millicent smiled as if she knew how people often

considered things, and remarked that very likely it was tidy comfortable work, but she could n't believe there was much to be seen in it. "Perhaps you'll say there's more than there is here," she went on, finding at last an effect of irritation, of reprehension, an implication of aggressive respectability, in the image of the patient dressmaker's sitting for so many years in her close brown little den with the foggy familiarities of Lomax Place on the other side of the pane. Millicent liked to think she herself was strong, yet she was not strong enough for that.

This allusion to her shrunken industry seemed to Miss Pynsent very cruel; but she reflected it was natural one should be insulted if one talked to a vulgar girl. She judged this young lady in the manner of a person who was not vulgar herself, and if there was a difference between them she was right in feeling it to be in her favour. Miss Pynsent's "cut," as I have intimated, was not truly fashionable, and in the application of gimp and the matching of colours she was not absolutely to be trusted; but morally she had the best taste in the world. "I have n't so much work as I used to have, if that's what you mean. My eyes are not so good and my health has failed with advancing years."

I know not to what extent Millicent was touched by the dignity of this admission, but she replied without embarrassment that what Miss Pynsent wanted was a smart young assistant, some nice girl of a "tasty" turn who would brighten up the business and give her new ideas. "I can see you've got the same old ones, always: I can tell that by the way you've stuck the braid on that dress;" and she directed a poke of her neat little umbrella at the drapery in the dressmaker's lap. She continued to patronise and exasperate her, and to offer her consolation and encouragement with the heaviest hand that had ever been applied to Miss Pynsent's sensitive surface. Poor Amanda ended by gazing at her as if she had been a public performer of some kind, a ballad-singer or a conjurer, and went so far as to ask herself whether the creature could be (in her own mind) the "nice girl" who was to regild the tarnished sign. Miss Pynsent had had assistants in the past — she had even once, for a few months, had a "forewoman"; and some of these damsels had been precious specimens, whose misdemeanours lived vividly in her memory. Never, all the same, in her worst hour of delusion, had she trusted her interests to such an exponent of the latest thing as this. She was quickly reassured as to Millicent's own views, perceiving more and more that she was a tremendous highflyer, who required a much larger field of action than the musty bower she now honoured, goodness only knew why, with her presence. Miss Pynsent held her tongue as she always did when the sorrow of her life had been touched, the thought of the slow, inexorable decline on which she had entered that day, nearly ten years before, when her hesitations and scruples resolved themselves into a hideous mistake. The deep conviction of error on this unspeakably important occasion had ached and throbbed within her ever since like an incurable disease. She had sown in her boy's mind the seeds of shame and rancour; she had made him conscious of his stigma, of his exquisitely vulnerable spot, and condemned him to know that for him the sun would never shine as it shone for most others. By the time he was sixteen years old she had learned — or believed she had learned — the judgement he had passed on her, and at that period she had lived through a series of horrible months, an ordeal in which every element of her old prosperity perished. She cried her eyes out, on coming to a sense of her blunder, so blinded and weakened herself with weeping that she might for a while have believed she should never be able to touch a needle again. She lost all interest in her work, and that play of invention which had always been her pride deserted her, together with the reputation of keeping the tidiest lodgings in Lomax Place. A couple of commercial gentlemen and a Welsh plumber of religious tendencies who for several years had made her establishment their home withdrew their patronage on the ground that the airing of her beds was not what it used to be, and disseminated cruelly this injurious legend. She ceased to notice or to care how sleeves were worn, and on the question of flounces and gores her mind was a blank. She fell into a grievous debility and then into a long, low, languid fever, during which Hyacinth tended her with a devotion that only made the wrong she had done him seem sharper, and that determined in Mr. Vetch, so soon as she was able to hold up her head a little, the impulse to come and sit with her through the dull hours of convalescence. She re-established to a certain extent, after a time, her connexion, so far as the letting of her rooms was concerned (from the other department of

her activity the tide had ebbed apparently for ever);
but nothing was the same again, and she knew it was
the beginning of the end. So it had gone on, and she
watched the end approach; she felt it very near indeed when a child she had seen playing in the gutters
came to flaunt it over her in silk and lace. She gave
a low, inaudible sigh of relief as Millicent at last got
up and stood there, smoothing the glossy cylinder of
her umbrella.

"Mind you give my love to Hyacinth," the girl said
with an assurance which showed all her insensibility
to tacit protests. "I don't care if you do guess that if
I've stopped so long it was in the hope he would be
dropping in to his tea. You can tell him I sat an hour,
on purpose, if you like; there's no shame in my wanting to see my childhood's sweetheart. He may know
I call him that!" Millicent continued with her show-
room laugh, as Miss Pynsent judged it to be; confer-
ring these permissions, successively, as if they were
great indulgences. "Do give him my best love and
tell him I hope he'll come and see me. I see you
won't tell him anything. I don't know what you're
afraid of; but I'll leave my card for him, all the
same." She drew forth a little bright-coloured
pocket-book, and it was with amazement that Miss
Pynsent saw her extract from it a morsel of engraved
pasteboard — so monstrous did it seem that one
of the squalid little Hennings should have lived to
display this emblem of social consideration. Millicent enjoyed the effect she produced as she laid the
card on the table, and gave another ringing peal
of mirth at the sight of her hostess's half-hungry,

half-astonished look. "What *do* you think I want to do with him? I could swallow him at a single bite!" she cried.

Poor Amanda gave no second glance at the document on the table, though she had perceived it contained, in the corner, her visitor's address, which Millicent had amused herself ingeniously with not mentioning: she only got up, laying down her work with an agitated hand, so that she should be able to see Miss Henning well out of the house. "You need n't think I shall put myself out to keep him in the dark. I shall certainly tell him you've been here, and exactly how you strike me."

"Of course you'll say something nasty — like you used to when I was a child. You usually let me 'ave it then, you know!"

"Ah well," said Miss Pynsent, nettled at this reminder of an acerbity which the girl's present development caused to appear absurdly ineffectual, "you're very different now, when I think what you've come from."

"What I've come from?" Millicent threw back her head and opened her eyes very wide, while all her feathers and ribbons nodded. "Did you want me to stick fast in this low place for the rest of my days? You've had to stay in it yourself, so you might speak civilly of it." She coloured and raised her voice and looked magnificent in her scorn. "And pray what have you come from yourself, and what has *he* come from — the mysterious 'Mr. Robinson' who used to be such a puzzle to the whole Plice? I thought perhaps I might clear it up, but you have n't told me that yet!"

Miss Pynsent turned straight away, covering her ears with her hands. "I've nothing to tell you! Leave my room — leave my house!" she cried with a trembling voice.

V

It was in this way she failed either to see or to hear the opening of the door of the room, which obeyed a slow, apparently cautious impulse given it from the hall and revealed the figure of a young man standing there with a short pipe in his teeth. There was something in his face which immediately told Millicent Henning he had heard her last tones resound into the passage. He entered as if, young as he was, he knew that when women were squabbling men were not called upon to be headlong, and now evidently wondered who the dressmaker's evident "match" might be. She recognised on the instant her old playmate, and without reflexion, confusion or diplomacy, in the fulness of her vulgarity and sociability, exclaimed at no lower pitch: "Gracious, Hyacinth Robinson, is *that* your form?"

Miss Pynsent turned round in a flash, but kept silent; then, very white and shaken, took up her work again and seated herself in her window. Hyacinth on his side stood staring — he blushed all over. He knew who she was but did n't say so; he only asked in a voice which struck the girl as quite different from the old one — the one in which he used to tell her she was beastly tiresome — "Is it of me you were speaking just now?"

"When I asked where you had come from? That was because we 'eard you in the 'all," said Milli-

74

cent smiling. "I suppose you've come from your work."

"You used to live in the Place — you always wanted to kiss me," the young man remarked with an effort not to show all the surprise and satisfaction he felt. "Did n't she live in the Place, Pinnie ?"

Pinnie, for all answer, fixed a pair of strange pleading eyes upon him, and Millicent broke out, with her recurrent laugh, in which the dressmaker had been right in discovering the note of affectation, "Do you want to know what you look like ? You look for all the world like a little plastered-up Frenchman! Don't he look like a funny little Frenchman, Miss Pynsent ?" she went on as if she were on the best possible terms with the mistress of the establishment.

Hyacinth caught a light from that afflicted woman; he saw something in her face that he knew very well by this time and in the sight of which he always found an odd, perverse, unholy relish. It seemed to say that she prostrated herself, that she did penance in the dust, that she was his to trample upon, to spit upon. He did neither of these things, but she was constantly offering herself, and her permanent humility, her perpetual abjection, was a vague counter-irritant to the soreness lodged in his own heart for ever and which had often at night made him cry with rage in his little room under the roof. Pinnie meant this to-day as a matter of course, and could only especially mean it in the presence of Miss Henning's remark about his looking like a Frenchman. He knew he looked like a Frenchman, he had often been told so before, and a large part of the time, often quite grandly, he felt like one — like one of those he had read about in Michelet and Carlyle. He had picked up their language with the most extraordinary facility, by the aid of one of his mates, a refugee from Paris, in the workroom, and of a second-hand dog's-eared dictionary bought for a shilling in the Brompton Road during one of his interminable, restless, melancholy, moody, yet all-observant strolls through London. He spoke it, he believed, by a natural impulse, caught the accent, the gesture, the movement of eyebrow and shoulder; so that on any occasion of his having to pass for a foreigner — there was no telling what might happen — he should certainly be able to do so to admiration, especially if he could borrow a blouse. He had never seen a blouse in his life, but he knew exactly the form and colour of such a garment and how it was worn. What the complications might be which should compel him to assume the disguise of a person of a social station lower still than his own he would not for the world have mentioned to you; but as they were very present to the mind of our imaginative, ingenious youth we shall catch a glimpse of them in the course of a further acquaintance with him. Actually, when there was no question of masquerading, it made him blush again that such a note should be struck by a loud, laughing, handsome girl who came back out of his past. There was more in Pinnie's weak eyes now than her usual rueful profession; there was a dumb intimation, almost as pathetic as the other, that if he cared to let her off easily he would n't detain their terrible visitor very long. He had no wish to do that; he kept the door open on purpose; he did n't enjoy talking to girls under Pinnie's eyes and could see that this one had every disposition to talk. So without responding to her observation about his appearance he said, not knowing exactly what to say: "Have you come back to live in the Place?"

"Heaven forbid I should ever do that!" cried Miss Henning with genuine emotion. "I must live near the establishment in which I'm employed."

"And what establishment is that now?" the young man asked, gaining confidence and perceiving in detail how handsome she was. He had n't roamed about London for nothing, and he knew that when a girl had such looks a jocular tone of address, a pleasing freedom, was *de rigueur;* so he added: "Is it the Bull and Gate or the Elephant and Castle?"

"A public-house? Well, you have n't got the politeness of a Frenchman at all events!" Her good-nature had come back to her perfectly, and her resentment of his imputation of her looking like a barmaid — a blowsy beauty who handled pewter — was tempered by her more and more curious consideration of Hyacinth's form. He was exceedingly "rum," but he had a stamp as sharp for her as that of a new coin and which also agreeably suggested value. Since he remembered so well that she had been fond of kissing him in their early days she would have liked to show herself prepared to repeat this graceful attention. But she reminded herself in time that her line should be religiously the ladylike, and she was content to exclaim simply: "I don't care what a man looks like so long as he knows a lot. That's the form *I* like!"

Miss Pynsent had promised herself the satisfaction of taking no further notice of her brilliant invader; but the temptation was great to expose her to Hyacinth, in mitigation of her brilliancy, by remarking sarcastically, according to opportunity, "Miss 'Enning would n't live in Lomax Plice for the world. She thinks it too dreadfully low."

"So it is; it's a beastly hole," said the young man.

The poor dressmaker's little dart fell to the ground and Millicent exclaimed jovially "Right you are!" while she directed to the object of her childhood's admiration an expression of face that put him more and more at his ease.

"Don't you suppose I know something?" he asked, planted before her with his little legs slightly apart and, with his hands behind him, making the open door waver to and fro.

"You? Oh, I don't care a straw what you know!" she said; and he had at any rate a mind sufficiently enriched to see what she meant by that. If she meant he was so good-looking that he might pass on this score alone her judgement was conceivable, though many women would strongly have dissented from it. He was as small as he had announced from the first — he had never got his growth — and she could easily see that he was not what she at least would call strong. His bones were small, his chest was narrow, his complexion pale, his whole figure almost childishly slight; and Millicent noted afterwards that he had a very delicate hand — the hand, as she said to

78

herself, of a gentleman. What she liked was his face and something jaunty and romantic, almost theatrical, in his whole little person. Miss Henning was not acquainted with any member of the dramatic profession, but she supposed vaguely that that was the way an actor would look in private life. Hyacinth's features were perfect; his eyes, large and much divided, had as their usual expression a kind of witty, almost an impertinent, candour, and a small, soft, fair moustache disposed itself upon his upper lip in a way that made him appear to smile even when his heart was heavy. The waves of his dense fine hair clustered round a forehead which was high enough to suggest remarkable things, and Miss Henning had observed that when he first appeared he wore his little soft circular hat in a way that left these frontal locks very visible. He was dressed in an old brown velveteen jacket and wore exactly the bright-coloured necktie which Miss Pynsent's quick fingers used of old to shape out of hoarded remnants of silk and muslin. He was shabby and work-stained, but an observant eye would have caught the hint of an "arrangement" in his dress (his appearance being plainly not a matter of indifference to himself) while a painter (not of the heroic) would have liked to make a sketch of him. There was something exotic in him, and yet, with his sharp young face, destitute of bloom but not of sweetness, and a certain conscious cockneyism that pervaded him, he was as strikingly as Millicent, in her own degree, a product of the London streets and the London air. He looked both ingenuous and slightly wasted, amused, amusing and indefinably

79

sad. Women had always found him touching, but he made them — so they had repeatedly assured him — die of laughing.

"I think you had better shut the door," said Miss Pynsent, meaning that he had better shut their departing visitor out.

"Did you come here on purpose to see us?" he went on, not heeding this injunction, of which he divined the spirit, and wishing the girl would take her leave so that he might go out again with her. He should like talking with her much better away from Pinnie, who evidently was ready to stick a bodkin into her for reasons he perfectly understood. He had seen plenty of them before, Pinnie's reasons, even where girls were concerned who were not nearly so good-looking as this one. She was always in a fearful "funk" about their getting hold of him and persuading him to make a marriage beneath his station. His station! — poor Hyacinth had often asked himself and enquired of Miss Pynsent what it could possibly be. He had thought of it bitterly enough, wondering how in the world he could marry "beneath" it. He would never marry at all — to that his mind was absolutely made up; he would never hand on to another the burden that had made his own young spirit so intolerably sore, the inheritance that had darkened the whole threshold of his manhood. All the more reason why he should have his compensation; why, if the soft society of women was to be enjoyed on other terms, he should cultivate it with a bold free mind.

"I thought I'd just give a look at the old shop;

I had an engagement not far off," Millicent said. "But I would n't have believed any one who had told me I should find you just where I left you."

"We needed you to look after us!" Miss Pynsent irrepressibly exclaimed.

"Oh, you're such a rattling swell yourself!" Hyacinth observed without heeding the dressmaker.

"None of *your* 'rattling' impudence! I'm as good a girl as there is in London." And to corroborate this Miss Henning went on: "If you were to offer to see me a part of the way home I'd tell you I don't knock about that way with gentlemen."

"I'll go with you as far as you like," Hyacinth replied simply, as if he knew how to treat that sort of speech.

"Well, it's only because I knew you as a baby!" And they went out together, Hyacinth careful not to look at poor Pinnie at all (he felt her glaring whitely and tearfully at him out of her dim corner — it had by this time grown too dusky to work without a lamp) and his companion giving her a cruelly familiar nod of farewell over her shoulder.

It was a long walk from Lomax Place to the quarter of the town in which (to be near the haberdashers of the Buckingham Palace Road) Miss Henning occupied a modest back room; but the influences of the hour were such as to make the excursion very agreeable to our young man, who liked the streets at all times, but especially at nightfall in the autumn, of a Saturday, when in the vulgar districts the smaller shops and open-air industries were doubly active, and big clumsy torches flared and smoked over hand-carts

81

and costermongers' barrows drawn up in the gutters. Hyacinth had roamed through the great city since he was an urchin, but his imagination had never ceased to be stirred by the preparations for Sunday that went on in the evening among the toilers and spinners, his brothers and sisters, and he lost himself in all the quickened crowding and pushing and staring at lighted windows and chaffering at the stalls of fishmongers and hucksters. He liked the people who looked as if they had got their week's wage and were prepared to lay it out discreetly; and even those whose use of it would plainly be extravagant and intemperate; and, best of all, those who evidently had n't received it at all and who wandered about disinterestedly and vaguely, their hands in empty pockets, watching others make their bargains and fill their satchels, or staring at the striated sides of bacon, at the golden cubes and triangles of cheese, at the graceful festoons of sausage, in the most brilliant of the windows. He liked the reflexion of the lamps on the wet pavements, the feeling and smell of the carboniferous London damp; the way the winter fog blurred and suffused the whole place, made it seem bigger and more crowded, produced halos and dim radiations, trickles and evaporations on the plates of glass. He moved in the midst of these impressions this evening, but he enjoyed them in silence, with an attention taken up mainly by his companion, and pleased to be already so intimate with a young lady whom people turned round to look at. She herself affected to speak of the rush and crush of the week's end with disgust: she said she liked the streets, but liked the respectable ones; she could n't abide the smell of fish, which the whole place seemed full of, so that she hoped they would soon get into the Edgeware Road, toward which they tended and which was a proper street for a lady. To Hyacinth she appeared to have no connexion with the long-haired little girl who, in Lomax Place, years before, was always hugging a smutty doll and courting his society; she was a stranger, a new acquaintance, and he observed her in suspense, wondering by what transitions she had reached her present pitch.

She enlightened him but little on this point, though she talked a great deal on a variety of subjects and mentioned to him her habits, her aspirations, her likes and dislikes — which last were as emphatic as the giggles of a person tickled. She was tremendously particular, difficult to please, he could see that; and she assured him she never put up with anything a moment after she had ceased to care for it. Especially was she particular about gentlemen's society, and she made it plain that a young fellow who wanted to have anything to say to her must be in receipt of wages amounting at the least to fifty shillings a week. Hyacinth assured her he did n't earn that as yet, and she remarked again that she made an exception for him because she knew all about him (or if not all at least a great deal) and he could see that her good-nature was equal to her beauty. She made such an exception that when, after they were moving down the Edgeware Road (which had still the brightness of late closing, but with more nobleness) he proposed she should enter a coffee-house with him and "take something" (he could hardly tell himself afterwards what brought him to this point) she acceded without a demur — without a demur even on the ground of his slender earnings. Slender as they were he had them in his pocket (they had been destined in some degree for Pinnie) and therefore felt equal to the occasion. Millicent partook profusely of tea and bread and butter, with a relish of raspberry jam, and thought the place most comfortable, though he himself, after finding himself ensconced, was visited by doubts of its propriety, suggested, among several things, by photographs, on the walls, of young ladies in tights. He himself was hungry, he had not yet had his tea, but he was too excited, too preoccupied to eat; the situation made him restless and gave him thrills; it seemed the beginning of something new and rare. He had never yet "stood" even a glass of beer to a girl of Millicent's stamp — a girl who rustled and glittered and smelt of musk — and if she should turn out as jolly a specimen of the sex as she seemed it might make a great difference in his leisure hours, in his evenings, in which he had often felt a likeness to great square blackboards uninscribed with a stroke of chalk. That it would also make a difference in his savings (he was under a pledge to Pinnie and to Mr. Vetch to put by something every week) it did n't concern him for the moment to reflect; and indeed, though he thought it odious and insufferable to be poor, the ways and means of ceasing to be so had hitherto left his fancy unstirred. He knew what Millicent's age must be, but felt her nevertheless older, much older, than himself — she seemed to know so much about London and about life; and this made it

84

still more of a sensation to be entertaining her like a young swell. He thought of it too in connexion with the question of the character of the establishment; if this character was what it easily might be she would perceive it as soon as he, and very likely it would be a part of the general initiation she had given him an impression of that she would n't mind so long as the tea was strong and the bread and butter thick. She described to him what had passed between Miss Pynsent and herself (she did n't call her Pinnie, and he was glad, for he would n't have liked it) before he came in, and let him know that she should never dare to come to the place again, as his mother would tear her eyes out. Then she checked herself. "But of course she ain't your mother! How stupid I am! I keep forgetting."

Hyacinth had, as he supposed, from far back cultivated a manner with which he could meet allusions of this kind: he had had first and last so many opportunities to practise it. Therefore he looked at his companion very steadily while he said: "My mother died many years ago; she was a great invalid. But Pinnie has been awfully good to me."

"My mother's dead too" — Miss Henning was prompt, as if "capping" it. "She died very suddenly. I dare say you remember her in the Plice." Then, while Hyacinth disengaged from the past the obscure figure of Mrs. Henning, of whom he mainly remembered that she used to strike him as cross and dirty, the girl added, smiling, but with more sentiment, "But I've had no Pinnie."

"You look as if you could take care of yourself."

"Well, I'm very confiding," said Millicent Henning. Then she asked what had become of Mr. Vetch. "We used to say that if Miss Pynsent was your mamma he was your papa. In our family we used to call him Miss Pynsent's young man."

"He's her young man still," Hyacinth returned. "He's our best friend — or supposed to be. He got me the place I'm in now. He lives by his fiddle, as he used to do."

Millicent looked a little at her companion, after which she observed, "I should have thought he would have got you a place at his theatre."

"At his theatre? That would have been no use. I don't play any instrument."

"I don't mean in the orchestra, you gaby! You'd look very nice in a fancy costume." She had her elbows on the table and her shoulders lifted, an attitude of extreme familiarity. He was on the point of replying that he did n't care for fancy costumes, he wished to go through life in his own character; but he checked himself with the reflexion that this was exactly what he was apparently destined not to do. His own character? He was to cover that up as carefully as possible; he was to go through life in a mask, in a borrowed mantle; he was to be every day and every hour an actor. Suddenly and with the utmost irrelevance Miss Henning enquired: "Is Miss Pynsent some relation? What gave her any right over you?"

Hyacinth had an answer ready for this question; he had determined to say as he had several times said before: "Miss Pynsent's an old friend of my family. My mother was very fond of her and she was very

86

fond of my mother." He repeated the formula now,
looking at the girl with the same inscrutable calmness, as he fancied; though a remark more to his taste
would have been that his mother was none of her business. But she was too handsome for such risks, and
she presented her large fair face to him across the
table with an air of solicitation to be cosy and comfortable. There were things in his heart and a torment and a hidden passion in his life which he should
be glad enough to lay open to some woman. He believed that perhaps this would be the cure ultimately;
that in return for something he might drop, syllable
by syllable, into some listening ear that would be
attached to some kissable cheek, certain other words
would be spoken to him which would make his pain
for ever less sharp. But what woman could he trust,
what ear would be both safe and happily enough
attached? How much did n't he already ask? The
answer was not in this loud fresh laughing creature,
whose sympathy could n't have the fineness he was
looking for, since her curiosity was vulgar. Hyacinth
objected to the vulgar as much as Miss Pynsent herself; in this respect she had long since discovered that
he was after her own heart. He had not at any rate
now taken up the subject of Mrs. Henning's death;
he felt himself incapable of researches into that lady
and had no desire for knowledge of Millicent's rela-
tionships. Moreover he always suffered, to sickness,
when people began to hover about the question of his
origin, the reasons why Pinnie had had the care of
him from a baby. Mrs. Henning had been repulsive,
but at least her daughter could speak of her. "Mr.

Vetch has changed his lodgings: he moved out of 17 three years ago," he said, to vary the topic. "He could n't stand the other people in the house; there was a man who played the accordeon."

Millicent, however, was but moderately interested in this anecdote, though wanting to know why people should like Mr. Vetch's fiddle any better. Then she added: "And I think that while he was about it he might have put you into something better than a book-binder's."

"He was n't obliged to put me into anything. It's a very good place."

"All the same, it is n't where I should have looked to find you," the girl declared, not so much in the tone of wishing to offer him tribute as of resentment at having miscalculated.

"Where should you have looked to find me? In the House of Commons? It's a pity you could n't have told me in advance what you would have liked me to be."

She faced him over her cup while she drank in ladylike sips. "Do you know what they used to say in the Plice? That your father was a lord."

"Very likely. That's the kind of rot they talk in that precious hole," the young man said without blenching. ·

"Well, perhaps he was," Millicent ventured.

"He may have been a prime-minister for all the good it has done me."

"Fancy your talking as if you did n't know!" said Millicent. ·

"Finish your tea — don't mind how I talk."

"Well, you *'ave* got a temper!" she archly retorted. "I should have thought you'd be a clerk at a banker's."

"Do they select them for their tempers?"

"You know what I mean. You used to be too clever to follow a trade."

"Well, I'm not clever enough to live on air."

"You might be, really, for all the tea you drink! Why did n't you go in for some high profession?"

"How was I to go in? Who the devil was to help me?" Hyacinth asked with a certain vibration.

"Have n't you got any relations?" said Millicent after a moment.

"What are you doing? Are you trying to make me swagger?"

When he spoke sharply she only laughed, not in the least ruffled, and by the way she looked at him seemed to like the effect. "Well, I'm sorry you're only a journeyman," she went on as she pushed away her cup.

"So am I," Hyacinth answered; but he called for the bill as if he had been an employer of labour. Then while they waited he remarked to his companion that he did n't believe she had an idea of what his work was and how charming it could be. "Yes, I get up books for the shops," he said when she had asserted that she perfectly understood. "But the art of the binder's an exquisite art."

"So Miss Pynsent told me. She said you had some samples at home. I should like to see them."

"You would n't know how good they are," he finely smiled.

89

He expected she would exclaim in answer that he was an impudent wretch, and for a moment she seemed on the point of doing so. But the words changed on her lips and she replied almost tenderly: "That's just the way you used to speak to me years ago in the Plice."

"I don't care about that. I hate all that time."

"Oh, so do I, if you come to that," said Millicent as if she could rise to any breadth of view. With which she returned to her idea that he had not done himself justice. "You used always to have your nose in something or other. I never thought you'd work with your 'ands."

This seemed to irritate him, and, having paid the bill and given threepence, ostentatiously, to the young woman with a languid manner and hair of an unnatural yellow who had waited on them, he said: "You may depend upon it I shan't do it an hour longer than I can help."

"What will you do then?"

"Oh, you'll see some day." In the street, after they had begun to walk again, he went on: "You speak as if I could have my pick. What was an obscure little beggar to do, buried in a squalid corner of London under a million of idiots? I had no help, no influence, no acquaintance of any kind with professional people, and no means of getting at them. I had to do something; I couldn't go on living on Pinnie. Thank God I help her now a little. I took what I could get." He spoke as if he had been touched by the imputation of having derogated.

Millicent seemed to imply that he defended himself

successfully when she said: "You express yourself like a reg'lar gentleman" — a speech to which he made no response. But he began to talk again afterwards, and, the evening having definitely set in, his companion took his arm for the rest of the way home. By the time he reached her door he had confided to her that in secret he wrote — quite as for publication; he was haunted with the dream of literary distinction. This appeared to impress her, and she branched off to remark, with the agreeable incoherence that characterised her, that she did n't care anything for a man's family if she liked the man himself; she thought families and that sort of rot were about played out. Hyacinth wished she would leave his origin alone; and while they lingered in front of her house before she went in he broke out:

"I've no doubt you're a jolly girl, and I'm very happy to have seen you again. But you've awfully little tact."

"*I* have little tact? You should see me work off an old jacket!"

He was silent a little, standing before her with his hands in his pockets. "It's a good job you're so lovely."

Millicent did n't blush at this compliment, and probably did n't understand all it conveyed, but she looked into his eyes a while, with all the smile that showed her teeth, and then came back more inconsequently than ever. "Come now, who are you?"

"Who am I? I'm a wretched little 'forwarder' in the shop."

"I did n't think I ever could fancy any one in that

line!" she competently cried. Then she let him
know she could n't ask him in, as she made it a point
not to receive gentlemen, but she did n't mind if she
took another walk with him and she did n't care if
she met him somewhere — if it were handy enough.
As she lived so far from Lomax Place she did n't care
if she met him half-way. So in the dusky by-street
in Pimlico, before separating, they took a casual tryst;
the most interesting, the young man felt, that had yet
been — he could scarcely call it granted him.

VI

ONE day shortly after this, at the bindery, his friend
Poupin, absent, had failed to send the explanation
customary in case of illness or domestic accident.
There were two or three men employed in the place
whose non-appearance, usually following close upon
pay-day, was better unexplained, was in fact an implication of moral feebleness; but as a general thing
Mr. Crookenden's establishment was a haunt of
punctuality and sobriety. Least of all had Eustache
Poupin been in the habit of asking for a margin.
Hyacinth knew how little indulgence he had ever
craved, and this was part of his admiration for the
extraordinary Frenchman, an ardent stoic, a cold
conspirator and an exquisite artist, who was by far
the most interesting person in the ranks of his acquaintance and whose conversation, in the workshop,
helped him sometimes to forget the smell of leather
and glue. His conversation! Hyacinth had had
plenty of that and had endeared himself to the passionate refugee by the solemnity and candour of his
attention. Poupin had come to England after the
Commune of 1871, to escape the reprisals of the
government of M. Thiers, and had remained there in
spite of amnesties and rehabilitations. He was a Republican of the old-fashioned sort, of the note of 1848,
humanity and idealistic, infinitely addicted to fra-
ternity and equality and inexhaustibly surprised and

exasperated at finding so little enthusiasm for them in the land of his exile. He had a marked claim upon Hyacinth's esteem and gratitude, for he had been his *parrain*, his protector at the bindery. When Anastasius Vetch found something for Miss Pynsent's young charge to do, it was through the Frenchman, with whom he had accidentally made acquaintance, that he found it.

When the boy was about fifteen years of age Mr. Vetch made him a present of the essays of Lord Bacon, and the purchase of this volume had important consequences for Hyacinth. Anastasius Vetch was a poor man, and the luxury of giving was for the most part denied him; but when once in a way he tasted it he liked the sensation to be pure. No man knew better the difference between the common and the rare, or was more capable of appreciating a book which opened well — of which the margin was not hideously chopped and of which the lettering on the back was sharp. It was only such a book that he could bring himself to offer even to a poor little devil whom a fifth-rate dressmaker (he knew Pinnie was fifth-rate) had rescued from the workhouse. So when it became a question of fitting the great Elizabethan with a new coat — a coat of full morocco discreetly, delicately gilt — he went with his little cloth-bound volume, a Pickering, straight to Mr. Crookenden, whom every one who knew anything about the matter knew to be a prince of binders, though they also knew that his work, limited in quantity, was mainly done for a particular bookseller and only through the latter's agency. Anastasius Vetch had no idea of paying the bookseller's commission, and though he could be lavish (for him) when he made a present, he was capable of taking an immense deal of trouble to save sixpence. He made his way into Mr. Crookenden's workshop, which was situated in a small superannuated square in Soho and where the proposal of so slender a job was received at first with chilling calm. Mr. Vetch, however, insisted; he explained with irresistible frankness the motive of his errand: the desire to obtain the best possible binding for the least possible money. He made his conception of the best possible binding so vivid, so exemplary, that the master of the shop at last confessed to that disinterested sympathy which, in favouring conditions, establishes itself between the artist and the connoisseur. Mr. Vetch's little book was put in hand as a particular service to an eccentric gentleman whose visit had been a smile-stirring interlude (for the circle of listening workmen) in a merely mechanical day; and when he went back three weeks later to see if the job were done he had the pleasure of finding that his injunctions, punctually complied with, had even been bettered. The work had been accomplished with a perfection of skill which made him ask whom he was to thank for it (he had been told that one man should do the whole of it) and in this manner he made the acquaintance of the most brilliant craftsman in the establishment, the incorruptible, the imaginative, the unerring Eustache Poupin.

In response to an appreciation which he felt not to be *banal* M. Poupin remarked that he had at home a small collection of experiments in morocco, russia, parchment, of fanciful specimens with which, for the love of the thing itself, he had amused his leisure hours and which he should be happy to show his interlocutor if the latter would do him the honour to call upon him at his lodgings in Lisson Grove. Mr. Vetch made a note of the address and, for the love of the thing itself, went one Sunday afternoon to see the binder's esoteric studies. On this occasion he made the acquaintance of Madame Poupin, a small, fat lady with a bristling moustache, the white cap of an *ouvrière*, a knowledge of her husband's craft that was equal to his own, and not a syllable of English save the words "What you think, what you think?" which she introduced with indefatigable frequency. He also discovered that his new acquaintance had been a political proscript and that he regarded the iniquitous fabric of Church and State with an eye scarcely more reverent than the fiddler's own. M. Poupin was an aggressive socialist, which Anastasius Vetch was not, and a constructive democrat (instead of being a mere scoffer at effete things) and a theorist and an optimist and a collectivist and a perfectionist and a visionary; he believed the day was to come when all the nations of the earth would abolish their frontiers and armies and custom-houses, and embrace on both cheeks and cover the globe with boulevards, radiating from Paris, where the human family would sit in groups at little tables, according to affinities, drinking coffee (not tea, *par exemple!*) and listening to the music of the spheres. Mr. Vetch neither prefigured nor desired this organised beatitude; he was fond of his cup of tea and only wanted to see the

British constitution a good deal simplified; he thought it a much overrated system, but his heresies rubbed shoulders sociably with those of the little bookbinder, and his friend in Lisson Grove became for him the type of the intelligent foreigner whose conversation gives wings to our heavy-footed culture. Poupin's humanitary zeal was as unlimited as his English vocabulary was the reverse, and the new friends agreed with each other enough, and not too much, to discuss, which was much better than an unspeakable harmony. On several other Sunday afternoons the fiddler went back to Lisson Grove, and having, at his theatre, as a veteran, a faithful servant, an occasional privilege, he was able to carry thither, one day in the autumn, an order for two seats in the second balcony. Madame Poupin and her husband passed a lugubrious evening at the English comedy, where they did n't understand a word that was spoken and consoled themselves by hanging on the agitated fiddle-stick of their friend in the orchestra. But this adventure failed to arrest the development of a friendship into which, eventually, Amanda Pynsent was drawn. Madame Poupin, among the cold insularies, lacked female society, and Mr. Vetch proposed to his amiable friend in Lomax Place to call upon her. The little dressmaker, who in the course of her life had known no Frenchwoman but the unhappy Florentine (so favourable a specimen till she began to go wrong) adopted his suggestion in the hope that she should get a few ideas from a lady whose appearance would doubtless exemplify (as Florentine's originally had done) the fine taste of her nation; but she found the

97

bookbinder and his wife a bewildering mixture of the brilliant and the relaxed, and was haunted long afterwards by the memory of the lady's camisole in some hideous print, her uncorseted overflow and her carpet slippers.

The acquaintance, none the less, was sealed three months later by a supper, one Sunday night, in Lisson Grove, to which Mr. Vetch brought his fiddle, at which Amanda presented to her hosts her adoptive son, and which also revealed to her that Madame Poupin could dress a Michaelmas goose if she could n't dress a fat Frenchwoman. This lady confided to the fiddler that she thought Miss Pynsent exceedingly *comme il faut — dans le genre anglais;* and neither Amanda nor Hyacinth had ever passed an evening of such splendour. It took its place, in the boy's recollection, beside the visit, years before, to Mr. Vetch's theatre. He drank in the remarks exchanged between that gentleman and M. Poupin. M. Poupin showed him his bindings, the most precious trophies of his skill, and it seemed to Hyacinth that on the spot he was initiated into a fascinating mystery. He handled the books for half an hour; Anastasius Vetch watched him without giving any particular sign. When therefore presently, Miss Pynsent consulted her friend for the twentieth time on the subject of Hyacinth's "career" — she spoke as if she were hesitating between the diplomatic service, the army and the church — the fiddler replied with promptitude: "Make him, if you can, what the Frenchman is." At the mention of a handicraft poor Pinnie always looked very solemn, yet when Mr.

Vetch asked her if she were prepared to send the boy
to one of the universities, or to pay the premium required for his being articled to a solicitor, or to make
favour on his behalf with a bank director or a mer-
chant prince, or, yet again, to provide him with a comfortable home while he should woo the muse and
await the laurels of literature — when, I say, he put
the case before her with this cynical, ironical lucidity
she only sighed and said that all the money she had
ever saved was ninety pounds, which, as he knew perfectly well, it would cost her his acquaintance for ever-
more to take out of the bank. The fiddler had in fact
declared to her in a manner not to be mistaken that
if she should divest herself, on the boy's account, of
this sole nest-egg of her old age, he would wash his
hands of her and her affairs. Her standard of success for Hyacinth was vague save on one point, as
regards which she was passionately, fiercely firm: she
was perfectly determined he should never go into a
small shop. She would rather see him a bricklayer
or a costermonger than dedicated to a retail business,
tying up candles at a grocer's or giving change for
a shilling across a counter. She would rather, she
declared on one occasion, see him articled to a shoemaker or a tailor.

A stationer in a neighbouring street had affixed to
his window a written notice that he was in want of
a smart errand-boy, and Pinnie, on hearing of it,
had presented Hyacinth to his consideration. The
stationer was a dreadful bullying man with a patch
over his eye, who seemed to think the boy would be
richly remunerated with three shillings a week; a con-

temptible measure, as it seemed to the dressmaker, of his rare abilities and acquirements. His schooling had been desultory, precarious, and had had a certain continuity mainly in his early years, while he was under the care of an old lady who combined with the functions of pew-opener at a neighbouring church the manipulation, in the Place itself, where she resided with her sister, a monthly nurse, of such pupils as could be spared (in their families) from the more urgent exercise of holding the baby and fetching the beer. Later, for a twelvemonth, Pinnie had paid five shillings a week for him at an "Academy" in a genteel part of Islington, where there was an "instructor in the foreign languages," a platform for oratory and a high social standard, but where Hyacinth suffered from the fact that almost all his mates were the sons of dealers in edible articles — pastry-cooks, grocers and fishmongers — and in this capacity subjected him to pangs and ignominious contrasts by bringing to school, for their exclusive consumption or for exchange and barter, various buns, oranges, spices and marine animals, which the boy, with his hands in his empty pockets and the sense of a savourless home in heart, was obliged to see devoured without his participation. Miss Pynsent would not have pretended he was highly educated in the technical sense of the word, but she believed that at fifteen he had read almost every book in the world. The limits of his reading had been in fact only the limits of his opportunity. Mr. Vetch, who talked with him more and more as he grew older, knew this, and lent him every volume he possessed or could pick up for the purpose. Reading was his extravagance, while the absence of any direct contact with a library repre- sented for him mainly the hard shock of the real; the shock, that is, he could most easily complain of. Mr. Vetch believed him subtly intelligent, and therefore thought it a woful pity that he could n't have further- ance in some liberal walk; but he would have thought it a greater pity still that a youth with that expression in his eyes should be condemned to measure tape or cut slices of cheese. He himself had no influence he could bring into play, no connexion with the great world of capital or the market of labour. That is he touched these mighty institutions at but one very small point — a point which, such as it was, he kept well in mind.

When Pinnie replied to the stationer round the corner, after he had mentioned the "terms" on which he was prepared to receive applications from errand- boys, that, thank her stars, she had n't sunk so low as that — so low as to sell her darling into slavery for three shillings a week — he felt that she only gave more florid expression to his own sentiment. Of course if Hyacinth did n't begin by carrying parcels he could n't hope to be promoted, through the more refined nimbleness of tying them up, to a position as accountant or manager; but both the fiddler and his friend — Miss Pynsent indeed only in the last resort — resigned themselves to the forfeiture of this pro- spect. Mr. Vetch saw clearly that a charming handi- craft was a finer thing than a vulgar "business," and one day after his acquaintance with Eustache Poupin had gone a considerable length he enquired of the fervid Frenchman if there were a chance of the lad's obtaining a footing, under his own wing, in Mr. Crookenden's workshop. There could be no better place for him to acquire a knowledge of the most elegant of the mechanical arts; and to be received into such an establishment and at the instance of such an artist would be a real start in life. M. Poupin meditated, and that evening confided his meditations to the companion who reduplicated all his thoughts and understood him better even than he understood himself. The pair had no children and had felt the deficiency; moreover they had heard from Mr. Vetch the dolorous tale of the boy's entrance into life. He was one of the disinherited, one of the expropriated, one of the exceptionally interesting; and moreover he was one of themselves, a child, as it were, of the inexhaustible France, an offshoot of the sacred race. It is not the most authenticated point in this veracious history, but there is strong reason to believe that tears were shed that night, in Lisson Grove, over poor Hyacinth Robinson. In a day or two M. Poupin replied to the fiddler that he had now been several years in *le vieux* "Crook's" employ; that during that time he had done work for him which he would have had *bien du mal* to get done by another, and had never asked for an indulgence, an allowance, a remission, an augmentation. It was time, if only for the dignity of the thing, he should ask for something, and he would make their little friend the subject of his demand. "*La société lui doit bien cela,*" he remarked afterwards, when, Mr. Crookenden proving dryly hospitable and the arrangement being formally complete, Mr. Vetch thanked him in his kindly, casual, bashful English way. He was paternal when Hyacinth began to occupy a place in the malodorous chambers in Soho; he took him in hand, made him a disciple, the recipient of a precious tradition, discovered in him a susceptibility to philosophic, to cosmic, as well as to technic truth. He taught him French and socialism, encouraged him to spend his evenings in Lisson Grove, invited him to regard Madame Poupin as a second, or rather as a third, mother, and in short made a very considerable mark on the boy's mind. He fostered and drew out the latent Gallicism of his nature, and by the time he was twenty Hyacinth, who had completely assimilated his influence, regarded him with a mixture of veneration and amusement. M. Poupin was the person who consoled him most when he was miserable; and he was very often miserable.

His staying away from his work was so rare that, in the afternoon, before he went home, Hyacinth walked to Lisson Grove to see what ailed him. He found his friend in bed with a plaster on his chest and Madame Poupin making *tisane* over the fire. The Frenchman took his indisposition solemnly but resignedly, like a man who believed that all illness was owing to the imperfect organisation of society, and lay covered up to his chin with a red cotton handkerchief bound round his head. Near his bed sat a visitor, a young man unknown to Hyacinth. Hyacinth naturally had never been to Paris, but he always supposed that the *intérieur* of his friends in Lisson Grove gave rather a vivid idea of that city. The two small rooms constituting their establishment contained a great many mirrors as well as little portraits (old-fashioned prints) of revolutionary heroes. The chimney-piece in the bedroom was muffled in some red drapery which appeared to Hyacinth extraordinarily magnificent; the principal ornament of the salon was a group of small and highly-decorated cups, on a tray, accompanied by gilt bottles and glasses, the latter still more diminutive — the whole intended for black coffee and liqueurs. There was no carpet on the floor, but rugs and mats of various shapes and sizes disposed themselves at the feet of the chairs and sofas; and in the sitting-room, where stood a wonderful gilt clock of the Empire, surmounted with a "subject" representing Virtue receiving a crown of laurel from the hands of Faith, Madame Poupin, with the aid of a tiny stove, a handful of charcoal and two or three saucepans, carried on a triumphant *cuisine*. In the windows were curtains of white muslin much fluted and frilled and tied with pink ribbon.

VII

"I'm suffering extremely, but we must all suffer so long as the social question is so abominably, so iniquitously neglected," Poupin remarked, speaking French and rolling toward Hyacinth his salient, excited-looking eyes, which always had the same declamatory, reclamatory, proclamatory, the same universally inaugurative expression, whatever his occupation or his topic. Hyacinth had seated himself near his friend's pillow, opposite the strange young man, who had been accommodated with a chair at the foot of the bed.

"Ah yes; with their filthy politics the situation of the *pauvre monde* is the last thing they ever think of!" his wife exclaimed from the fire. "There are times when I ask myself how long it will go on."

"It will go on till the measure of their imbecility, their infamy, is full. It will go on till the day of justice, till the reintegration of the despoiled and disinherited, is ushered in with a force that will shake the globe."

"Oh, we always see things go on; we never see them change," said Madame Poupin, making a very cheerful clatter with a big spoon in a saucepan.

"We may not see it, but *they'll* see it," her husband returned. "But what do I say, my children? I do see it," he pursued. "It's before my eyes in its radiant reality, especially as I lie here — the revendication, the rehabilitation, the rectification."

Hyacinth ceased to pay attention, not because he had a differing opinion about what M. Poupin called the *avènement* of the disinherited, but, on the contrary, precisely on account of his familiarity with that prospect. It was the constant theme of his French friends, whom he had long since perceived to be in a state of chronic spiritual inflammation. For them the social question was always in order, the political question always abhorrent, the disinherited always present. He wondered at their zeal, their continuity, their vivacity, their incorruptibility; at the abundant supply of conviction and prophecy they always had on hand. He believed that at bottom he was sorer than they, yet he had deviations and lapses, moments when the social question bored him and he forgot not only his own wrongs, which would have been pardonable, but those of the people at large, of his brothers and sisters in misery. They, however, were perpetually in the breach, and perpetually consistent with themselves and, what is more, with each other. Hyacinth had heard that the institution of marriage in France was lightly considered, but he was struck with the closeness and intimacy of the union in Lisson Grove, the passionate identity of interest: especially on the day when M. Poupin informed him, in a moment of extreme but not indiscreet expansion, that the lady was his wife only in a spiritual, affectional sense. There were hypocritical concessions and debasing superstitions of which this exalted pair had wholly disapproved. Hyacinth knew their vocabulary by heart and could have said everything, in the same words, that on any given occasion M. Poupin was likely to say. He knew that "they," in their phraseology, was a comprehensive allusion to every one in the world but the people — though who, exactly, in their length and breadth, the people were was less definitely established. He himself was of this sacred body, for which the future was to have such compensations; and so of course were his French friends, and so was Pinnie, and so were most of the inhabitants of Lomax Place and the workmen in old Crook's shop. But was old Crook himself, who wore an apron rather dirtier than the rest of them and was a master-hand at "forwarding," yet who, on the other side, was the occupant of a villa all but detached, at Putney, with a wife known to have secret aspirations toward a page in buttons? Above all was Mr. Vetch, who earned a weekly wage, and not a large one, with his fiddle, but who had mysterious affinities of another sort, reminiscences of a phase in which he smoked cigars, had a hat-box and used cabs — besides visiting Boulogne? Anastasius Vetch had interfered in his life, atrociously, at a terrible crisis; but Hyacinth, who strove to cultivate justice in his own conduct, believed he had acted conscientiously, and tried to esteem him, the more so as the fiddler evidently felt he had something to make up to him for and had ever treated him with marked benevolence. He believed in short that Mr. Vetch took a sincere interest in him and if he should meddle again would meddle in a different way: he used to see him sometimes look at him with the kindest eyes. It would make a difference therefore if he were of the people or not, inasmuch as on the day of the great revenge it would only be the people who should be

THE PRINCESS CASAMASSIMA

saved. It was for the people the world was made: whoever was not of them was against them; and all others were cumberers, usurpers, exploiters, *accapareurs*, as M. Poupin used to say. Hyacinth had once put the question directly to Mr. Vetch, who looked at him a while through the fumes of his eternal pipe and then said: "Do you think I'm an aristocrat?"

"I did n't know but you were a bourgeois," the young man answered.

"No, I'm neither. I'm a Bohemian."

"With your evening dress, every night?"

"My dear boy," said the fiddler, "those are the most confirmed."

Hyacinth was only half satisfied with this, for it was by no means definite to him that Bohemians were also to be saved; if he could be sure perhaps he would become one himself. Yet he never suspected Mr. Vetch of being a governmental agent, though Eustache Poupin had told him that there were a great many who looked a good deal like that: not of course with any purpose of incriminating the fiddler, whom he had trusted from the first and continued to trust. The governmental agent in extraordinary disguises, the wondrous *mouchard* of M. Poupin's view, became a very familiar type to Hyacinth, and though he had never caught one of the infamous brotherhood in the act there were plenty of persons to whom, on the very face of the matter, he had no hesitation in attributing the character. There was nothing of the Bohemian, at any rate, about the Poupins, whom Hyacinth had now known long enough not to be surprised at the

way they combined the socialistic passion, a red-hot
impatience for the general rectification, with an extraordinary decency of life and a worship of proper
work. The Frenchman spoke habitually as if the
great swindle practised upon the people were too
impudent to be endured a moment longer, and yet
he found patience for the most exquisite "tooling"
and took a book in hand with the deliberation of one
who should believe that everything was immutably
constituted. Hyacinth knew what he thought of
priests and theologies, but he had the religion of conscientious craftsmanship and he reduced the boy, on
his side, to a kind of prostration before his delicate
wonder-working fingers. "What will you have?
J'ai la main parisienne," M. Poupin would reply
modestly when Hyacinth's admiration broke out; and
he was good enough, after he had seen a few specimens of what our hero could do, to inform him that
he had the same happy conformation. "There's no
reason why you should n't be a good workman, *il n'y
a que ça;*" and his own life was practically governed
by this conviction. He delighted in the use of his
hands and his tools and the exercise of his taste, which
was faultless, and Hyacinth could easily imagine how
it must torment him to spend a day on his back. He
ended by perceiving, however, that consolation was
on this occasion in some degree conveyed by the presence of the young man who sat at the foot of the
bed and with whom M. Poupin exhibited such signs
of acquaintance as to make our hero wonder why he
had not seen him before, nor even heard of him.

"What do you mean by force that will shake the

globe?" the young man enquired, leaning back in his chair with raised arms and his interlocked hands, behind him, supporting his head. M. Poupin had spoken French, which he always preferred to do, the insular tongue being an immense tribulation to him; but his visitor spoke English, and Hyacinth immediately took in that there was nothing French about *him* — M. Poupin could never tell him he had *la main parisienne.*

"I mean a force that will make the bourgeois go down into their cellars and hide, pale with fear, behind their barrels of wine and their heaps of gold!" cried M. Poupin, rolling terrible eyes.

"And in this country, I hope, in their coal-bins. *La-la*, we shall find them even there," his wife remarked.

"'89 was an irresistible force," said M. Poupin. "I believe you would have thought so if you had been there."

"And so was the entrance of the Versaillais, which sent you over here ten years ago," the young man returned. He saw Hyacinth was watching him and he met his eyes, smiling a little, in a way that added to our hero's interest.

"*Pardon, pardon*, I resist!" cried Eustache Poupin, glaring, in his improvised nightcap, out of his sheets; and Madame repeated that they resisted — she believed well that they resisted! The young man burst out laughing; whereupon his host declared with a dignity which even his recumbent position did n't abate that it was really frivolous of him to ask such questions as that, knowing as he did — what he did know.

"Yes, I know — I know," said the young man good-naturedly, lowering his arms and thrusting his hands into his pockets while he stretched his long legs a little. "But everything is yet to be tried."

"Oh the trial will be on a great scale — *soyez tranquille!* It will be one of those experiments that constitute a proof."

Hyacinth wondered what they were talking about, and perceived that it must be something important, for the stranger was not a man who would take an interest in anything else. Hyacinth was immensely struck with him, could see he was remarkable, and felt slightly aggrieved that he should be a stranger: that is that he should be apparently a familiar of Lisson Grove and yet that M. Poupin should not have thought his young friend from Lomax Place worthy up to this time to be made acquainted with him. I know not to what degree the visitor in the other chair discovered these reflexions in Hyacinth's face, but after a moment, looking across at him, he said in a friendly yet just slightly diffident way, a way our hero liked: "And do you know too?"

"Do I know what?" asked Hyacinth in wonder.

"Oh, if you did you would!" the young man exclaimed and laughed again. Such a rejoinder from any one else would have irritated our sensitive hero, but it only made him more curious about his interlocutor, whose laugh was loud and extraordinarily gay.

"*Mon ami*, you ought to present *ces messieurs*," Madame Poupin remarked.

"*Ah ça*, is that the way you trifle with state

secrets?" her husband cried without heeding her. Then he went on in a different tone: "M. Hyacinthe is a gifted child, *un enfant très-doué*, in whom I take a tender interest — a child who has an account to settle. Oh, a thumping big one! Is n't it so, *mon petit?*"

This was very well meant, but it made Hyacinth blush, and, without knowing exactly what to say, he murmured shyly: "Oh, I only want them to let me alone!"

"He's very young," said Eustache Poupin.

"He's the person we have seen in this country whom we like best," his wife added.

"Perhaps you're French," suggested the strange young man.

The trio seemed to Hyacinth to be waiting for his answer to this; it was as if a listening stillness had fallen. He found it a difficult pass, partly because there was something exciting and embarrassing in the attention of the other visitor, and partly because he had never yet had to decide that important question. He did n't really know if he were French or were English, or which of the two he should prefer to be. His mother's blood, her suffering in an alien land, the unspeakable, irremediable misery that consumed her in a place and among a people she must have execrated — all this made him French; yet he was conscious at the same time of qualities that did n't mix with it. He had spun to the last fineness, long ago, a legend about his mother, built it up slowly, adding piece to piece, in passionate musings and broodings, when his cheeks burned and his eyes filled;

but there were times when it wavered and faded, when it ceased to console him and he ceased to trust it. He had had a father too, and his father had suffered as well, and had fallen under a blow, and had paid with his life; and him also he felt in his spirit and his senses, when the effort to think it out did n't simply end in darkness and confusion, challenging still even while they baffled, and inevitable freezing horror. At any rate he seemed rooted in the place where his wretched parents had expiated, and he knew nothing of any other. Moreover when old Poupin said "M. Hyacinthe," as he had often done before, he did n't altogether enjoy it; he thought it made his name, which he liked well enough in English, sound like the name of a hairdresser. Our young friend was under a cloud and a stigma, but he was not yet prepared to admit he was ridiculous. "Oh, I dare say I ain't anything," he replied in a moment.

"*En v'là des bêtises!*" cried Madame Poupin. "Do you mean to say you're not as good as any one in the world? I should like to see!"

"We all have an account to settle, don't you know?" said the strange young man.

He evidently meant this to be encouraging to Hyacinth, whose quick desire to avert M. Poupin's allusions had not been lost on him; but our hero could see that he himself would be sure to be one of the first to be paid. He would make society bankrupt, but he would be paid. He was tall and fair and good-natured looking, but you could n't tell — or at least Hyacinth could n't — if he were handsome or ugly, with his large head and square forehead, his thick, straight hair, his heavy mouth and rather vulgar nose, his admirably clear steady eyes, light-coloured and set very deep; for despite a want of fineness in some of its parts his face had a marked expression of intelligence and resolution, spoke somehow, as if it had showed you his soul drawing deep and even breaths, of a state of moral health. He was dressed as a workman in his Sunday toggery, having evidently put on his best to call in Lisson Grove, where he was to meet a lady, and wearing in particular a necktie which was both cheap and pretentious and of which Hyacinth, who noticed everything of that kind, observed the crude false blue. He had very big shoes — the shoes almost of a country labourer — and spoke with a provincial accent which Hyacinth believed to be that of Lanca-shire. This did n't suggest cleverness, but it did n't prevent Hyacinth from feeling sure he was the re-verse of stupid, that he probably indeed had a large easy brain quite as some people had big strong fists. Our little hero had a great desire to know superior persons, and he interested himself on the spot in this quiet stranger whose gravity, by any fine balance, showed, like that of a precious metal, in the small piece as well as in the big. He had the complexion of a ploughboy and the glance of a commander-in-chief, and might have been a distinguished young *savant* in the disguise of an artisan. The disguise would have been very complete, for he had several brown stains on his fingers. Hyacinth's curiosity on this occasion was both excited and gratified; for after two or three allusions, which he did n't understand, had been

made to a certain place where Poupin and their friend
had met and expected to meet again, Madame Poupin
exclaimed that it was a shame not to take in M. Hyacinthe, who, she would answer for it, had in him the
making of one of the pure.

"All in good time, in good time, *ma bonne*," the
worthy invalid replied. "M. Hyacinthe knows I
count on him, whether or no I make him an *interne*
to-day or only wait a little longer."

"What do you mean by an *interne?*" Hyacinth
asked.

"*Mon Dieu*, what shall I say!" — and Eustache
Poupin stared at him solemnly from his pillow.
"You're very sympathetic, but I'm afraid you're too
young."

"One is never too young to contribute one's *obole*,"
said Madame Poupin.

"Can you keep a secret?" asked the other guest,
but not as if he thought it probable.

"Is it a plot — a conspiracy?" Hyacinth broke out.

"He asks that as if he were asking if it's a plum-
pudding," said M. Poupin. "It isn't good to eat, and
we don't do it for our amusement. It's terribly serious, my child."

"It's a group of workers to which he and I and
a good many others belong. There's no harm in
telling him that," the young man went on.

"I advise you not to tell it to Mademoiselle; she's
quite in the old ideas," Madame Poupin suggested
to Hyacinth, tasting her *tisane*.

Hyacinth sat baffled and wondering, looking from
his fellow-labourer in Soho to his new acquaintance

opposite. "If you've some plan, something to which one can give one's self, I think you might have told me," he remarked in a moment to Poupin.

The latter merely viewed him a little as if he were a pleasing object and then said to the strange young man: "He's a little jealous of you. But there's no harm in that; it's of his age. You must know him, you must like him. We'll tell you his history some other day; it will make you feel that he belongs to us of necessity. It's an accident that he has n't met you here before."

"How could *ces messieurs* have met when M. Paul never comes? He does n't spoil us!" Madame Poupin cried.

"Well, you see I've my little sister at home to take care of when I ain't at the works," M. Paul explained. "This afternoon it was just a chance; there was a lady we know came in to sit with her."

"A lady — a real lady?"

"Oh yes, every inch," smiled M. Paul.

"Do you like them to thrust themselves into your apartment like that because you've the *désagrément* of being poor? It seems to be the custom in this country, but it would n't suit me at all," Madame Poupin continued. "I should like to see one of *ces dames* — the real ones — coming in to sit with me!"

"Oh, you're not a cripple; you've got the use of your legs!"

"Yes, and of my arms!" cried the Frenchwoman.

"This lady looks after several others in our court and she reads to my sister."

"Oh, well, you're patient, you other English."

"We shall never do anything without that," said M. Paul with undisturbed good-humour.

"You're perfectly right; you can't say that too often. It will be a tremendous job and only the strong will prevail," his host murmured a little wearily, turning his eyes to Madame Poupin, who approached slowly, holding the *tisane* in rather a full bowl and tasting it again and yet again as she came.

Hyacinth had been watching his fellow-visitor with deepening interest; a fact of which M. Paul apparently became aware, for he volunteered presently, giving a little nod in the direction of the bed, "He says we ought to know each other. I'm sure I've nothing against it. I like to know folk if they're likely to be worth it."

Hyacinth was too pleased with this even to take it up; it seemed to him for a moment that he could n't touch it gracefully enough. But he said with sufficient eagerness: "Will you tell me all about your plot?"

"Oh, it's no plot. I don't think I care much for plots." And with his mild, steady, light-blue English eye, M. Paul certainly had not much the appearance of a conspirator.

"Is n't it a new era?" asked Hyacinth, rather disappointed.

"Well, I don't know; it's just a taking of a stand on two or three points."

"*Ah bien, voilà du propre;* between us we've thrown him into a fever!" cried Madame Poupin, who had put down her bowl on a table near her husband's bed and was bending over him with her hand on his forehead. Her patient was flushed, he had

117

closed his eyes, and it was evident there had been more than enough conversation. Madame Poupin announced as much, with the addition that if the young men wished to make acquaintance they must do it outside; their friend must be perfectly quiet. They accordingly withdrew with apologies and promises to return for further news on the morrow, and two minutes later Hyacinth found himself standing face to face with his companion on the pavement in front of M. Poupin's residence, under a street-lamp which struggled ineffectually with the brown winter dusk.

"Is that your name, M. Paul?" he asked as he looked up at him.

"Oh bless you, no; that's only her Frenchified way of putting it. My name *is* Paul, though — Paul Muniment."

"And what's your trade?" Hyacinth demanded with a jump into familiarity; for his friend seemed to have told him a great deal more than was usually conveyed in that item of information.

Paul Muniment looked down at him from above broad shoulders. "I work for a firm of wholesale chemists at Lambeth."

"And where do you live?"

"I live over the water too; in the far south of London."

"And are you going home now?"

"Oh yes, I'm going to toddle."

"And may I toddle with you?"

Mr. Muniment considered him further and then gave a laugh. "I'll carry you if you like."

"Thank you; I expect I can walk as far as you," said Hyacinth.

"Well, I admire your spirit and I dare say I shall like your company."

There was something in his face, taken in connexion with the idea that he was concerned in the taking of a stand — it offered our quick youth the image of a rank of bristling bayonets — which made Hyacinth feel the desire to go with him till he dropped; and in a moment they started away together and took the direction Muniment had mentioned. They discoursed as they went, exchanging a great many opinions and anecdotes; but they reached the southwesterly court in which the young chemist lived with his infirm sister before he had told Hyacinth anything definite about the "points" of his reference or Hyacinth, on his side, had detailed the circumstances involved in his being, according to M. Poupin, one of the disinherited. Hyacinth did n't wish to press, would n't for the world have appeared indiscreet, and moreover, though he had taken so great a fancy to Muniment, was not quite prepared as yet to be pressed himself. Therefore it failed to become very clear how his companion had made Poupin's acquaintance and how long he had enjoyed it. Paul Muniment nevertheless was to a certain extent communicative, especially on the question of his living in a very poor little corner. He had his sister to keep — she could do nothing for herself; and he paid a low rent because she had to have doctors and doses and all sorts of little comforts. He spent a bob a week for her on flowers. It was better too when you got upstairs, and from the back windows you could see the dome of Saint Paul's. Audley Court, with its pretty name, which reminded Hyacinth of Tennyson, proved to be a still dingier nook than Lomax Place; and it had the further drawback that you had to penetrate a narrow alley, a passage between high black walls, to enter it. At the door of one of the houses the young men paused, lingering a little, and then Muniment said: "I say, why should n't you come up? I like you well enough for that, and you can see my sister; her name's Rosy." He spoke as if this would be a great privilege and added, for the joke, that Rosy enjoyed a call from a gentleman of all things. Hyacinth needed no urging, and he groped his way at his companion's heels up a dark staircase which appeared to him — for they stopped only when they could go no further — the longest and steepest he had ever ascended. At the top Paul Muniment pushed open a door, but exclaimed "Hullo, have you gone to roost?" on perceiving the room on the threshold of which they stood to be unlighted.

"Oh dear, no; we're sitting in the dark," a small bright voice instantly replied. "Lady Aurora's so kind; she's here still."

The voice came out of a corner so pervaded by gloom that the speaker was indistinguishable. "Well now, that's beautiful!" Paul Muniment rejoined. "You'll have a party then, for I've brought some one else. We're poor, you know, but honest, and not afraid of showing up, and I dare say we can manage a candle."

At this, in the dim firelight, Hyacinth saw a tall

figure erect itself — a figure angular and slim, crowned with a large vague hat and a flowing umbrageous veil. This unknown person gave a singular laugh and said: "Oh I brought some candles; we could have had a light if we had wished." Both the tone and the purport of the words announced to Hyacinth that they proceeded from Lady Aurora.

VIII

PAUL MUNIMENT took a match out of his pocket and lighted it on the sole of his shoe; after which he applied it to a tallow candle which stood in a tin receptacle on the low mantel-shelf. This enabled Hyacinth to perceive a narrow bed in a corner and a small object stretched upon it — an object revealed to him mainly by the bright fixedness of a pair of large eyes, of which the whites were sharply contrasted with the dark pupil and which gazed at him across a counterpane of gaudy patchwork. The brown room seemed crowded with heterogeneous objects and presented moreover, thanks to a multitude of small prints, both plain and coloured, fastened all over the walls, a highly-decorated appearance. The little person in the corner had the air of having gone to bed in a picture-gallery, and as soon as Hyacinth became aware of this his impression deepened that Paul Muniment and his sister were very wonderful people. Lady Aurora hovered before him with an odd drooping, swaying erectness, and she laughed a good deal, vaguely and shyly, as for the awkwardness of her being found still on the premises. "Rosy, girl, I've brought you a visitor," Hyacinth's guide soon said. "This young man has walked all the way from Lisson Grove to make your acquaintance." Rosy continued to look at the visitor from over her counterpane, and he felt slightly embarrassed, for he had never yet been presented to a young lady in her position. "You must n't mind her being in bed — she's always in bed," her brother went on. "She's in bed just the same as a little slippery trout's in the water."

"Dear me, if I did n't receive company because I was in bed, there would n't be much use, would there, Lady Aurora?"

Rosy put this question in a light, gay tone, with a dart of shining eyes at her companion, who replied at once with still greater hilarity and in a voice which struck Hyacinth as strange and affected: "Oh mercy, no; it seems quite the natural place!" Then she added: "And it's such a lovely bed, such a comfortable bed!"

"Indeed it is, when your ladyship makes it up," said Rosy; while Hyacinth wondered at this strange phenomenon of a peer's daughter (for he knew she must be that) performing the functions of a housemaid.

"I say now, you have n't been doing that again to-day?" Muniment asked, punching the mattress of the invalid with a vigorous hand.

"Pray, who would if I did n't?" Lady Aurora enquired. "It only takes a minute if one knows how." Her manner was jocosely apologetic and she seemed to plead guilty to having been absurd; in the dim light Hyacinth thought he saw her blush as if she were much embarrassed. In spite of her blushing her appearance and manner suggested to him a personage in a comedy. She sounded the letter *r* as a *w*.

"I can do it beautifully. I often do it, when Mrs.

Major does n't come up," Paul Muniment said, continuing to thump his sister's couch in an appreciative but somewhat subversive manner.

"Oh, I've no doubt whatever!" Lady Aurora exclaimed quickly. "Mrs. Major must have so very much to do."

"Not in the making-up of beds, I'm afraid; there are only two or three, down there, for so many," the young man returned loudly and with a kind of inconsequent cheerfulness.

"Yes, I've thought a great deal about that. But there would n't be room for more, you know," said Lady Aurora, this time with all gravity.

"There's not much room for a family of that sort anywhere — thirteen people of all ages and sizes," her host observed. "The world's pretty big, but there does n't seem room."

"We're also thirteen at home," Lady Aurora hastened to mention. "We're also rather crowded."

"Surely you don't mean at Inglefield?" Rosy demanded from her dusky nook.

"I don't know about Inglefield. I'm so much in town." Hyacinth could see that Inglefield was a subject she wished to turn off, and to do so she added: "We too are of all ages and sizes."

"Well, it's fortunate you're not all *your* size!" Paul Muniment declared with a freedom at which Hyacinth was rather shocked and which led him to suspect that though his new friend was a very fine fellow a delicate tact was not his main characteristic. Later he explained this by the fact that he was rural and provincial and had not had, like himself, the benefit of the life of a capital; and later still he wished to know what, after all, such a character as that had to do with tact or with compliments, and why its work in the world was not most properly performed by the simple exercise of a rude manly strength.

At this familiar allusion to her stature Lady Aurora turned hither and thither a little confusedly; Hyacinth saw her high, lean figure almost rock in the dim little room. Her commotion carried her to the door, and with ejaculations of which it was difficult to guess the meaning she was about to depart when Rosy detained her, having evidently much more social art than Paul. "Don't you see it's only because her ladyship's standing up that she's so, you gawk? *We're* not thirteen, at any rate, and we've got all the furniture we want, so there's a chair for every one. Do be seated again, Lady Aurora, and help me to entertain this gentleman. I don't know your name, sir; perhaps my brother will mention it when he has collected his wits. I'm very glad to see you, though I don't see you very well. Why should n't we light one of her ladyship's candles? It's very different to that common thing."

Hyacinth thought Miss Muniment very charming; he had begun to make her out better by this time, and he watched her small wan, pointed face, framed on the pillow by thick black hair. She was a diminutive dark person, pale and wasted with a lifelong infirmity; Hyacinth thought her manner denoted high accomplishment — he judged it impossible to tell her age. Lady Aurora pleaded that she ought to have gone, long since; but she seated herself nevertheless on the chair that Paul pushed toward her.

"Here's a go!" this young man exclaimed to the other guest. "You told me your name, but I've clean forgotten it." Then when Hyacinth had pronounced it again he said to his sister: "That won't tell you much; there are bushels of Robinsons in the north. But you'll like him, he's all right; I met him at the Poupins." "Puppin" would represent the sound by which he designated the French bookbinder, and that was the name by which Hyacinth always heard him called at Crookenden's. Hyacinth knew how much nearer to the right thing he himself came.

"Your name, like mine, represents a flower," said the little woman in the bed. "Mine is Rose Muniment and her ladyship's is Aurora Langrish. That means the morning or the dawn; it's the most beautiful of all, don't you think?" Rose Muniment addressed this question to Hyacinth while Lady Aurora gazed at her shyly and mutely and as if admiring her manner, her self-possession and flow of conversation. Her brother lighted one of the visitor's candles and the girl went on without waiting for Hyacinth's response. "Isn't it right she should be called the dawn when she brings light where she goes? The Puppins are the charming foreigners I've told you about," she explained to her friend.

"Oh, it's so pleasant knowing a few foreigners!" Lady Aurora exclaimed with a spasm of expression. "They're often so very fresh."

"Mr. Robinson's a sort of foreigner and he's very fresh," said Paul Muniment. "He meets Mr. Puppin quite on his own ground. If I had his gift of tongues it would bring me on."

"I'm sure I should be very happy to help you with your French. I feel the advantage of knowing it," Hyacinth remarked finely, becoming conscious that his declaration drew the attention of Lady Aurora toward him; so that he wondered what he could go on to say to keep at that level. This was the first time he had encountered socially a member of that aristocracy to which he had now for a good while known it was Miss Pynsent's theory that he belonged; and the occasion was interesting in spite of the lady's appearing to have so few of the qualities of her caste. She was about thirty years of age; her nose was large and, in spite of the sudden retreat of her chin, her face long and lean. She had the manner of extreme near-sightedness; her front teeth projected from her upper gums, which she revealed when she smiled, and her fair hair, in tangled silky skeins (Rose Muniment thought it too lovely) drooped over her pink cheeks. Her clothes looked as if she had worn them a good deal in the rain, and the note of a certain disrepair in her apparel was given by a hole in one of her black gloves, through which a white finger gleamed. She was plain and diffident and she might have been poor; but in the fine grain and sloping, shrinking slimness of her whole person, the delicacy of her curious features and a kind of cultivated quality in her sweet, vague, civil expression, there was a suggestion of race, of long transmission, of an organism that had resulted from fortunate touch after touch. She was not a common woman; she was one of the caprices of an aristocracy. Hyacinth did n't define her in this manner to himself, but he received from her the impression that if she was a simple creature (which he learned later she was not) aristocracies were yet complicated things. Lady Aurora remarked that there were many delightful books in French, and he proclaimed it a torment to know that (as he did very well) when you saw no way to getting hold of them. This led Lady Aurora to say after a moment's hesitation that she had a good lot of her own and that if he liked she should be most happy to lend them to him. Hyacinth thanked her — thanked her even too much, and felt both the kindness and the brilliant promise of the offer (he knew the exasperation of having volumes in his hands, for external treatment, which he could n't take home at night, having tried that method surreptitiously during his first weeks at old Crook's and come very near being sacked in consequence) while he wondered how such a system could be put into practice; whether she would expect him to call at her house and wait in the hall till the books were sent out to him. Rose Muniment exclaimed that that was her ladyship all over — always wanting to make up to people for being less lucky than herself: she would take the shoes off her feet for any one that might take a fancy to them. At this the visitor declared that she would stop coming to see her if the girl caught her up that way for everything; and Rosy, without heeding the remonstrance, explained to Hyacinth that she thought it the least she could do to give what she had. She was so ashamed of being rich that she wondered the lower

classes did n't break into Inglefield and take possession of all the treasures in the Italian room. She was
a tremendous socialist; she was worse than any one
— she was worse even than Paul.

"I wonder if she's worse than me," Hyacinth returned at a venture, not understanding the allusions
to Inglefield and the Italian room, which Miss Muniment made as if she knew all about these places.
After learning more of the world he remembered this
tone of Muniment's sister — he was to have plenty
of observation of it on other occasions — as that of
a person in the habit of visiting the nobility at their
country-seats; she talked about Inglefield as if she
had stayed there.

"Hullo, I did n't know you were so advanced!"
exclaimed the master of the scene, who had been sitting silent and sidewise in a chair that was too narrow
for him, his big arm hugging the back. "Have we
been entertaining an angel unawares?"

Hyacinth made out he was chaffing him, but he
knew the way to face that sort of thing was to exaggerate one's meaning. "You did n't know I was
advanced? Why, I thought that was the principal
thing about me. I think I go about as far as any one."

"I thought the principal thing about you was that
you knew French," Paul Muniment said with an air
of derision which showed him he would n't put that
ridicule upon him unless he liked him, at the same
time that it revealed to him how he had come within
an ace of posturing.

"Well, I don't know it for nothing. I'll say something that will take your head off if you don't look

out — just the sort of thing they say so well in French."

"Oh, do say something of that kind; we should enjoy it so much!" cried Rosy in perfect good faith and clasping her hands for expectation.

The appeal was embarrassing, but Hyacinth was saved from the consequences of it by a remark from Lady Aurora, who quavered out the words after two or three false starts, appearing to address him, now that she spoke to him directly, with a sort of over-done consideration. "I should like so very much to know — it would be so interesting — if you don't mind — how far exactly you do go." She threw back her head very far and thrust her shoulders forward, and if her chin had been more adapted to such a purpose would have appeared to point it at him.

This challenge was hardly less alarming than the other, for he was far from being ready with an impressive formula. He replied, however, with a candour in which he tried as far as possible to sink his vagueness: "Well, I'm very strong indeed. I think I see my way to conclusions from which even Monsieur and Madame Poupin would shrink. Poupin, at any rate; I'm not so sure about his wife."

"I should like so much to know Madame," Lady Aurora murmured as if politeness demanded that she should content herself with this answer.

"Oh, Puppin is n't strong," said Muniment; "you can easily look over his head! He has a sweet assortment of phrases — they 're really pretty things to hear, some of them; but he has n't had a new idea these thirty years. It 's the old stock that has been withering in the window. All the same he warms one up; he has a spark of the sacred fire. The principal conclusion Mr. Robinson sees his way to," he added to Lady Aurora, "is that your father ought to have his head chopped off and carried on a pike."

"Ah yes, the French Revolution."

"Lord, I don't know anything about your father, my lady!" Hyacinth interposed.

"Did n't you ever hear of the Earl of Inglefield?" cried Rose Muniment.

"He's one of the best," said Lady Aurora as if she were pleading for him.

"Very likely, but he's a landlord, and he has an hereditary seat and a park of five thousand acres all to himself, while we're bundled together into this sort of kennel." Hyacinth admired the young man's consistency till he saw he was amusing himself; after which he still admired the way he could mix that up with the tremendous opinions it must have been certain he entertained. In his own imagination he associated bitterness with the revolutionary passion; but the young chemical expert, at the same time that he was planning far ahead, seemed capable of turning revolutionists themselves into ridicule even for the entertainment of the revolutionised.

"Well, I've told you often enough that I don't go with you at all," said Rose Muniment, whose recumbency appeared not in the least to interfere with her universal participation. "You'll make a tremendous mistake if you try to turn everything round. There ought to be differences, and high and low, and there always will be, true as ever I lie here. I think it's against everything, pulling down them that's above."

"Everything points to great changes in this country, but if once our Rosy's against them how can you be sure? That's the only thing that makes me doubt," her brother went on, looking at her with a placidity which showed the habit of indulgence.

"Well, I may be ill, but I ain't buried, and if I'm content with my position — such a position as it is — surely other folk might be with theirs. Her ladyship may think I'm as good as her if she takes that notion; but she'll have a deal to do to make *me* believe it."

"I think you're much better than I, and I know very few people so good as you," Lady Aurora brought out, blushing not for her opinions but for her timidity. It was easy to see that though she was original she would have liked to be even more original than she was. She was conscious, however, that such a declaration might appear rather gross to persons who did n't see exactly how she meant it; so she added, as quickly as her hesitating manner permitted, to cover it up: "You know there's one thing you ought to remember, *à propos* of revolutions and changes and all that sort of thing; I just mention it because we were talking of some of the dreadful things that were done in France. If there were to be a great disturbance in this country — and of course one hopes there won't — it would be my impression that the people would behave in a different way altogether."

"What people do you mean?" Hyacinth allowed himself to enquire.

"Oh, the upper class, the people who've got all the things."

"We don't call them the *people*," observed Hyacinth, reflecting the next instant that his remark was a little primitive.

"I suppose you call them the wretches, the scoundrels!" Rose Muniment suggested, laughing merrily.

"All the things, but not all the brains," her brother said.

"No indeed, are n't they stupid?" exclaimed her ladyship. "All the same, I don't think they'd all go abroad."

"Go abroad?"

"I mean like the French nobles who emigrated so much. They'd stay at home and resist; they'd make more of a fight. I think they'd fight very hard."

"I'm delighted to hear it, and I'm sure they'd win!" cried Rosy.

"They would n't collapse, don't you know," Lady Aurora continued. "They'd struggle till they were beaten."

"And you think they'd be beaten in the end?" Hyacinth asked.

"Oh dear, yes," she replied with a familiar confidence at which he was greatly surprised. "But of course one hopes it won't happen."

"I infer from what you say that they talk it over a good deal among themselves, to settle the line they'll take," said Paul Muniment.

But Rosy intruded before Lady Aurora could answer. "I think it's wicked to talk it over, and I'm sure we have n't any business to talk it over here!

133

When her ladyship says the aristocracy will make a fine stand I like to hear her say it and I think she speaks in a manner that becomes her own position. But there's something else in her tone which, if I may be allowed to say so, I think a great mistake. If her ladyship expects, in case of the lower classes coming up in that odious manner, to be let off easily, for the sake of the concessions she may have made in advance, I'd just advise her to save herself the disappointment and the trouble. They won't be a bit the wiser and they won't either know or care. If they're going to trample over their betters it is n't on account of her having seemed to give up everything to us here that they'll let *her* off. They'll trample on her just the same as on the others, and they'll say she has got to pay for her title and her grand relations and her fine appearance. Therefore I advise her not to waste her good-nature in trying to let herself down. When you're up so high as that you've got to stay there; and if the powers above have made you a lady the best thing you can do is to hold up your head. I can promise your ladyship *I* would!"

The close logic of this speech and the quaint self-possession with which the little bedridden speaker delivered it struck Hyacinth as amazing and confirmed his idea that the brother and sister were a most extraordinary pair. It had a terrible effect on poor Lady Aurora, by whom so stern a lesson from so humble a quarter had evidently not been expected and who sought refuge from her confusion in a series of pleading gasps, while Paul Muniment, with his humorous density, which was deliberate, and acute too, not seeing, or at any rate not heeding, that she had been sufficiently snubbed by his sister, inflicted a fresh humiliation in saying "Rosy's right, my lady. It's no use trying to buy yourself off. You can't do enough; your sacrifices don't count. You spoil your fun now and you don't get it made up to you later. To all you people nothing will ever be made up. Eat your pudding while you have it; you may n't have it long."

Lady Aurora listened to him with her eyes on his face, and as they rested there Hyacinth scarcely knew what to make of her expression. Afterwards he thought he could attach a meaning to it. She got up quickly when Muniment had ceased speaking; the movement suggested she had taken offence and he would have liked to show her he thought she had been rather roughly used. But she gave him no chance, not glancing at him for a moment. Then he saw he was mistaken and that if she had flushed considerably it was only with the excitement of pleasure, the enjoyment of such original talk and of seeing her friends at last as free and familiar as she wished them to be. "You're the most delightful people — I wish every one could know you!" she broke out. "But I must really be going." She went to the bed and bent over Rosy and kissed her.

"Paul will see you as far as you like on your way home," this young woman remarked.

Lady Aurora protested, but Paul, without protesting in return, only took up his hat and smiled at her as if he knew his duty. On this her ladyship said: "Well, you may see me downstairs; I forgot it was so dark."

"You must take her ladyship's own candle and you must call a cab," Rosy directed.

"Oh, I don't go in cabs. I walk."

"Well, you may go on the top of a 'bus if you like; you can't help being superb," Miss Muniment declared, watching her sympathetically.

"Superb? Oh mercy!" cried the poor devoted, grotesque lady, leaving the room with Paul, who told Hyacinth to wait for him a little. She neglected to take leave of our young man, and he asked himself what was to be hoped from that sort of people when even the best of them — those that wished to be agreeable to the *demos* — reverted inevitably to the supercilious. She had said no more about lending him her books.

IX

"SHE lives in Belgrave Square; she has ever so many brothers and sisters; one of her sisters is married to Lord Warmington," Rose Muniment instantly began, not apparently in the least discomposed at being left alone with a strange young man in a room which was now half dark again, thanks to her brother's having carried off the second and more brilliant candle. She was so interested for the time in telling Hyacinth the history of Lady Aurora that she appeared not to remember how little she knew about himself. Her ladyship had dedicated her life and her pocket-money to the poor and sick; she cared nothing for parties and races and dances and picnics and cards and life in great houses, the usual amusements of the aristocracy: she was like one of the saints of old come to life again out of a legend. She had made their acquaintance, Paul's and hers, about a year before, through a friend of theirs, such a fine brave young woman, who was in Saint Thomas's Hospital for a surgical operation. She had been laid up there for weeks during which Lady Aurora, always looking out for those who could n't help themselves, used to come and talk to her and read to her, till the end of her time in the ward, when the poor girl, parting with her kind friend, told her how she knew of another unfortunate creature (for whom there was no place there, because she was incurable) who would be mighty thankful for any little

attention of that sort. She had given Lady Aurora
the address in Audley Court and the very next day
her ladyship had knocked at their door. It was n't
because she was poor — though in all conscience they
were pinched enough — but because she had so little
satisfaction in her limbs. Lady Aurora came very
often, for several months, without meeting Paul, because he was always at his work; but one day he came
home early on purpose to find her, to thank her for
her goodness, and also to see (Miss Muniment rather
shyly intimated) if she were really so good as his extravagant little sister made her out. Rosy had a
triumph after that: Paul had to admit that her ladyship was beyond anything that any one in his waking
senses would believe. She seemed to want to give up
everything to those who were below her and never to
expect any thanks at all. And she was n't always
preaching and showing you your duty; she wanted
to talk to you sociable-like, as if you were just her
own sister. And *her* own sisters were the highest in
the land, and you might see her name in the newspapers the day they were presented to the Queen.
Lady Aurora had been presented too, with feathers
in her head and a long tail to her gown; but she had
turned her back on it all with a kind of terror — a
sort of shivering sinking state which she had often
described to Miss Muniment. The day she had first
seen Paul was the day they became so intimate, the
three of them together — if she might apply such
a word as that to such a peculiar connexion. The
little woman, the little girl, as she lay there (Hyacinth
scarce knew how to characterise her) told our young

man a very great secret, in which he found himself
too much interested to think of criticising so precipitate a confidence. The secret was that, of all the
people she had ever seen in the world, her ladyship
thought Rosy's Paul the very cleverest. And she had
seen the greatest, the most famous, the brightest of
every kind, for they all came to stay at Inglefield,
thirty and forty of them at once. She had talked with
them all and heard them say their best (and you could
fancy how they would try to give it out at such a place
as that, where there was nearly a mile of conserva-
tories and a hundred wax candles were lighted at
a time) and at the end of it all she had made the
remark to herself — and she had made it to Rosy too
— that there was none of them had such a head on
his shoulders as the young man in Audley Court.
Rosy would n't spread such a rumour as that in the
court itself, but she wanted every friend of her
brother's (and she could see Hyacinth was a real one
by the way he listened) to know what was thought of
him by them that had an experience of intellect. She
did n't wish to give it out that her ladyship had lowered herself in any manner to a person that earned
his bread in a dirty shop (clever as he *might* be) but
it was easy to see she minded what he said as if he
had been a bishop — or more indeed, for she did n't
think much of bishops, any more than Paul himself,
and that was an idea she had got from him. Oh, she
took it none so ill if he came back from his work before she had gone, and to-night Hyacinth could see
for himself how she had lingered. This evening, she
was sure, her ladyship would let him walk home with

her half the way. This announcement gave Hyacinth the prospect of a considerable session with his communicative hostess; but he was very glad to wait, for he was vaguely, strangely excited by her talk, fascinated by the little queer-smelling, high-perched interior, encumbered with relics, treasured and polished, of a poor north-country home, bedecked with penny ornaments and related in so unexpected a manner to Belgrave Square and the great landed estates. He spent half an hour with Paul Muniment's small, odd, sharp, crippled, chattering sister, who gave him an impression of education and native wit (she expressed herself far better than Pinnie or than Milly Henning) and who startled, puzzled and at the same time rather distressed him by the manner in which she referred herself to the most abject class — the class that prostrated itself, that was in a fever and flutter, in the presence of its betters. That was Pinnie's attitude of course, but Hyacinth had long ago perceived that his adoptive mother had generations of plebeian patience in her blood, and that though she had a tender soul she had not a truly high spirit. He was more entertained than afflicted, however, by Miss Muniment's tone, and he was thrilled by the frequency and familiarity of her allusions to a kind of life he had often wondered about; this was the first time he had heard it described with that degree of authority. By the nature of his mind he was perpetually, almost morbidly conscious that the circle in which he lived was an infinitesimally small shallow eddy in the roaring vortex of London, and his imagination plunged again and again into the flood that whirled past it and round it, in the hope of being carried to some brighter, happier vision — the vision of societies where, in splendid rooms, with smiles and soft voices, distinguished men, with women who were both proud and gentle, talked of art, literature and history. When Rosy had delivered herself to her complete satisfaction on the subject of Lady Aurora she became more quiet, asking as yet, however, no straight questions of her guest, whom she seemed to take very much for granted. He presently remarked that she must let him come very soon again, and he added, to explain this wish: "You know you seem to me very curious people."

Miss Muniment did n't in the least repudiate the imputation. "Oh yes, I dare say we seem very curious. I think we're generally thought so; especially me, being so miserable and yet so lively." And she laughed till her bed creaked again.

"Perhaps it's lucky you're ill; perhaps if you had your health you'd be all over the place," Hyacinth suggested. And he went on candidly: "I can't make it out, your being so up in everything."

"I don't see why you need make it out! But you would, perhaps, if you had known my father and mother."

"Were they such a rare lot?"

"I think you'd say so if you had ever been in the mines. Yes, in the mines, where the filthy coal 's dug out. That's where my father came from — he was working in the pit when he was a child of ten. He never had a day's schooling in his life, but he climbed up out of his black hole into daylight and air, and he invented a machine, and he married my mother, who came out of Durham, and (by her people) out of the pits and the awfulness too. My father had no great figure, but *she* was magnificent — the finest woman in the country and the bravest and the best. She's in her grave now, and I could n't go to look at it even if it were in the nearest church-yard. My father was as black as the coal he worked in: I know I'm just his pattern, barring that *he* did have his legs, when the liquor had n't got into them. Yet between him and my mother, for grand high in-telligence, there was n't much to choose. But what's the use of brains if you have n't got a backbone? My poor father had even less of that than I, for with me it's only the body that can't stand up, and with him it was the very nature. He invented, for use in machine-shops, a mechanical improvement — a new kind of beam-fixing, whatever that is — and he sold it at Bradford for fifteen pounds: I mean the whole right and profit of it and every hope and comfort of his family. He was always straying and my mother was always bringing him back. She had plenty to do, with me a puny ailing brat from the moment I opened my eyes. Well, one night he strayed so far that he never came home, or only came a loose bloody bundle of clothes. He had fallen into a gravel-pit, he did n't know where he was going. That's the reason my brother won't ever touch so much as you could wet your finger with, and that I've only a drop once a week or so in the way of a strengthener. I take what her ladyship brings me, but I take no more. If she could but have come to us before my mother went —

that would have been a saving! I was only nine when my father died, and I'm three years older than Paul. My mother did for us with all her might, and she kept us decent — if such a useless little mess as me can be said to be decent. At any rate she kept me alive, and that's a proof she was handy. She went to the wash-tub, and she might have been a queen as she stood there with her bare arms in the foul linen and her long hair braided on her head. She was terrible hand-some, but he'd have been a bold man that had taken on himself to tell her so. And it was from her we got our education — she was determined we should rise above the common. You might have thought, in her position, that she could n't go into such things, but she was a rare one for keeping you at your book. She could hold to her idea when my poor father could n't, and her idea for us was that Paul should get learning and should look after me. You can see for yourself that that's what has come of it. How he got it's more than I can say, as we never had a penny to pay for it; and of course my mother's head would n't have been of much use if he had n't had a head himself. Well, it was all in the family. Paul was a boy that would learn more from a yellow poster on a wall or a time-table at a railway station than many a young fellow from a year at college. That was his only col-lege, poor lad — picking up what he could. Mother was taken when she was still needed, nearly five years ago. There was an epidemic of typhoid, and of course it must pass me over, the goose of a thing — only that I'd have made a poor feast — and just lay that really grand character on her back. Well, she never again made it ache over her soapsuds, straight and broad as it was. Not having seen her, you would n't believe," said Rose Muniment in conclusion; "but I just wanted you to understand that our parents had jolly good brains at least to give us."

Hyacinth listened to this eloquence — the clearest statement of anything he had ever heard made by a woman — with the deepest interest, and without being in the least moved to allow for filial exaggeration; inasmuch as his impression of the brother and sister was such as it would have taken a much more marvellous tale to account for. The very way Rose Muniment talked of brains made him feel this; she pronounced the word as if she were distributing prizes for intellectual eminence from off a platform. No doubt the weak inventor and the strong worker had been fine specimens, but that did n't diminish the merit of their highly original offspring. The girl's insistence on her mother's virtues (even now that her age had become more definite to him he thought of her as a girl) touched in his heart a chord that was always ready to throb — the chord of melancholy aimless wonder as to the difference it would have made for his life to have had some rich warm presence like that in it.

"Are you very fond of your brother?" he enquired after a little.

The eyes of his hostess glittered at him. "If you ever quarrel with him you'll see whose side I shall take."

"Ah, before that I shall make you like *me*."

"That's very possible, and you'll see how I shall fling you over!"

144

"Why then do you object so to his views — his ideas about the way the people are to come up?"

"Because I think he'll get over them."

"Never — never!" cried Hyacinth. "I've only known him an hour or two, but I deny that with all my strength."

"Is that the way you're going to make me like you — contradicting me so?" Miss Muniment asked with familiar archness.

"What's the use, when you tell me I shall be sacrificed? One might as well perish for a lamb as for a sheep."

"I don't believe you're a lamb at all. Certainly you're not if you want all the great people pulled down and the most dreadful scenes enacted."

"Don't you believe in human equality? Don't you want anything done for the groaning, toiling millions — those who have been cheated and crushed and bamboozled from the beginning of time?"

Hyacinth asked this question with considerable heat, but the effect of it was to send his companion off into a new ring of laughter. "You say that just like a man my brother described to me three days ago, a little man at some club whose hair stood up — Paul imitated the way he raved and stamped. I don't mean that you do either, but you use almost the same words as him." Hyacinth scarce knew what to make of this allusion or of the picture offered him of Paul Muniment casting ridicule on those who spoke in the name of the down-trodden. But Rosy went on before he had time to do more than reflect that there would evidently be great things to learn about her brother:

145

"I have n't the least objection to seeing the people improved, but I don't want to see the aristocracy lowered an inch. I like so much to look at it up there."

"You ought to know my Aunt Pinnie — she's just such another benighted idolater!" Hyacinth returned.

"Oh, you're making me like you very fast! And pray who's your Aunt Pinnie?"

"She's a dressmaker and a charming little woman. I should like her to come and see you."

"I'm afraid I'm not in her line — I never had on a dress in my life. But, as a charming woman, I should be delighted to see her," Miss Muniment hastened to add.

"I'll bring her some day," he said; and then he went on rather incongruously, for he was irritated by the girl's optimism, thinking it a shame her sharpness should be enlisted on the wrong side. "Don't you want, for yourself, a better place to live in?"

She jerked herself up and for a moment he thought she would jump out of her bed at him. "A better place than this? Pray how could there be a better place? Every one thinks it's lovely; you should see our view by daylight — you should see everything I've got. Perhaps you're used to something very fine, but Lady Aurora says that in all Belgrave Square there is n't such a cosy little room. If you think I'm not perfectly content you're very much mistaken!"

Such an attitude could only exasperate him, and his exasperation made him indifferent to the mistake of his having appeared to sniff at Miss Muniment's quarters. Pinnie herself, submissive as she was, had spared him that sort of displeasure; she groaned over

the dinginess of Lomax Place sufficiently to remind
him that she had not been absolutely stultified by
misery. "Don't you sometimes make your brother
very cross?" he asked, smiling, of his present entertainer.

"Cross? I don't know what you take us for! I
never saw him lose his temper in his life."

"He must be a rum customer! Does n't he really
care for — for what we were talking about?"

For a space Rosy was silent; then she replied:
"What my brother really cares for — well, one of
these days, when you know, you 'll tell me."

Hyacinth stared. "But is n't he tremendously
deep in —" What should he call the mystery?

"Deep in what?"

"Well, in what's going on beneath the surface.
Does n't he belong to important things?"

"I'm sure I don't know what he belongs to — you
may ask him!" cried Rosy, who laughed gaily again
as the opening door re-admitted the subject of their
conversation. "You must have crossed the water
with her ladyship," she pursued. "I wonder who
enjoyed their walk most."

"She's a handy old girl and she has a goodish
stride," said the young man.

"I think she's in love with you simply, Mr. Muniment."

"Really, my dear, for an admirer of the aristocracy
you allow yourself a license," Paul scoffed, smiling
at Hyacinth.

Hyacinth got up, feeling that really he had paid
a long visit; his curiosity was far from satisfied, but

147

there was a limit to the time one should spend in a young lady's sleeping apartment. "Perhaps she is; why not?" he struck out.

"Perhaps she is then; she's daft enough for anything."

"There have been fine folks before who have patted the people on the back and pretended to enter into their life," Hyacinth said. "Is she only playing with that idea or is she in earnest?"

"In earnest — in terrible deadly earnest, my dear fellow! I think she must be rather crowded out at home."

"Crowded out of Inglefield? Why, there's room for three hundred!" Rosy broke in.

"Well, if that's the kind of mob that's in possession, no wonder she prefers Camberwell. We must be kind to the poor lady," Paul added in a tone that Hyacinth noticed. He attributed a remarkable meaning to it; it seemed to say that people such as he were now so sure of their game that they could afford to be magnanimous; or else it expressed a prevision of the doom that hung over her ladyship's head. Muniment asked if Hyacinth and Rosy had got on together, and the girl replied that Mr. Robinson had made himself most agreeable. "Then you must tell me all about him after he goes, for you know I don't know him much myself," said her brother.

"Oh yes, I'll tell you everything — you know how I like describing."

Hyacinth found himself amused at the young lady's account of his efforts to please her, the fact being that he had only listened to her own eager discourse without opening his mouth; but Paul, whether or no guessing the truth, said to him all pertinently: "It's very wonderful — she can describe things she has never seen. And they're just like the reality."

"There's nothing I've never seen," Rosy declared. "That's the advantage of my lying here in such a manner. I see everything in the world."

"You don't seem to see your brother's meetings — his secret societies and his revolutionary clubs. You put that aside when I asked you."

"Oh, you must n't ask her that sort of thing," said Paul, lowering at Hyacinth with a fierce frown — an expression he perceived in a moment to be facetiously assumed.

"What am I to do then, since you won't tell me anything definite yourself?"

"It will be definite enough when you get hanged for it!" Rosy exclaimed mockingly.

"Why do you want to poke your head into ugly black holes?" Muniment asked, laying his hand on Hyacinth's shoulder and shaking it gently.

"Don't you belong to the party of action?" our young man gravely demanded.

"Look at the way he has picked up all the silly bits of catchwords!" Paul cried in not unkindly derision to his sister. "You must have got that precious phrase out of the newspapers, out of some drivelling leader. Is that the party you want to belong to?" he went on with his clear eyes ranging over his diminutive friend.

"If you'll show me the thing itself I shall have no more occasion to mind the newspapers," Hyacinth

149

candidly pleaded, rejoicing all the while to feel himself in such a relation. It was his view of himself, and not an unfair one, that his was a character that would never sue for a favour; but now he felt that in any connexion with Paul Muniment such a law would be suspended. This rare man he could go on his knees to without a sense of humiliation.

"What thing do you mean, infatuated, deluded youth?" Paul pursued, refusing to be serious.

"Well, you know you do go to places you had far better keep out of, and that often when I lie here and listen to steps on the stairs I'm sure they are coming in to make a search for your papers," Miss Muniment lucidly interposed.

"The day they find my papers, my dear, will be the day you'll get up and dance."

"What did you ask me to come home with you for?" Hyacinth demanded as he twirled his hat. It was an effort for a moment to keep the tears from his eyes; he saw himself forced to put such a different construction on his new friend's hospitality. He had had a happy impression that Muniment had divined in him a possible associate of a high type in a subterranean crusade against the existing order of things, whereas it now came over him that the real use he had been put to was to beguile an hour for a pert invalid. That was all very well, and he would sit by Miss Rosy's bedside, were it a part of his service, every day in the week; only in such a case it should be his reward to enjoy the confidence of her brother. This young man justified at the present juncture the high estimate Lady Aurora Langrish had formed of his

intelligence: whatever his natural reply to Hyacinth's
question would have been he invented straight off
a better one and said at random, smiling and not
knowing exactly what his visitor had meant —

"What did I ask you to come with me for? To see
if you'd be afraid."

What there was to be afraid of was to Hyacinth a
quantity equally vague; but he answered quickly
enough: "I think you've only to try me to see."

"I'm sure that if you introduce him to some of
your low wicked friends he'll be quite satisfied after
he has looked round a bit," Miss Muniment remarked
irrepressibly.

"Those are just the kind of people I want to know,"
Hyacinth rang out.

His sincerity appeared to touch his friend. "Well,
I see you're a good 'un. Just meet me some night."

"Where, where?" asked Hyacinth eagerly.

"Oh, I'll tell you where when we get away from
her." And Muniment led him good-humouredly out.

X

SEVERAL months after Hyacinth had made his acquaintance Millicent Henning remarked that it was high time our hero should take her to some first-class place of amusement. He proposed hereupon the Canterbury Music Hall; at which she tossed her head and affirmed that when a young lady had done for a young man what she had done for him the least he could do was to give her an evening at some theatre in the Strand. Hyacinth would have been a good deal at a loss to say exactly what she had done for him, but it was familiar to him by this time that she regarded him as under great obligations. From the day she had come to look him up in Lomax Place she had taken a position, largely, in his life, and he had seen poor Pinnie's wan countenance grow several degrees more blank. Amanda Pynsent's forebodings had been answered to the letter; the flaring cometary creature had become a fixed star. She had never spoken to him of Millicent but once, several weeks after her interview with the girl; and this had not been in a tone of rebuke, for she had divested herself for ever of any maternal prerogative. Tearful, tremulous, deferential enquiry was now her only weapon, and nothing could be more humble and circumspect than the manner in which she made use of it. He was never at home of an evening, at present, and he had mysterious ways of spending his Sundays, with

which church-going had nothing to do. The time
had been when often, after tea, he sat near the lamp
with the dressmaker and, while her fingers flew, read
out to her the works of Dickens and of Scott; happy
hours of vain semblance that he had forgotten the
wrong she had done him, so that she could almost
forget it herself. But now he gulped down his tea so
fast that he hardly took off his hat while he sat there,
and Pinnie, with her quick eye for all matters of costume, noticed that he wore it still more gracefully
askew than usual, cocking it with a victorious exalted air. He hummed to himself; he fingered his
moustache; he looked out of window when there was
nothing to look at; he seemed preoccupied, launched
in intellectual excursions, half anxious and half in
spirits. During the whole winter Miss Pynsent explained everything by four words murmured beneath
her breath: "That beastly forward jade!" On the
single occasion, however, on which she had sought
relief from her agitation in an appeal to Hyacinth
she did n't trust herself to designate the girl by epithet or title.

"There's only one thing I want to know," she said
to him in a manner which might have seemed casual
if in her silence, knowing her as well as he did, he had
not already perceived the implication of her thought.
"Does she expect you to marry her, dearest?"

"Does who expect me? I should like to see the
woman who does!"

"Of course you know who I mean. The one that
came after you — and picked you right up — from
the other end of London." And at the remembrance

of that insufferable scene poor Pinnie flamed for a moment. "Are n't there plenty of vulgar fellows in that low part where she lives without her ravaging over here? Why can't she stick to her own beat, I should like to know?" Hyacinth had flushed at the question, and she had seen something in his face to make her change her tone. "Just promise me this, my precious child: that if you get into any sort of mess with that piece you 'll immediately confide it to your poor old Pinnie."

"My poor old Pinnie sometimes makes me quite sick," he remarked for answer. "What sort of a mess do you suppose I shall get into?"

"Well, suppose she does come it over you that you promised to marry her?"

"You don't know what you 're talking about. She does n't want to marry any one — the way she sees it."

"Then how the dickens does she see it?"

"Do you imagine I 'd tell a lady's secrets?" the young man returned.

"Oh laws, if she was a lady I should n't be afraid!" said Pinnie.

"Every woman's a lady when she has placed herself under one's protection," Hyacinth declared with his little manner of a man of the great world.

"Under your protection? Oh I say!" cried Pinnie, staring. "And pray who 's to protect you?"

As soon as she had said this she repented, because it seemed just the sort of exclamation that would have made Hyacinth bite her head off. One of the things

she loved him for, however, was that he gave you
touching surprises in this line, had sudden inconsist-
encies of temper that were all for your advantage.
He was by no means always mild when he ought to
have been, but he was sometimes heavenly when he
need n't have been at all. At such moments Pinnie
wanted to kiss him and had often tried to make Mr.
Vetch understand what fascinating traits of character she was always noting in their young friend.
This particular one was rather difficult to describe,
and Mr. Vetch never would admit that he understood, or that he had observed anything that seemed
to correspond to the dressmaker's somewhat confused psychological sketch. It was a comfort to her
in these days, and almost the only one she had, that
she was sure Anastasius Vetch understood a good
deal more than he felt bound to acknowledge. He
was always up to his old game of being a great deal
cleverer than cleverness itself required; and it consoled her present weak, pinched feeling to know that,
though he still talked of the boy as if it would be
a pity to take him too seriously, that was n't the way
he thought of him. He also took him seriously and
had even a certain sense of duty in regard to him.
Miss Pynsent went so far as to say to herself that the
fiddler probably had savings and that no one had
ever known of any one else belonging to him. She
would n't have mentioned it to Hyacinth for the
world, for fear of leading up to a disappointment; but she had visions of a foolscap sheet
folded away in some queer little bachelor's box
(she could n't fancy what men kept in such

places) on which the youth's name would have been written down in very big letters before a solicitor.

"Oh, I'm unprotected in the nature of things," he replied, smiling at his too scrupulous companion. Then he added: "At any rate, it is n't from that girl any danger will come to me."

"I can't think why you like her," Pinnie remarked as if she had spent on the question treasures of impartiality.

"It's jolly to hear one woman on the subject of another," Hyacinth said. "You're kind and good and yet you're ready — !" He gave a sigh as for long experience.

"Well, what am I ready to do? I'm not ready to see you gobbled up before my eyes!"

"You need n't be afraid. She won't drag me to the altar."

"And pray does n't she think you good enough — for one of the beautiful 'Ennings?"

"You don't understand, my poor Pinnie," he wearily pleaded. "I sometimes think there is n't a single thing in life that you understand. One of these days she'll marry an alderman."

"An alderman — that creature?"

"An alderman or a banker or a bishop or some of that bloated kind. She does n't want to end her career to-day — she wants to begin it."

"Well, I wish she'd take you later!" the dressmaker returned.

Hyacinth said nothing for a little, but then broke out: "What are you afraid of? Look here, we had

better clear this up once for all. Are you afraid of my
marrying a girl out of a shop ?"

"Oh, you would n't, would you ?" cried Pinnie
with conciliatory eagerness. "That's the way I like
to hear you talk!"

"Do you think I'd marry any one who would
marry *me* ?" Hyacinth went on. "The kind of girl
who'd look at me is the kind of girl I'd never look
at." He struck Pinnie as having thought it all out;
which did n't surprise her, as she had been familiar
from his youth with his way of following things up.
But she was always delighted when he made a remark that showed he was conscious of being of fine
clay — flashed out an allusion to his not being what
he seemed. He was not what he seemed, but even
with Pinnie's valuable assistance he had not suc-
ceeded in representing to himself very definitely what
he was. She had placed at his disposal for this purpose a passionate idealism which, employed in some
case where it could have consequences, might have
been termed profligate and which yet never cost her
a scruple or a compunction.

"I'm sure a princess might look at you and be
none the worse!" she declared in her delight at this
assurance, more positive than any she had yet received, that he was safe from the worse danger. This
the dressmaker considered to be the chance of his
marrying some person of her own base order.
Still it came over her that his taste might be
lowered, and before the subject was dropped, on
the present occasion, she said that of course he
must be quite aware of all that was wanting to

such a girl as Millicent 'Enning — who visibly wasn't
worth any struggle for her aspirate.

"Oh, I don't bother about what's wanting to her.
I'm content with what she has."

"Content, dearest — how do you mean?" the little
dressmaker quavered. "Content to make an intimate
friend of her?"

"It's impossible I should discuss these matters with
you," Hyacinth grandly enough replied.

"Of course I see that. But I should think she'd
bore you sometimes," Miss Pynsent threw off cun-
ningly.

"She does, I assure you, to extinction!"

"Then why do you spend every evening with her?"

"Where should you like me to spend my evenings?
At some beastly public-house — or at the Italian
opera?" His association with Miss Henning was not
so close as that, but nevertheless he wouldn't take
the trouble to prove to poor Pinnie that he enjoyed
her society only two or three times a week; that on
other evenings he simply strolled about the streets
(this boyish habit clung to him) and that he had even
occasionally the resource of going to the Poupins' or
of gossiping and smoking a pipe at some open house-
door, when the night was not cold, with a fellow-
mechanic. Later in the winter, after he had made
Paul Muniment's acquaintance, the aspect of his life
changed considerably, though Millicent continued to
be exceedingly mixed up with it. He hated the taste
of liquor and still more the taste of the places where
it was sold; besides which the types of misery and
vice that one was liable to see collected in them

frightened and harrowed him, made him ask himself questions that pierced the deeper because they were met by no answer. It was both a blessing and a drawback to him that the delicate, charming character of the work he did at old Crook's, under Eustace Poupin's influence, was a kind of education of the taste, trained him in the finest discriminations, in the recognition of the rare and the hatred of the cheap. This made the brutal, garish, stodgy decoration of public-houses, with their deluge of gaslight, their glittering brass and pewter, their lumpish woodwork and false colours, detestable to him. He had been still very young when the "gin-palace" ceased to convey to him an idea of the palatial.

For this unfortunate but remarkably-organised youth every displeasure or gratification of the visual sense coloured his whole mind, and though he lived in Pentonville and worked in Soho, though he was poor and obscure and cramped and full of unattainable desires, nothing in life had such an interest or such a price for him as his impressions and reflexions. They came from everything he touched, they made him vibrate, kept him thrilled and throbbing, for most of his waking consciousness, and they constituted as yet the principal events and stages of his career. Fortunately they were often an immense amusement. Everything in the field of observation suggested this or that; everything struck him, penetrated, stirred; he had in a word more news of life, as he might have called it, than he knew what to do with — felt sometimes as he could have imagined an overwhelmed man of business to whom the post brought too many letters. The man of business indeed could keep a secretary, but what secretary could have cleared up for Hyacinth some of the strange communications of life? He liked to talk about these things, but it was only a few here and there he could discuss with Milly. He allowed Miss Pynsent to imagine that his hours of leisure were almost exclusively dedicated to this young lady, because, as he said to himself, if he were to account to her for every evening in the week it would make no difference — she would stick to her suspicion; and he referred this perversity to the general weight of misconception under which he at this crude period of his growth held it was his lot to languish. It did n't matter if one was a little more or a little less misunderstood. He might indeed have remembered it mattered to Pinnie, who, after her first relief at hearing him express himself so properly on the subject of a matrimonial connexion with Miss Henning, allowed her faded, kind, weak face little by little to lengthen out to its old solemnity. This came back as the days went on, for it was n't much comfort that he did n't want to marry the young woman in Pimlico when he allowed himself to be held as tight as if he did. For the present, however, she simply said "Oh well, if you see her as she is I don't care what you do" — a sentiment implying a certain moral recklessness on the part of the good little dressmaker. She was irreproachable herself, but she had lived more than fifty years in a world of wickedness; like so many London women of her class and kind she had little sentimental softness for her own sex, whose general "paying" seemed the simplest and most natural arrangement; and she judged it quite a minor evil that Millicent should be left lamenting if only Hyacinth might get out of the scrape. Between a young person who had taken a gross risk and a premature, lowering marriage for her beloved little boy she very well knew which she preferred. It should be added that her view of Millicent's power to look after herself was such as to make it absurd to pity her in advance. Pinnie thought Hyacinth the cleverest young man in the, or at least in their, world, but her state of mind implied that the young lady in Pimlico was cleverer. Her ability, at any rate, was of a kind that precluded the knowledge of suffering, whereas Hyacinth's was somehow fairly founded on it.

By the time he had enjoyed for three months the acquaintance of the brother and sister in Audley Court the whole complexion of his life seemed changed; it was pervaded by an element of romance which overshadowed, though by no means eclipsing, the brilliant figure of Miss Henning. It was pitched in a higher key altogether and appeared to command a view of horizons equally fresh and vast. Millicent therefore shared her dominion without knowing exactly what it was that drew her old playfellow off and without indeed demanding of him an account she was not on her own side prepared to give. Hyacinth was, in the language of the circle in which she moved, her personal fancy, and she was content to fill as regards himself the same eminent and somewhat irresponsible position. She had the assurance that she was a beneficent friend: fond of him and

careful of him as an elder sister might be; warning
him as no one else could do against the dangers of the
town; putting that stiff common sense, of which she
was convinced that she possessed an extraordinary
supply, at the service of his incurable verdancy;
looking after him generally as no one, poor child, had
ever done. Millicent made light of the dingy dressmaker in this view of her friend's meagre little past
(she thought Pinnie no better than a starved cat) and
enjoyed herself immensely in the character of guide
and philosopher. She felt that character never so
high as when she pushed the young man with a
robust elbow or said to him "Well, you *are* a sharp
'un, you are!" Her theory of herself, as we know,
was that she was the "best sort" in the world, as well
as one of the greatest beauties and quickest wits, and
there could be no better proof of her kindness of heart
than her disinterested affection for a snippet of a
bookbinder. Her sociability was certainly immense,
and so were her vanity, her grossness, her presumption, her appetite for beer, for buns, for entertainment of every kind. She represented for Hyacinth
during this period the eternal feminine, and his taste,
considering he was fastidious, will be wondered at;
the judgement will be that she did n't represent it very
favourably.

It may easily be believed that he criticised his
inclination even while he gave himself up to it, and
that he often wondered he should find so much to
attract in a girl in whom he found so much to condemn. She was vulgar, clumsy and grotesquely ignorant; her conceit was proportionate and she had n't

a grain of tact or of quick perception. And yet there was something so elementally free in her, by his loose measure, she carried with such an air the advantages she did possess, that her figure constantly mingled itself even with those bright visions hovering before him after Paul Muniment had opened a queerly-placed but far-reaching window. She was bold and generous and incalculable, and if she was coarse she was neither false nor cruel. She laughed with the laugh of the people and if you hit her hard enough would cry with their tears. When he himself was not letting his imagination wander among the haunts of the aristocracy and stretching it in the shadow of an ancestral beech to read the last number of the *Revue des Deux Mondes* he was occupied with contemplations of a very different kind; he was absorbed in the struggles and sufferings of the millions whose life flowed in the same current as his and who, though they constantly excited his disgust and made him shrink and turn away, had the power to chain his sympathy, to raise it to passion, to convince him for the time at least that real success in the world would be to do something with them and for them. All this, strange to say, was never so vivid as in Millicent's company — which is a proof of his fantastic, erratic way of seeing things. She had no such ideas about herself; they were almost the only ideas she did n't have. She had no theories about redeeming or uplifting the people; she simply loathed them, for being so dirty, with the outspoken violence of one who had known poverty and the strange bedfellows it makes in a very different degree from Hyacinth, brought up (with Pinnie to put sugar in his tea and let him never want for neckties) like a regular little swell.

Millicent, to hear her talk, only asked to keep her skirts clear and marry some respectable tea-merchant. But for our hero she was magnificently plebeian, in the sense that implied loud recklessness of danger and the qualities that shine forth in a row. She summed up the sociable humorous ignorant chatter of the masses, their capacity for offensive and defensive passion, their instinctive perception of their strength on the day they should really exercise it; and as much as any of this their ideal of something smug and prosperous, where washed hands and oiled hair and plates in rows on dressers and stuffed birds under glass and family photographs of a quite similar effect would symbolise success. She was none the less plucky for being at bottom a shameless Philistine, ambitious of a front garden with rockwork; and she presented the plebeian character in none the less plastic a form. Having the history of the French Revolution at his fingers' ends, Hyacinth could easily see her (if there should ever be barricades in the streets of London) with a red cap of liberty on her head and her white throat bared so that she should be able to shout the louder the Marseillaise of that hour, whatever it might be. If the festival of the Goddess of Reason should ever be enacted in the British Capital — and Hyacinth could consider such possibilities without a smile, so much was it a part of the little religion he had to remember always that there was no knowing what might happen — if this solemnity, I say, should be revived in Hyde Park, who was

better designated than Miss Henning to figure in a
grand statuesque manner as the heroine of the occasion? It was plain she had laid her inconsequent
admirer under a peculiar spell, since he could associate her with such scenes as that while she consumed
beer and buns at his expense. If she had a weakness
it was for prawns; and she had, all winter, a plan for
his taking her down to Gravesend, where this luxury
was cheap and abundant, when the fine long days
should arrive. She was never so frank and facetious
as when she dwelt on the details of a project of this
kind; and then Hyacinth was reminded afresh that
it was an immense good fortune for him she was so
handsome. If she had been ugly he could n't have
listened to her; but the rare bloom and grand style of
her person glorified even her accent, interfused her
cockney genius with prismatic hues, gave her a large
and constant impunity.

XI

SHE desired at last to raise their common experience to a loftier level, to enjoy what she called a high-class treat. Their commerce had been condemned for the most part to go forward in the streets, the wintry, dusky, foggy streets, which looked bigger and more numerous in their perpetual obscurity and in which everything was covered with damp, gritty smut, an odour extremely agreeable to Miss Henning. Happily she shared Hyacinth's relish of vague perambulation and was still more addicted than he to looking into the windows of shops, before which, in long, contemplative halts, she picked out freely the articles she should n't mind having put up for her. He invariably pronounced the objects of her selection hideous and made no scruple to assure her she had the worst taste of any girl in the place. Nothing he could say to her affronted her so much, for her pretensions in the way of a cultivated judgement were boundless. Had not indeed her natural aptitude been fortified, in the neighbourhood of Buckingham Palace (there was scarcely anything they did n't sell in the great shop of which she was an ornament) by daily contact with the freshest products of modern industry ? Hyacinth laughed this establishment to scorn and made the point that there was nothing in it from top to bottom that a real artist would look at. She enquired with answering derision if this were a description of his own few inches; but in reality she was fascinated as much as she was provoked by his attitude of being difficult to please, of seeing indescribable differences among the smartest things. She had given herself out originally as very knowing, but he could make her gape with doubts. When once in a while he pointed out a commodity that he condescended to like (this did n't happen often, because the only shops in which there was a chance of his making such a discovery were closed at nightfall) she stared and bruised him with her elbow, declaring that if any one should give her such a piece of rubbish she would sell it for fourpence. Once or twice she asked him to be so good as to explain to her in what its superiority consisted — she could n't rid herself of a suspicion that there might be something in his judgement and was angry at not finding herself as positive as any one. Then he would reply that it was no use attempting to tell her; she would n't understand and had better continue to admire the insipid productions of an age that had lost the sense of fineness — a phrase she remembered, proposing to herself even to make use of it on some future occasion, but was quite unable to interpret.

When her companion demeaned himself in this manner it was not with a view of strengthening the tie that united him to his childhood's friend; but the effect followed on Millicent's side and the girl was proud to think herself in possession of a young man whose knowledge was of so high an order that it was inexpressible. In spite of her vanity she was not so convinced of her perfection as not to be full of un-

167

gratified aspirations; she had an idea it might be to her advantage some day to exhibit a sample of that learning; and at the same time, when, in consideration for instance of a jeweller's gas-lighted display in Great Portland Street, Hyacinth lingered for five minutes in perfect silence and she delivered herself according to her wont at such junctures, she was a thousand miles from guessing the perverse sentiments that made it impossible for him to speak. She could long for things she was not likely to have; envy other people for possessing them and say it was a "regular shime"; draw brilliant pictures of what she should do with them if she did have them; and pass immediately, with a mind unencumbered by superfluous inductions, to some other topic equally intimate and personal. The sense of privation with her was often extremely acute; but she could always put her finger on the remedy. With her fellow-sufferer the case was very different; the remedy for him was terribly vague and inaccessible. He was liable to moods in which the sense of exclusion from all he would have liked most to enjoy in life settled on him like a pall. They had a bitterness, but they were not invidious — they were not moods of vengeance, of imaginary spoliation: they were simply states of paralysing melancholy, of infinite sad reflexion, in which he felt how in this world of effort and suffering life was endurable, the spirit able to expand, only in the best conditions, and how a sordid struggle in which one should go down to the grave without having tasted them was not worth the misery it would cost, the dull demoralisation it would involve.

In such hours the great roaring indifferent world of London seemed to him a huge organisation for mocking at his poverty, at his inanition; and then its vulgarest ornaments, the windows of third-rate jewellers, the young man in a white tie and a crush-hat who dandled by on his way to a dinner-party in a hansom that nearly ran over one — these familiar phenomena became symbolic, insolent, defiant, took on themselves to make him smart with the sense that *he* was above all out of it. He felt moreover that there was neither consolation nor refutation in saying to himself that the immense majority of mankind were out of it with him and appeared to put up well enough with the annoyance. That was their own affair; he knew nothing of their reasons or their resignation, and if they chose neither to rebel nor to compare he at least, among the disinherited, would keep up the standard. When these fits were on our young man his brothers of the people fared, collectively, very ill at his hands; their function then was to represent in massive shape precisely the grovelling interests which attracted one's contempt, and the only acknowledge-ment one owed them was for the completeness of the illustration. Everything which in a great city could touch the sentient faculty of a youth on whom nothing was lost ministered to his conviction that there was no possible good fortune in life of too "quiet" an order for him to appreciate — no privi-lege, no opportunity, no luxury to which he might n't do full justice. It was not so much that he wanted to enjoy as that he wanted to know; his desire was n't to be pampered but to be initiated. Sometimes of a Saturday in the long evenings of June and July he made his way into Hyde Park at the hour when the throng of carriages, of riders, of brilliant pedestrians was thickest; and though lately, on two or three of these occasions, he had been accompanied by Miss Henning, whose criticism of the scene was rich and distinct, a tremendous little drama had taken place privately on the stage of his inner consciousness. He wanted to drive in every carriage, to mount on every horse, to feel on his arm the hand of every pretty woman in the place. In the midst of this his sense was vivid that he belonged to the class whom the "bloated" as they passed did n't so much as rest their eyes on for a quarter of a second. They looked at Millicent, who was safe to be looked at anywhere and was one of the handsomest girls in any company, but they only reminded him of the high human walls, the deep gulfs of tradition, the steep embankments of privilege and dense layers of stupidity fencing the "likes" of him off from social recognition.

And this was not the fruit of a morbid vanity on his part, or of a jealousy that could n't be intelligent; his personal discomfort was the result of an intense admiration for what he had missed. There were individuals whom he followed with his eyes, with his thoughts, sometimes even with his steps; they seemed to tell him what it was to be the flower of a high civilisation. At moments he was aghast when he reflected that the cause he had secretly espoused, the cause from which M. Poupin and Paul Muniment (especially the latter) had within the last few months drawn aside the curtain, proposed to itself to bring about a state of things in which that particular scene would be impossible. It made him even rather faint to think that he must choose; that he could n't (with any respect for his own consistency) work underground for the enthronement of the democracy and yet continue to enjoy in however platonic a manner a spectacle which rested on a hideous social inequality. He must either suffer with the people as he had suffered before, or he must apologise to others, as he sometimes came so near doing to himself, for the rich; inasmuch as the day was certainly near when these two mighty forces would come to a death-grapple. Hyacinth thought himself obliged at present to have reasons for his feelings; his intimacy with Paul Muniment, which had now grown very great, laid a good deal of that sort of responsibility upon him. Muniment laughed at his reasons whenever he produced them, but appeared to expect him nevertheless to have them ready on demand, and Hyacinth had ever a desire to do what he expected. There were times when he said to himself that it might very well be his fate to be divided to the point of torture, to be split open by sympathies that pulled him in different ways; for had n't he an extraordinarily mingled current in his blood, and from the time he could remember was n't there one half of him always either playing tricks on the other or getting snubs and pinches from it?

That dim, dreadful, confused legend of his mother's history, as regards which what Pinnie had been able to tell him when he first began to question her was at once too much and too little — this stupefying explanation had supplied him first and last with a hundred different theories of his identity. What he knew, what he guessed had sickened and what he did n't know tormented him; but in his illuminated ignorance he had fashioned forth an article of faith. This had gradually emerged from the depths of darkness in which he found himself plunged as a consequence of the challenge he had addressed to Pinnie — while he was still only a child — on the memorable day that had transformed the whole face of his future. It was one January afternoon when he had come in from a walk. She was seated at her lamp, as usual, with her work, and had begun to tell him of a letter one of the lodgers had got describing the manner in which his brother-in-law's shop at Nottingham had been rifled by burglars. He had listened to her story, standing in front of her, and then by way of response had suddenly said to her: "Who was that awful woman you took me to see ever so long ago?" The expression of her white face as she looked up at him, her fear of such an attack all dormant after so many years — this strange, scared, sick glance was a thing he could never forget, any more than the tone, with her breath failing her, in which she had repeated "That awful woman?"

"That woman in the prison years ago — how old was I? — who was dying and who kissed me so, as I've never been kissed, as I never shall be again! Who *was* she, who WAS she?" Poor Pinnie, to do her justice, had made, after she recovered her breath, a gallant fight: it had lasted a week; it was to leave her spent and sore for ever after, and before it was over Anastasius Vetch had been called in. At his instance she had retracted the falsehoods with which she had previously tried to put the boy off, and had made at last a confession and a report which he was satisfied to believe as complete as her knowledge. Hyacinth could never have told you why the crisis had occurred on such a day, why his question had broken out at that particular moment. The strangeness of the matter to himself was that the germ of his curiosity should have developed so slowly; that the haunting wonder which now, as he looked back, appeared to fill his whole childhood, should only after so long an interval have crept up to the air. It was only of course little by little that he had recovered his bearings in his new and more poignant consciousness; little by little that he had reconstructed his antecedents, taken the measure, so far as was possible, of his heredity. His having the courage to disinter from the *Times* in the reading-room of the British Museum a report of his mother's trial for the murder of Lord Frederick Purvis, which was very copious, the affair having been quite a *cause célèbre;* his resolution in sitting under that splendid dome and, with his head bent to hide his hot eyes, going through every syllable of the ghastly record had been an achievement of comparatively recent years. There were certain things Pinnie knew that appalled him; and there were others, as to which he would have given his hand to have some light, that it made his heart ache supremely to find she was honestly ignorant of. He scarce understood what sort of favour Mr. Vetch wished to make with him (as a compensation for the precious part he had played in the business years before) when the fiddler permitted himself to pass judgement on the family of the wretched young nobleman for not having provided in some manner for the infant child of his assassin. Why should they have provided when it was evident they had refused absolutely to recognise his lordship's responsibility? Pinnie had to admit this under Hyacinth's terrible cross-questioning; she could n't pretend with any show of evidence that Lord Whiteroy and the other brothers (there had been no less than seven, most of them still living) had at the time of the trial given any symptom of believing Florentine Vivier's asseverations. That was their affair; he had long since made up his mind that his own was very different. One could n't believe at will, and fortunately, in the case, he had no effort to make; for from the moment he began to consider the established facts (few as they were and poor and hideous) he regarded himself immutably as the son of the recreant and sacrificed Lord Frederick.

He had no need to reason about it; all his nerves and pulses pleaded and testified. His mother had been a daughter of the wild French people — all Pinnie could tell him of her parentage was that Florentine had once mentioned that in her extreme childhood her father, his gun in his hand, had fallen in the blood-stained streets of Paris on a barricade; but on the other side it took an English aristocrat to account for him, though a poor specimen apparently had to suffice. This, with its further implications, became Hyacinth's article of faith; the reflexion that he was a bastard involved in a remarkable manner the reflexion that he was a gentleman. He was conscious he did n't hate the image of his father as he might have been expected to do; and he supposed this was because Lord Frederick had paid so tremendous a penalty. It was in the exaction of that penalty that the moral proof for him resided; his mother would n't have armed herself on account of any injury less cruel than the passage of which her miserable baby was the living sign. She had avenged herself because she had been thrown over, and the bitterness of that wrong had been in the fact that he, hopeless brat, lay there in her lap. *He* was the one properly to have been sacrificed: that remark our young man often made to himself. That his judgement of the whole question was passionate and personal and took little account of any disturbing conflict of evidence is proved by the importance he attached for instance to the name by which his mother had told poor Pinnie (when this excellent creature consented to take him) that she wished him to be called. Hyacinth had been the name of her father, a republican clockmaker, the martyr of his opinions, whose memory she professed to worship; and when Lord Frederick had insinuated himself into her confidence he had had reasons for preferring to be known as plain Mr. Robinson — reasons, however, into which, in spite of the light thrown upon them at the trial, it was difficult after so many years to enter.

Hyacinth had never known of Mr. Vetch's saying more than once to Pinnie "If her contention as regards that dissolute young swell was true why did n't

she make the child bear his real name instead of his
false one ?" — an enquiry which the dressmaker had
answered, with some ingenuity, by remarking that
she could n't call him after a man she had murdered,
as one must suppose her unwilling to publish to
every one his connexion with a crime that had been
so much talked about. If Hyacinth had assisted at
this little discussion it is needless to say that he would
have sided with Miss Pynsent; though that his judgement was independently formed is proved by the fact
that Pinnie's fearfully indiscreet attempts at condol-
ence should not have made him throw up his version
in disgust. It was after the complete revelation that
he understood the romantic innuendoes with which
his childhood had been surrounded and of which he
had never caught the meaning; they having seemed
but a feature of the general fact of the poor woman's
professional life — so much cutting and trimming and
shaping and embroidering, so much turning and alter-
ing and doing-up. When it came over him that she
had for years made a fool of him to himself and to
others he could have beaten her for grief and shame;
and yet before he administered this rebuke he had to
remember that she only chattered (though she professed to have been extraordinarily dumb) about
a matter over which he spent nine tenths of his own
time in all gloomily brooding. When she tried to
console him for the horror of his mother's history by
descanting on the glory of the Purvises and remind-
ing him that he was related through them to half the
aristocracy of England he felt her to be turning the
tragedy of his life into a monstrous farce; and yet he

none the less continued to cherish the belief that he was a gentleman born. He allowed her to tell him nothing about the family in question, and his impracticability on this subject was one of the reasons of the deep dejection of her later years. If he had only let her idealise him a little to himself she would have felt she was making up by so much for her grand mistake. He sometimes saw the name of his father's kin in the newspaper, but he then always cast the sheet away. He had nothing to ask of them and wished to prove to himself that he could ignore them (who had been willing to let him die like a rat) as completely as they ignored him. A thousand times yes, he was with the people and every possible vengeance of the people as against such shameless egoism as that; but all the same he was happy to feel he had blood in his veins that would account for the finest sensibilities.

He had no money to pay for places at a theatre in the Strand, Millicent Henning having made it clear to him that on this occasion she expected something better than the pit. "Should you like the royal box or a couple of stalls at ten bob apiece?" he asked of her on a note of that too uniform irony which formed the basis of almost all their talk. She had replied that she would content herself with a seat in the second balcony, in the very front; and as such a position involved an expenditure still beyond his compass he waited one night on Mr. Vetch, to whom he had already more than once had recourse in moments of pecuniary embarrassment. His relations with the caustic fiddler were of the oddest and much easier

when put to the proof than in theory. Mr. Vetch had
let him know—long before this and with the purpose
of covering Pinnie to the utmost — the part he had
played at the crisis of that question of her captive's
being taken to call on Mrs. Bowerbank; and Hyacinth, in the face of this information, had asked with
some sublimity what the devil the fiddler had had to
do with his private affairs. Their neighbour had replied that it was not as an affair of his but as an affair
of Pinnie's he had considered the matter; and our
hero had afterwards let it drop, though he had never
been formally reconciled to so officious a critic. Of
course his feeling on this head had been immensely
modified by the trouble Mr. Vetch had taken to get
him a place with old Crook; and at the period of
which I write it had long been familiar to him that
the author of that benefit did n't care a straw what
he thought of his advice at the dark hour and in fact
took a perverse pleasure in "following" the career of
a youth put together of such queer pieces. It was
impossible to Hyacinth not to be conscious that this
projected attention was kindly; and to-day, at any
rate, he would have declared that nothing could have
made up to him for not knowing the truth, horrible
as it might be. His miserable mother's embrace
seemed to furnish him with an inexhaustible fund of
motive, and in the conditions that was a support.
What he chiefly objected to in Mr. Vetch was the
betrayed habit of still regarding him as extremely
juvenile; he would have got on much better with a
better recognition of his being already a man of the
world. The obscure virtuoso knew an immense deal

178

about society and seemed to know the more because he never swaggered — it was only little by little you discovered it; but that was no reason for his looking as if his chief boon in life was a private diverting commentary on the conversation of his young friend. Hyacinth felt that he gave considerable evidence of patience with this when he occasionally asked his fellow-resident in Lomax Place to lend him half-a-crown. Somehow circumstances had of old tied them together, and though this partly vexed the little book-binder it also touched him; he had more than once solved the problem of deciding how to behave (when the fiddler exasperated him) by simply asking of him some substantial service. Mr. Vetch had never once refused. It was satisfactory to Hyacinth to remember as much when knocking at his door late, after allowing him time to come home from the theatre. He knew his habits: he never went straight to bed, but sat by his fire an hour, smoking his pipe, mixing a grog and reading some old book. Hyacinth could tell when to go up by the light in his window, which he could see from a court behind.

"Oh, I know I have n't been to see you for a long time," he said in response to the remark with which his neighbour greeted him; "and I may as well tell you immediately what has brought me at present — in addition to the desire to ask after your health. I want to take a young lady to the theatre."

Mr. Vetch was habited in a tattered dressing-gown; his apartment smelt strongly of the liquor he was consuming. Divested of his evening-gear he looked to our hero so plucked and blighted as on the spot to

THE PRINCESS CASAMASSIMA

settle his claims in the event of a social liquidation; he too was unmistakeably a creditor. "I'm afraid you find your young lady rather expensive."

"I find everything expensive," said Hyacinth as if to finish that subject.

"Especially, I suppose, your secret societies."

"What do you mean by that?" the young man asked with a fine stare.

"Why, you told me in the autumn that you were just about to join a few."

"A few? How many do you suppose?" But our friend checked himself. "Do you suppose if I had been serious I'd tell?"

"Oh dear, oh dear!" sighed Mr. Vetch. Then he went on: "You want to take her to my shop, eh?"

"I'm sorry to say she won't go there. She wants something in the Strand: that's a great point. She wants very much to see *The Pearl of Paraguay*. I don't wish to pay anything, if possible; I'm sorry to say I have n't a penny. But as you know people at the other theatres and I've heard you say that you do each other little favours from place to place, *à charge de revanche*, it occurred to me you might be able to get me an order. The piece has been running a long time and most people (except poor devils like me) must have seen it: therefore there probably is n't a rush."

Mr. Vetch listened in silence and presently said: "Do you want a box?"

"Oh no; something more modest."

"Why not a box?" asked the fiddler in a tone the youth knew.

"Because I have n't the clothes people wear in that sort of place, — if you must have such a definite reason."

"And your young lady — has *she* the clothes ?"

"Oh, I dare say; she seems to have everything."

"Where does she get 'em ?"

"Oh, I don't know. She belongs to a big shop; she has to be fine."

"Won't you have a pipe ?" Mr. Vetch asked, pushing an old tobacco-pouch across the table; and while the young man helped himself he puffed a while in silence. "What will she do with you ?" he finally asked.

"What will who do with me ?"

"Your big beauty — Miss Henning. I know all about her from Pinnie."

"Then you know what she 'll do with me!" Hyacinth returned with rather a scornful laugh.

"Yes, but, after all, it does n't very much matter."

"I don't know what you 're talking about," said Hyacinth.

"Well, now the other thing — what do they call it ? the Subterranean ? — are you very deep in that ?" the fiddler went on as if he had not heard him.

"Did Pinnie tell you also about that ?"

"No, our friend Puppin has told me a good deal. He knows you 've put your head into something. Besides, I see it," said Mr. Vetch.

"How do you see it, pray ?"

"You 've got such a speaking eye. Any one can tell, to look at you, that you 've taken some oath on bloody bones, that you belong to some terrible gang.

You seem to say to every one 'Slow torture won't induce me to tell where it meets!'"

"You won't get me an order then?" Hyacinth said in a moment.

"My dear boy, I offer you a box. I take the greatest interest in you."

They smoked together a while and at last Hyacinth remarked: "It has nothing to do with the Subterranean."

"Is it more terrible, more deadly secret?" his companion asked with extreme seriousness.

"I thought you pretended to be a radical," Hyacinth returned.

"Well, so I am — of the old-fashioned, constitutional, milk-and-water, jog-trot sort. I'm not an exterminator."

"We don't know what we may be when the time comes," Hyacinth observed more sententiously than he intended.

"Is the time coming then, my dear young friend?"

"I don't think I've a right to give you any more of a warning than that," smiled our hero.

"It's very kind of you to do so much, I'm sure, and to rush in here at the small hours for the purpose. Meanwhile, in the few weeks or months or years, or whatever they are, that are left, you wish to crowd in all possible enjoyment with the young ladies: that's a very natural inclination." To which Mr. Vetch irrelevantly added: "Do you see many foreigners?"

"Yes, a good many."

"And what do you think of them?"

"Oh, all sorts of things. I rather like Englishmen best."

"Mr. Muniment for example?"

"I say, what do you know about *him*?" Hyacinth asked.

"I've seen him at the Puppins'. I know you and he are as thick as thieves."

"He'll distinguish himself some day very much," said Hyacinth, who was perfectly willing and indeed very proud to be thought a close ally of a highly original man.

"Very likely — very likely. And what will *he* do with you?" the fiddler enquired.

Hyacinth got up; they looked at each other hard. "Do get me two good places in the second balcony."

Mr. Vetch replied that he would do what he could, and three days afterwards he handed his young friend the coveted order. He accompanied it with the injunction "You had better put in all the fun you can, you know!"

BOOK SECOND

XII

HYACINTH and his companion took their seats with extreme promptitude before the curtain rose on *The Pearl of Paraguay*. Thanks to Millicent's eagerness not to be late they encountered the discomfort which had constituted her main objection to going into the pit: they waited for twenty minutes at the door of the theatre, in a tight, stolid crowd, before the official hour of opening. Millicent, bareheaded and powerfully laced, presented a splendid appearance and, on Hyacinth's part, gratified a youthful, ingenuous pride of possession in every respect save a tendency, while ingress was denied them, to make her neighbours feel her elbows and to comment loudly and sarcastically on the situation. It was more clear to him even than it had been before that she was a young lady who in public places might easily need a champion or an apologist. Hyacinth knew there was only one way to apologise for a "female" when the female was attached very closely and heavily to one's arm, and was reminded afresh of how little constitutional aversion Miss Henning had to a row. He had an idea she might think his own taste ran even too little in that direction, and entertained visions of violent confused scenes in which he should in some way distinguish himself: he scarcely knew in what way and imagined himself more easily routing some hulking adversary by an exquisite application of the retort courteous

187

than by flying at him with a pair of very small fists.

By the time they had reached their places in the balcony she was rather flushed and a good deal ruffled; but she had composed herself in season for the rising of the curtain on the farce preceding the melodrama and which the pair had had no intention of losing. At this stage a more genial agitation took possession of her and she surrendered her sympathies to the horse-play of the traditional prelude. Hyacinth found it less amusing, but the theatre, in any conditions, was full of sweet deception for him. His imagination projected itself lovingly across the footlights, gilded and coloured the shabby canvas and battered accessories, losing itself so effectually in the fictive world that the end of the piece, however long or however short, brought with it something of the alarm of a stoppage of his personal life. It was impossible to be more friendly to the dramatic illusion. Millicent, as the audience thickened, rejoiced more largely and loudly, held herself as a lady, surveyed the place as if she knew all about it, leaned back and leaned forward, fanned herself with majesty, gave her opinion upon the appearance and coiffure of every woman within sight, abounded in question and conjecture and produced from her pocket a little paper of peppermint-drops of which under cruel threats she compelled Hyacinth to partake. She followed with attention, though not always with success, the complicated adventures of the Pearl of Paraguay through scenes luxuriantly tropical, in which the male characters wore sombreros and stilettos and the ladies either

danced the cachucha or fled from licentious pursuit;
but her eyes wandered intermittently to the occu-
pants of the boxes and stalls, concerning several of
whom she had theories which she imparted to Hyacinth, while the play went on, greatly to his discomfiture, he being unable to conceive of such levity. She
had the pretension of knowing who every one was;
not individually and by name, but as regards their
exact social station, the quarter of London in which
they lived and the amount of money they were prepared to spend in the neighbourhood of Buckingham
Palace. She had seen the whole town pass through
her establishment there, and though Hyacinth, from
his infancy, had been watching it at his own point
of view, his companion made him feel all the characteristic points he had missed. Her interpretations
differed from his largely in being so very bold and
irreverent. Miss Henning's observation of the London world had not been of a nature to impress her
with its high moral tone, and she had a free off-hand
cynicism which imposed itself. She thought most
ladies hypocrites and had in all ways a low opinion of
her own sex, which more than once before this she
had justified to Hyacinth by narrating observations
of a surprising kind gathered during her career as
a shop-girl. There was a pleasing inconsequence
therefore in her being moved to tears in the third act
of the play, when the Pearl of Paraguay, dishevelled
and distracted, dragging herself on her knees, im-
plored the stern hidalgo her father to believe in
her innocence in spite of circumstances appearing to
condemn her — a midnight meeting with the wicked

189

hero in the grove of cocoanuts. It was at this crisis none the less that she asked Hyacinth who his friends were in the principal box on the left of the stage and let him know that a gentleman seated there had been watching him at intervals for the past half-hour.

"Watching *me*! I like that! When I want to be watched I take you with me."

"Of course he has looked at me," Millicent answered as if she had no interest in denying that. "But you're the one he wants to get hold of."

"To get hold of!"

"Yes, you ninny: don't hang back. He may make your fortune."

"Well, if you'd like him to come and sit by you I'll go and take a walk in the Strand," said Hyacinth, entering into the humour of the occasion but not seeing from where he was placed any gentleman in the box. Millicent explained that the mysterious observer had just altered his position; he had gone to the back, which must have had considerable depth. There were other persons there, out of sight; she and Hyacinth were too much on the same side. One of them was a lady concealed by the curtain; her arm, bare save for its bracelets, was visible at moments on the cushioned ledge. Hyacinth saw it in effect reappear there, and even while the piece proceeded regarded it with a certain interest; but till the curtain fell at the end of the act there was no further symptom that a gentleman wished to get hold of him.

"Now do you say it's me he's after?" Millicent asked abruptly, giving him a sidelong dig while the fiddlers in the orchestra began to scrape their instruments for the interlude.

"Of course; I'm only the pretext," Hyacinth replied, after he had looked a moment, in a manner which he flattered himself was a proof of quick self-possession. The gentleman designated by his friend was once more at the front and leaning forward with his arms on the edge. Hyacinth saw he was looking straight at him, and our young man returned his gaze — an effort not rendered the more easy by the fact that after an instant he recognised him.

"Well, if he knows us he might give some sign, and if he does n't he might leave us alone," Millicent declared, abandoning the distinction she had made between herself and her companion. She had no sooner spoken than the gentleman complied with the first-mentioned of these conditions; he smiled at Hyacinth across the house — he nodded to him with unmistakeable friendliness. Millicent, perceiving this, glanced at the young man from Lomax Place and saw that the demonstration had brought a deep colour to his cheek. He was blushing, flushing; whether with pleasure or embarrassment did n't immediately appear. "I say, I say — is it one of your grand relations?" she promptly asked. "Well, I can stare as well as him;" and she told Hyacinth it was a "shime" to bring a young lady to the play when you had n't so much as an opera-glass for her to look at the company. "Is he one of those lords your aunt was always talking about in the Plice? Is he your uncle or your grandfather or your first or second cousin? No, he's too young for your grandfather. What a pity I can't see if he looks like you!"

At any other time Hyacinth would have thought these enquiries in the worst possible taste, but now he was too much given up to other reflexions. It pleased him that the gentleman in the box should recognise and notice him, because even so small a fact as this was an extension of his social existence; but it no less surprised and puzzled him, producing altogether, in his easily-excited organism, an agitation of which, in spite of his attempted self-control, the air he had for Millicent was the sign. They had met three times, he and his fellow-spectator; but they had met in quarters that, to Hyacinth's mind, would have made a furtive wink, a mere tremor of the eyelid, a more judicious reference to the fact than so public a salutation. Our friend would never have permitted himself to greet him first, and this was not because the gentleman in the box belonged — conspicuously as he did so — to a different walk of society. He was apparently a man of forty, tall, lean and loose-jointed; he fell into lounging, dawdling attitudes and even at a distance looked lazy. He had a long, amused, contented face, unadorned with moustache or whisker, and his brown hair, parted at the side, came forward on either temple in a rich, well-brushed lock, after the fashion of the portraits of 1820. Millicent had a glance of such range and keenness that she was able to make out the details of his evening-dress, of which she appreciated the "form"; to observe the character of his large hands· and to note that he continually smiled at something, that his eyes were extraordinarily light in colour and that in spite of the dark, well-marked brows arching over them his fine skin never had produced and never would produce a beard of any strength. Our young lady pronounced him mentally a "swell" of the first magnitude and wondered more than ever where he had picked up Hyacinth. Her companion seemed to echo her thought when he exclaimed with a little surprised sigh, almost an exhalation of awe: "Well, I had no idea he was one of that lot!"

"You might at least tell me his name, so that I shall know what to call him when he comes round to speak to us," the girl said, provoked at her companion's reserve.

"Comes round to speak to us — a chap like that!" Hyacinth echoed.

"Well, I'm sure if he had been your own brother he could n't have grinned at you more! He may want to make my acquaintance after all; he won't be the first."

The gentleman had once more retreated from sight, and there was that amount of evidence of the intention she imputed to him. "I don't think I'm at all clear that I've a right to tell his name." Hyacinth spoke responsibly, yet with all disposition to magnify an incident which deepened the brilliancy of the entertainment he had been able to offer Miss Henning. "I met him in a place where he may not like to have it known he goes."

"Do you go to places that people are ashamed of? Is it one of your political clubs, as you call them, where that dirty young man from Camberwell, Mr.

193

Monument (what do you call him?), fills your head with ideas that'll bring you to no good? I'm sure your friend over there does n't look as if he'd be on *your* side."

Hyacinth had indulged in this reflexion himself; but the only answer he made to Millicent was: "Well then, perhaps he'll be on yours!"

"Laws, I hope *she* ain't one of the aristocracy!" Millicent exclaimed with apparent irrelevance; and following the direction of her eyes Hyacinth saw that the chair his mysterious acquaintance had quitted in the stage-box was now occupied by a lady hitherto invisible — not the one who had given them a glimpse of her shoulder and bare arm. This was an ancient personage muffled in a voluminous and crumpled white shawl — a stout, odd, foreign-looking woman with a fair, nodding, wiggy head. She had a placid, patient air and a round wrinkled face in which, how-ever, a pair of small bright eyes moved quickly enough. Her rather soiled white glóves were too large for her, and round her head, horizontally arranged as if to keep her wig in its place, she wore a narrow band of tinsel decorated in the middle of the forehead by a jewel which the rest of her appearance would lead the spectator to suppose false. "Is the old woman his mother? Where did she dig up her clothes? They look as if she had hired them for the evening. Does *she* come to your wonderful club too? I dare say she cuts it fine, don't she?" Millicent went on; and when Hyacinth suggested sportively that the old lady might be not the gentleman's mother but his wife or his fancy of the moment she declared that in

that case, were he to come to see them, she should n't
fear for herself. No wonder he wanted to get out of
that box! The party in the wig — and what a wig!
— was sitting there on purpose to look at them, but
she could n't say she was particularly honoured by
the notice of such an old guy. Hyacinth pretended
he quite liked her appearance and admired in her
a charm of her own; he offered to bet another paper
of peppermints that if they could find out she would
be some tremendous old dowager, some one with
a handle to her name. To this Millicent replied with
an air of experience that she had never thought the
greatest beauty was in the upper class; and her companion could see she was covertly looking over her
shoulder to watch for his strange clubmate and that
she would be disappointed if he did n't come. This
idea did n't make Hyacinth jealous, for his mind was
occupied with another side of the business; and if he
offered sportive suggestions it was because he was
really excited, was dazzled, by an incident of which
the reader will have failed as yet to perceive the
larger relations. What moved him was not the pleasure of being patronised by a rich man; it was simply
the prospect of new experience — a sensation for
which he was always ready to exchange any present
boon; and he was convinced that if the gentleman
with whom he had conversed in a small occult back
room in Bloomsbury as Captain Godfrey Sholto —
the Captain had given him his card — had in more
positive fashion than by Millicent's supposing it
come out of the stage-box to see him, he would bring
with him rare influences. His view of this possibility

made suspense akin to preparation; therefore when at the end of a few minutes he became aware that his young woman, with her head turned, was taking the measure of some one who had come in behind them, he felt fate to be doing for him by way of a change as much as could be expected. He got up in his place, but not too soon to see that Captain Sholto had been standing there a moment in contemplation of Millicent and that she on her side had performed with deliberation the ceremony of appraising him. The Captain had his hands in his pockets and wore his crush-hat pushed a good deal back. He laughed to the young couple in the balcony in the friendliest way, as if he had known them both for years, and Millicent could see on a nearer view that he was a fine distinguished easy genial gentleman, at least six feet high in spite of a habit or an affectation of carrying himself in a casual relaxed familiar manner. Hyacinth felt a little, after the first, as if he were treating them rather too much as a pair of children on whom he had stolen to startle them; but this impression was speedily removed by the air with which he said, laying his hand on our hero's shoulder as he stood in the little passage at the end of the bench where the holders of Mr. Vetch's order occupied the first seats: "My dear fellow, I really thought I must come round and speak to you. My spirits are all gone with this brute of a play. And those boxes are fearfully stuffy, you know," he added — quite as if Hyacinth had had at least an equal experience of that part of the theatre.

"It's hot enough here too," Millicent's companion

returned. He had suddenly become much more conscious of the high temperature, of his proximity to the
fierce chandelier, and he mentioned that the plot of
the play certainly was unnatural, though he thought
the piece rather well acted.

"Oh, it's the good old stodgy British tradition.
This is the only place where you find it still, and even
here it can't last much longer; it can't survive old
Baskerville and Mrs. Ruffler. 'Gad, how old they
are! I remember her, long past her prime, when I
used to be taken to the play, as a boy, in the Christ-
mas holidays. Between them they must be something like a hundred and eighty, eh? I believe one's
supposed to cry a good deal about the middle," Captain Sholto continued in the same friendly familiar
encouraging way, addressing himself to Millicent,
upon whom indeed his eyes had rested almost unin-
terruptedly from the start. She sustained his glance
with composure, but with just enough of emphasised
reserve to intimate (what was perfectly true) that she
was not in the habit of conversing with gentlemen
with whom she was unacquainted. She turned away
her face at this (she had already given the visitor the
benefit of a good deal of it) and left him, as in the
little passage he leaned against the parapet of the
balcony with his back to the stage, facing toward
Hyacinth, who was now wondering, with rather more
vivid a sense of the relations of things, what he had
come for. He wanted to do him honour in return
for his civility, but did n't know what one could talk
of at such short notice to a person whom he immediately perceived to be, and the more finely that

it was all unaggressively, a man of the world. He instantly saw Captain Sholto did n't take the play seriously, so that he felt himself warned off that topic, on which otherwise he might have had much to say. On the other hand he could n't in the presence of a third person allude to the matters they had discussed at the "Sun and Moon"; nor might he suppose his visitor would expect this, though indeed he impressed him as a man of humours and whims, disposed to amuse himself with everything, including esoteric socialism and a little bookbinder who had so much more of the gentleman about him than one would expect. Captain Sholto may have been slightly embarrassed, now that he was completely launched in his attempt at fraternisation, especially after failing to elicit a smile from Millicent's rare respectability; but he left to Hyacinth the burden of no initiative and went on to say that it was just this prospect of the dying-out of the old British tradition that had brought him to-night. He was with a friend, a lady who had lived much abroad, who had never seen anything of the kind and who liked everything that was characteristic. "You know the foreign school of acting's a very different affair," he said again to Millicent, who this time replied "Oh yes, of course," and, considering afresh the old woman in the box, reflected that she looked as if there were nothing in the world that she at least had n't seen.

"We've never been abroad," Hyacinth candidly said while he looked into his friend's curious light-coloured eyes, the palest in tint he had ever encountered.

"Oh well, there's a lot of nonsense talked about that!" Captain Sholto replied; on which Hyacinth remained uncertain of his reference and Millicent decided to volunteer a remark.

"They're making a tremendous row on the stage. I should think it would be very bad in those boxes." There was a banging and thumping behind the curtain, the sound of heavy scenery pushed about.

"Oh yes, it's much better here every way. I think you've the best seats in the house," said their visitor. "I should like very much to finish my evening beside you. The trouble is I 've ladies — a pair of them," he pursued as if he were seriously considering this possibility. Then laying his hand again on Hyacinth's shoulder he smiled at him a moment and indulged in a still greater burst of frankness. "My dear fellow, that's just what, as a partial reason, has brought me up here to see you. One of my ladies has a great desire to make your acquaintance!"

"To make my acquaintance?" Hyacinth felt himself turn pale; the first impulse he could have in connexion with such an announcement as that — and it lay far down in the depths of the unspeakable — was a conjecture that it had something to do with his parentage on his father's side. Captain Sholto's smooth bright face, irradiating such unexpected advances, seemed for an instant to swim before him. The Captain went on to say that he had told the lady of the talks they had had, that she was immensely interested in such matters — "You know what I mean, she really is" — and that as a consequence of what he had said she had begged him to come and ask — a — his young friend (Hyacinth saw in a moment that the Captain had forgotten his name) to look in at her if he did n't mind.

"She has a tremendous desire to meet some one who looks at the whole business from your standpoint, don't you see? And in her position she scarcely ever has a chance, she does n't come across them — to her great annoyance. So when I spotted you tonight she immediately declared I must introduce you at any cost. I hope you don't mind just for a quarter of an hour. I ought perhaps to tell you that she's a person used to having nothing refused her. 'Go up and bring him down,' you know, as if it were the simplest thing in the world. She's really very much in earnest: I don't mean about wishing to see you — that goes without saying — but about our whole job, yours and mine. Then I should add — it does n't spoil anything — that she's the most charming woman in the world, simply! Honestly, my dear boy, she's perhaps the most remarkable woman in Europe."

So Captain Sholto delivered himself, with the highest naturalness and plausibility, and Hyacinth, listening, felt that he himself ought perhaps to resent the idea of being served up for the entertainment of capricious not to say presumptuous triflers, but that somehow he did n't, and that it was more worthy of the part he aspired to play in life to meet such occasions calmly and urbanely than to take the trouble of avoidance. Of course the lady in the box could n't be sincere; she might think she was, though even that was questionable; but you did n't really care for

200

the cause exemplified in the guarded back room in Bloomsbury when you came to the theatre in that style. It was Captain Sholto's style as well, but it had been by no means clear to Hyacinth hitherto that *he* really cared. All the same this was no time for going into the question of the lady's sincerity, and at the end of sixty seconds our young man had made up his mind that he could afford to indulge her. None the less, I must add, the whole proposal continued to make things dance, to appear fictive and phantasmagoric; so that it sounded in comparison like a note of reality when Millicent, who had been turning from one of the men to the other, exclaimed —

"That's all very well, but who's to look after *me*?" Her assumption of the majestic had broken down and this was the cry of nature.

Nothing could have been pleasanter and more charitable to her alarm than the manner in which Captain Sholto reassured her. "My dear young lady, can you suppose I've been unmindful of that? I've been hoping that after I've taken down our friend and introduced him you might allow me to come back and in his absence occupy his seat."

Hyacinth was preoccupied with the idea of meeting the most remarkable woman in Europe; but at this juncture he looked at Millicent Henning with some curiosity. She rose grandly to the occasion. "I'm much obliged to you, but I don't know who you are."

"Oh, I'll tell you all about that!" the Captain benevolently cried.

"Of course I should introduce you," said Hyacinth,

and he mentioned to Miss Henning the name of his distinguished acquaintance.

"In the army?" the young lady enquired as if she must have every guarantee of social position.

"Yes — not in the navy! I've left the army, but it always sticks to one."

"Mr. Robinson, is it your intention to leave me?" Millicent asked in a tone of the highest propriety.

Hyacinth's imagination had taken such a flight that the idea of what he owed to the beautiful girl who had placed herself under his care for the evening had somehow effaced itself. Her words put it before him in a manner that threw him quickly and consciously back on his honour; yet there was something in the way she uttered them that made him look at her harder still before he replied: "Oh dear, no — of course it would never do. I must put off to some other opportunity the honour of making the acquaintance of your friend," he added to their visitor.

"Ah, my dear fellow, we might manage it so easily now," this gentleman murmured with evident disappointment. "It's not as if Miss — a — Miss — a — were to be alone."

It flashed upon Hyacinth that the root of the project might be a desire of Captain Sholto to insinuate himself into Millicent's good graces; then he wondered why the most remarkable woman in Europe should lend herself to that design, consenting even to receive a visit from a little bookbinder for the sake of furthering it. Perhaps after all she was not the most remarkable; still, even at a lower estimate, of what advantage could such a complication be to her?

To Hyacinth's surprise Millicent's face made acknowledgement of his implied renunciation; and she said to Captain Sholto as if she were considering the matter very impartially: "Might one know the name of the lady who sent you?"

"The Princess Casamassima."

"Laws!" cried Millicent Henning. And then quickly, as if to cover up this crudity: "And might one also know what it is, as you say, that she wants to talk to him about?"

"About the lower orders, the rising democracy, the spread of ideas and all that."

"The lower orders? Does she think we belong to them?" the girl demanded with a strange provoking laugh.

Captain Sholto was certainly the readiest of men. "If she could see you she'd think you one of the first ladies in the land."

"She'll never see me!" Millicent replied in a manner which made it plain that she at least was not to be whistled for.

Being whistled for by a princess presented itself to Hyacinth as an indignity endured gracefully enough by the heroes of several French novels in which he had found a thrilling interest; nevertheless he said incorruptibly to the Captain, who hovered there like a Mephistopheles converted to inscrutable good: "Having been in the army you'll know that one can't desert one's post."

The Captain, for the third time, laid his hand on his young friend's shoulder, and for a minute his smile rested in silence on Millicent Henning. "If

I tell you simply I want to talk with this young lady, that certainly won't help me particularly, and there's no reason why it should. Therefore I'll tell you the whole truth: I want to talk with her about *you!*" And he patted Hyacinth in a way which conveyed at once that this idea must surely commend him to the young man's companion and that he himself liked him infinitely.

Hyacinth was conscious of the endearment, but he put before Millicent that he would do just as she liked; he was determined not to let a member of a justly-doomed patriciate suppose he held any daughter of the people cheap. "Oh, I don't care if you go," said Miss Henning. "You had better hurry — the curtain's going to rise."

"That's charming of you! I'll rejoin you in three minutes!" Captain Sholto exclaimed.

He passed his hand into Hyacinth's arm, and as our hero lingered still, a little uneasy and questioning Millicent always with his eyes, the girl spoke with her bright boldness: "That kind of princess — I should like to hear all about her."

"Oh, I'll tell you that too," the Captain returned with his perfect ease as he led his young friend away. It must be confessed that Hyacinth also rather wondered what kind of princess she was, and his suspense on this point made his heart beat fast when, after traversing steep staircases and winding corridors, they reached the small door of the stage-box.

XIII

His first consciousness after his companion had opened it was of his proximity to the stage, on which the curtain had now again risen. The play was in progress, the actors' voices came straight into the box, and it was impossible to speak without disturbing them. This at least was his inference from the noiseless way his conductor drew him in and, without announcing or introducing him, simply pointed to a chair and whispered: "Just drop into that; you'll see and hear beautifully." He heard the door close behind him and became aware that Captain Sholto had already retreated. Millicent would at any rate not be left long to languish in solitude. Two ladies were seated in the front of the box, which was so large that there was a considerable space between them; and as he stood there, where Captain Sholto had planted him — they appeared not to have noticed the opening of the door — they turned their heads and looked at him. The one on whom his eyes first rested was the odd party he had already viewed at a distance; she looked queerer still on a closer view and gave him a little friendly gratified nod. The other was partly overshadowed by the curtain of the box, drawn forward with the intention of shielding her from the observation of the house; she had still the air of youth, and the simplest way to express the instant effect upon Hyacinth of her fair face of welcome is to say that she dazzled him. He remained as Sholto had left him, staring rather confusedly and not moving an inch; whereupon the younger lady put out her hand — it was her left, the other rested on the ledge of the box — with the expectation, as he perceived, to his extreme mortification, too late, that he would give her his own. She converted the gesture into a sign of invitation and beckoned him silently but graciously to move his chair forward. He did so and seated himself between the two; then for ten minutes he stared straight before him at the stage, not turning his eyes sufficiently even to glance up at Millicent in the balcony. He looked at the play, but was far from seeing it; he had no sense of anything but the woman who sat there, close to him, on his right, with a fragrance in her garments and a light about her which he seemed to see even while his head was averted. The vision had been only of a moment, but it hung before him, threw a vague white mist over the proceedings on the stage. He was consciously embarrassed, overturned and bewildered; he made a great effort to collect himself, to consider the situation lucidly. He wondered if he ought to speak, to look at her again, to behave differently in some way; if she would take him for a clown, for an idiot; if she were really as beautiful as she had seemed or it were only a superficial glamour which a renewed inspection would dissipate. While he so pondered the minutes lapsed and neither of his hostesses spoke; they watched the play in perfect stillness, so that he divined this to be the proper thing and that he himself must remain dumb until a word should be addressed him. Little by little he recovered himself, took possession of his predicament and at last transferred his eyes to the Princess. She immediately perceived this and returned his glance with a bright benevolence. She might well be a princess — it was impossible to conform more to the finest evocations of that romantic word. She was fair, shining, slender, with an effortless majesty. Her beauty had an air of perfection; it astonished and lifted one up, the sight of it seemed a privilege, a reward. If the first impression it had given Hyacinth was to make him feel strangely transported he need still not have set that down to his simplicity, for this was the effect the Princess Casamassima produced on persons of a wider experience and greater pretensions. Her dark eyes, blue or grey, something that was not brown, were as kind as they were splendid, and there was an extraordinary light nobleness in the way she held her head. That head, where two or three diamond stars glittered in the thick, delicate hair which defined its shape, suggested to Hyacinth something antique and celebrated, something he had admired of old — the memory was vague — in a statue, in a picture, in a museum. Purity of line and form, of cheek and chin and lip and brow, a colour that seemed to live and glow, a radiance of grace and eminence and success — these things were seated in triumph in the face of the Princess, and her visitor, as he held himself in his chair trembling with the revelation, questioned if she were really of the same substance with the humanity he had hitherto known. She might be divine, but he could see she understood human needs — that she wished him to be at his ease and happy; there was something familiar in her benignity, as if she had seen him many times before. Her dress was dark and rich; she had pearls round her neck and an old rococo fan in her hand. He took in all these things and finally said to himself that if she wanted nothing more of him he was content, he would like it to go on; so pleasant was it to be enthroned with fine ladies in a dusky, spacious receptacle which framed the bright picture of the stage and made one's own situation seem a play within the play. The act was a long one, and the repose in which his companions left him might have been a calculated charity, to enable him to get used to them, to see how harmless they were. He looked at Millicent in the course of time and saw that Captain Sholto, seated beside her, had not the same standard of propriety, inasmuch as he made a remark to her every few minutes. Like himself the young lady in the balcony was losing the play, thanks to her so keeping her eyes on her friend from Lomax Place, whose position she thus endeavoured to gauge. He had quite given up the Paraguayan complications; by the end of the half-hour his attention might have come back to them had he not then been engaged in wondering what the Princess would say to him after the descent of the curtain — or if she would say anything. The consideration of this problem as the moment of the solution drew nearer made his heart again beat fast. He watched the old lady on his left and supposed it was natural a princess should have an attendant — he took for granted she was an attendant — as different as possible from herself. This ancient dame was without majesty or grace; huddled together with her hands folded on her stomach and her lips protruding, she solemnly followed the performance. Several times, however, she turned her head to Hyacinth, and then her expression changed; she repeated the jovial, encouraging, almost motherly nod with which she had greeted him on his making his bow and by which she appeared to wish to intimate that, better than the serene beauty on the other side, she could enter into the full anomaly of his situation. She seemed to argue that he must keep his head and that if the worst should come to the worst she was there to look after him. Even when at last the curtain descended it was some moments before the Princess spoke, though she rested her smile on her guest as if she were considering what he would best like her to say. He might at that instant have guessed what he discovered later — that among this lady's faults (he was destined to learn they were numerous) not the least eminent was an exaggerated fear of the commonplace. He expected she would make some remark about the play, but what she said was, very gently and kindly, "I like to know all sorts of people."

"I should n't think you 'd find the least difficulty in that," Hyacinth replied.

"Oh, if one wants anything very much it 's sure to be difficult. Every one is n't so obliging as you."

Hyacinth could think immediately of no proper answer to this, but the old lady saved him the trouble by declaring with a foreign accent: "I think you were

most extraordinarily good-natured. I had no idea
you'd come — to two strange women."

"Yes, we're strange women," said the Princess
musingly.

"It's not true she finds things difficult; she makes
every one do everything," her companion went on.

The Princess glanced at her and then remarked to
Hyacinth: "Her name is Madame Grandoni." The
tone was not familiar, but there was a happy shade
in it, as if he had really taken so much trouble for
them that it was but just he should be entertained
a little at their expense. It seemed to imply also that
Madame Grandoni's fitness for supplying such entertainment was obvious.

"But I'm not Italian — ah no!" the old lady cried.
"In spite of my name I'm an honest, ugly, unfortunate German. But *cela n'a pas d'importance*. She also,
with such a name, isn't Italian either. It's an accident; the world's full of accidents. But she isn't
German, poor lady, any more." Madame Grandoni
appeared to have entered into the Princess's view,
and Hyacinth thought her exceedingly droll. In a moment she added: "That was a very charming person
you were with."

"Yes, she's very charming," Hyacinth replied, not
sorry to have a chance to say it.

The Princess made no remark on this subject, and
Hyacinth saw not only that from her position in the
box she could have had no glimpse of Millicent, but
that she would never take up such an allusion as that.
It was as if she had not heard it that she asked: "Do
you find the play very interesting?"

He hesitated, then told the simple truth. "I must confess I've lost the whole of this last act."

"Ah, poor bothered young man!" cried Madame in Grandoni. "You see — you see!"

"What do I see?" the Princess enquired. "If you're annoyed at being here now you'll like us later; probably at least. We take a great interest in the things you care for. We take a great interest in the people," the Princess went on.

"Oh, allow me, allow me, and speak only for yourself!" the elder lady interposed. "I take no interest whatever in the people; I don't understand them and I know nothing about them. An honourable nature, of any class, I always respect; but I won't pretend to a passion for the ignorant masses, because I have it not. Moreover that does n't touch the gentleman."

The Princess Casamassima had a clear faculty of completely ignoring things of which she wished to take no account; it was not in the least the air of contempt, but thoughtful, tranquil, convenient absence, after which she came back to the point where she wished to be. She made no protest against her companion's speech, but said to Hyacinth, as if vaguely conscious she had been committing herself in some absurd way: "She lives with me; she's everything to me; she's the best woman in the world."

"Yes, fortunately, with many superficial defects I'm as good as good bread," Madame Grandoni conceded.

Hyacinth was by this time less embarrassed than when he had presented himself, but he was not less mystified; he wondered afresh if he were not being

practised on for some inconceivable end: so strangely
did it strike him that two such products of another
world than his own should of their own movement
take the trouble to explain each other to a dire little
bookbinder. This idea made him flush; it might
have come over him that he had fallen into a trap.
He was conscious he looked frightened, and he was
conscious the moment afterwards that the Princess
noticed it. This was apparently what made her say:
"If you've lost so much of the play I ought to tell
you what has happened."

"Do you think he would follow that any more?"
Madame Grandoni asked.

"If you would tell me — if you would tell me — !"
And then Hyacinth stopped. He had been going to
say "If you would tell me what all this means and
what you want of me it would be more to the point!"
but the words died on his lips and he sat staring, for
the woman at his right hand was simply too beautiful. She was too beautiful to question, to judge by
common logic; and how could he know moreover
what was natural to a person in that exaltation of
grace and splendour? Perhaps it was her habit to
send out every evening for some witless stranger
to amuse her; perhaps that was the way the foreign
aristocracy lived. There was no sharpness in her
face — for the present hour at least: there was nothing but luminous charity, yet she looked as if she
knew what was going on in his mind. She made
no eager attempt to reassure him, but there was
a world almost of direct tenderness in the tone in
which she said: "Do you know I'm afraid I've

already forgotten what they have been doing — ?
It's terribly complicated; some one or other was
hurled over a precipice."

"Ah, you're a brilliant pair," Madame Grandoni
declared with a laugh of long experience. "I could
describe everything. The person who was hurled
over the precipice was the virtuous hero, and you'll
see him in the next act all the better for it."

"Don't describe anything; I've so much to ask."
Hyacinth had looked away in tacit deprecation at
hearing himself "paired" with the Princess, and he
felt she was watching him. "What do you think
of Captain Sholto?" she went on suddenly, to his
surprise, if anything in his position could excite surprise more than anything else; and as he hesitated,
not knowing what to say, she added: "Isn't he a very
curious type?"

"I know him very little." But he had no sooner
uttered the words than it struck him they were far
from brilliant, were poor and flat and very little calculated to satisfy the Princess. Indeed he had said
nothing at all that could place him in a favourable
light; so he continued at a venture: "I mean I've
never seen him at home." That sounded still more
silly.

"At home? Oh, he's never at home; he's all over
the world. To-night he was as likely to have been in
Paraguay for instance — though what a place to be!"
she smiled — "as here. He is what they call a cos-
mopolite. I don't know if you know that species;
very modern, more and more frequent and exceedingly tiresome. I prefer the Chinese. He had told

213

me he had had a lot of very interesting talk with you. That was what made me say: 'Oh, do ask him to come in and see me. A little interesting talk, that would be a change!'"

"She's very complimentary to me!" said Madame Grandoni.

"Ah my dear, you and I, you know, we never talk: we understand each other without that!" Then the Princess pursued, addressing herself to Hyacinth: "Do you never admit women?"

"Admit women — ?"

"Into those séances — what do you call them? — those little meetings that Captain Sholto describes to me. I should like so much to be present. Why not?"

"I have n't seen any ladies," Hyacinth said. "I don't know if it's a rule, but I've seen nothing but men"; and he subjoined, smiling, though he thought the dereliction rather serious and could n't understand the part Captain Sholto was playing, nor, considering the grand company he kept, how he had originally secured admittance into the subversive little circle in Bloomsbury: "You know I'm not sure he ought to go about reporting our proceedings."

"I see. Perhaps you think he's a spy, an *agent provocateur* or something of that sort."

"No," said Hyacinth after a moment. "I think a spy would be more careful — would disguise himself more. Besides, after all, he has heard very little." He spoke as with mild amusement.

"You mean he has n't really been behind the scenes?" the Princess asked, bending forward a little and now covering the young man steadily with her

214

beautiful deep eyes, as if by this time he must have got used to her and would n't flinch from such attention. "Of course he has n't," she said of herself, however, "and he never will be. He knows that, and that it's quite out of his power to tell any real secrets. What he repeated to me was interesting, but of course I could see there was nothing the authorities anywhere could put their hand on. It was mainly the talk he had had with you which struck him so very much, and which struck me, as I tell you. Perhaps you did n't know how he was drawing you out."

"I'm afraid that's rather easy," said Hyacinth with perfect candour; for it came over him that he *had* chattered with a vengeance in Bloomsbury and had thought it natural enough there that his sociable fellow-visitor should offer him cigars and attach importance to the views of a clever and original young artisan.

"I'm not sure that I find it so! However, I ought to tell you that you need n't have the least fear of Captain Sholto. He's a perfectly honest man, so far as he goes; and even if you had trusted him much more than you appear to have done he'd be incapable of betraying you. However, don't trust him: not because he's not safe, but because — !" She took herself up. "No matter, you'll see for yourself. He has gone into that sort of thing simply to please me. I should tell you, merely to make you understand, that he would do anything for that. That's his own affair. I wanted to know something, to learn something, to ascertain what really is going on; and for a woman everything of that sort's so difficult,

215

especially for a woman in my position, who's tire-somely known and to whom every sort of bad faith is sure to be imputed. So Sholto said he would look into the subject for me. Poor man, he has had to look into so many subjects! What I particularly wanted was that he should make friends with some of the leading spirits, really characteristic types." The Princess's voice was low and rather deep, but her tone perfectly natural and easy, with a charm-ing assumption — for you could call it nothing else — of more wonderful things than he could count. Her manner of speaking was in fact altogether new to her listener, for whom the pronunciation of her words and the very punctuation of her sentences were the revelation of what he supposed to be society — the very Society to the destruction of which he was dedicated.

"Surely Captain Sholto does n't suppose *I'm* a leading spirit!" he exclaimed with the resolve not to be laughed at any more than he could help.

"He told me you were very original."

"He does n't know, and — if you'll allow me to say so — I don't think *you* know. How should you? I'm one of many thousands of young men of my class — you know, I suppose, what *that* is — in whose brains certain ideas are fermenting. There's nothing original about me at all. I'm very young and very ignorant; it's only a few months since I began to talk of the possibility of a social revolution with men who have considered the whole ground much more than I could possibly do. I'm a mere particle," Hyacinth wound up, "in the grey immensity of the people. All

I pretend to is my good faith and a great desire that justice shall be done."

The Princess listened to him intently and her attitude made him feel how little *he*, in comparison, expressed himself like a person who had the habit of conversation; he seemed to himself to betray ridiculous effort, to stammer and emit vulgar sounds. For a moment she said nothing, only looking at him with her exquisite smile. "I do draw you out!" she exclaimed at last. "You're much more interesting to me than if you were an exception." At these last words Hyacinth flinched a hair's breadth; the movement was shown by his dropping his eyes. We know to what extent he really regarded himself as of the stuff of the common herd. The Princess doubtless guessed it as well, for she quickly added: "At the same time I can see you're remarkable enough."

"What do you think I'm remarkable for?"

"Well, you've general ideas."

"Every one has them to-day. They have them in Bloomsbury to a terrible degree. I've a friend (who understands the matter much better than I) who has no patience with them: he declares they're our folly, our danger and our bane. A few very special ideas — if they're the right ones — are what we want."

"Who's your friend?" the Princess asked abruptly.

"Ah, Christina, Christina!" Madame Grandoni murmured from the other side of the box.

Christina took no notice of her, and Hyacinth, not understanding the warning and only remembering how personal women always are, replied: "A young man who lives in Camberwell and who's in the employ of a big wholesale chemist."

If he had designed in this description of his friend a stronger dose than his hostess would be able to digest he was greatly mistaken. She seemed to gaze tenderly at the picture suggested by his words, and she immediately enquired if the young man were also clever and if she might n't hope to know him. Had n't Captain Sholto seen him, and if so why had n't he spoken of him too? When Hyacinth had replied that Captain Sholto had probably seen him, but, as he believed, had had no particular conversation with him, the Princess asked with startling frankness if her visitor would n't bring the person so vividly described some day to see her.

Hyacinth glanced at Madame Grandoni, but that worthy woman was engaged in a survey of the house through an old-fashioned eyeglass with a long gilt handle. He had perceived much before this that the Princess Casamassima had no desire for vain phrases, and he had the good taste to feel that from himself to such a great lady compliments, even had he wished to pay them, would have had no suitability. "I don't know whether he would be willing to come. He's the sort of man that in such a case you can't answer for."

"That makes me want to know him all the more. But you'll come yourself at all events, eh?"

Poor Hyacinth murmured something about the unexpected honour; after all he had a French heredity and it was n't so easy for him to say things as ill as his other idiom mainly required. But Madame Grandoni, laying down her eyeglass, almost took the

words out of his mouth with the cheerful exhortation:
"Go and see her — go and see her once or twice.
She'll treat you like an angel."

"You must think me very peculiar," the Princess
remarked sadly.

"I don't know what I think. It will take a good
while."

"I wish I could make you trust me — inspire you
with confidence," she went on. "I don't mean only
you personally, but others who think as you do.
You'd find I'd go with you — pretty far. I was
answering just now for Captain Sholto; but who in
the world's to answer for *me?*" And her sadness
merged itself in a smile that affected Hyacinth as
indescribably magnanimous and touching.

"Not I, my dear, I promise you!" her ancient
companion ejaculated with a laugh which made the
people in the stalls look up at the box.

Her spirit was contagious; it gave Hyacinth the
audacity to say to her "I'd trust *you,* if you did!"
though he felt the next minute that this was even
a more familiar speech than if he had expressed a
want of confidence.

"It comes then to the same thing," said the Princess. "She wouldn't show herself with me in public
if I weren't respectable. If you knew more about me
you'd understand what has led me to turn my attention to the great social question. It's a long story and
the details wouldn't interest you; but perhaps some
day, if we have more talk, you'll put yourself a little
in my place. I'm very serious, you know; I'm not
amusing myself with peeping and running away. I'm

convinced that we're living in a fool's paradise, that the ground's heaving under our feet."

"It's not the ground, my dear; it's you who are turning somersaults," Madame Grandoni interposed.

"Ah you, my friend, you've the happy faculty of believing what you like to believe. I have to believe what I see."

"She wishes to throw herself into the revolution, to guide it, to enlighten it," Madame Grandoni said to Hyacinth, speaking now with imperturbable gravity.

"I'm sure she could direct it in any sense she would wish!" the young man responded in his glow. The pure, high dignity with which the Princess had just spoken and which appeared to cover a suppressed tremor of passion set his pulses throbbing, and though he scarcely saw what she meant — her aspirations appearing as yet so vague — her tone, her voice, her wonderful face showed she had a generous soul.

She answered his eager declaration with a serious smile and a melancholy head-shake. "I've no such pretensions and my good old friend's laughing at me. Of course that's very easy; for what in fact can be more absurd on the face of it than for a woman with a title, with diamonds, with a carriage, with servants, with a position, as they call it, to sympathise with the upward struggles of those who are below? 'Give all that up and we'll believe you,' you've a right to say. I'm ready to give them up the moment it will help the cause; I assure you that's the least difficulty. I don't want to teach, I want to learn; and above all I want to know *à quoi m'en tenir*. Are we on the eve of great changes or are we not? Is everything that's gathering force underground, in the dark, in the night, in little hidden rooms, out of sight of governments and policemen and idiotic 'statesmen' — heaven save them! — is all this going to burst forth some fine morning and set the world on fire? Or is it to sputter out and spend itself in vain conspiracies, be dissipated in sterile heroisms and abortive isolated movements? I want to know *à quoi m'en tenir*," she repeated, fixing her visitor with more brilliant eyes and almost as if he could tell her on the spot. Then suddenly she added in quite a different tone: "Pardon me, I've an idea you know French. Did n't Captain Sholto tell me so?"

"I've some little acquaintance with it," Hyacinth replied. "I've French blood in my veins."

She considered him as if he had proposed to her some attaching problem. "Yes, I can see you're not *le premier venu*. Now your friend, of whom you were speaking, is a chemist; and you yourself — what's your occupation?"

"I'm just a bookbinder."

"That must be delightful. I wonder if you'd bind me some books."

"You'd háve to bring them to our shop, and I can do there only the work that's given out to me. I might manage it by myself at home," Hyacinth freely professed.

"I should like that better. And what do you call home?"

"The place I live in, in the north of London: a little street you certainly never heard of."

"What is it called?"

"Lomax Place, at your service," he laughed.

She seemed to reflect his innocent gaiety; she was n't a bit afraid to let him see she liked him. "No, I don't think I've heard of it. I don't know London very well; I have n't lived here long. I've spent most of my life abroad. My husband's a foreigner, a South Italian. We don't live always together. I have n't the manners of this country — not of any class, have I, eh? Oh this country — there's a great deal to be said about it and a great deal to be done, as you of course understand better than any one. But I want to know London; it interests me more than I can say — the huge, swarming, smoky, human city. I mean real London, the people and all their sufferings and passions; not Park Lane and Bond Street. Perhaps you can help me — it would be a great kindness: that's what I want to know men like you for. You see it is n't idle, my having given you so much trouble to-night."

"I shall be very glad to show you all I know. But it is n't much and above all it is n't pretty," said Hyacinth.

"Whom do you live with in Lomax Place?" she asked, a little oddly, by way of allowance for this.

"Captain Sholto's leaving the young lady — he's coming back here," Madame Grandoni announced, inspecting the balcony with her instrument. The orchestra had been for some time playing the overture to the following act.

Hyacinth had just hesitated. "I live with a dressmaker."

"With a dressmaker? Do you mean — do you mean — ?" But the Princess paused.

"Do you mean she's your wife?" asked Madame Grandoni more bravely.

"Perhaps she gives you rooms," the Princess suggested.

"How many do you think I have? She gives me everything, or has done so in the past. She brought me up; she's the best little woman in the world."

"You had better command a dress of her," Madame Grandoni threw off.

"And your family, where are they?" the Princess continued.

"I have no family."

"None at all?"

"None at all. I never had."

"But the French blood you speak of and which I see perfectly in your face—you have n't the English expression or want of expression — that must have come to you through some one."

"Yes, through my mother."

"And she's dead?"

"Long ago."

"That's a great loss, because French mothers are usually so much to their sons." The Princess looked at her painted fan as she opened and closed it; after which she said: "Well then, you'll come some day. We'll arrange it." Hyacinth felt the answer to this could be only a silent inclination of his utmost stature, and to make it he rose from his chair. As he stood there, conscious he had stayed long enough and yet not knowing exactly how to withdraw, the Princess, with her fan closed, resting upright on her knee, and her hands clasped on the end of it, turned up her strange lovely eyes at him and said: "Do you think anything will occur soon?"

"Will occur — ?"

"That there'll be a crisis — that you'll make yourselves felt?"

In this beautiful woman's face there was to his bewildered perception something at once inspiring, tempting and mocking; and the effect of her expression was to make him say rather clumsily "I'll try and ascertain — " as if she had asked him whether her carriage were at the door.

"I don't quite know what you're talking about; but please don't have it for another hour or two. I want to see what becomes of the Pearl!" Madame Grandoni interposed.

"Remember what I told you: I'd give up everything — everything!" And the Princess kept looking up at him. Then she held out her hand, and this time he knew sufficiently what he was about to take it.

When he bade good-night to Madame Grandoni the old lady sounded at him with a comical sigh "Well, she *is* respectable!" and out in the lobby when he had closed the door of the box behind him he found himself echoing these words and repeating mechanically "She *is* respectable!" They were on his lips as he stood suddenly face to face with Captain Sholto, who grasped his shoulder once more and shook him in that free yet insinuating manner for which this officer appeared remarkable.

"My dear fellow, you were born under a lucky star."

"I never supposed it," said Hyacinth, changing colour.

"Why what in the world would you have? You've the faculty, the precious faculty, of inspiring women with an interest — but an interest!"

"Yes, ask them in the box there! I behaved like an awful muff," Hyacinth declared, overwhelmed now with a sense of opportunities missed.

"They won't tell me that. And the lady upstairs?"

"Well," said Hyacinth gravely, "what about her?"

"She would n't talk to me of anything but you. You may imagine how I liked it!"

"I don't like it either. But I must go up."

"Oh yes, she counts the minutes. Such a charming person!" Captain Sholto added with more propriety of tone. As Hyacinth left him he called out: "Don't be afraid — you'll go far."

When the young man took his place in the balcony beside Millicent she gave him no greeting nor asked any question about his adventures in the more privileged part of the house. She only turned her fine complexion upon him for some minutes, and as he himself was not in the mood to begin to chatter the silence continued — continued till after the curtain had risen on the last act of the play. Millicent's attention was now evidently not at her disposal for the stage, and in the midst of a violent scene which included pistol-shots and shrieks she said at last to her companion: "She's a tidy lot, your Princess, by what I learn."

225

"Pray what do you know about her?"

"I know what that fellow told me."

"And what may that have been?"

"Well, she's a bad 'un as ever was. Her own husband has had to turn her out of the house."

Hyacinth remembered the allusion the lady herself had made to her matrimonial situation; in spite of which he would have liked to be able to reply to Miss Henning that he did n't believe a word of it. He withheld the doubt and after a moment simply remarked: "Well, I don't care."

"You don't care? Well, I do then!" Millicent cried. And as it was impossible in view of the performance and the jealous attention of their neighbours to continue the conversation at this pitch, she contented herself with ejaculating in a somewhat lower key at the end of five minutes during which she had been watching the stage: "Gracious, what dreadful common stuff!" Hyacinth then wondered if Captain Sholto had given her this formula.

XIV

HE did n't mention to Pinnie or Mr. Vetch that he
had been taken up by a great lady; but he mentioned
it to Paul Muniment, to whom he now confided a
great many things. He had at first been in considerable fear of his straight loud north-country friend,
who showed signs of cultivating logic and criticism
in a degree that was hostile to fine loose talk; but he
discovered in him later a man to whom one could say
anything in the world if one did n't think it of more
importance to be sympathised with than to be understood. For a revolutionist he was strangely unexas-
perated, was indulgent even to contempt. The sight
of all the things he wanted to change had seemingly
no power to irritate him, and if he joked about questions that lay very near his heart his humour had
no ferocity — the fault Hyacinth sometimes found
with it rather was that it was innocent to puerility.
Our hero envied his power of combining a care for
the wide misery of mankind with the apparent state
of mind of the cheerful and virtuous young workman
who of a Sunday morning has put on a clean shirt
and, not having taken the gilt off his wages the night
before, weighs against each other, for a happy day,
the respective attractions of Epping Forest and
Gravesend. He never dragged in with the least snarl
his personal lot and his daily life; it had not seemed
to occur to him for instance that "society" was really

responsible for the condition of his sister's spinal column, though Eustache Poupin and his wife (who practically, however, were as patient as he) did everything they could to make him say so, believing evidently that it would relieve him. Apparently he cared nothing for women, talked of them rarely and always decently, and had never a sign of a sweetheart save in so far as Lady Aurora Langrish might pass for one. He never drank a drop of beer nor touched a pipe; he always had a clear tone, a fresh cheek and a merely, an imperturbably intelligent eye, and once excited on Hyacinth's part a kind of elderbrotherly indulgence by the open-mouthed glee and credulity with which, when the pair were present, in the sixpenny gallery, at Astley's, at an equestrian pantomime, he followed the tawdry spectacle. He once pronounced the young bookbinder a suggestive little beggar, and Hyacinth's opinion of him was by this time so exalted that the remark had almost the value of a patent of nobility. Our hero treated himself to a high unlimited faith in him; he had always dreamed of some grand friendship and this was the best opening he had yet encountered. No one could entertain a sentiment of that sort more nobly, more ingeniously than Hyacinth, or cultivate with more art the intimate personal relation. It disappointed him sometimes that his confidence was not more unreservedly repaid; that on certain important points of the socialistic programme Muniment would never commit himself and had not yet shown the *fond du sac*, as Eustache Poupin called it, to so ardent an admirer. He answered particular appeals freely enough, and answered them occasionally in a manner that made Hyacinth jump, as when in reply to a question about his attitude on capital punishment he said that so far from wishing it abolished he should go in for extending it much further — he should impose it on those who habitually lied or got drunk; but his friend had always a feeling that he kept back his best card and that even in the listening circle in Bloomsbury, when only the right men were present, there were unspoken conclusions in his mind which he did n't as yet think any one good enough to be favoured with. So far therefore from suspecting him of any real poverty of programme Hyacinth was sure he had extraordinary things in his head; that he was thinking them out to the logical end, wherever it might land him; and that the night he should produce them with the door of the club-room guarded and the company bound by a tremendous oath the others would look at each other, gasp and turn pale.

"She wants to see you; she asked me to bring you; she was very serious," our young man meanwhile said, reporting his interview with the ladies in the box at the play; which, however, now that he looked back upon it, seemed as queer as a dream and not much more likely than that sort of experience to have a continuation in one's waking hours.

"To bring me — to bring me where?" asked Muniment. "You talk as if I were a sample out of your shop or a little dog you had for sale. Has she ever seen me? Does she think I'm smaller than you? What does she know about me?"

"Well, principally that you're a friend of mine — that's enough for her."

"Do you mean it ought to be enough for me that she's a friend of yours? I've a notion you'll have some queer ones before you've done; a good many more than I have time to talk to. And how can I go to see a delicate female with those paws?" Muniment said as he exhibited ten work-stained fingers.

"Buy a pair of gloves — " Hyacinth recognised the serious character of this obstacle. But after a moment he added: "No, you ought n't to do that. She wants to see dirty hands."

"That's easy enough, good Lord! She need n't send for me for the purpose. But is n't she making game of you?"

"It's very possible, but I don't see what good it can do her."

"You're not obliged to find excuses for the pampered classes. Their bloated luxury begets evil, impudent desires; they're capable of doing harm for the sake of harm. Besides, is she genuine?"

"If she is n't, what becomes of your explanation?" Hyacinth asked.

"Oh, it does n't matter; at night all cats are grey. Whatever she is, she's an idle, bedizened trifler; perhaps even a real profligate female."

"If you had seen her you would n't talk of her that way."

"God forbid I should see her then, if she's going to corrupt me!"

"Do you suppose she'll corrupt *me?*" Hyacinth demanded with an expression of face and a tone of voice which produced on his friend's part an explosion of mirth.

"How can she, after all, when you're already such a little mass of corruption?"

"You don't think that — ?" and Hyacinth looked very grave.

"Do you mean that if I did I would n't say it? Have n't you noticed that I say what I think?"

"No, you don't, not half of it: you're as dark as a fish."

Paul Muniment glanced at his friend as if rather struck with the penetration of that remark; then he said: "Well then, if I should give you the other half of my opinion of you do you think you'd fancy it?"

"I'll save you the trouble. I'm a very clever, conscientious, promising young chap, and any one would be proud to claim me as a friend."

"Is that what your Princess told you? She must be a precious piece of goods!" Paul exclaimed. "Did she pick your pocket meanwhile?"

"Oh yes; a few minutes later I missed a silver cigar-case engraved with the arms of the Robinsons. Seriously," Hyacinth continued, "don't you consider it possible that a woman of that class should want to know what's going on among the like of us?"

"It depends on what class you mean."

"Well, a woman with a lot of wonderful jewels and wonderful scents and the manners of an angel. I wonder if even the young ladies in the perfumery shops have such manners — they can't have such pearls. It's queer of course, that sort of interest, but it's conceivable; why not? There may be unselfish natures; there may be disinterested feelings."

"And there may be fine ladies in an awful funk about their jewels and even about their manners. Seriously, as you say, it's perfectly conceivable. I'm not in the least surprised at the aristocracy being curious to know what we're up to and wanting very much to look into it. In their place I should be very uneasy, and if I were a woman with angelic manners very likely I too should be glad to get hold of a soft susceptible little bookbinder and pump him dry, bless his tender heart!"

"Are you afraid I'll tell her secrets?" cried Hyacinth, flushing with virtuous indignation.

"Secrets? What secrets could you tell her, my pretty lad?"

Hyacinth turned away. "You don't trust me—you never have."

"We will, some day — don't be afraid," said Muniment, who evidently had no intention of harshness, at least in respect to Hyacinth, a thing that appeared impossible to him. "And when we do you'll cry with disappointment."

"Well, *you* won't," Hyacinth returned. And then he asked if his friend thought the Princess Casamassima a spy of spies — the devil she'd have to be! — and why, if she were in that line, Sholto was not, since it must be supposed he was not when they had seen fit to let him walk in and out, at any rate, at the place in Bloomsbury. Muniment did n't even know whom he meant, not having had any relations with the gentleman; but he summoned a sufficient image after his companion had described the Captain's appearance. He then remarked with his usual geniality that he did n't take him for anything worse than a jackass; but even if he had edged himself into the place with every intention to betray them what handle could he possibly get — what use against them could he make of anything he had seen or heard? If he had a fancy to dip into working-men's clubs (Paul remembered now the first night he came; he had been brought by that German cabinet-maker who always had a bandaged neck and smoked a pipe with a bowl as big as a stove); if it amused him to put on a bad hat and inhale foul tobacco and call his "inferiors" "my dear fellow"; if he thought that in doing so he was getting an insight into the people and going halfway to meet them and preparing for what was coming — all this was his own affair and he was very welcome, though a man must be a flat who would spend his evening in a hole like that when he might enjoy his comfort in one of those flaming big shops, full of armchairs and flunkies, in Pall Mall. And what did he see after all in Bloomsbury? Nothing but a remarkably stupid "social gathering" where there were clay pipes and a sanded floor and not half enough gas and the principal papers; and where the men, as any one would know, were advanced radicals and mostly advanced idiots. He could pat as many of them on the back as he liked and say the House of Lords would n't last till midsummer; but what discoveries would he make? He was simply on the same lay as Hyacinth's Princess; he was nervous and scared and thought he would see for himself.

233

"Oh, he is n't the same sort as the Princess. I'm sure he's in a very different line!" Hyacinth objected.

"Different of course; she's a handsome woman, I suppose, and he's an ugly man; but I don't think that either of them will save us or spoil us. Their curiosity's natural, but I've other things to do than to show them over: therefore you can tell her Serene Highness that I'm much obliged."

Hyacinth reflected a moment and then said: "You show Lady Aurora over; you seem to wish to give her the information she desires; therefore what's the difference? If it's right for her to take an interest why is n't it right for my Princess?"

"If she's already yours what more can she want?" Muniment asked. "All I know of Lady Aurora and all I look at is that she comes and sits with Rosy and brings her tea and waits on her. If the Princess will do as much I'll see what *I* can do; but apart from that I shall never take a grain of interest in her interest in the masses — or in this particular mass!" And Paul, with his discoloured thumb, designated his own substantial person. His tone was disappointing to Hyacinth, who was surprised at his not appearing to think the incident at the theatre more remarkable and romantic. He seemed to regard his mate's explanation of the passage as all-sufficient; but when a moment later he made use, in referring to the mysterious lady, of the expression that she was "quaking" that critic broke out: "Never in the world; she's not afraid of anything!"

"Ah, my lad, not afraid of you, evidently!"

Hyacinth paid no attention to this coarse sally, but

resumed with a candour that was proof against further ridicule: "Do you think she can do me a hurt of any kind if we follow up our acquaintance?"

"Yes, very likely, but you must hit her back and give it to her badly. That's your line, you know — to go in for what's going, to live your life, to gratify the 'sex.' I'm an ugly, grimy brute, I've got to watch the fires and mind the shop; but you're one of those taking little beggars who *must* run about and see the world. You ought to be an ornament to society, like a young man in an illustrated story-book. Only you know," Muniment added in a moment, "if she should hurt you very much I *would* have a go at her!"

Hyacinth had been intending for some time to take Pinnie to call on the prostrate damsel in Audley Court, to whom he had promised that his benefactress (he had told Rose Muniment she was his god-mother — it sounded so right) should pay this civility; but the affair had been delayed by wan hesitations on the part of the dressmaker, the poor woman having hard work to imagine to-day that there were people in London forlorn enough for her countenance to be of value to them. Her social curiosity had quite died out and she knew she no longer made the same figure in public as when her command of the fashions enabled her to illustrate them in her own little person by the aid of a good deal of whalebone. Moreover she felt that Hyacinth had strange friends and still stranger opinions; she suspected him of taking an un-natural interest in politics and of being somehow not on the right side, little as she knew about parties or causes; and she had a vague conviction that this kind

235

cf perversity only multiplied the troubles of the poor, who, according to theories which Pinnie had never reasoned out but which in her breast were as deep as religion, ought always to be of the same way of thinking as the rich. They were unlike them enough in their poverty without trying to add other differences. When at last she accompanied Hyacinth to Camberwell one Saturday evening at midsummer it was in a sighing, sceptical, second-best manner; but if he had told her he wished it she would have gone with him to a soirée at a scavenger's. There was no more danger of Rose Muniment's being out than that one of the bronze couchant lions in Trafalgar Square should have walked down Whitehall; but he had let her know in advance and he perceived, as he opened her door in obedience to a quick, shrill summons, that she had had the happy thought of inviting Lady Aurora to help her entertain Miss Pynsent. Such at least was the inference he drew from seeing her ladyship's memorable figure rise before him for the first time since their meeting there. He presented his companion to their reclining hostess, and Rosy immediately repeated her name to the representative of Belgrave Square. Pinnie curtseyed down to the ground as Lady Aurora put out her hand to her, and then slipped noiselessly into a chair beside the bed. Lady Aurora laughed and fidgeted in a friendly, cheerful, yet at the same time rather pointless manner, and Hyacinth gathered that she had no recollection of having seen him. His attention, however, was mainly given to Pinnie: he watched her jealously, to see if on this important occasion she would n't put forth a certain stiff, quaint, polished politeness of which she possessed the secret and which made him liken her extraction of the sense of things to the nip of a pair of old-fashioned silver sugar-tongs. Not only for Pinnie's sake but for his own as well he wished her to figure as a superior little woman; so he hoped she would n't lose her head if Rosy should begin to talk about Inglefield. She was evidently much impressed by Rosy and kept repeating, "Dear, dear!" under her breath while the small strange person in the bed rapidly explained to her that there was nothing in the world she would have liked so much as to follow *her* delightful profession, but that she could n't sit up to it, and had never had a needle in her hand but once, when at the end of three minutes it had dropped into the sheets and got into the mattress, so that she had always been afraid it would work out again and stick into her: which it had n't done yet and perhaps never would — she lay so quiet, pushing it about so little. "Perhaps you'd think it's me that trimmed the little handkerchief I wear round my neck," Miss Muniment said; "perhaps you'd think I could n't do less, lying here all day long with complete command of my time. Not a stitch of it. I'm the finest lady in London; I never lift my finger for myself. It's a present from her ladyship — it's her ladyship's own beautiful needlework. What do you think of that? Have you ever met any one so favoured before? And the work — just look at the work and tell me how it strikes you." The girl pulled off the bit of muslin from her neck and thrust it at Pinnie, who looked at it confusedly and gasped "Dear,

237

dear, dear!" partly in sympathy, partly as if, in spite of the consideration she owed every one, those were very odd proceedings.

"It's very badly done; surely you see that," said Lady Aurora. "It was only a joke."

"Oh yes, everything's a joke!" cried the irrepressible invalid — "everything except my state of health; that's admitted to be serious. When her ladyship sends me five shillings' worth of coals it's only a joke; and when she brings me a bottle of the finest port, that's another; and when she climbs up seventy-seven stairs (there are seventy-seven, I know perfectly, though I never go up or down) to spend the evening with me at the height of the London season, that's the best of all. I know all about the London season though I never go out, and I appreciate what her ladyship gives up. She's very jocular indeed, but fortunately I know how to take it. You can see it would n't do for me to be touchy, can't you, Miss Pynsent?"

"Dear, dear, I should be so glad to make you anything myself; it would be better — it would be better — !" poor Pinnie floundered.

"It would be better than my poor work. I don't know how to do that sort of thing in the least," said Lady Aurora.

"I'm sure I did n't mean that, my lady — I only meant it would be more convenient. Anything in the world she might fancy," the dressmaker went on as if it were a question of the invalid's appetite.

"Ah, you see I don't wear things — only a flannel jacket to be a bit tidy," Miss Muniment returned.

"I go in only for smart counterpanes, as you can see for yourself;" and she spread her white hands complacently over her coverlet of brilliant patchwork. "Now does n't that look to you, Miss Pynsent, as if it might be one of her ladyship's jokes?"

"Oh my good friend, how can you? I never went so far as that!" Lady Aurora interposed with visible anxiety.

"Well, you 've given me almost everything; I sometimes forget. This only cost me sixpence; so it comes to the same thing as if it had been a present. Yes, only sixpence in a raffle in a bazaar at Hackney, for the benefit of the Wesleyan Chapel three years ago. A young man who works with my brother and lives in that part offered him a couple of tickets; and he took one and I took one. When I say 'I' of course I mean he took the two; for how should I find (by which I naturally mean how should *he* find) a sixpence in that little cup on the chimney-piece unless he had put it there first? Of course my ticket took a prize, and of course, as my bed 's my dwelling-place, the prize was a beautiful counterpane of every colour of the rainbow. Oh there never was such luck as mine!" Rosy chattered, flashing her gay demented eyes at Hyacinth as if to irritate him with her contradictious optimism.

"It 's very lovely, but if you 'd like another for a change I 've got a great many pieces," Pinnie remarked with a generosity which made the young man feel she was acquitting herself finely.

Rose Muniment laid her little hand on the dressmaker's arm and responded straight: "No, not a change, not a change. How can there be a change when there's already everything? There's everything here — every colour that was ever seen or invented or dreamed of since the world began." And with her other hand she stroked affectionately her variegated quilt. "You've a great many pieces, but you have n't as many as there are here; and the more you should patch them together the more the whole thing would resemble this dear dazzling old friend. I've another idea, very very charming, and perhaps her ladyship can guess what it is." Rosy kept her fingers on Pinnie's arm and, smiling, turned her brilliant eyes from one of her female companions to the other as to associate and blend them as closely as possible in their interest in her. "In connexion with what we were talking about a few minutes ago — could n't your ladyship just go a little further in the same line?" Then as Lady Aurora looked troubled and embarrassed, blushing at being called upon to answer a conundrum, as it were, so publicly, her infirm friend came to her assistance. "It will surprise you at first, but it won't when I've explained it: my idea is just simply a sweet pink dressing-gown!"

"A sweet pink dressing-gown!" Lady Aurora repeated.

"With a neat black trimming! Don't you see the connexion with what we were talking of before our good visitors came in?"

"That would be very pretty," said Pinnie. "I've made them like that in my time. Or a carefully-selected blue trimmed with white."

240

"No, pink and black, pink and black — to suit my complexion. Perhaps you did n't know I *have* a complexion; but there are very few things I lack! Anything at all I should fancy, you were so good as to say. Well now, I fancy that! Your ladyship does see the connexion by this time, does n't she?"

Lady Aurora looked distressed, as if she felt she certainly ought to see it but was not sure that even yet it did n't escape her, and as if at the same time she were struck with the fact that this sudden evocation might result in a strain on the small dressmaker's resources. "A pink dressing-gown would certainly be very becoming and Miss Pynsent would be very kind," she said; while Hyacinth made the mental comment that it was a largeish order, since Pinnie would have obviously to furnish the materials as well as the labour. The amiable coolness with which the invalid laid her under contribution was, however, to his sense, quite in character, and he reflected that after all when you were flat on your back like that you had the right to reach out your hands (it was n't far you could reach at best) and grab what you could get. Pinnie declared she knew just the article Miss Muniment wanted and that she would undertake to make a perfect duck of it; and Rosy went on to say that she must explain of what use such an article would be, but for this purpose there must be another guess. She would give it to Miss Pynsent and Hyacinth — as many times as they liked: what *had* she and Lady Aurora been talking about before they came in? She clasped her hands and her eyes shone with her eagerness while she continued to turn them from Lady Aurora to the dressmaker. What would they imagine? What would they think natural, delightful, magnificent — if one could only end at last by making out the right place to put it? Hyacinth suggested successively a cage of Java sparrows, a music-box and a shower-bath — or perhaps even a full-length portrait of her ladyship; and Pinnie looked at him askance in a frightened way, as if perchance he were joking too broadly. Rosy at last relieved their suspense and announced: "A sofa, just a sofa now! What do you say to that? Do you suppose that idea could have come from any one but her ladyship? She must have all the credit of it; she came out with it in the course of conversation. I believe we were talking of the peculiar feeling that comes just under the shoulder-blades if one never has a change. She mentioned it as she might have mentioned just the right sort of rub — there *are* such wrong sorts! — or another spoonful of that American stuff. We're thinking it over and one of these days, if we give plenty of time to the question, we shall find the place, the very nicest and snuggest of all and no other. I hope *you* see the connexion with the pink dressing-gown," she pursued to Pinnie, "and I hope you see the importance of the question 'Shall anything go?' I should like you to look round a bit and tell me what you would answer if I were to say to you '*Can* anything go?'"

XV

"I'm sure there's nothing *I* should like to part with,"
Pinnie returned; and while she surveyed the scene
Lady Aurora, with discretion, to lighten Amanda's
responsibility, got up and turned to the window,
which was open to the summer evening and admitted
still the last rays of the long day. Hyacinth, after a
moment, placed himself beside her, looking out with
her at the dusky multitude of chimney-pots and the
small black houses roofed with grimy tiles. The
thick warm air of a London July floated beneath
them, suffused with the everlasting uproar of the
town, which appeared to have sunk into quietness but
again became a mighty voice as soon as one listened
for it; here and there, in poor windows, glimmered
a turbid light, and high above, in a clearer smokeless zone, a sky still fair and luminous, a faint silver
star looked down. The sky was the same that
bent far away in the country over golden fields and
purple hills and gardens where nightingales sang;
but from this point of view everything that covered
the earth was ugly and sordid and seemed to
express or to represent the weariness of toil. Presently, to Hyacinth's astonishment, Lady Aurora
said to him: "You never came after all to get the
books."

"Those you kindly offered to lend me? I did n't
know it was an understanding."

243

She gave an uneasy laugh. "I've picked them out; they're quite ready."

"It's awfully kind of you," the young man hastened to say. "I'll come and get them some day with pleasure." He was n't very sure he would, but it was the least he could profess.

"She'll tell you where I live, you know," Lady Aurora went on with a movement of her head in the direction of the bed, as if she were too shy to mention it herself.

"Oh, I've no doubt she knows the way — she could tell me every street and every turn!" Hyacinth laughed.

"She has made me describe to her very often how I come and go," his companion concurred. "I think few people know more about London than she. She never forgets anything."

"She's a wonderful little witch — she terrifies me!" he acknowledged.

Lady Aurora turned her modest eyes on him. "Oh, she's so good, she's so patient!"

"Yes, and so preternaturally wise and so awfully all there."

"Ah, she's immensely clever," said her ladyship. "Which do you think the cleverer?"

"The cleverer?"

"Of the girl or her brother."

"Oh, I think he'll be some day prime minister of England."

"Do you really? I'm so glad!" she cried with a flush of colour. "I do rejoice if you think that will be possible. You know it ought to be if things were right."

Hyacinth had not professed this high faith for the purpose of playing on her ladyship's feelings, but when he felt her intense agreement it was as if he had been making sport of her. Still he said no more than he believed when he observed in a moment that he had the greatest expectations of Paul Muniment's future: he was sure the world would hear of him, that England would need him, that the public some day would acclaim him. It was impossible to know him without feeling he was very strong and must play some important part.

"Yes, people would n't believe — they would n't believe." She abounded in his sense and he could measure the good he did her. It was moreover a pleasure to himself to place on record his opinion of his friend; it seemed to make that opinion more clear, to give it the force of an invocation or a prophecy. This was especially the case when he asked why on earth nature had endowed Paul Muniment with such extraordinary powers of mind, and powers of body too — because he was as strong as a horse — if it had n't been intended he should do something supreme for his fellow-men. Hyacinth confided to her ladyship that he thought the people in his own class generally very stupid — distinctly what he should call third-rate minds. He wished it had n't been so, for heaven knew he felt kindly to them and only asked to cast his lot with theirs; but he was obliged to confess that centuries of poverty, of ill-paid toil, of bad insufficient food and wretched housing had n't a favourable effect on the higher faculties. All the more reason that when there was a splendid exception like

their friend it should count for a tremendous force —
it had so much to make up for, so many to act for.
And then Hyacinth repeated that in his own low walk
of life people had really not the faculty of thought;
their minds had been simplified — reduced to two or
three elements. He saw that such judgements made
his fellow-guest very uncomfortable; she turned about,
she twisted herself vaguely as if she wished to protest,
but she was far too considerate to interrupt him. He
had no wish to worry her, but there were times when
he could n't withstand the perverse satisfaction of
insisting on his lowliness of station, of turning the
knife in the wound inflicted by such explicit reference, and of letting it be seen that if his place in the
world was immeasurably small he at least had no
illusions about either himself or his species. Lady
Aurora replied as quickly as possible that she knew
a great deal about the poor — not the poor after the
fashion of Rosy, but the terribly, hopelessly poor,
with whom she was more familiar than Hyacinth
would perhaps believe — and that she was often
struck with their great talents and their quick wit,
with their command of conversation really of much
more interest to her than most of what one usually
heard in drawing-rooms. She often found them immensely clever.

Hyacinth smiled at her and said: "Ah when you
get to the lowest depths of poverty they may become
rich and rare again. But I'm afraid I have n't gone
so far down. In spite of my opportunities I don't
know many absolute paupers."

"I know a great many." Lady Aurora hesitated

as if she did n't like to swagger, but she brought it out. "I dare say I know more than any one." There was something touching and beautiful to Hyacinth in this simple and diffident claim: it confirmed his impression that she was in some mysterious, incongruous and even slightly ludicrous manner a true heroine, a creature of a noble ideal. She perhaps guessed he was indulging in reflexions that might be favourable to her, for she said precipitately the next minute, as if there were nothing she dreaded so much as the danger of a compliment: "I think your aunt's so very attractive — and I'm sure dear Rosy thinks so." No sooner had she spoken than she blushed again; it appeared to have occurred to her that he might suppose she wished to contradict him by presenting this case of his aunt as a proof that the baser sort, even in a prosaic upper layer, were not without redeeming points. There was no reason why she should not have had this intention; so without sparing her he replied:

"You mean she's an exception to what I was saying?"

She stammered a little; then at last, as if, since he would n't spare her, she would n't spare him either: "Yes, and you're an exception too; you'll not make me believe you're wanting in intelligence. The Muniments don't think so," she added.

"No more do I myself; but that does n't prove that exceptions are not frequent. I've blood in my veins that's not the blood of the people."

"Oh, I see," said Lady Aurora sympathetically. And with a smile she went on: "Then you're all the more of an exception — in the upper class!"

Her way of taking it was the kindest in the world, but it did n't blind Hyacinth to the fact that from his own point of view he had been extraordinarily indiscreet. He had believed a moment before that he would have been proof against the strongest temptation to refer to the mysteries of his lineage, inasmuch as if made in a boastful spirit (and he had no desire as yet to treat it as an exercise in humility) any such reference would inevitably contain an element of the grotesque. He had never opened his lips to any one about his birth since the dreadful days when the question was discussed with Mr. Vetch's assistance in Lomax Place; never even to Paul Muniment, never to Millicent Henning nor to Eustache Poupin. He had his impression that people had ideas about him, and with some of Miss Henning's he had been made acquainted: these were of such a nature that he sometimes wondered if the tie uniting him to her were not on her own side a secret determination to satisfy her utmost curiosity before she had done with him. But he flattered himself he was impenetrable, and none the less he had begun to swagger idiotically the first time a temptation (really to call a temptation) presented itself. He turned crimson as soon as he had spoken, partly at the sudden image of what he had to swagger about and partly at the absurdity of a challenge from the model of civility before him. He hoped she did n't particularly regard what he had said — and indeed she gave no sign whatever of being startled by his claim to a pedigree, she had too much quick delicacy for that; she appeared to notice only the symptoms of confusion that followed. But as soon as possible he gave himself a lesson in humility by remarking: "I gather you spend most of your time among the poor and I'm sure you carry blessings with you. But I frankly confess I don't understand a lady's giving herself up to people like us when there's no obligation. Wretched company we must be when there's so much better to be had."

"I like it very much — you don't understand."

"Precisely — that's what I say. Our little friend on the bed is perpetually talking about your house, your family, your splendours, your gardens and greenhouses. They must be magnificent of course — "

"Oh, I wish she would n't; really I wish she would n't. It makes one feel dreadfully!" Lady Aurora interposed with vehemence.

"Ah, you had better give her her way; it's such a pleasure to her."

"Yes, more than to any of us!" sighed her ladyship helplessly.

"Well, how can you leave all those beautiful things to come and breathe this beastly air, surround yourself with hideous images and associate with people whose smallest fault is that they're ignorant, brutal and dirty? I don't speak of the ladies here present," Hyacinth added with the manner which most made Millicent Henning (who at once admired and hated it) wonder where on earth he had got it.

"Oh, I wish I could make you understand!" cried Lady Aurora, looking at him with troubled, appealing eyes and as if he were unexpectedly discouraging.

"But when all's said I think I do understand! Charity exists in your nature as a kind of passion."

"Yes, yes, it's a kind of passion!" her ladyship repeated eagerly, all thankful for the word. "I don't know if it's charity — I don't mean that. But whatever it is it's a passion — it's my life — it's all I care for." She faltered as if there might be something indecent in the confession or uncertain in the recipient; and then evidently was mastered by the comfort of being able to justify herself for an eccentricity that had excited notice, as well as by the luxury of discharging her soul of a long accumulation of intense things. "Already when I was fifteen years old I wanted to sell all I had and give to the poor. And ever since I've wanted to do something: it has seemed as if my heart would break if I should n't be able!"

Hyacinth was struck with a great respect, which however did n't prevent his presently saying, though in words that sounded patronising even to himself: "I suppose you're very religious."

She looked away into the thickening dusk, at the smutty housetops, the blurred emanation of lamplight above the streets. "I don't know. One has one's ideas. Some of them may be strange. I think a great many clergymen do good, but there are others I don't like at all. I dare say we had too many always at home; my father likes them so particularly. I think I've known too many bishops, I've had the church too much on my back. I dare say they would n't think at home, you know, that one was quite what one ought to be; but of course they consider me very odd in every way, as there's no doubt I am. I should tell you that I don't tell them everything; for what's the use when people don't understand? We're twelve at home and eight of us girls; and if you think it's so very splendid, and *she* thinks so, I should like you both to try it for a little! My father is n't rich and there's only one of us, Eva, married, and we're not at all handsome, and — oh there are all kinds of things," the young woman went on, looking round at him an instant through her sense of being launched. "I don't like society, and neither would you if you were to see the kind there is in London — at least in some parts," Lady Aurora added considerately. "I dare say you would n't believe all the humbuggery and the tiresomeness that one has to go through. But I've got out of it; I do as I like, though it has been rather a struggle. I have my liberty, and that's the greatest blessing in life except the reputation of being queer, and even a little mad, which is a greater advantage still. I'm a little mad, you know; you need n't be surprised if you hear it. That's because I stop in town when they go into the country; all the autumn, all the winter, when there's no one here (except three or four millions) and the rain drips, drips, drips from the trees in the big dull park where my people live. I dare say I ought n't to say such things to you, but, as I tell you, I'm quite a proper lunatic and I might as well keep up the character. When one's one of eight daughters and there's very little money (for any of *us* at least) and nothing to do but to go out with three or four others in mackintoshes, one can easily go off one's head. Of course there's the village, and it's not at all a nice one, and there are the people to look after, and goodness knows they're in want of it; but one must work with the vicarage, and at the vicarage are four more daughters, all old maids, and it's dreary and dreadful and one has too much of it, for they don't understand what one thinks or feels or a single word one says to them. Besides, they *are* stupid, I admit, the country poor; they're very very dense. I like Camberwell better," said Lady Aurora, smiling and taking breath at the end of her nervous, hurried, almost incoherent speech, of which she had delivered herself pantingly, with strange intonations and contortions, as if afraid that from one moment to the other she would repent, not of her confidence but of her egotism.

It placed her for Hyacinth in an unexpected light, making him feel that her awkward aristocratic spinsterhood was the cover of tumultuous passions. No one could have less the appearance of being animated by a vengeful irony; but he saw this timorous, scrupulous, though clearly all generous, creature to be evidently most a person not to spare, wherever she could prick them, the institutions among which she had been brought up and against which she had violently reacted. He had always supposed a reactionary to mean a backslider from the liberal faith, but Rosy's devotee gave a new value to the term; she appeared to have been driven to her present excesses by the squire and the parson and the conservative influences of that upper-class British home which our young man had always held the highest fruit of civilisation. It was clear that her ladyship was an original, and an original with force; but it gave Hyacinth a real pang to hear her make light of Inglefield (especially the park) and of the opportunities that must have abounded in Belgrave Square. It had been his belief that in a world of suffering and injustice these things were if not the most righteous at least the most fascinating. If they did n't give one the finest sensations where were such sensations to be had? He looked at Lady Aurora with a face that was a tribute to her sudden vividness while he said: "I can easily understand your wanting to do some good in the world, because you 're a kind of saint."

"A very curious kind!" laughed her ladyship.

"But I don't understand your not liking what your position gives you."

"I don't know anything about my position. I want to live!"

"And do you call *this* life?"

"I 'll tell you what my position is if you want to know: it 's the deadness of the grave!"

Hyacinth was startled by her tone, but he nevertheless laughed back at her: "Ah, as I say, you 're a regular saint!" She made no reply, for at that moment the door opened and Paul Muniment's tall figure emerged from the blackness of the staircase into the twilight, now very faint, of the room. Lady Aurora's eyes as they rested on him seemed to declare that such a vision as that at least was life. Another person as tall as himself appeared behind him, and Hyacinth recognised with astonishment their insinuating friend Captain Sholto. Paul had brought him up for Rosy's entertainment, being ready, and more than ready, always to introduce any one in the world, from the prime minister to the common hangman, who might give that young lady a sensation. They must have met at the "Sun and Moon," and if the Captain, some accident smoothing the way, had made him half as many advances as he had made some other people, Hyacinth could see that it would n't take long for Paul to lay him under contribution. But what the mischief was the Captain up to? It can't be said that our young man arrived this evening at an answer to that question. The occasion proved highly festal and the hostess rose to it without lifting her head from the pillow. Her brother introduced Captain Sholto as a gentleman who had a great desire to know extraordinary people, and she made him take possession of the chair at her bedside, out of which Miss Pynsent quickly edged herself, and asked him who he was and where he came from and how Paul had made his acquaintance and whether he had many friends in Camberwell. Sholto had not the same grand air that hovered about him at the theatre; he was dressed with ingenious cheapness, to an effect coinciding, however different the cause, with poor Hyacinth's own; but his disguise prompted our young man to wonder what made him so unmistakeably a gentleman in spite of it — in spite too of his rather overdoing the manner of being appreciative even to rapture and thinking everything and every one most charming and curious. He stood out, in poor Rosy's tawdry little room, among her hideous attempts at decoration, and looked to Hyacinth a being from another sphere, playing over the place and company a smile (one could n't call it false or unpleasant, yet it was distinctly not natural) of which he had got the habit in camps and courts. It became intense when it rested on our hero, whom he greeted as he might have done a dear young friend from whom he had been long and painfully separated. He was easy, he was familiar, he was exquisitely benevolent and bland — he was altogether a problem.

Rosy was a match for him, however; he evidently did n't puzzle her in the least and she thought his visit the most natural thing in the world. She expressed all the gratitude decency required, but appeared to assume that people who climbed her stairs would always find themselves repaid. She remarked that her brother must have met him for the first time that day, since the way he sealed a new acquaintance was usually by bringing the person immediately to call on her. And when the Captain said that if she did n't like them he supposed the poor wretches were dropped on the spot she admitted that this would be true if it ever happened she disapproved: as yet, however, she had not been obliged to draw the line. This was perhaps partly because he had n't brought up any of his awful firebrands, the people he knew for unmentionable reasons. Of such in general she had a very small opinion, and she would n't conceal from Captain Sholto that she hoped he was n't one of them. Rosy spoke as if her brother represented the Camberwell district in the House of Commons and she had discovered that a parliamentary career lowered the moral tone. The Captain nevertheless entered quite into her views and told her that it was as common friends of Mr. Hyacinth Robinson Mr. Muniment and he had come together; they were both so fond of him that this had immediately constituted a kind of tie. On hearing himself commemorated in such a brilliant way Mr. Hyacinth Robinson averted his head; he saw Captain Sholto might be trusted to make as great an effort for Rosy's entertainment as he gathered he had made for Milly Henning's that evening at the theatre. There were not chairs enough to go round, and Paul fetched a three-legged stool from his own apartment, after which he undertook to make tea for the company with the aid of a tin kettle and a spirit-lamp — these implements having been set out, flanked by half a dozen cups, in honour, presumably, of the little dressmaker, who had come such a distance. The little dressmaker, Hyacinth observed with pleasure, fell into earnest conversation with Lady Aurora, who bent over her, flushed, smiling, stammering and apparently so nervous that Pinnie, in comparison, was majestic and serene. They communicated presently to Hyacinth a plan they had arrived at as by a quick freemasonry, the idea that Miss Pynsent should go home to Belgrave Square with her ladyship and settle certain preliminaries in regard to the pink dressing-gown, toward which, if Miss Pynsent assented, her ladyship hoped to be able to contribute sundry brown "breadths" that had proved their quality in honourable service and might be dyed to the proper hue. Pinnie, Hyacinth could see, was in a state of religious exaltation; the visit to Belgrave Square and the idea of co-operating in such a manner with the nobility were privileges she could n't take solemnly enough. The latter

256

luxury indeed she began to enjoy without delay, Lady Aurora suggesting that Mr. Muniment might be rather awkward about making tea and that they should take the business off his hands. Paul gave it up to them with a pretence of compassion for their conceit and the observation that at any rate it took two women to supplant one man; and Hyacinth drew him to the window to ask where he had encountered Sholto and how he liked him.

They had met in Bloomsbury, as Hyacinth supposed, and Sholto had made up to him very much as a country curate might make up to an archbishop. He wanted to know what he thought of this and that: of the state of the labour market at the East End, of the terrible case of the old woman who had starved to death at Walham Green, of the practicability of more systematic out-of-door agitation and of the prospect of their getting one of their own men — one of the Bloomsbury lot — into the House. "He was mighty civil," Muniment said, "and I don't find that he has yet picked my pocket. He looked as if he would like me to suggest that *he* should stand as one of our own men, one of the Bloomsbury lot. He asks too many questions, but makes up for it by not paying any attention to the answers. He told me he'd give the world to see a really superior working-man's 'interior.' I didn't know at first just where he proposed to cut me open: he wanted a favourable specimen, one of the best; he had seen one or two that he didn't believe to be up to the average. I suppose he meant Schinkel's, the cabinetmaker's, neat home, and he wanted to compare. I told him I didn't know

257

what sort of a specimen my place would be, but that
he was welcome to look in and that it contained at
any rate one or two original features. I expect he has
found that's the case — with Rosy and the noble
lady. I wanted to show him off to Rosy; he's good
for that if he is n't good for anything else. I told him
we expected a little company this evening, so it might
be a good time; and he assured me that to mingle in
such an occasion as that was the dream of his existence. He seemed in a rare hurry, as if I were going
to show him a hidden treasure, and insisted on driving me over in a hansom. Perhaps his idea is to introduce the use of cabs among the working-classes;
certainly I 'll work to return him if that's to be his
platform. On our way over he talked to me about
you; told me you were an intimate friend of his."

"What did he say about me?" Hyacinth asked
with promptness.

"Vain little beggar!"

"Did he call me that?" said Hyacinth ingenuously.

"He said you were simply astonishing."

"Simply astonishing?" Hyacinth repeated.

"For a person of your low extraction."

"Well, I may be rum, but he is certainly rummer.
Don't you think so now you know him?"

Paul eyed his young friend. "Do you want to
know what he is? He's a tout."

"A tout? What do you mean?"

"Well, a cat's-paw, if you like better."

Hyacinth stared. "For whom, pray?"

"Or a deep-sea fisherman, if you like better still.
I give you your choice of comparisons. I made them

up as we came along in the hansom. He throws his nets and hauls in the little fishes — the pretty little shining, wriggling fishes. They are all for *her;* she swallows 'em down."

"For her? Do you mean the Princess?"

"Who else should I mean? Take care, my tadpole!"

"Why should I take care? The other day you told me not to."

"Yes, I remember. But now I see more."

"Did he speak of her? What did he say?" Hyacinth eagerly asked.

"I can't tell you now what he said, but I'll tell you what I guessed."

"And what's that?"

They had been talking of course in a very low tone, and their voices were covered by Rosy's chatter in the corner, by the liberal laughter with which Captain Sholto accompanied it, and by the much more discreet, though earnest, intermingled accents of Lady Aurora and Miss Pynsent. But Muniment spoke more softly still — Hyacinth felt a kind of suspense — as he replied in a moment: "Why, she's a monster!"

"A monster?" repeated our young man, from whom, this evening, his friend was destined to draw ejaculations and echoes.

Paul glanced toward the Captain, who was apparently more and more engaged by Rosy. "In him I think there's no great harm. He's only a patient angler."

It must be admitted that Captain Sholto justified

to a certain extent this definition by the manner in which he baited his hook for such little facts as might help him to a more intimate knowledge of his host and hostess. When the tea was made Rosy asked Miss Pynsent to be so good as to hand it about. They must let her poor ladyship rest a little, must n't they? — and Hyacinth could see that in her innocent but inveterate self-complacency she wished to reward and encourage the dressmaker, draw her out and present her still more by offering her this graceful exercise. Sholto sprang up, however, and begged Pinnie to let him relieve her, taking a cup from her hand; and poor Pinnie, who noted in a moment that he was some kind of uncanny masquerader, who was bewildered by the strange mixture of elements that surrounded her and unused to being treated like a duchess (for the Captain's manner was a triumph of respectful gallantry), collapsed on the instant into a chair, appealing to Lady Aurora with a frightened smile and conscious that, deeply versed as she might be in the theory of decorum, she had no precedent that could meet such an occasion. "Now how many families would there be in such a house as this, and what should you say about the sanitary arrangements? Would there be others on this floor — what is it, the third, the fourth? — beside yourselves, you know, and should you call it a fair example of a tenement of its class?" It was with such enquiries as this that the good gentleman beguiled their tea-drinking, while Hyacinth made the reflexion that, though he evidently meant them very well, they were characterised by a want of fine tact, by too patronis-

ing a curiosity. The Captain invited information as
to the position in life, the avocations and habits of the
other lodgers, the rent they paid, their relations with
each other, both in and out of the family. "Now
would there be a good deal of close packing, do you
suppose, and any perceptible want of — a — sobriety?"

Paul Muniment, who had swallowed his cup of tea
at a single gulp — there was no offer of a second —
gazed out of the window into the dark, which had
now come on, with his hands in his pockets, whistling,
impolitely, no doubt, but with extreme animation.
He had the manner of having made over their visitor
altogether to Rosy and of thinking that whatever that
personage said or did was all so much grist to her
indefatigable little mill. Lady Aurora writhed in her
pain, and it is a proof of the degree to which our slight
hero had the instincts of a man of the world that he
guessed exactly how vulgar she thought this new
acquaintance. She was doubtless rather vexed also
— Hyacinth had learned this evening that Lady
Aurora could be vexed — at the alacrity of Rosy's
responses: the little person in the bed gave the Captain every satisfaction, considered his questions as
a proper tribute to humble respectability and supplied him, as regards the population of Audley Court,
with statistics and anecdotes picked up by mysterious processes of her own. At last her ladyship, on
whom Paul Muniment had not been at pains to be-
stow much conversation, took leave of her, signifying
to Hyacinth that for the rest of the evening she would
assume the care of Miss Pynsent. Pinnie might have

been consciously laid bare for monstrous rites now that she was really about to be transported to Belgrave Square, but Hyacinth was sure she would acquit herself only the more honourably; and when he offered to call for her there later on she reminded him under her breath and with a small sad smile of the many years during which, after nightfall, she had carried her work, pinned up in a cloth, about London.

Paul Muniment, according to his habit, lighted Lady Aurora downstairs, and Captain Sholto and Hyacinth were alone for some minutes with Rosy; which gave the former, taking up his hat and stick, an opportunity to say to his young friend: "Which way are you going? Not my way, by chance?" Hyacinth saw that he hoped for his company, and he became conscious that, strangely as Paul had indulged him and too promiscuously investigating as he had just shown himself, this ingratiating character was not more easy to resist than he had been the other night at the theatre. The Captain bent over Rosy's bed as if she had been a fine lady on a satin sofa, promising to come back very soon and very often, and the two men went downstairs. On their way they met their host coming up, and Hyacinth felt rather ashamed, he could scarce tell why, that his friend should see him marching off with the "tout." After all, if Paul had brought him to see his sister might not Paul's pupil and devotee at least walk with him? "I'm coming again, you know, very often. I dare say you'll find me a great bore!" the Captain announced as he bade good-night to Muniment.

"Your sister's a most interesting creature, one of the most interesting creatures I've ever seen, and the whole thing, you know, exactly the type of place I wanted to get at, only much more — really much more — original and curious. It has been a jolly glimpse — a grand success!"

And the Captain felt his way down the dusky shaft, while Paul Muniment, above, gave him the benefit of rather a wavering candlestick and answered his civil speech with an "Oh well, you take us as you find us, you know!" and an outburst of frank but not unfriendly laughter.

Half an hour later Hyacinth found himself in Captain Sholto's chambers, seated on a big divan covered with Persian rugs and cushions and smoking the most expensive cigar that had ever touched his lips. As they left Audley Court the Captain had taken his arm and they had walked along together in a desultory, colloquial manner, till on Westminster Bridge (they had followed the embankment beneath Saint Thomas's Hospital) Sholto brought out: "By the way, why shouldn't you come home with me and see my little place? I've a few things that might amuse you — some pictures, some odds and ends I've picked up, and a few bindings; you might tell me what you think of them." Hyacinth assented without demur; he had still in his ear the reverberation of the Captain's enquiries in Rosy's room, and he saw no reason why he on his side shouldn't embrace an occasion of ascertaining how, as his companion would have said, a man of fashion would live now.

This particular specimen lived in a large old-fashioned house in Queen Anne Street, of which he occupied the upper floors, where he had filled the high wainscoted rooms with the spoils of travel and the ingenuities of modern taste. There was not a country in the world he appeared not to have ransacked, and to Hyacinth his trophies represented a wonderfully long purse. The whole establishment, from the low-voiced inexpressive valet who, after he had poured brandy into tall tumblers, solemnised the very popping of soda-water corks, to the quaint little silver receptacle in which he was invited to deposit the ashes of his cigar, was such a revelation for our appreciative youth that he felt himself hushed and depressed, so poignant was the thought that it took thousands of things he then should never possess nor know to make a civilised being. He had often in evening walks wondered what was behind the walls of certain ample bright-windowed houses in the West End, and now he got an idea. The first effect of the idea was to lay him rather flat.

"Well now, tell me what you thought of our friend the Princess," the Captain said, thrusting out the loose yellow slippers his servant had helped to exchange for his shoes. He spoke as if he had been waiting impatiently for the proper moment to ask that question, so much might depend on the answer.

"She's beautiful — beautiful," Hyacinth answered almost dreamily while his eyes wandered all over the room.

"She was so interested in all you said to her; she'd like so much to see you again. She means to write to you — I suppose she can address to the 'Sun and

Moon'?—and I hope you'll go to her house if she proposes a day."

"I don't know—I don't know. It seems so strange."

"What seems strange, my dear chap?"

"Everything! My sitting here with you; my introduction to that lady; the idea of her wanting, as you say, to see me again and of her writing to me; and this whole place of yours, with all its dim rich curiosities hanging on the walls and glinting in the light of that rose-coloured lamp. You yourself too — you're strangest of all."

The Captain looked at him so silently and so fixedly, through the fumes of their tobacco, after he had made this last charge that Hyacinth thought he was perhaps offended; but this impression was presently dissipated by further signs of sociability and hospitality, and Sholto took occasion later to let him know how important it was, in the days they were living in, not to have too small a measure of the usual, destined as they certainly were — "in the whole matter of the relations of class with class and all that sort of thing, you know" — to witness some very startling developments. The Captain spoke as if, for his part, he were a child of his age (so that he only wanted to see all it could show him) down to the points of his yellow slippers. Hyacinth felt that he himself had not been very satisfactory about the Princess; but as his nerves began to tremble a little more into tune with the situation he repeated to his host what Milly had said about her at the theatre — asked if this young lady had correctly understood

him in believing she had been turned out of the house
by her husband.

"Yes, he literally pushed her into the street — or
into the garden; I believe the scene took place in the
country. But perhaps Miss Henning did n't mention, or perhaps I did n't, that the Prince would at
the present hour give everything he owns in the world
to get her back. Fancy such an absurd scene!" said
the Captain, laughing in a manner that struck Hyacinth as rather profane.

He stared with dilated eyes at this picture, which
seemed to demand a comparison with the only incident of the sort that had come within his experience
— the forcible ejection of intoxicated females from
public-houses. "That magnificent being — what had
she done?"

"Oh, she had made him feel he was an ass!" the
Captain answered promptly. He turned the conversation to Miss Henning; said he was so glad Hyacinth
gave him an opportunity to speak of her. He got on
with her famously; perhaps she had told him. They
became immense friends — *en tout bien tout honneur,
s'entend*. Now, *there* was another London type, plebeian but brilliant; and how little justice one usually
did it, how magnificent it was! But she of course was
a wonderful specimen. "My dear fellow, I've seen
many women, and the women of many countries,"
the Captain went on, "and I've seen them as intimately as you like, and I know what I'm talking
about; and when I tell you that that one — that
one — !" Then he suddenly paused, laughing in his
democratic way. "But perhaps I'm going too far:

you must always pull me up, you know, when I do. At any rate I congratulate you; I do right heartily. Have another cigar. Now what sort of — a — salary would she receive at her big shop, you know ? I know where it is; I mean to go there and buy some pocket-handkerchiefs."

Hyacinth knew neither how far Captain Sholto had been going, nor exactly on what he congratulated him; and he pretended at least an equal ignorance on the subject of Millicent's pecuniary gains. He did n't want to talk about her moreover, nor about his own life; he wanted to talk about the Captain's and to elicit information that would be in harmony with his romantic chambers, which reminded one somehow of certain of Bulwer's novels. His host gratified this pretension most liberally and told him twenty stories of things of interest, often of amazement, that had happened to him in Albania, in Madagascar and even in Paris. Hyacinth induced him easily to talk about Paris (from a different point of view from M. Poupin's) and sat there drinking in enchantments. The only thing that fell below the high level of his entertainment was the bindings of his friend's books, which he told him frankly, with the conscience of an artist, were not up to the mark. After he left Queen Anne Street he was quite too excited to go straight home; he walked about with his mind full of images and strange speculations till the grey London streets began to clear with the summer dawn.

XVI

THE aspect of South Street, Mayfair, on a Sunday afternoon in August, is not enlivening, yet the Prince had stood for ten minutes gazing out of the window at the genteel vacancy of the scene; at the closed blinds of the opposite houses, the lonely policeman on the corner, covering a yawn with a white cotton hand, the low-pitched light itself, which seemed conscious of an obligation to observe the decency of the British Sabbath. Our personage, however, had a talent for that kind of attitude; it was one of the things by which he had exasperated his wife; he could remain motionless, with the aid of some casual support for his high, lean person, considering serenely and inexpressively any object that might lie before him and presenting his aristocratic head at a favourable angle, for periods of extraordinary length. On first coming into the room he had given some attention to its furniture and decorations, perceiving at a glance that they were rich and varied; some of the things he recognised as old friends, odds and ends the Princess was fond of, which had accompanied her in her remarkable wanderings, while others were unfamiliar and suggested vividly that she had not ceased to "collect." He made two reflexions: one was that she was living as expensively as ever; the other that, however this might be, no one had such a feeling as she for the *mise-en-scène* of life, such a talent for arranging a room. She had always, wherever she was, the most charming room in Europe.

It was his impression that she had taken the house in South Street but for three months; yet, gracious heaven, what had she not put into it? The Prince asked himself this question without violence, for that was not to be his line to-day. He could be angry to a point at which he himself was often frightened, but he honestly believed this to be only when he had been baited past endurance, so that as a usual thing he was really as mild and accommodating as the extreme urbanity of his manner appeared to announce. There was indeed nothing to suggest to the world in general that he was an impracticable or vindictive nobleman: his features were not regular and his complexion had a bilious tone; but his dark brown eye, which was at once salient and dull, expressed benevolence and melancholy; his head drooped from his long neck in a considerate, attentive style; and his close-cropped black hair, combined with a short, fine, pointed beard, completed his resemblance to some old portrait of a personage of distinction under the Spanish dominion at Naples. To-day at any rate he had come in conciliation, almost in humility, and that is why he did n't permit himself even to murmur at the long delay he had to accept. He knew very well that if his wife should consent to take him back it would be only after a probation to which this little wait in her drawing-room was a trifle. It was a quarter of an hour before the door opened, and even then it was not the Princess who appeared, but only Madame Grandoni.

Their greeting was at first all a renouncement of

words. She came to him with both hands out-stretched, and took his own and held them a while, looking up at him with full benignity. She had elongated her florid, humorous face to a degree that was almost comical, and the pair might have passed, in their silent solemnity, for acquaintances meeting in a house in which last obsequies were about to take place. It was indeed a house on which death had descended, as he very soon learned from Madame Grandoni's expression; something had perished there for ever and he might proceed to bury it as soon as he liked. His wife's ancient German friend, however, was not a person to sustain that note very long, and when, after she had made him sit down on the sofa be-side her, she shook her head slowly and definitely several times, it was with a brow on which a more genial appreciation of the facts had already begun to appear.

"Never — never — never?" said the Prince in a deep hoarse voice, a voice at variance with his attenuated capacity. He had much of the complexion which in late-coming members of long-descended races we qualify to-day as effete; but his tone might have served for the battle-cry of some deep-chested fighting ancestor.

"Surely you know your wife as well as I," she replied in Italian, which she evidently spoke with facility, though with a strong guttural accent. "I've been talking with her: that's what has made me keep you. I've urged her to see you. I've told her that this could do no harm and would pledge her to nothing. But you know your wife," Madame Gran-doni repeated with an intensity now much relaxed.

Prince Casamassima looked down at his boots. "How can one ever know a person like that? I hoped she'd see me five little minutes."

"For what purpose? Have you anything to propose?"

"For what purpose? To rest my eyes on her beautiful face."

"Did you come to England for that?"

"For what else should I have come?" the Prince asked as he turned his blighted gaze to the opposite side of South Street.

"In London, such a day as this, *già*," said the old lady sympathetically. "I'm very sorry for you; but if I had known you were coming I'd have written to you that you might spare yourself the pain."

He gave a deep interminable sigh. "You ask me what I wish to propose. What I wish to propose is that my wife should n't kill me inch by inch."

"She'd be much more likely to do that if you lived with her!" Madame Grandoni cried.

"*Cara amica*, she does n't appear to have killed you," the melancholy nobleman returned.

"Oh, me? I'm past killing. I'm as hard as a stone. I went through my miseries long ago; I suffered what you've not had to suffer; I wished for death many times and I survived it all. Our troubles don't kill us, *Principe mio;* it's we who must try to kill them. I've buried not a few. Besides Christina's fond of me, the devil knows why!" Madame Grandoni added.

"And you're so good to her," said the Prince, who laid his hand on her fat wrinkled fist.

"*Che vuole?* I've known her so long. And she has some such great qualities."

"Ah, to whom do you say it?" And he gazed at his boots again, for some moments, in silence. Suddenly he resumed: "How does she look to-day?"

"She always looks the same: like an angel who came down from heaven yesterday and has been rather disappointed in her first day on earth!"

The Prince was evidently a man of a simple nature, and Madame Grandoni's rather violent metaphor took his fancy. His face lighted up a little and he replied with eagerness: "Ah, she's the only woman I've ever seen whose beauty never for a moment falls below itself. She has no bad days. She's so handsome when she's angry!"

"She's very handsome to-day, but she's not angry," said the old lady.

"Not when my name was announced?"

"I was not with her then; but when she sent for me and asked me to see you it was quite without passion. And even when I argued with her and tried to persuade her (and she does n't like that, you know) she was still perfectly quiet."

"She hates me, she despises me too much, eh?"

"How can I tell, dear Prince, when she never mentions you?"

"Never, never?"

"That's much better than if she railed at you and abused you."

"You mean it should give me more hope for the future?" the young man asked quickly.

His old friend had a pause. "I mean it's better

for *me*," she answered with a laugh of which the friendly ring covered as much as possible her equivocation.

"Ah, you like me enough to care," he murmured as he turned on her his sad grateful eyes.

"I'm very sorry for you. *Ma che vuole?*"

The Prince had apparently nothing to suggest and only exhaled in reply another gloomy groan. Then he enquired if his wife pleased herself in that country and if she intended to pass the summer in London. Would she remain long in England and — might he take the liberty to ask? — what were her plans? Madame Grandoni explained that the Princess had found the English capital much more to her taste than one might have expected, and that as for plans she had as many or as few as she had always had. Had he ever known her to carry out any arrangement or to do anything of any kind she had prepared or promised? She always at the last moment did the other thing, the one that had been out of the question; and it was for this Madame Grandoni herself privately made her preparations. Christina, now that everything was over, would leave London from one day to the other; but they should n't know where they were going till they arrived. The old lady concluded by asking if the Prince himself liked England. He thrust forward his full lips. "How can I like anything? Besides, I've been here before; I've many friends."

His companion saw he had more to say to her, to extract from her, but that he was hesitating nervously because he feared to incur some warning, some rebuff with which his dignity — in spite of his position of discomfiture, really very great — might find it difficult to square itself. He looked vaguely round the room and presently remarked: "I wanted to see for myself how she's living."

"Yes, that's very natural."

"I've heard — I've heard — " And Prince Casamassima stopped.

"You've heard great rubbish, I've no doubt." Madame Grandoni watched him as if she foresaw what was coming.

"She spends a terrible deal of money," said the young man.

"Indeed she does." The old lady knew that, careful as he was of his very considerable property, which at one time had required much nursing, his wife's prodigality was not what lay heaviest on his mind. She also knew that expensive and luxurious as Christina might be she had never yet exceeded the income settled upon her by the Prince at the time of their separation — an income determined wholly by himself and his estimate of what was required to maintain the social consequence of his name, for which he had a boundless reverence. "She thinks she's a model of thrift — that she counts every shilling," Madame Grandoni continued. "If there's a virtue she prides herself upon it's her economy. Indeed it's the only thing for which she takes any credit."

"I wonder if she knows that I" — he just hesitated, then went on — "spend almost nothing at all. But I'd rather live on dry bread than that in a country like this, in this great English society, she should n't make a proper appearance."

"Her appearance is all you could wish. How can it help being proper with me to set her off ?"

"You're the best thing she has, dear friend. So long as you're with her I feel a certain degree of security; and one of the things I came for was to extract from you a promise that you won't leave her."

"Ah, let us not tangle ourselves up with promises!" Madame Grandoni exclaimed. "You know the value of any engagement one may take with regard to the Princess; it's like promising you I'll stay in the bath when the hot water's on. When I begin to be scalded I've to jump out — naked as I may naturally be. I'll stay while I can, but I should n't stay if she were to do certain things." Madame Grandoni uttered these last words with a clear emphasis, and for a minute she and her companion looked deep into each other's eyes.

"What things do you mean ?"

"I can't say what things. It's utterly impossible to predict on any occasion what Christina will do. She's capable of giving us great surprises. The things I mean are things I should recognise as soon as I saw them, and they would make me leave the house on the spot."

"So that if you've not left it yet — ?" he asked with extreme eagerness.

"It's because I've thought I may do some good by staying."

He seemed but half content with this answer; nevertheless he said in a moment: "To me it makes all the difference. And if anything of the kind you speak of should happen, that would be only the greater reason for your staying. — You might interpose, you might arrest — " He stopped short before her large Germanic grimace.

"You must have been in Rome more than once when the Tiber had overflowed, *è vero ?* What would you have thought then if you had heard people telling the poor wretches in the Ghetto, on the Ripetta, up to their knees in liquid mud, that they ought to interpose, to arrest ?"

"*Capisco bene,*" said the Prince, dropping his eyes. He appeared to have closed them, for some moments, as if under a slow spasm of pain. "I can't tell you what torments me most," he presently went on — "the thought that sometimes makes my heart rise into my mouth. It's a haunting fear." And his pale face and disturbed respiration might indeed have been those of a man before whom some horrible spectre had risen.

"You need n't tell me. I know what you mean, my poor friend."

"Do you think then there *is* a danger — that she'll drag my name, do what no one has ever dared to do ? That I'd never forgive," he declared almost under his breath; and the hoarseness of his whisper lent it a great effect.

Madame Grandoni hastily wondered if she had not better tell him (as it would prepare him for the worst) that his wife cared about as much for his name as for any old label on her luggage; but after an instant's reflexion she reserved this information for another hour. Besides, as she said to herself, the Prince ought already to know perfectly to what extent Christina attached the idea of an obligation or an interdict to her ill-starred connexion with an ignorant and superstitious Italian race whom she despised for their provinciality, their parsimony and their futility (she thought their talk the climax of childishness) and whose fatuous conception of their importance in the great modern world she had on various public occasions sufficiently riddled with her derision. She finally contented herself with remarking: "Dear Prince, your wife's a very proud woman."

"Ah, how could my wife be anything else? But her pride's not my pride. And she has such ideas, such opinions! Some of them are monstrous."

Madame Grandoni smiled. "She does n't think it so necessary to have them when you're not there."

"Why then do you say that you enter into my fears — that you recognise the stories I've heard?"

I know not whether the good lady lost patience with his pressure; at all events she broke out with a certain sharpness. "Understand this, understand this: Christina will never consider you — your name, your illustrious traditions — in any case in which she does n't consider herself much more!"

The Prince appeared to study for a moment this somewhat ambiguous yet portentous phrase; then he slowly got up with his hat in his hand and walked about the room softly, solemnly, as if suffering from his long thin feet. He stopped before one of the windows and took another survey of South Street; then turning he suddenly asked in a voice into which he had evidently endeavoured to infuse a colder curiosity: "Is she admired in this place? Does she see many people?"

"She's thought very strange of course. But she sees whom she likes. And they mostly bore her to death!" Madame Grandoni conscientiously added.

"Why then do you tell me this country pleases her?"

The old woman left her place. She had promised Christina, who detested the sense of being under the same roof with her husband, that the latter's visit should be kept within narrow limits; and this movement was intended to signify as kindly as possible that it had better terminate. "It's the common people who please her," she returned with her hands folded on her crumpled satin stomach and her ancient eyes, still keen for all comedy, raised to his face. "It's the lower orders, the *basso popolo*."

"The *basso popolo*?" The Prince stared at this fantastic announcement.

"The *povera gente*," pursued his friend, amused at his dismay.

"The London mob — the most horrible, the most brutal — ?"

"Oh, she wishes to raise them."

"After all, something like that's no more than I had heard," said the Prince gravely.

"*Che vuole?* Don't trouble yourself; it won't be for long!"

Madame Grandoni saw this comforting assurance lost upon him; his face was turned to the door of the room, which had been thrown open, and all his attention given to the person who crossed the threshold. She transferred her own to the same quarter and recognised the little artisan whom Christina had, in a manner so extraordinary and so profoundly characteristic, drawn into her box that night at the theatre — afterwards informing her old friend that she had sent for him to come and see her.

"Mr. Robinson!" the butler, who had had a lesson, announced in a loud colourless tone.

"It won't be for long," Madame Grandoni repeated for the Prince's benefit; but it was to Mr. Robinson the words had the air of being addressed.

Hyacinth stood, while she signalled to the servant to leave the door open and wait, looking from the queer old lady, who was as queer as before, to the tall foreign gentleman (he recognised his foreignness at a glance) whose eyes seemed to challenge him, to devour him; wondering if he had made some mistake and needing to remind himself that he had the Princess's note in his pocket, with the day and hour as clear as her magnificent script could make them.

"Good-morning, good-morning. I hope you're well," said Madame Grandoni with quick friendliness, but turning her back upon him at the same time in order to ask of their companion, in the other idiom, as she extended her hand: "And don't you leave London soon — in a day or two ?"

The Prince made no answer; he still scanned the little bookbinder from head to foot, as if wondering who the deuce he could be. His eyes seemed to Hyacinth to search for the small neat bundle he ought to have had under his arm and without which he was incomplete. To the reader, however, it may be confided that, dressed more carefully than he had ever been in his life before, stamped with that extraordinary transformation which the British Sunday often operates in the person of the wage-earning cockney, with his handsome head uncovered and the heat of wonder in his fine face, the young man from Lomax Place might have passed for anything rather than a carrier of parcels. "The Princess wrote to me, madam, to come and see her," he said as a prompt precaution; in case he should have incurred the reproach of undue precipitation.

"Oh yes, I dare say." And Madame Grandoni guided the Prince to the door with an expression of the desire he might have a comfortable journey back to Italy.

But he stood stiff there; he appeared to have jumped to a dark conclusion about Mr. Robinson. "I must see you once more. I must. It's impossible — !"

"Ah well, not in this house, you know."

"Will you do me the honour to meet me then?" And as the old lady hesitated he added with sudden intensity: "Dearest friend, I beg you on my knees!" After she had agreed that if he would write to her proposing a day and place she would see him were it possible, he raised her ancient knuckles to his lips and, without further notice of Hyacinth, turned away. She bade the servant announce the other visitor to the Princess, and then approached Mr. Robinson, rubbing her hands and smiling, her head very much to one side. He smiled back at her vaguely; he

did n't know what she might be going to say. What
she said was, to his surprise —

"My poor young man, may I take the liberty of
asking your age?"

"Certainly, madam; I'm twenty-four."

"And I hope you're industrious, and temperate in
all ways and — what do you call it in English? —
steady."

"I don't think I'm very wild," said Hyacinth without offence. He thought the old woman patronising,
but he forgave her.

"I don't know how one speaks in this country to
young men like you. Perhaps one's considered meddling or impertinent."

"I like the way you speak," Hyacinth hastened to
profess.

She stared, and then with a comical affectation of
dignity: "You're very good. I'm glad it amuses
you. You're evidently intelligent and clever," she
went on, "and if you're disappointed it will be a
pity."

"How do you mean if I'm disappointed?"

"Well, I dare say you expect great things when
you come into a house like this. You must tell me if
I upset you. I'm very old-fashioned and I'm not
of this country. I speak as one speaks to young men
like you in other places."

"I'm not so easily upset!" Hyacinth assured her
with a flight of imagination. "To expect anything
one must know something, one must understand:
is n't it so? And I'm here without knowing, without
understanding. I've come only because a lady who

seems to me very beautiful and very kind has done me the honour to send for me."

Madame Grandoni examined him a moment as if struck by his good looks, by something delicate stamped on him everywhere. "I can see you're very clever, very intelligent; no, you're not like the young men I mean. All the more reason —!" And she paused, giving a short sigh. Her case might have been all too difficult. "I want to warn you a little, and I don't know how. If you were a young Roman it would be different."

"A young Roman?"

"That's where I live properly, in the Eternal City. If I hurt you, you can explain it that way. No, you're not like them "

"You don't hurt me — please believe that; you interest me very much," said Hyacinth, to whom it did n't occur that he himself might seem patronising. "Of what do you want to warn me?"

"Well — only to advise you a little. Don't give up anything."

"What can I give up?"

"Don't give up *yourself*. I say that to you in your interest. I think you've some honest little trade — I forget what. But whatever it may be remember that to do it well is the best thing; better than paying extraordinary visits, better even than being liked by Princesses!"

"Ah yes, I see what you mean!" Hyacinth returned, exaggerating a little. "I'm very fond of my trade indeed, I assure you."

"I'm delighted to hear it. Hold fast to it then

and be quiet; be diligent and good and get on. I gathered the other night that you're one of the young men who want everything changed — I believe there are a great many in Italy and also in my own dear old Deutschland, and who even think it useful to throw bombs into innocent crowds and shoot pistols at their rulers or at any one. I won't go into that. I might seem to be speaking for myself, and the fact is that for myself I don't care; I'm so old that I may hope to spend the few days that are left me without receiving a bullet. But before you go any further please think a little whether you're right."

"It is n't just that you should impute to me ideas which I may not have," said Hyacinth, turning very red but taking more and more of a fancy, all the same, to Madame Grandoni. "You talk at your ease about our ways and means, but if we were only to make use of those that you would like to see — !" And while he blushed, smiling, the young man shook his head two or three times with great significance.

"I should n't like to see any!" the old lady cried. "I like people to bear their troubles as one has done one's self. And as for injustice, you see how kind I am to you when I say to you again Don't, don't, give anything up. I'll tell them to send you some tea," she added as she took her way out of the room, presenting to him her round, low, aged back and dragging over the carpet a scanty and lustreless train.

XVII

He had been warned by Mr. Vetch as to what brilliant women might do with him — it was only a word on the old fiddler's lips, but the word had had a point; he had been warned by Paul Muniment, and now he was admonished by a person supremely well placed for knowing: a fact that could n't fail to deepen the emotion which, any time these three days, had made him draw his breath more quickly. That emotion, nevertheless, did n't actually make him fear remote consequences; as he looked over the Princess Casamassima's drawing-room and inhaled an air that seemed to him inexpressibly delicate and sweet he hoped his adventure would throw him on his mettle only half as much as the old lady had wished to intimate. He considered, one after the other, the different chairs, couches and ottomans the room contained — he wished to treat himself to the most sumptuous — and then for reasons he knew best sank into a seat covered with rose-coloured brocade and of which the legs and frame appeared of pure gold. Here he sat perfectly still, only with his heart beating very sensibly and his eyes coursing again and again from one object to another. The splendours and suggestions of Captain Sholto's apartment were thrown completely into the shade by the scene before him, and as the Princess did n't scruple to keep him waiting twenty minutes (during which

284

the butler came in and set out on a small table a glittering tea-service) Hyacinth had time to count over
the innumerable *bibelots* (most of which he had never
dreamed of) involved in the character of a woman
of high fashion and to feel that their beauty and oddity revealed not only whole provinces of art, but
refinements of choice on the part of their owner,
complications of mind and — almost — terrible
depths of temperament.

When at last the door opened and the servant,
reappearing, threw it far back as to make a wide
passage for a person of the importance of his mistress, Hyacinth's suspense became very acute; it was
much the same feeling with which, at the theatre, he
had sometimes awaited the entrance of a celebrated
actress. In this case the actress was to perform for
him alone. There was still a moment before she
came on, and when she arrived she was so simply
dressed — besides his seeing her now on her feet —
that she looked quite a different figure. She approached him rapidly and a little stiffly and shyly,
but in the prompt manner in which she shook hands
was an evident desire to be very direct and perfectly
easy. She might have been another person, but that
person had a beauty even more radiant; the fairness
of her face shone forth at our young man as if to dissipate any doubts assailing and bewildering him as
to the reality of the vision bequeathed to him by his
former interview. And in this peculiar high grace of
her presence he could n't have told you if she struck
him as more proud or more kind.

"I've kept you a long time, but it's supposed not

usually to be a bad place, my salon; there are various things to look at and perhaps you've noticed some of them. Over on that side for instance is rather a curious collection of miniatures." She spoke abruptly, quickly, as if conscious that their communion might be awkward and she were trying to strike instantly (to conjure that element away) the sort of note that would make them both most comfortable. Quickly too she sat down before her tea-tray and poured him out a cup, which she handed him without asking if he would have it. He accepted it with a trembling hand, though he had no desire for it; he was too nervous to swallow the tea, but it would n't have appeared to him possible to decline. When he had murmured that he had indeed looked at all her things, but that it would take hours to do justice to such treasures, she asked if he were fond of works of art; immediately adding, however, that she was afraid he had not many opportunities of seeing them, though of course there were the public collections, open to all. He replied with perfect veracity that some of the happiest moments of his life had been spent at the British Museum and the National Gallery, and this fact appeared to interest her greatly, so that she straightway begged him to tell her what he thought of certain pictures and antiques. In this way it was that in an incredibly short time, as appeared to him, he found himself discussing the Bacchus and Ariadne and the Elgin Marbles with one of the most remarkable women in Europe. It was true that she herself talked most, passing precipitately from one point to another, putting questions and not waiting

for answers, describing and qualifying things, expressing feelings, by the aid of phrases that he had never
heard before but which seemed to him illuminating
and happy — as when for instance she asked what
art was, after all, but a synthesis made in the interest
of pleasure, or said that she did n't like England in
the least, but absurdly loved it. It did n't occur to
him to think these discriminations pedantic. Suddenly she threw off "Madame Grandoni told me you
saw my husband."

"Ah, was the gentleman your husband?"

"Unfortunately! What do you think of him?"

"Oh, I can't think—!" Hyacinth decently pleaded.

"I wish I could n't either! I have n't seen him for
nearly three years. He wanted to see me to-day, but
I refused."

"Ah!" — and the young man stared, not knowing
how he ought to receive so unexpected a confidence.
Then as the suggestions of inexperience are sometimes the happiest of all he spoke simply what was in
his mind and said gently: "It has made you — naturally — nervous." Later on, when he had left the
house, he wondered how at that stage he could have
ventured on such a familiar remark.

But she had taken it with a quick, surprised laugh.
"How do you know that?" Before he had time to
tell she added: "Your saying that — that way —
shows me how right I was to ask you to come to see
me. You know I hesitated. It shows me you 've
perceptions; I guessed as much the other night at the
theatre. If I had n't I would n't have asked you.
I may be wrong, but I like people who understand

what one says to them, and also what one does n't say."

"Don't think I understand too much. You might easily exaggerate that," Hyacinth declared conscientiously.

"You confirm completely my first impression," the Princess returned, smiling in a way that showed him he really amused her. "We shall discover the limits of your comprehension! I *am* atrociously nervous. But it will pass. How's your cousin the dressmaker?" she enquired abruptly. And when Hyacinth had briefly given some account of poor Pinnie — *described her as tolerably well for her*, but old and tired and sad and not very successful — she exclaimed impatiently "Ah, well, she's not the only one!" and came back with irrelevance to the former question. "It's not only my husband's visit — absolutely unexpected! — that has made me fidgety, but the idea that now you've been so kind as to come here you may wonder why, after all, I made such a point of it, and even think any explanation I might be able to give you entirely insufficient."

"I don't want any explanation," said Hyacinth with a sense of great presence of mind.

"It's charming of you to say that, and I shall take you at your word. Explanations usually make things worse. All the same I don't want you to think (as you might have done so easily the other evening) that I wish only to treat you as a curious animal."

"I don't care how you treat me!" he smiled.

There was a considerable silence, after which she pursued: "All I ask of my husband is to let

288

me alone. But he won't. He won't return my indifference."

Hyacinth wondered what reply he ought to make
to such an announcement as that, and it seemed to
him the least civility demanded was that he should
say — as he could with such conviction — "It can't
be easy to be indifferent to you."

"Why not if I'm odious? I *can* be — oh there's
no doubt of that! However, I can honestly say that
with the Prince I've been exceedingly reasonable and
that most of the wrongs — the big ones, those that
settled the question — have been on his side. You
may tell me of course that that's the pretension of
every woman who has made a mess of her marriage.
But ask Madame Grandoni."

"She'll tell me it's none of my business."

"Very true — she might!" the Princess inconsequently laughed. "And I don't know either why I
should bore you with my domestic affairs; except
that I've been wondering what I could do to show
you confidence in return for your showing so much
in me. As this matter of my separation from my husband happens to have been turned uppermost by his
sudden descent on me I just mention it, though the
subject's tiresome enough. Moreover I ought to let
you know that I've very little respect for distinctions
of class — the sort of thing they make so much of in
this country. They're doubtless convenient in some
ways, but when one has a reason — a reason of feeling — for overstepping them, and one allows one's
self to be deterred by some dreary superstition about
one's place or some one else's place, then I think it's

ignoble. It always belongs to one's place not to be a poor creature. I take it that if you're a socialist you think about this as I do; but lest by chance, as the sense of those differences is the English religion, it may have rubbed off even on you (though I'm more and more impressed with the fact that you're scarcely more British than I am): lest you should in spite of your theoretic democracy be shocked at some of the applications that I, who cherish the creed, am capable of making of it, let me assure you without delay that in that case we should n't get on together at all and had better part company before we go further." She paused long enough for Hyacinth to declare with a great deal of emphasis that he was n't easily shocked; and then restlessly, eagerly, as if it relieved her to talk and made their queer conjunction less abnormal that she should talk most, she arrived at the point that she wanted to know the *people*, and know them intimately — the toilers and strugglers and sufferers — because she was convinced they were the most interesting portion of society, and at the question "What could really be in worse taste than for me to carry into such an undertaking a pretension of greater delicacy and finer manners? If I must do that," she continued, "it's simpler to leave them alone. But I can't leave them alone; they press on me, they haunt me, they fascinate me. There it is — after all it's very simple: I want to know them and I want you to help me."

"I'll help you with pleasure to the best of my humble ability. But you'll be awfully disappointed," Hyacinth said. Very strange it seemed to him that within so few days two ladies of rank should have found occasion to express to him the same mysterious longing. A breeze from a thoroughly unexpected quarter was indeed blowing through the aristocracy. Nevertheless, though there was much of the same accent of passion in the Princess Casamassima's communication that there had been in Lady Aurora's, and though he felt bound to discourage his present interlocutress as he had done the other, the force that drove her struck him as a very different mixture from the shy, conscientious, anxious heresies of Rose Muniment's friend. The temper varied in the two women as much as the aspect and the address, and that perhaps made their curiosity the more significant.

"I have n't the least doubt of it," this investigator answered; "there's nothing in life in which I've not been awfully disappointed. But disappointment for disappointment I shall like it better than some others. You'll not persuade me either that among the people I speak of characters and passions and motives are not more natural, more complete, more *naïfs*. The upper classes are so deadly *banals*. My husband traces his descent from the fifth century, and he's the greatest bore in Europe. That's the kind of people I was condemned to by my marriage. Oh, if you knew what I've been through you'd allow that intelligent mechanics (of course I don't want to know idiots) would be a pleasant change. I must begin with some one — nust n't I? — so I began the other night with you!" As soon as she had uttered these words the Princess added a correction with the consciousness of her mistake in her face. It made that face, to Hyacinth, more nobly, tenderly beautiful. "The only objection to you individually is that you've nothing of the people about you — to-day not even the dress." Her eyes wandered over him from head to foot, and their recognitions made him ashamed. "I wish you had come in the clothes you wear at your work."

"You see you do regard me as a curious animal," he returned.

It was perhaps to contradict this that, after a moment, she began to tell him more about her domestic affairs. He ought to know who she was, unless Captain Sholto had told him; and she mentioned her parentage — American on the mother's side, Italian on the father's — and how she had led from her youngest years a wandering Bohemian life in a thousand different places (always in Europe, she had never been in America and knew very little about it, though she wanted greatly to cross the Atlantic) and largely at one period in Rome. She had been married by her people, in a mercenary way, for the sake of a fortune and a great name, and it had turned out as badly as her worst enemy could have wished. Her parents were dead, luckily for them, and she had no one near her of her own except Madame Grandoni, who belonged to her only in the sense that she had known her as a girl; was an association of her — what should she call them? — her uneasy but innocent years. Not that she had ever been very innocent; she had had a horrible education. However, she had known a few good people — people she respected then; but Madame Grandoni was the only one who had stuck to her. She too was liable to leave her any day; the Princess appeared to intimate that her destiny might require her to take some step which would test severely the old woman's attachment. It would detain her too long to make him understand the stages by which she had arrived at her present state of mind: her disgust with a thousand social arrangements, her rebellion against the selfishness, the corruption, the iniquity, the cruelty, the imbecility of the people who all over Europe had the upper hand. If he could have seen her life, the *milieu* in which she had for several years been condemned to move, the evolution of her opinions (Hyacinth was delighted to hear her use that term) would strike him as perfectly logical. She had been humiliated, outraged, tortured; she considered that she too was one of the numerous class who could be put on a tolerable footing only by a revolution. At any rate she had some self-respect left, and there was still more that she wanted to recover; the only way to arrive at which was to throw herself into some effort that would make her forget her own affairs and comprehend the troubles and efforts of others. Hyacinth listened to her with a wonderment which, as she went on, was transformed into willing submission; she seemed so natural, so vivid, so exquisitely generous and sincere. By the time he had been with her half an hour she had made the situation itself easy and usual, and a third person who should have joined them at this moment would have noticed nothing to suggest that friendly social intercourse between little bookbinders and Neapolitan princesses was not in London a matter of daily occurrence.

Hyacinth had seen plenty of women who chattered about themselves and their affairs — a vulgar garrulity of confidence was indeed a leading characteristic of the sex as he had hitherto learned to know it — but he was quick to perceive that the great lady who now took the trouble to open herself to him was not of a gossiping habit; that she must be on the contrary, as a general thing, proudly, ironically reserved, even to the point of passing with many people for a model of the unsatisfactory. It was very possible she was capricious; yet the fact that her present sympathies and curiosities might be a caprice wore in her visitor's eyes no sinister aspect. Why was it not a noble and interesting whim, and why might n't he stand for the hour at any rate in the silvery moonshine it cast on his path ? It must be added that he was far from taking in everything she said, some of her allusions and implications being so difficult to seize that they mainly served to reveal to him the limits of his own acquaintance with life. Her words evoked all sorts of shadowy suggestions of things he was condemned not to know, touching him most when he had not the key to them. This was especially the case with her reference to her career in Italy, on her husband's estates, and her relations with his family, who considered that they had done her a great honour in receiving her into their august circle (putting the best face on a bad business) after they had moved heaven and earth to keep her out of it. The position made for her among such people and what she had had to suffer from their family tone, their opinions and customs (though what these might be remained vague to her listener) had evidently planted in her soul a lasting resentment and contempt; and Hyacinth gathered that the force of reaction and revenge might carry her far, make her modern and democratic and heretical *à outrance* — lead her to swear by Darwin and Spencer and all the scientific iconoclasts as well as by the revolutionary spirit. He surely need n't have been so sensible of the weak spots in his comprehension of the Princess when he could already surmise that personal passion had counted for so much in the formation of her views. This induction, however, which had no harshness, did n't make her affect him any the less as a creature compounded of the finest elements; brilliant, delicate, complicated, but complicated with something divine.

It was not till after he had left her that he became conscious she had forced him to talk in spite of talking so much herself. He drew a long breath as he reflected that he had n't made quite such an ass of himself as might very well have happened; he had been saved by the thrill of his interest and admiration, which had not gone to his head and prompted him to show that he too in his improbable little way was remarkable, but had kept him in a state of anxious, conscious tension, as if the occasion had been a great appointed solemnity, some initiation more formal than any he believed practised even in the grimmest subterranean circles. He had said indeed much more than he had warrant for when she questioned him on his "radical" affiliations; he had spoken as if the movement were vast and mature, whereas in fact, so far at least as he was as yet concerned with it and could answer for it from personal knowledge, it was circumscribed by the hideously-papered walls of the little club-room at the "Sun and Moon." He reproached himself with this laxity, but it had not been engendered by pride. He was only afraid of disappointing his hostess too much, of making her say "Why in the world then did you come to see me if you've nothing more remarkable to put before me?" — a question to which of course he would have had an answer ready but for its being so impossible to say he had never asked to come and that his coming was her own affair. He wanted too much to come a second time to have the courage to make that speech. Nevertheless when she exclaimed, changing the subject abruptly, as she always did, from something else they had been talking about, "I wonder if I shall ever see you again!" he replied with perfect sincerity that it was scarce possible for him to believe anything so delightful could be repeated. There were some kinds of happiness that to many people never came at all, and to others could come only once. He added: "It's very true I had just that feeling after I left you the other night at the theatre. And yet here I am!"

"Yes, there you are," said the Princess thoughtfully — as if this might be a still graver and more embarrassing fact than she had yet supposed it. "I take it there's nothing essentially inconceivable in my seeing you again; but it may very well be that you'll never again find it so pleasant. Perhaps that's the happiness that comes but once. At any rate, you know, I'm going away."

"Oh yes, of course; every one leaves town —!" Hyacinth rose to that occasion.

"Do *you*, Mr. Robinson?" the Princess asked.

"Well, I don't as a general thing. Nevertheless it's possible that this year I may get three or four days at the seaside. I should like to take my old lady. I've done it before."

"And except for that shall you be always at work?"

"Yes; but you must understand that I love my work. You must understand that it's a great blessing for a young fellow like me to have it."

"And if you did n't have it what would you do? Should you starve?"

"Oh, I don't think I should starve," our friend replied judicially.

She looked a little chagrined, but after a moment pursued: "I wonder whether you'd come to see me in the country somewhere."

"Oh cracky!" Hyacinth exclaimed, catching his breath. "You're so kind I don't know what to do."

"Don't be *banal*, please. That's what other people are. What's the use of my looking for something fresh in other walks of life if you're going to be *banal* too? I ask if you'd come."

He could n't have said at this moment whether he were plunging or soaring. "Yes, I think I'd come. I don't know at all how I should do it — there

297

would be several obstacles; but wherever you should call for me I'd come."

"You mean you can't leave your work like that? You might lose it if you did, and then be in want of money and much embarrassed?"

"Yes, there would be little difficulties of that kind. You see that immediately, in practice, great obstacles and complications come up when it's a question of a person like you making friends with a person like me."

"That's the way I like you to talk," said the Princess with a pitying gentleness that struck her visitor as quite sacred. "After all I don't know where I shall be. I've got to pay stupid visits myself, visits where the only comfort will be that I shall make the people jump. Every one here thinks me exceedingly odd — as there's no doubt I am! I might be ever so much more so if you'd only help me a little. Why shouldn't I have my bookbinder after all? In attendance, you know — it would be awfully *chic*. We might have immense fun, don't you think so? No doubt it will come. At any rate I shall return to London when I've got through that *corvée;* I shall be here next year. In the mean time don't forget me," she went on as she rose to her feet. "Remember on the contrary that I expect you to take me into the slums — into very bad places." Why the idea of these scenes of misery should have lighted up her face is more than may be explained; but she smiled down at Hyacinth — who even as he stood up was of slightly smaller stature — with all her strange high radiance. Then in a manner almost equally quaint she added a reference to what she had said a moment before. "I recognise perfectly the obstacles in practice as you call them; but though I'm not by nature persevering, and am really very easily put off, I don't consider they'll prove insurmountable. They exist on my side as well, and if you'll help me to overcome mine I'll do the same for you with yours."

These words, repeating themselves again and again in his consciousness, appeared to give him wings, to help him to float and soar as he turned that afternoon out of South Street. He had at home a copy of Tennyson's poems — a single comprehensive volume, with a double column on the page, in a tolerably neat condition despite much handling. He took it to pieces that same evening, and during the following week, in his hours of leisure, at home in his little room, with the tools he kept there for private use and a morsel of delicate, blue-tinted Russia leather of which he obtained possession at old Crook's, he devoted himself to the task of binding the book as perfectly as he knew how. He worked with passion, with religion, and produced a masterpiece of firmness and finish, of which his own appreciation was as high as that of M. Poupin when at the end of the week he exhibited to him the fruit of his toil, and much more freely expressed than that of old Crook himself, who grunted approbation but was always too long-headed to create precedents. Hyacinth carried the volume to South Street as an offering to the Princess, hoping she would not yet have left London; in which case he would ask the servant to deliver it to her along with a little note he had sat up all night to compose. But the majestic major-domo in charge of the house, opening the door yet looking down at him as if from a second-story window, took the life out of his vision and erected instead of it, by a touch, a high blank wall. The Princess had been absent for some days; her representative was so good as to inform the young man with the parcel that she was on a visit to a " Juke" in a distant part of the country. He offered however to receive and even to forward anything Hyacinth might wish to leave; but our hero felt a sudden indisposition to launch his humble tribute into the vast, the possibly cold unknown of a "jucal" circle. He decided to retain his little package for the present; he would offer it to her when he should see her again, and he retreated without giving it up. Later on it seemed to create a manner of material link between the Princess and himself, and at the end of three months it had almost come to appear not that the exquisite book was an intended present from his own hand, but that it had been placed in that hand by the most remarkable woman in Europe. Rare sensations and impressions, moments of acute happiness, almost always, with our young man, in retrospect, became rather mythic and legendary; and the superior piece of work he had done after seeing her last, in the immediate heat of his emotion, turned to a virtual proof and gage — as if a ghost in vanishing from sight had left a palpable relic.

XVIII

THE matter touched him but indirectly, yet it may
concern the reader more closely to know that before
the visit to the Duke took place Madame Grandoni
granted to Prince Casamassima the private interview
she had promised him on that sad Sunday afternoon.
She crept out of South Street after breakfast — a repast which under the Princess's roof was served in the
foreign fashion at twelve o'clock — crossed the sultry
solitude into which at such a season that precinct
resolves itself, and entered the Park, where the grass
was already brown and a warm, smoky haze pre-
vailed, a tepid and tasteless *réchauffé*, as it struck our
old friend, of the typical London fog. The Prince
met her by appointment at the gate and they went
and sat down together under the trees beside the
drive, amid a wilderness of empty chairs and with
nothing to distract their attention from an equestrian
or two left over from the cavalcades of a fortnight
before and whose vain agitation in the saddle the
desolate scene threw into high relief. They remained
there nearly an hour, though Madame Grandoni, in
spite of her leaning to friendly interpretations,
could n't have told herself what comfort it was to her
afflicted companion. She had nothing to say to him
that could better his case as he bent his mournful
gaze on a prospect not after all perceptibly improved
by its not being Sunday, and could only feel that with

301

her he must seem to himself to be nearer his wife —
to be touching something she had touched. She
wished he would resign himself more, but she was
willing to minister to that thin illusion, little as she
approved of the manner in which he had conducted
himself at the time of the last sharp crisis in the remarkable history of his relations with Christina. He
had conducted himself after the fashion of a spoiled
child, a child with a bad little nature, in a rage; he
had been fatally wanting in dignity and wisdom and
had given the Princess an advantage which she took
on the spot and would keep for ever. He had acted
without manly judgement, had put his uncles upon
her (as if she cared for his uncles, powerful prelate
as one of them might be!), had been suspicious and
jealous on exactly the wrong occasions — occasions
as to which her resentment of it had been just
and in particular had been showy. He had not been
clever enough or strong enough to make good his
valid rights, and had transferred the whole quarrel
to ground where his wife was far too accomplished
a combatant not to obtain the appearance of victory.

There was another reflexion for Madame Grandoni to make as her interview with her dejected
friend prolonged itself. She could make it the more
freely as, besides being naturally quick and appreciative, she had always, during her Roman career, in the
dear old days (mixed with bitterness as they had been
for her) lived with artists, archæologists, ingenious
strangers, people who abounded in good talk, threw
out ideas and played with them. It came over her

that really, even if things had not reached that particular crisis, Christina's active, various, ironical mind, with all its audacities and impatiences, could not have tolerated long the simple deadly dulness of the Prince's company. The old lady had begun on meeting him: "Of course what you want to know at once is whether she has sent you a message. No, my poor friend, I must tell you the truth. I asked her for one, but she assures me she has nothing whatever, of any kind, to say to you. She knew I was coming out to see you — I have n't done so *en cachette*. She does n't like it, but she accepts the necessity for this once, since you've made the mistake, as she considers it, of approaching her again. We talked of you last night after your note came to me — for five minutes; that is I talked in my independent way and Christina was good enough to listen. At the end she spoke briefly, with perfect calmness and the appearance of being the most reasonable woman in the world. She did n't ask me to repeat it to you, but I do so because it's the only substitute I can offer you for a message. 'I try to occupy my life, my mind, to create interests, in the odious position in which I find myself; I endeavour to get out of myself, my small personal disappointments and troubles, by the aid of such poor faculties as I possess. There are things in the world more interesting after all, and I hope to succeed in giving my attention to them. It appears to me not too much to ask that the Prince on his side should make the same conscientious effort — and leave me contentedly alone!' Those were your wife's remarkable words; they're all I have to give you."

After she had given them Madame Grandoni felt a pang of regret; the Prince turned upon her a face so white, bewildered and wounded. It had seemed to her they might form a wholesome admonition, but she now saw that, as coming from his wife, they were cruel, and she herself felt almost cruel for having repeated them. What they amounted to was an exquisite taunt of his mediocrity — a mediocrity after all neither a crime nor a design nor a preference. How could the Prince occupy himself, what interests could he create and what faculties, gracious heaven, did he possess? He was as ignorant as one of the dingy London sheep browsing before them, and as contracted as his hat-band. His expression became pitiful; it was as if he dimly measured the insult, felt it more than saw it — felt he could n't plead incapacity without putting his wife largely in the right. He gazed at Madame Grandoni, his face worked, and for a moment she thought he was going to cry right out. But he said nothing — perhaps because he was afraid of that — so that suffering silence, during which she gently laid her hand on his own, remained his sole answer. He might doubtless do so much he did n't that when Christina touched on this she was unanswerable. The old lady changed the subject: told him what a curious country England was in so many ways; offered information as to their possible movements during the summer and autumn, which within a day or two had taken more form. But at last, as if he had not heard her, he broke out on the identity of the young man who had come in the day he called, just as he was going.

Madame Grandoni risked the truth. "He was the Princess's bookbinder."

"Her bookbinder? Do you mean one of her lovers?"

"Prince, how can you dream she'll ever live with you again?" the old lady asked in reply to this.

"Why then does she have him in her drawing-room — announced like an ambassador, carrying a hat in his hand like mine? Where were his books, his bindings? I should n't say this to *her*," he added as if the declaration justified him.

"I told you the other day that she's making studies of the people — the lower orders. The young man you saw is a study." She could n't help laughing out as she gave her explanation this turn; but her mirth elicited no echo.

"I've thought that over — over and over; but the more I think the less I understand. Would it be your idea that she's quite crazy? I must tell you I don't care if she is!"

"We're all quite crazy, I think," said Madame Grandoni; "but the Princess no more than the rest of us. No, she must try everything; at present she's trying democracy, she's going all lengths in radicalism."

"*Santo Dio!*" murmured the young man. "And what do they say here when they see the bookbinder?"

"They have n't seen him and perhaps they won't. But if they do it won't matter, because here everything's forgiven. That a person should be extraordinary in some way of his own — and a woman as

305

much as a man — is all they want. A bookbinder will do as well as anything else."

The Prince mused a while. "How can she bear the dirt, the bad smell?"

"I don't know what you're talking about. If you mean the young man you saw at the house — I may tell you, by the way, that it was only the first time he had been there and that the Princess had only seen him once — if you mean the little bookbinder he is n't dirty, especially what *we* should call. The people of that kind here are not like our dear Romans. Every one has a sponge as big as your head; you can see them in the shops."

"They're full of gin; their faces are awful, are purple," said the Prince; after which he immediately asked: "If she had only seen him once how could he have come into her drawing-room that way?"

His friend looked at him a little sternly. "Believe at least what *I* say, my poor friend! Never forget that this was how you spoiled your affairs most of all — by treating a person (and such a person!) as if, as a matter of course, she lied. Christina has many faults, but she has n't that one; that's why I can live with her. She'll speak the truth always."

It was plainly not agreeable to the Prince to be reminded so sharply of his greatest mistake, and he flushed a little as Madame Grandoni spoke. But he did n't admit his error and she doubted if he even saw it. At any rate he remarked rather grandly, like a man who has still a good deal to say for himself: "There are things it's better to conceal."

"It all depends on whether you're afraid. Christina never is. Oh, I grant you she's very perverse, and when the entertainment of watching her, to see how she'll carry out some of her inspirations, is not stronger than anything else I lose all patience with her. When she does n't charm she can only exasperate. But, as regards yourself, since you're here and I may n't see you again for a long time or perhaps ever (at my age — I'm a hundred and twenty!) I may as well give you the key of certain parts of your wife's conduct. It may make her seem to you a little less fantastic. At the bottom then of much that she does is the fact that she's ashamed of having married you."

"Less fantastic?" the young man repeated, staring.

"You may say that there can be nothing more extravagant — as even more insane — than that. But you know — or if not it is n't for want of her having told you — how the Princess considers that in the darkest hour of her life she sold herself for a title and a fortune. She regards her doing so as such a horrible piece of frivolity that she can't for the rest of her days be serious enough to make up for it."

"Yes, I know she pretends to have been forced. And does she think she's so serious now?"

"The young man you saw the other day thinks so," the old woman smiled. "Sometimes she calls it by another name: she says she has thrown herself with passion into being 'modern.' That sums up the greatest number of things that you and your family are not."

"Yes, we're not anything of that low sort, thank God! *Dio mio, Dio mio!*" groaned the Prince. He

307

seemed so exhausted by his reflexions that he remained sitting in his chair after his companion, lifting her crumpled corpulence out of her own, had proposed that they should walk about a little. She had no ill-nature, but she had already noticed that whenever she was with Christina's husband the current of conversation made her, as she phrased it, bump against him. After administering these small shocks she always steered away, and now, the Prince having at last got up and offered her his arm, she tried again to talk with him of things he could consider without bitterness. She asked him about the health and habits of his uncles, and he replied for the moment with the minuteness he had been taught that in such a case courtesy demanded; but by the time that at her request they had returned to the gate nearest South Street (she wished him to come no further) he had prepared a question to which she had not opened the way. "And who and what then is this English captain? About him there's a great deal said."

"This English captain?"

"Godfrey Gerald Cholto — you see I know a good deal about him," said the Prince, articulating the English names with difficulty.

They had stopped near the gate, on the edge of Park Lane, and a couple of predatory hansoms dashed at them from opposite quarters. "I thought that was coming, and at bottom it's he who has occupied you most!" Madame Grandoni exclaimed with a sigh. "But in reality he's the last one you need trouble about. He doesn't count the least little bit."

"Why does n't he count?"

"I can't tell you — except that some people don't, you know. He does n't even think he does."

"Why not, when she receives him always — lets him go wherever she goes?"

"Perhaps that's just the reason. When people give her a chance to get tired of them she takes it rather easily. At any rate you need n't be any more jealous of him than you are of me. He's a convenience, a *factotum*, but he works without wages."

"Is n't he then in love with her?"

"Naturally. He has however no hope."

"Ah, poor gentleman!" said the Prince lugubriously.

"He accepts the situation better than you. He occupies himself — as she has strongly recommended him in my hearing to do — with other women!"

"Oh the brute!" the Prince exclaimed. "At all events he sees her."

"Yes, but she does n't see *him!*" laughed Madame Grandoni as she turned away.

XIX

THE pink dressing-gown that Pinnie had engaged to make for Rose Muniment became in Lomax Place a conspicuous object, supplying poor Amanda with a constant theme for reference to one of the great occasions of her life — her visit to Belgrave Square with Lady Aurora after their meeting at Rosy's bedside. She detailed this episode minutely to her companion, repeating a thousand times that her ladyship's affability was beyond anything she could have expected. The grandeur of the house in Belgrave Square figured in her recital as something oppressive and fabulous, tempered though it had been by shrouds of brown holland and the nudity of staircases and saloons of which the trappings had been put away. "If it's so noble when they're out of town what can it be when they're all there together and everything's out?" she enquired suggestively; and she permitted herself to be restrictive only on two points, one of which was the state of Lady Aurora's gloves and bonnet-strings. If she had n't been afraid to appear to notice the disrepair of these objects she should have been so happy to offer to do any little mending. "If she'd only come to me every week or two I'd keep up her rank for her," said Pinnie, who had visions of a needle that positively flashed in the disinterested service of the aristocracy. She added that her ladyship got all dragged out with her long expeditions to Camber-

well; she might be in tatters for all they could do to
help her, at the top of those dreadful stairs, with that
strange sick creature (she was too unnatural) thinking only of her own finery and talking about her complexion. If she wanted pink she should have pink;
but to Pinnie there was something almost unholy in
it, like decking out a corpse or dressing up the cat.
This was the second perversity that left Miss Pynsent cold; it could n't be other than difficult for her
to enter into the importance her ladyship appeared
to attach to those pushing people. The girl was
unfortunate certainly, stuck up there like a puppy on
a shelf, but in her ladyship's place she would have
found some topic more in keeping while they walked
about under those tremendous gilded ceilings. Lady
Aurora, seeing how she was struck, showed her all
over the house, carrying the lamp herself and telling
an old woman who was there — a "confidential"
housekeeper, a person with ribbons in her cap who
would have pushed Pinnie out if you could push with
your eyes — that they would do very well without
her. If the pink dressing-gown, in its successive
stages of development, filled up the little brown parlour (it was terribly long on the stocks) making such
a pervasive rose-coloured presence as had not been
seen there for many a day, this was evidently because
it was associated with Lady Aurora, not because it
was dedicated to her humble friend.

One day when Hyacinth came home Pinnie at once
announced to him that her ladyship had been there to
look at it—to pass judgement before the last touches
were conferred. The dressmaker intimated that in

such a case as that her judgement was rather wild and she seemed to have embarrassing ideas about pockets. Whatever could poor Miss Muniment want of pockets and what had she to put in them? But Lady Aurora had evidently found the garment far beyond anything she expected, and she had been more affable than ever and had wanted to know about every one in the "Plice": not in a meddling, prying way, either, like some of those condescending swells, but quite as if the poor people were the high ones and she was afraid her curiosity might be "presumptious." It was in the same discreet spirit that she had invited Amanda to relate her whole history and had expressed an interest in the career of her young friend.

"She said you had charming manners," Miss Pynsent hastened to remark; "but on my life, Hyacinth Robinson, I never mentioned a scrap that it could give you pain that any one should talk about." There was an heroic explicitness in this, on Pinnie's part, for she knew in advance just how Hyacinth would look at her — fixedly, silently, hopelessly, as if she were still capable of tattling horribly (with the idea that her revelations would increase her importance) and putting forward this hollow theory of her supreme discretion to cover it up. His eyes seemed to say it all: "How can I believe you, and yet how can I prove you're lying? I'm very helpless, for I can't prove that without applying to the person to whom your incorrigible folly has probably led you to brag, to throw out mysterious and tantalising hints. You know of course that I'd never condescend to that." Pinnie suffered acutely from this imputation, yet exposed herself to it often, because she could never deny herself the pleasure, keener still than her pain, of letting Hyacinth know he was appreciated, admired and, for those "charming manners" commended by Lady Aurora, even all but wondered at in so many words; and this kind of interest always appeared to imply a suspicion of his secret — something which, when he expressed to himself the sense of it, he called, resenting it at once and finding a certain softness in it, "a beastly *attendrissement.*" When Pinnie went on to say to him that Lady Aurora appeared to feel a certain surprise at his never yet having come to Belgrave Square for the famous books he reflected that he must really wait upon her without more delay if he wished to keep up his reputation as a man of the world; and meanwhile he considered much the extreme oddity of this new phase of his life which had opened so suddenly from one day to the other: a phase in which his society should have become indispensable to ladies of high rank and the obscurity of his condition only an attraction the more. They were taking him up then one after the other and were even taking up poor Pinnie as a means of getting at him; so that he wondered with gaiety and irony if it meant that his destiny was really seeking him out — that the aristocracy, recognising a mysterious affinity (with that fineness of *flair* for which they were remarkable) were coming to him to save him the trouble of coming to them.

It was late in the day (the beginning of an October evening) and Lady Aurora was at home. Hyacinth had made a mental calculation of the time at which she would have risen from dinner; the operation of "rising from dinner" having always been, in his imagination, for some reason or other, highly characteristic of the nobility. He was ignorant of the fact that Lady Aurora's principal meal consisted of a scrap of fish and a cup of tea served on a little stand in the dismantled breakfast-parlour. The door was opened for Hyacinth by the invidious old lady whom Pinnie had described and who listened to his appeal, conducted him through the house and ushered him into her ladyship's presence without the smallest relaxation of a pair of tightly-closed lips. His good hostess was seated in the little breakfast-parlour by the light of a couple of candles and apparently immersed in a collection of crumpled papers and account-books. She was ciphering, consulting memoranda, taking notes; she had had her head in her hands and the silky entanglement of her hair resisted the rapid effort she made to smooth herself down as she saw the little bookbinder come in. The impression of her fingers remained in little rosy streaks on her pink skin. She exclaimed instantly "Oh, you've come about the books — it's so very kind of you"; and she hurried him off to another room, to which, as she explained, she had had them brought down for him to choose from. The effect of this precipitation was to make him suppose at first that she might wish him to execute his errand as quickly as possible and take himself off; but he presently noted that her nervousness and her shyness were of an order that would always give false ideas. She wanted him to stay, she wanted to talk with him and she had rushed with

314

him at the books in order to gain time and composure
for exercising some subtler art. Hyacinth, staying
half an hour, became more and more convinced that
her ladyship was, as he had ventured to pronounce
her on the occasion of their last meeting, a regular
saint. He was privately a little disappointed in the
books, though he selected three or four, as many as
he could carry, and promised to come back for others:
they denoted on Lady Aurora's part a limited acquaintance with French literature and even a certain
puerility of taste. There were several volumes of
Lamartine and a set of the spurious memoirs of the
Marquise de Créqui; but for the rest the little library
consisted mainly of Marmontel and Madame de Gen-
lis, Le Récit d'une Sœur and the tales of M. J. T. de
Saint-Germain. There were certain members of an
intensely modern school, advanced and consistent
realists of whom Hyacinth had heard and on whom
he had long desired to put his hand; but evidently
none of them had ever stumbled into Lady Aurora's
candid collection, though she did possess a couple of
Balzac's novels, which by ill luck happened to be
just those our young man had read more than once.

There was nevertheless something very agreeable
to him in the moments he passed in the big, dim,
cool, empty house, where, at intervals, monumental
pieces of furniture — not crowded and miscellaneous,
as he had seen the appurtenances of the Princess —
loomed and gleamed, and Lady Aurora's fantastic
intonations awakened echoes which gave him a sense
of privilege, of rioting, decently, in the absence of
prohibitory presences. She spoke again of the poor

315

people in the south of London and of the Muniments in particular; evidently the only fault she had to find with these latter was that they were not poor enough — not sufficiently exposed to dangers and privations against which she could step in. Hyacinth liked her for this, even though he wished she would talk of something else — he hardly knew what, unless it was that, like Rose Muniment, he wanted to hear more about Inglefield. He did n't mind, with the poor, going into questions of their state — it even gave him at times a strange savage satisfaction; but he saw that in discussing them with the rich the interest must inevitably be less: the rich could n't consider poverty in the light of experience. Their mistakes and illusions, their thinking they had got hold of the sensations of want and dirt when they had n't at all, would always be more or less irritating. It came over Hyacinth that if he found this deficient perspective in Lady Aurora's deep conscientiousness it would be a queer enough business when he should come to pretending to hold the candlestick for the Princess Casamassima.

His present hostess said no word to him about Pinnie, and he guessed she must have wished to place him on the footing on which people don't express approbation or surprise at the decency or good-breeding of each other's relatives. He saw how she would always treat him as a gentleman and that even if he should be basely ungrateful she would never call his attention to the fact that she had done so. He should n't have occasion to say to her, as he had said to the Princess, that she regarded him as a curious animal; and it gave him at once the sense of learning more about life, a sense always delightful to him, to perceive there were such different ways (which implied still a good many more) of being a lady of rank. The manner in which Lady Aurora appeared to wish to confer with him on the great problems of pauperism and reform might have implied he was a benevolent nobleman (of the type of Lord Shaftesbury) who had endowed many charities and was noted, in philanthropic schemes, for the breadth of his views. It was not less present to him that Pinnie might have tattled, put forward his claims to high consanguinity, than it had been when the dressmaker herself descanted on her ladyship's condescensions; but he remembered now that he too had only just escaped being asinine when, the other day, he flashed out an allusion to his accursed origin. At all events he was much touched by the delicacy with which the earl's daughter comported herself, simply assuming that he was "one of themselves"; and he reflected that if she did know his history (he was sure he might pass twenty years in her society without discovering if she did) this shade of courtesy, this natural tact, coexisting even with extreme awkwardness, illustrated that "best breeding" which he had seen alluded to in novels portraying the aristocracy. The only remark on Lady Aurora's part that savoured in the least of looking down at him from a height was when she said cheerfully and encouragingly: "I suppose one of these days you'll be setting up in business for yourself." This was not so cruelly patronising that he could n't reply with a smile equally free from any sort of impertinence: "Oh dear, no, I shall never do that. I should make a great mess of any attempt to carry on a business. I've no turn at all for that sort of thing."

Lady Aurora looked a little surprised. "Oh, I see; you don't like — you don't like —!" She hesitated: he saw she was going to say he did n't like the idea of going in to that extent for a trade; but he stopped her in time from imputing to him a sentiment so foolish and declared what he meant to be simply that his one faculty was the faculty of doing his little piece of work, whatever it was, of liking to do it skilfully and prettily, and of liking still better to get his money for it when done. His conception of "business" or of rising in the world did n't go beyond that. "Oh yes, I can fancy!" her ladyship exclaimed; but she looked at him a moment with eyes which showed that he puzzled her, that she did n't quite understand his tone. Before he left her she asked him abruptly (nothing had led up to it) what he thought of Captain Sholto, whom she had seen that other evening in Audley Court. Did n't he think him a very odd sort of person? Hyacinth confessed to this impression; whereupon Lady Aurora went on anxiously, eagerly: "Don't you consider him decidedly vulgar?"

"How can I know?"

"You can know perfectly — as well as any one!" Then she added: "I think it's a pity they should form relations with any one of that kind."

"They" of course meant Paul Muniment and his sister. "With a person who may be vulgar?" — Hyacinth regarded this solicitude as exquisite. "But

318

think of the people they know — think of those they're surrounded with — think of all Audley Court!"

"The poor, the unhappy, the labouring classes? Oh, I don't call *them* vulgar!" cried her ladyship with radiant eyes. The young man, lying awake a good deal that night, laughed to himself, on his pillow, not unkindly, at her fear that he and his friends would be contaminated by the familiar of a princess. He even wondered if she would n't find the Princess herself a bit vulgar.

XX

It must not be supposed that his relations with Millicent had remained unaffected by the remarkable incident that had brushed her with its wing at the theatre. The whole occurrence had made a great impression on the young lady from Pimlico; he never saw her, for weeks afterwards, that she had not an immense deal to say about it; and though it suited her to cultivate the shocked state at the crudity of such proceedings and to denounce the Princess for a bold-faced foreigner, of a kind to which any one who knew anything of what could go on in London would give a wide berth, it was easy to see she enjoyed having rubbed shoulders across the house with a person so splendid and having found her own critical estimate of her friend confirmed in such high quarters. She professed to draw her warrant for her low opinion of the lady in the box from information given her by Captain Sholto as he sat beside her — information of which at different moments she gave a different version; her notes of it having nothing in common save that they were alike unflattering to the Princess. Hyacinth had many doubts of the Captain's having talked indiscreetly; it would be in such a case such a very unnatural thing for him to do. He *was* unnatural — that was true — and he might have told Millicent, who was capable of having plied him with questions, that his distinguished friend was separated from her husband; but, for the rest, it was more probable that the girl had given the rein to a fine faculty of free invention of which he had had frequent glimpses, under pressure of her primitive half-childish, half-plebeian impulse of destruction, the instinct of pulling down what was above her, the reckless energy that would, precisely, make her so effective in revolutionary scenes. Hyacinth (it has been mentioned) did n't consider that Millicent was false, and it struck him as a proof of positive candour that she should make up absurd, abusive stories about a person as to whom she only knew that she disliked her and could hope for no esteem, and indeed for no recognition of any kind, in return. When people were fully false you did n't know where you stood with them, and on such a point as this Miss Henning could never be accused of leaving you in obscurity. She said little else about the Captain and did n't pretend to repeat the remainder of his conversation, taking on her air of grand indifference when Hyacinth amused himself with repaying her criticism of his new acquaintance by drawing a sufficiently derisive portrait of hers.

His line was that Sholto's admiration for the high-coloured beauty in the second balcony had been at the bottom of the whole episode: he had persuaded the Princess to pretend she was a revolutionist and should like therefore to confer with the little firebrand above in order that he might slip into the seat of this too easily deluded youth. At the same time it never occurred to our young man to conceal the fact that the lady in the box had followed him up; he contented himself with saying that this had been no part of the original plot, but a simple result — not unnatural after all — of his showing so much more charm than might have been expected. He described with sportive variations his visit in South Street, conscious that he would never feel the need, with his childhood's friend, of glossing over that sort of experience. She might make him a scene of jealousy and welcome — there were things that would have much more terror for him than that; her jealousy, with its violence, its energy, even a certain inconsequent, dare-devil humour that played through it, entertained him, emphasised the frankness, the passion and pluck he admired her for. He should never be on the footing of sparing Miss Henning's susceptibilities; how fond she might really be of him he could n't take upon himself to say, but her affection would never assume the form of that sort of delicacy, and their intercourse was plainly foredoomed to be an exchange of thumps and concussions, of sarcastic shouts and mutual *défis*. He liked her, at bottom, strangely, absurdly; but after all it was only well enough to torment her — she could bear so much — not well enough to spare her. Of any actual ground for the girl's jealousy of the Princess he never thought; it could n't occur to him to weigh against each other the sentiments he might excite in such opposed bosoms or those that the spectacle of either emotion might have kindled in his own. He had no doubt his share of fatuity, but he found himself unable to associate mentally a great lady and a bouncing shop-girl in a contest for a prize which should have anything of *his* figure. How could they show the least common mark — even so small a one as a desire to possess themselves of Hyacinth Robinson? A fact he did n't impart to Millicent and could have no wish to impart to her was the different matter of his pilgrimage to Belgrave Square. He might be in love with the Princess (how could he qualify as yet the bewildered emotion she had produced in him?) and he certainly never would conceive a passion for poor Lady Aurora; yet it would have given him pain much greater than any he felt in the other case to hear Milly make free with the ministering angel of Audley Court. The distinction was perhaps somehow in her appearing really not to touch or arrive at the Princess at all, whereas Lady Aurora was within her range and compass.

After paying him that visit at his rooms Hyacinth lost sight of Captain Sholto, who had not again reappeared at the "Sun and Moon," the little tavern which presented so common and casual a face to the world, but offered in its unsuspected rear a security still unimpugned to machinations going down to the very bottom of things. Nothing was more natural than that the Captain should be engaged at this season in the recreations of his class; and our young man took for granted that if he were not hanging about the Princess on that queer footing as to which one had a secret hope one should some day command more light, he was probably buffeting breezy northern seas on a yacht or creeping after stags in the Highlands; our hero's acquaintance with the light literature of his country being such as to assure him that in one or other of these occupations people of leisure, during the autumn, were necessarily immersed. If the Captain were giving his attention to neither he must have started for Albania, or at least for Paris. Happy Captain, Hyacinth mused, while his imagination followed him through vivid exotic episodes and his restless young feet continued to tread, through the stale flat weeks of September and October, the familiar pavements of Soho, Islington and Pentonville, and the shabby sinuous ways that unite these regions of labour. He had told the Princess he sometimes had a holiday at this period and that there was a chance of his escorting his respectable companion to the seaside; but as it turned out at present the spare cash for such an excursion was wanting. Hyacinth had indeed for the moment an exceptionally keen sense of the lack of this convenience and was forcibly reminded that the society of agreeable women was a direct and constant appeal to the pocket. He not only had n't a penny, but was much in debt, owed pence and shillings, as he would have largely put it, all over the place, and the explanation of his pinched feeling was in a vague half-remorseful, half-resigned reference to the numerous occasions when he had had not to fail of funds under penalty of disappointing a young lady whose needs were positive, and especially to a certain high crisis (as it might prove to be) in his destiny when it had come over him that one could n't call on a princess just as one was. So this year he did n't ask old Crook for the week which some of the other men took — Eustache Poupin, who had never quitted London since his arrival, launched himself precisely that summer, supported by his brave wife, into the

British unknown on the strength of a return ticket to Worthing—simply because he should n't know what to do with it. The best way not to spend money, though no doubt not the best in the world to make it, was still to take one's daily course to the old familiar shabby shop where, as the days shortened and November thickened the air to a livid yellow, the uncovered flame of the gas, burning often from the morning on, lighted up the ugliness in which the hand of practice endeavoured to disengage a little beauty — the ugliness of a dingy belittered interior, of battered dispapered walls, of work-tables stained and hacked, of windows opening into a foul drizzling street, of the bared arms, the sordid waistcoat-backs, the smeared aprons, the personal odour, the patient obstinate irritating shoulders and vulgar narrow inevitable faces of his fellow-labourers. Our young friend's relations with his comrades would form a chapter by itself, but all that may be said of the matter here is that the clever little operator from Lomax Place had in a manner a double identity and that much as he lived in Mr. Crookenden's establishment he lived out of it still more. In this busy, pasty, sticky, leathery little world, where wages and beer were the main objects of consideration, he played his part in a way that marked him as a queer lot, but capable of queerness in the line of equanimity too. He had n't made good his place there without discovering that the British workman, when animated by the spirit of mirth, has rather a heavy hand, and he tasted of the practical joke in every degree of violence. During his first year he dreamed, with secret

THE PRINCESS CASAMASSIMA

passion and suppressed tears, of a day of bliss when at last they would let him alone — a day which arrived in time, for it is always an advantage to be clever if one be only clever enough. Hyacinth was sufficiently so to have invented a *modus vivendi* in respect to which M. Poupin said to him *"Enfin vous voilà ferme!"* (the Frenchman himself, terribly *éprouvé* at the beginning, had always bristled with firmness and opposed to insular grossness a refined dignity) and under the influence of which the scenery of Soho figured a daily dusky exhibition of projected shadows, confined to the passive part of life and giving no hostages to reality, or at least to ambition, save an insufficient number of shillings on Saturday night and stray spasmodic reminiscences of delicate work that might have been more delicate still, as well as of such applications of the tool as he flattered himself unsurpassed unless by the supreme Eustache.

One evening in November he had after discharging himself of a considerable indebtedness to Pinnie still a sovereign in his pocket — a sovereign that seemed to spin there under the equal breath of a dozen different lively uses. He had come out for a walk with a vague intention of pushing as far as Audley Court; and lurking within this nebulous design, on which the damp breath of the streets, making objects seem that night particularly dim and places particularly far, had blown a certain chill, was a sense of how nice it would be to take something to Rose Muniment, who delighted in a sixpenny present and to whom he had n't for some time rendered any such homage. At last, after he had wandered a while, hesitating be-

tween the pilgrimage to Lambeth and the possibility
of still associating the two or three hours with those
perhaps in some lucky way or other at Millicent
Henning's disposal, he reflected that if a sovereign
was to be pulled to pieces it was a simplification to get
it changed. He had struck through the region of
Mayfair, partly with the preoccupation of a short cut
and partly from an instinct of self-defence; if one was
in danger of spending one's money with a rush it
was so much gained to plunge into a quarter where,
at that hour especially, there were no shops for little
bookbinders. Hyacinth's victory, however, was imperfect when it occurred to him to turn into a public-
house in order to convert his gold into convenient
silver. When it was a question of entering these
establishments he selected in preference the most
decent; he never knew what unpleasant people he
might find on the other side of the swinging door.
Those which glitter at intervals amid the residential
gloom of the large district abutting on Grosvenor
Square partake of the general gentility of the neighbourhood, so that our friend was not surprised (he
had passed into the compartment marked "private
bar") to see but a single drinker leaning against the
counter on which, with his request very civilly enun-
ciated, he put down his sovereign. He was surprised
on the other hand when, glancing up again, he became aware that this lonely reveller was Captain
Godfrey Sholto.

"Why, my dear boy, what a remarkable coincidence!" the Captain exclaimed. "For once in five
years that I come into a place like this!"

"I don't come in often myself. I thought you were in Madagascar," Hyacinth said.

"Ah, because I've not been at the 'Sun and Moon'? Well, I've been constantly out of town, you know. And then — don't you see what I mean? — I want to be tremendously careful. That's the way to get on, is n't it? But I dare say you don't believe in my discretion!" Sholto laughed. "What shall I do to make you understand? I say, have a brandy and soda," he continued as if this might assist Hyacinth's comprehension. He seemed a trifle flurried and, were it possible to imagine such a thing of so independent and whimsical a personage, the least bit abashed or uneasy at having been found in such a low place. Yet it was not any lower than the "Sun and Moon." He was dressed on this occasion according to his station, without the pot-hat and the shabby jacket, and Hyacinth looked at him with the pang of the felt charm that a good tailor would add to life. Our hero was struck more than ever before with his being the type of man whom, as he strolled about observing people, he had so often regarded with wonder and envy — the sort of man of whom one said to one's self that he was the "finest white," feeling that he and his like had the world in their pocket. Sholto requested the barmaid to please not dawdle in preparing the brandy and soda Hyacinth had thought to ease off the situation by accepting: this indeed was perhaps what the finest white would naturally do. And when the young man had taken the glass from the counter did n't he appear to encourage him not to linger as he drank it and to smile down at him very kindly and amusedly, as if the combination of so small a book-binder and so big a tumbler were sufficiently droll? The Captain took time however to ask how he had spent his autumn and what was the news in Bloomsbury; he further enquired about those jolly people across the river. "I can't tell you what an impression they made on me — that evening you know." After this he went on suddenly and irrelevantly: "And so you're just going to stay on for the winter quietly?" Our hero stared: he wondered what other high course could be imputed to him; he could n't reflect immediately that this was the sort of thing the finest whites said to each other when they met after their fashionable dispersals, and that his friend had only been guilty of a momentary inadvertence. In point of fact the Captain recovered himself. "Oh, of course you've got your work, and that sort of thing"; and, as Hyacinth did n't succeed in swallowing at a gulp the contents of his big tumbler he asked him presently if he had heard anything from the Princess. Our youth replied that he could have no news except what the Captain might be good enough to give him; but he added that he had been to see her just before she left town.

"Ah, you did go? That was quite right — jolly right."

"I went because she very kindly wrote me to come."

"Ah, she wrote to you to come?" The Captain fixed him a moment with his curious colourless eyes. "Do you know you're a devilish privileged mortal?"

"Certainly I know it." Hyacinth blushed and felt

foolish; the barmaid, who had heard this odd couple talking of a princess, was staring at him too with her elbows on the counter.

"Do you know there are people who'd give their heads that she should write them to come?"

"I've no doubt of it whatever!" — and he took refuge in a laugh that sounded less natural than he would have liked, and wondered if his interlocutor were n't precisely one of these people. In this case the barmaid might well stare; for deeply convinced as our young man might be that he was the son of Lord Frederick Purvis, there was really no end to the oddity of his being preferred — and by a princess — to Captain Sholto. If anything could have re-enforced at that moment his sense of this anomaly it would have been the indescribably gentlemanly way, implying all sorts of common initiations, in which his companion went on.

"Ah well, I see you know how to take it! And if you're in correspondence with her why do you say you can hear from her only through me? My dear fellow, I'm not in correspondence with her. You might think I'd naturally be, but I'm not." He subjoined as Hyacinth had laughed again in a manner that might have passed for ambiguous: "So much the worse for me — is that what you mean?" Hyacinth replied that he himself had had the honour of hearing from the Princess but once, and mentioned her having told him how her letter-writing came on only in fits, when it was sometimes very profuse: there were months together that she did n't touch a pen. "Oh, I can imagine what she told you!" the Captain knowingly returned. "Look out for the next fit! She's visiting about, you know — at a lot of great houses. It's a great thing to be somewhere with her — an immense comedy." He remarked that he had heard, now he remembered, that she either had taken or was thinking of taking a place in the country for a few months, and he added that if Hyacinth did n't propose to finish his brandy and soda they might as well turn out. Hyacinth's thirst had been very superficial, and as they turned out the Captain observed by way of explanation of his having been found in a public-house (it was the only attempt of this kind he made) that any friend of his would always know him by his love of rum out-of-the-way nooks. "You must have noticed that," he said — "my taste for exploration. If I had n't explored I never should have known you, should I? That was rather a nice little girl in there; did you twig her good bust? It's a pity they always have such beastly hands." Hyacinth had instinctively made a motion to go southward, but Sholto, passing a hand into his arm, led him the other way. The house they had quitted was near a corner, which they rounded, the Captain pushing forward as if there were some reason for haste. His haste was checked however by a prompt encounter with a young woman who, coming in the opposite direction, turned the angle as briskly as themselves. At this moment he gave his friend a great jerk, but not before Hyacinth had caught a glimpse of the young woman's face — it seemed to flash upon him out of the dusk — and given quick voice to his surprise.

"Hullo, Millicent!" This was the simple cry that

331

THE PRINCESS CASAMASSIMA

escaped from his lips while the Captain, still going on, but threw off "What's the matter? Who's your pretty friend?" Hyacinth declined to go on and repeated Miss Henning's baptismal name so loudly that the young woman, who had passed them without looking back, was obliged to stop. Then he saw he was not mistaken, though Millicent gave no audible response. She stood looking at him with her head very high, and he approached her, disengaging himself from Sholto, who however hung back only an instant before joining them. Hyacinth's heart had suddenly begun to beat very fast; there was a sharp shock in the girl's turning up just in that place at that moment. Yet when she began to laugh, and with violence, and to ask him why he should look at her as if she were a kicking horse, he recognised that there was nothing so very extraordinary, after all, in a casual meeting between persons who were such frequenters of the London streets. Millicent had never concealed the fact that she "trotted about" on various errands at night; and once when he had said to her that the less a respectable young woman took the evening air alone the better for her respectability she had asked how respectable he thought she pretended to be and had remarked that if he would make her a present of a brougham or even call for her three or four times a week in a cab she would doubtless preserve more of her social purity. She could turn the tables quickly enough and she exclaimed now, professing on her own side great astonishment:

"Whatever are you prowling about here for? You're after no good, I'll be bound!"

332

"Good evening, Miss Henning; what a jolly meeting!" said the Captain, removing his hat with a humorous flourish.

"Oh, how d'ye do?" Millicent returned as if not at once placing him.

"Where were you going so fast? What are you doing?" asked Hyacinth, who had looked from one to the other.

"Well, I never did see such a manner — from one that knocks about like *you!*" cried Miss Henning. "I'm going to see a friend of mine — a lady's-maid in Curzon Street. Have you anything to say to that?"

"Don't tell us — don't tell us!" Sholto interposed after she had spoken — and she had not, however slightly, hesitated. "I at least disavow the indiscretion. Where may not a charming woman be going when she trips with a light foot through the deepening dusk?"

"I say, what are you talking about?" the girl demanded with dignity of Hyacinth's companion. She spoke as if with a resentful suspicion that her foot had not really been felt to be light.

"On what errand of mercy, on what secret ministration?" the Captain laughed.

"Secret yourself!" cried Millicent. "Do you two always hunt in couples?"

"All right, we'll turn round and go with you as far as your friend's," Hyacinth said.

"All right," Millicent replied.

"All right," the Captain added; and the three took their way together in the direction of Curzon Street. They walked for a few moments in silence, though

333

the Captain whistled, and then Millicent suddenly turned to Hyacinth.

"You have n't told me where *you* were going yet, you know."

"We met in that public-house," the Captain said, "and were each so ashamed of being found in such a place by the other that we tumbled out together without much thinking what we should do with ourselves."

"When he's out with me he pretends he can't abide them houses," Miss Henning declared. "I wish I had looked in that one to see who was there."

"Well, she's rather nice," the Captain went on. "She told me her name was Georgiana."

"I went to get a piece of money changed," Hyacinth said with the sense of a certain dishonesty in the air and glad he at least could afford to speak the truth.

"To get your grandmother's nightcap changed! I recommend you to keep your money together — you 've none too much of it!" Millicent exclaimed.

"Is that the reason you 're playing me false?" Hyacinth flashed out. He had been thinking with still intentness as they walked; at once nursing and strangling a kindled suspicion. He was pale with the idea that he had been bamboozled, yet was able to say to himself that one must allow in life, thank goodness, for the element of coincidence, and that he might easily put himself immensely in the wrong by making a groundless charge. It was only later that he pieced his impressions together and saw them — as it appeared — justify each other; at present, as soon as he had uttered it, he was almost ashamed of his quick retort to Millicent's taunt. He ought at least to have waited to see what Curzon Street would bring forth.

The girl broke out on him immediately, repeating "False, false?" with high derision and wanting to know whether that was the way to knock a lady about in public. She had stopped short on the edge of a crossing and she went on with a voice so uplifted that he was glad they were in a street apt to be empty at such an hour: "You're a pretty one to talk about falsity when a woman has only to leer at you out of an opera-box!"

"Don't say anything about *her*," the young man interposed, trembling.

"And pray why not about 'her,' I should like to know? You don't pretend she's a decent woman, I suppose?" Millicent's laughter rang through the quiet neighbourhood.

"My dear fellow, you know you *have* been to her," Captain Sholto wonderfully smiled.

Hyacinth turned on him staring and at once provoked and baffled by his ambiguous part in an incident it was doubtless possible to magnify but not possible to treat as perfectly simple. "Certainly I've been to the Princess Casamassima, thanks to you. When you came and pressed me to go, when you dragged me, do you make it a reproach? Who the devil are you, anyway, and what do you want of me?" our hero cried — his mind flooded in a moment with everything in the Captain that had puzzled and worried and escaped him. This swelling tide obliterated on the spot everything that had beguiled.

335

"My dear fellow, whatever I am I'm not an ass," this gentleman replied with imperturbable good-humour. "I don't reproach you with anything. I only wanted to put in a word as a peacemaker. My good friends — my good friends," and he laid a hand in his practised way on Hyacinth's shoulder while with the other pressed to his heart he bent on the girl a face of gallantry which had something paternal in it: "I'm determined this absurd misunderstanding shall end as lovers' quarrels ought always to end."

Hyacinth withdrew himself from the Captain's touch and said to Millicent: "You're not really jealous of — of any one. You pretend that only to throw dust in my eyes."

To this sally Miss Henning returned him an answer which promised to be lively, but the Captain swept it away in the profusion of his protests. He declared them a dear delightful abominable pair; he pronounced it rarely interesting to see how in people of their sort the prime passions lay near the surface; he almost pushed them into each other's arms and then wound up with proposing that they should all terminate their little differences by proceeding together to the Pavilion music-hall, the nearest place of entertainment in that neighbourhood, leaving the lady's-maid in Curzon Street to dress her mistress's wig in peace. He has been presented to the reader as an accomplished man, and it will doubtless be felt that the picture is justified by his having eventually placed this idea in so attractive a light that his companions entered a hansom with him and rattled toward the haunt of pleasure, Hyacinth sandwiched, on the edge of the seat, between the others. Two or three times our young man's ears burned; he felt that if there was an understanding between them they had now, behind him, a rare opportunity for carrying it out. If this understanding flourished at his expense the whole evening constituted for them indeed an opportunity, and that thought rendered his diversion but scantly absorbing, though at the Pavilion the Captain engaged a big private box and ordered ices brought in. Hyacinth cared so little for his little pink pyramid that he suffered Millicent to consume it after she had disposed of her own. It was present to him, however, that if he should make a fool of himself the folly would be of a very gross kind, and this is why he withheld a question repeatedly on his lips — the impulse to demand of his entertainer why the mischief he had hurried him so out of the public-house if he had not been waiting there preconcertedly for Millicent. We know that in Hyacinth's eyes one of this young lady's compensatory merits had been that she was not deceitful, and he asked himself if a girl could change that way from one month to the other. This was optimistic, but, all the same, before leaving the Pavilion he decided with one of his highest flights of intelligence that he could quite well see what Lady Aurora had meant by calling Captain Sholto vulgar.

XXI

PAUL MUNIMENT had fits of silence while the others were talking; but on this occasion he had not opened his lips for half an hour. When he talked Hyacinth listened almost to the retention of breath, and when he said nothing watched him fixedly, listening to the others only through the medium of his candid countenance. At the "Sun and Moon" Muniment paid very little attention to his young friend, doing nothing that should cause it to be perceived they were particular pals; and Hyacinth even divined him at moments bored or irritated by the serious manner in which his small worrying bookbinder could n't conceal from the world that he regarded him. He wondered if this were a system, a calculated prudence, on Muniment's part, or only a manifestation of the superior brutality latent in his composition and which, without an intention of direct harshness, was naturally impatient of palaver. There was plenty of palaver at the "Sun and Moon"; there were nights when a blast of imbecility seemed to blow over the place and one felt ashamed to be associated with so much crude fatuity and flat-faced vanity. Then every one, with two or three exceptions, made an ass of himself, thumping the table and repeating over some inane phrase which appeared for the hour to constitute the whole furniture of his mind. There were men who kept saying "Them was my words in the month of

February last, and what I say I stick to — what I say I stick to;" and others who perpetually enquired of the company "And what the plague am I to do with seventeen bob — with seventeen bloody bob ? What am I to do with them — will ye tell me that ?" an interrogation which in truth usually ended by producing a ribald reply. There were still others who remarked to satiety that if it was not done to-day it would have to be done to-morrow, and several who constantly proclaimed their opinion that the only way was to pull up the Park rails again, just to haul 'em straight up. A little shoemaker with red eyes and a greyish face, whose appearance Hyacinth deplored, scarcely ever expressed himself but in the same form of words: "Well, are we in earnest or ain't we in earnest ? — that's the thing *I* want to know." He was terribly in earnest himself, but this was almost the only way he had of showing it; and he had much in common (though they were always squabbling) with a large red-faced man, of uncertain attributes and stertorous breathing, who was understood to know a good deal about dogs, had fat hands and wore on his forefinger a big silver ring containing some one's hair — Hyacinth believed it to be that of a terrier snappish in life. He had always the same refrain: "Well now are we just starving or ain't we just starving ? I should like the v'ice of the company on that question."

When the tone fell as low as this Paul Muniment held his peace save for whistling a little and leaning back with his hands in his pockets and his eyes on the table. Hyacinth often supposed him to be on the point of breaking out and letting the company know what he thought of them — he had a perfectly clear vision of what he must think: but Muniment never compromised his popularity to that degree; he judged it — this he once told his young comrade — too valuable a weapon, so that he cultivated the faculty of patience, which had the advantage of showing one more and more that one must do one's thinking for one's self. His popularity indeed struck Hyacinth as rather an uncertain amount, and the only mistake he had seen a symptom of on his friend's part was a tendency to overestimate it. Muniment thought many of their colleagues asinine, but it was Hyacinth's belief that he himself knew still better how asinine they were; and this inadequate conception supported in some degree on Paul's part his theory of his influence — an influence that would be stronger than any other on the day he should choose to exert it. Hyacinth only wished that day would come; it would n't be till then, he was sure, that they would all know where they were and that the good they were striving for, blindly, obstructedly, in a kind of eternal dirty intellectual fog, would pass from the stage of crude discussion and mere sore, sharp, tantalising desirableness into that of solid, seated reality. Muniment was listened to unanimously when he spoke and much talked about, usually with a knowing, implicit allusiveness, when he was absent; it was generally admitted he could see further than most. But it was suspected he wanted to see further than was necessary; as one of the most inveterate frequenters of the club remarked one evening, if a man could see as far as he could 'eave a brick this was far enough. There was an idea he had nothing particular to complain of personally, or perhaps that if he had he did n't complain of it — an attitude which could only contain the germs of a latent disaffection. Hyacinth was aware of being himself exposed to the same imputation; but he could n't help it — it would have been impossible to him to keep up his character for sincerity by revealing at the "Sun and Moon" the condition of his wardrobe or by announcing that he had n't had a penn'orth of bacon for six months. There were members of the club who were apparently always in the enjoyment of involuntary leisure — narrating the vainest peregrinations in search of a job, the cruellest rebuffs, the most vivid anecdotes of the insolence of office. They made Hyacinth uncomfortably conscious at times that if *he* should be out of work it would be wholly by his own fault; that he held in his hand a fine bread-winning tool on which he might absolutely count. He was also not unadvised however that his position in this little band of malcontents (it was small only if measured by the numbers gathered on any one occasion; he liked to think it large in its latent possibilities, its mysterious ramifications and affiliations) was peculiar and distinguished: it would be favourable if he should develop the kind of energy and assurance that would help him to make use of it. He had an intimate conviction — the proof of it was in the air, in the sensible facility of his footing at the "Sun and Moon" — that Eustache Poupin had taken on himself to disseminate the anecdote of his origin, of his mother's disaster; in consequence of which, as the victim of social infamy, of heinous laws, it was conceded to him that he had a larger account to settle even than most. He was *ab ovo* a revolutionist, and that balanced against his smart neckties, a certain suspicious security that was perceived in him as to the *h* (he had had from his earliest years a natural command of it) and the fact that he possessed the sort of hand on which there is always a premium — an accident somehow to be guarded against in a thorough-going system of equality. He never challenged Poupin on the subject, for he owed the Frenchman too much to reproach him with any officious step that was meant in kindness; and moreover his fellow-labourer at old Crook's had said to him, as if to anticipate such an impugnment of his discretion: "Remember, my child, that I'm incapable of drawing aside any veil that you may have preferred to drop over your lacerated personality. Your moral dignity will always be safe with me. But remember at the same time that among the disinherited there's a mystic language which dispenses with proofs — a freemasonry, a reciprocal divination: they understand each other at half a word." It was at half a word then in Bloomsbury that Hyacinth had been understood; but there was a certain delicacy in him that forbade him to push his advantage, to treat implications of sympathy, none the less definite for being awkward and obscure, as steps in the ladder of success. He had no wish to be a leader because his mother had murdered her lover and died in penal servitude: these circumstances recommended intentness, but they also imposed modesty. When the gathering at the "Sun and Moon" was at its best and its temper seemed really an earnest of what was the basis of all its calculations — that the people was only a sleeping lion, already breathing shorter and beginning to stretch its limbs and stiffen its claws — at these hours, some of them thrilling enough, Hyacinth waited for the voice that should allot him the particular part he was to play. His ambition was to play it with brilliancy, to offer an example — an example even that might survive him — of pure youthful, almost juvenile, consecration. He was conscious of no commission to give the promises, to assume the responsibilities, of a redeemer, and he had no envy of the man on whom this burden should rest. Muniment indeed might carry it, and it was the first article of his faith that to help him to carry it the better he himself was ready for any sacrifice. Then it was — on these nights of intenser vibration—that he waited for the sacred sign.

They came oftener this second winter, for the season was terribly hard; and as in that lower world one walked with one's ear nearer the ground the deep perpetual groan of London misery seemed to swell and swell and form the whole undertone of life. The filthy air reached the place in the damp coats of silent men and hung there till it was brewed to a nauseous warmth, and ugly serious faces squared themselves through it, and strong-smelling pipes contributed their element in a fierce dogged manner which appeared to say that it now had to stand for everything — for bread and meat and beer, for shoes and blankets and the poor things at the pawnbroker's and the smokeless chimney at home. Hyacinth's colleagues affected him as wiser then, as more richly permeated with intentions boding ill to the satisfied classes; and though the note of popularity was still most effectively struck by the man who could demand oftenest, unpractically, "What the hell am I to do with half a quid?" it was brought home to our hero on more than one occasion that revolution was ripe at last. This was especially the case on the evening I began by referring to, when Eustache Poupin squeezed in and announced, as if it were a great piece of news, that in the east of London that night there were forty thousand men out of work. He looked round the circle with his dilated foreign eye as he took his place: he seemed to address the company individually as well as collectively and to make each man responsible for hearing him. He owed his position at the "Sun and Moon" to the brilliancy with which he represented the political exile, the magnanimous immaculate citizen wrenched out of bed at dead of night, torn from his hearthstone, his loved ones and his profession and hurried across the frontier with only the coat on his back. Poupin had performed in this character now for many years, but had never lost the bloom of the outraged proscript, and the passionate pictures he had often drawn of the bitterness of exile were moving even to those who knew with what success he had set up his household gods in Lisson Grove. He was recognised as suffering everything for his opinions; and his hearers in Bloomsbury, who even in their most infuriated hours felt as Britons, appeared never to have made the subtle reflexion, though they

made many others, that there was a want of tact in
his calling on them to sympathise with him for being
one of themselves. He imposed himself by the eloquence of his assumption that if one were not in the
beautiful supreme France one was nowhere worth
speaking of, and ended by producing an impression
that that country had a quite supernatural charm.
Muniment had once said to Hyacinth that he was
sure Poupin would be very sorry to be enabled to go
home again (as he really might from one week to the
other, the Republic being so indulgent and the am-
nesty to the Communards constantly extended) for
over there he could n't be a refugee; and however this
might be he certainly flourished a good deal in London on the basis of this very fact that he so suffered
from it.

"Why do you tell us that as if it was so very striking? Don't we know it and have n't we known it
always? But you're right; we behave as if we knew
nothing at all," said Mr. Schinkel, the German cabinet-maker who had originally introduced Captain
Sholto to the "Sun and Moon." He had a long, un-
healthy, benevolent face and greasy hair, and constantly wore an untidy bandage round his neck, as if
for a local ailment. "You remind us — that's very
well; but we shall forget it in half an hour. We're not
serious."

"*Pardon, pardon;* for myself I don't admit that!"
Poupin replied, striking the table with his finger-tips
several times, very fast. "If I'm not serious I'm
nothing."

"Oh no, you're something," said the German,

smoking his monumental pipe with a contemplative air. "We're all something, but I'm not sure it's anything very useful."

"Well, things would be worse without us. I'd jolly rather be in here, in *this* kind of muck, than outside," remarked the fat man who understood dogs.

"Certainly, it's very pleasant, especially if you've your beer; but not so pleasant over there at the Docks, where fifty thousand people starve. It's a very unpleasant night," the cabinet-maker went on.

"How can it be worse?" Eustache Poupin asked while he looked at the German as to make him responsible for the fat man's reflexion. "It's so bad that the imagination recoils, refuses — !"

"Oh, we don't care for the imagination!" the fat man declared. "We want a compact body in marching order."

"What do you call a compact body?" the little grey-faced shoemaker demanded. "I dare say you don't mean your kind of body."

"Well, I know what I mean," said the fat man severely.

"That's a grand thing. Perhaps one of these days you'll tell us."

"You'll see it for yourself perhaps, before that day comes," the gentleman with the silver ring rejoined. "Perhaps when you do you'll remember."

"Well, you know, Schinkel says we don't," said the shoemaker, nodding at the cloud-compelling German.

"I don't care a bloody rap what no man says!" the dog-fancier exclaimed, gazing straight before him.

"They say it's a bad year — the blockheads in the

newspapers," Mr. Schinkel went on, addressing himself to the company at large. "They say that on purpose — to convey the impression that there are such things as good years. I ask the company, has any gentleman present ever happened to notice that article? The good year's yet to come: it might begin to-night, if we like: it all depends on our being able to be serious for a few hours. But that's too much to expect. Mr. Muniment's very serious; he looks as if he was waiting for the signal, but he does n't speak — he never speaks if I want particularly to hear him. He only deliberates very deeply—oh I'm sure. But it's almost as bad to think without speaking as to speak without thinking."

Hyacinth always admired the cool, easy way in which Muniment comported himself when the attention of the public was directed at him. These manifestations of curiosity or of hostility would have put him out immensely himself. When a lot of people, especially the kind of people collected at the "Sun and Moon," looked at him or listened to him all at once, he always blushed and stammered, feeling that if he could n't have a million of spectators (which would have been inspiring) he should prefer to have but two or three; there was something rather awful in twenty.

Muniment smiled an instant good-humouredly; then after a moment's hesitation, looking across at the German and the German only, as if his remark were worth noticing but it did n't matter if the others did n't understand the reply, he said simply: "Hoffendahl's in London."

347

"Hoffendahl? *Gott in Himmel!*" the cabinet-maker exclaimed, taking the pipe out of his mouth. And the two men exchanged a longish glance. Then Mr. Schinkel remarked: "That surprises me, *sehr*. Are you very sure?"

Muniment continued for a little to look at him. "If I keep quiet half an hour, with so many valuable suggestions flying all round me, you think I say too little. Then if I open my head to give out three words you appear to think I say too much."

"Ah no, on the contrary — I want you to say three more. If you tell me you've seen him I shall be perfectly satisfied."

"Upon my word I should hope so! Do you think he's the kind of bloke a fellow says he has seen?"

"Yes, when he has n't!" said Eustache Poupin, who had been listening. Every one was listening now.

"It depends on the fellow he says it to. Not even here?" the German asked.

"Oh here!" Paul Muniment exclaimed in a peculiar tone while he resumed his muffled whistle again.

"Take care — take care; you 'll make me think you have n't!" cried Poupin with his excited expression.

"That's just what I want," said Muniment.

"*Nun*, I understand," the cabinet-maker remarked, restoring his pipe to his lips after an interval almost as momentous as the stoppage of a steamer in mid-ocean.

"*'Ere*, 'ere?" repeated the small shoemaker indignantly. "I dare say it's as good as the place he came from. He might look in and see what he thinks of it."

"That's a place you might tell us a little about now," the fat man suggested as if he had been waiting for his chance.

Before the shoemaker had time to notice this challenge some one enquired with a hoarse petulance who the bloody blazes they were talking about; and Mr. Schinkel took upon himself to reply that they were talking about a man who had n't done what he had done by simply exchanging abstract ideas, however valuable, with his friends in a respectable pot-house.

"What the devil has he done then?" some one else demanded; and Muniment replied quietly that he had spent twelve years in a Prussian prison and was consequently still an object of a good deal of interest to the police.

"Well, if you call that very useful I must say I prefer a pot-house!" cried the shoemaker, appealing to all the company and looking, as it appeared to Hyacinth, particularly hideous.

"*Doch, doch*, it's useful," the German remarked philosophically among his yellow clouds.

"Do you mean to say you're not prepared for that yourself?" Muniment asked of the shoemaker.

"Prepared for that? I thought we were going to smash that sort of shop altogether; I thought that was the main part of the job."

"They'll smash best who've been inside," the German said; "unless they've only gone bad, like fish too long caught. But Hoffendahl's all there yet."

349

"Ah no; no smashing, no smashing of any valuable property," Muniment went on. "There are no wrong places — there are only wrong uses for them. We want to keep them standing and even to put up a few more; but the difference will be that we shall put the correct sort into them."

"I take your idea — that Griffin's one of the correct sort," the fat man remarked, indicating the shoemaker.

"I thought we was going to 'ave their 'eads — all that bloomin' lot!" Mr. Griffin protested; while Eustache Poupin began to enlighten the company as to the great Hoffendahl, one of the purest martyrs of their cause, a man who had been through everything — who had been scarred and branded, tortured, almost flayed, and had never given his would-be butchers the names they wanted. Was it possible they did n't remember that great combined assault, early in the sixties, which took place in four Continental cities at once and which in spite of every effort to smother it up — there had been editors and journalists transported even for hinting at it — had done more for the social question than anything before or since? "Through 'im being served in the manner you describe?" some one asked with plainness; to which Poupin replied that it was one of those failures that are more glorious than any success. Muniment said that the affair had been only a flash in the pan, but that the great value of it was this — that whereas some forty persons (and of both sexes) had been engaged in it, only one had been seized and had suffered. It had been Hoffendahl himself who was collared. Certainly he had suffered much, he had suffered for every one; but from that point of view — that of the economy of material — the thing had been a rare success.

"Do you know what I call the others? I call 'em bloody sneaks!" the fat man cried; and Eustache Poupin, turning to Muniment, expressed the hope that he did n't really approve of such a solution — did n't consider that an economy of heroism was an advantage to any cause. He himself esteemed Hoffendahl's attempt because it had shaken, more than anything — except of course the Commune — had shaken it since the French Revolution, the rotten fabric of the actual social order, and because that very fact of the impunity, the invisibility of the persons concerned in it had given the predatory classes, had given all Europe, a shudder that had not yet subsided; but for his part, he must regret that some of the associates of the devoted victim had not come forward and insisted on sharing with him his tortures and his captivity.

"*Ç'aurait été d'un bel exemple!*" said the Frenchman with an impressive moderation of statement which made even those who could n't understand him see he was saying something fine; while the cabinet-maker observed that in Hoffendahl's place any of them would have stood out just the same. He did n't care if they set it down to self-love (Mr. Schinkel called it "loaf") but he might say that he himself would have done so if he had been trusted and had been bagged.

"I want to have it all drawn up clear first; then I'll

go in," said the fat man, who seemed to think it was expected of him to be reassuring.

"Well, who the dickens is to draw it up, eh? That's what we happen to be talking about," returned his antagonist the shoemaker.

"A fine example, old man? Is that your idea of a fine example?" Muniment, with his amused face, asked of Poupin. "A fine example of asininity! Are there capable people, in such plenty, about the place?"

"Capable of greatness of soul, I grant you not."

"Your greatness of soul is usually greatness of blundering. A man's foremost duty is not to get collared. If you want to show you're capable, that's the way."

At this Hyacinth suddenly felt himself moved to speak. "But some one must be caught always, must he not? Has n't some one always been?"

"Oh, I dare say you'll be if you like it!" Muniment replied without looking at him. "If they succeed in potting you, do as Hoffendahl did, and do it as a matter of course; but if they don't, make it your supreme duty, make it your religion, to lie close and keep yourself for another go. The world's full of unclean beasts whom I shall be glad to see shovelled away by the thousand; but when it's a question of honest men and men of courage I protest against the idea that two should be sacrificed where one will serve."

"*Trop d'arithmétique — trop d'arithmétique!* — That's fearfully English!" Poupin cried.

"No doubt, no doubt; what else should it be? You

shall never share my fate if I have a fate and I can prevent it!" Muniment laughed.

Poupin stared at him and his coarse mirth, as if he thought the English frivolous as well as calculating; then he rejoined: "If I suffer I trust it may be for suffering humanity, but I trust it may also be for France."

"Oh, I hope you ain't going to suffer any more for France," said Mr. Griffin. "Has n't it done that insatiable old country of yours some good by this time, all you 've had to put up with ?"

"Well, I want to know what Hoffendahl has come over for; it 's very kind of him, I 'm sure. What 's he going to do for *us* ? — that 's what *I* want to know," brought out in a loud argumentative tone a personage at the end of the table most distant from Muniment's place. His name was Delancey and he gave himself out as holding a position in a manufactory of soda-water; but Hyacinth had a secret belief that he was really a hairdresser — a belief connected with a high lustrous curl or crest which he wore on the summit of his large head, as well as with the manner in which he thrust over his ear, as if it were a barber's comb, the pencil addressed to his careful note-taking on the discussions conducted at the "Sun and Moon." His opinions were distinct and frequently expressed; he had a watery (Muniment had once called it a soda-watery) eye and a personal aversion to a lord. He desired to change everything except religion, of which he approved.

Muniment answered that he was unable to say as yet what the German revolutionist had come to England for, but that he hoped to be able to give some information on the matter the next time they should meet. It was very certain Hoffendahl had n't come for nothing, and he would undertake to declare that they would all feel within a short time that he had given a lift to the cause they had at heart. He had had a great experience, which they might very well find it useful to appeal to. If there was a way for them then and there he would be sure to know the way. "I quite agree with the majority of you — as I take it to be," Muniment went on in his fresh, cheerful, reasonable manner — "I quite agree with you that the time has come to settle upon it and to follow it. I quite agree with you that the actual state of things is" — he paused a moment and then went on in the same pleasant tone — "is infamous and hellish."

These remarks were received with a differing demonstration: some of the company declaring that if the Dutchman cared to come round and smoke a pipe they 'd be glad to see him — perhaps he 'd show where the thumbscrews had been put on; others being strongly of the opinion that they did n't want any more advice — they had already had advice enough to turn a donkey's stomach. What they wanted was to put forth their might without any more palaver; to do for something or for some one; to go out somewhere and smash something on the spot — why not? — smash it that very night. While they sat still and talked there were about half a million of people in London that did n't know where the hell the morrow's meal was to come from; what they wanted to

354

do, unless they were just a collection of pettifogging old women, was to show them where to get it, to take it to them with heaped-up hands. Hyacinth listened, with a divided attention, to interlaced iterations, while the talk blew hot and cold; there was a genuine emotion, a quick pulse of high fever, to-night in the rear of the "Sun and Moon," and he felt the contagion of excited purpose. But he was following a train of his own; he was wondering what Muniment had in reserve (for certainly Paul but played with the company) and his imagination, quickened by the sense of impending relations with the heroic Hoffendahl and the discussion as to the alternative duty of escaping or of facing one's fate, had launched itself into possible perils — into the idea of how he might in a given case settle for himself that question of paying for the lot. The loud, contradictory, vain, unpractical babble went on about him, but he was definitely conscious only that the project of breaking into the bakers' shops was well before the assembly and was receiving a vigorous treatment, and that there was likewise a good deal of reference to the butchers and grocers and even to the fishmongers. He was in a state of inward exaltation, possessed by an intense desire to stand face to face with the sublime Hoffendahl, to hear his voice and touch his mutilated hand. He was ready for anything: he knew he was himself safe to breakfast and dine, if poorly still sufficiently, and that his colleagues were perhaps even more crude and clumsy than usual; but a breath of popular passion had warmed his cheek and his heart, and he seemed to see, immensely magnified, the monstrosity of the great ulcers and sores of London — the sick, eternal misery crying out the darkness in vain, confronted with granaries and treasure-houses and places of delight where shameless satiety kept guard. In such a mood as this he felt there was no need to consider, to reason: the facts themselves were as imperative as the cry of the drowning, since while pedantry gained time did n't starvation and anguish gain it too ? He knew Muniment disapproved of delay, that he held the day had come for a forcible rectification of horrible inequalities. In the last conversation they had had together his judicious friend had given him a more definite warrant than ever before for numbering him in the party of immediate action, though indeed he remarked on this occasion, once more, that that particular formula the little bookbinder appeared to have taken such a fancy to was mere gibberish. He hated this sort of pretentious label; it was fit only for politicians and amateurs. None the less he had been as plain as possible on the point that their game must be now to frighten society, and frighten it effectually; to make it believe that the swindled classes were at last fairly in league — had really grasped the idea that, closely combined, they would be irresistible. They were not in league and they had n't in their totality grasped any idea at all — Muniment was not slow to make that equally plain. All the same society was scareable, and every great scare was a gain for the people. If Hyacinth had needed warrant to-night for a faith transcending logic he would have found it in his recall of this quiet profession; but his friend's words came back to him mainly to make him wonder what that friend had in his head just now. He took no part in any vociferation; he had called Schinkel to come round and sit beside him, and the two appeared to confer together in honest ease while the brown atmosphere grew denser, the passing to and fro of firebrands more lively and the flush of faces more portentous. What Hyacinth would have liked to know most of all was why Muniment had not mentioned to him first that Hoffendahl was in London and that he had seen him; for he *had* seen him, though he had dodged Schinkel's question — of that Hyacinth instantly felt sure. He would ask for more information later; and meanwhile he wished, without resentment, but with a patient conscious ache, that Muniment would treat him with a little more confidence. If there were a secret in regard to Hoffendahl — and there evidently was: Muniment, quite rightly, though he had dropped the announcement of his arrival for a certain effect, had no notion of sharing the rest of what he knew with that raw roomful — if there were something to be silent and devoted about Hyacinth ardently hoped that to him in particular would a chance be given to show how he could practise this superiority. He felt hot and nervous; he got up suddenly and, through the dark tortuous greasy passage communicating with the outer world, went forth into the street. The air was foul and sleety but refreshed him, and he stood in front of the public-house and smoked another pipe. Bedraggled figures passed in and out and a damp tattered wretched man with a spongy purple face, who had been thrust suddenly across the threshold, stood and whimpered in the brutal blaze of the row of lamps. The puddles glittered roundabout and the silent vista of the street, bordered with low black houses, stretched away in the wintry drizzle to right and left, losing itself in the huge tragic city where unmeasured misery lurked beneath the dirty night, ominously, monstrously still, only howling, for its pain, in the heated human cockpit behind him. Ah what could he do ? What opportunity would rise ? The blundering divided counsels he had been listening to but made the helplessness of every one concerned more abject. If he had a definite wish while he stood there it was that that exalted deluded company should pour itself forth with Muniment at its head and surge through the sleeping world and gather the myriad miserable out of their slums and burrows, should roll into the selfish squares and lift a tremendous hungry voice and awaken the gorged indifferent to a terror that would bring them down. He lingered a quarter of an hour, but this grand treat gave no sign of coming off, and he finally returned to the noisy club-room in a state of tormented wonder as to what better idea than this very bad one (which seemed to our young man to have at the least the merit that it *was* an idea) Muniment could be revolving in that too-comprehensive brain of his.

As he re-entered the place he saw the meeting was breaking up in disorder, or at all events in confusion, and that certainly no organised attempt at the rescue of any number of victims would take place that night. All the men were on their feet and were turning away amid a shuffle of benches and chairs, a hunch of shabby shoulders, a frugal abatement of flaring gas

358

and a varied vivacity of disgust and resignation. The moment after Hyacinth came in Mr. Delancey, the supposititious hairdresser, jumped upon a chair at the far end of the room and shrieked out an accusation which made every one stop and stare at him.

"Well, I want you all to know what strikes me before we part company. There is n't a man in the blessed lot of you that is n't afraid of his bloody skin — afraid, afraid, afraid! I'll go anywhere with any one, but there is n't another, by G——, by what I can make out! There is n't a mother's son of you that'll risk his precious bones!"

This little oration affected Hyacinth like a quick blow in the face: it seemed to leap at him personally, as if a three-legged stool or some hideous hob-nailed boot had been shied at him. The room surged round, heaving up and down, while he was conscious of a loud explosion of laughter and scorn, of cries of "Order, order!" of some clear word of Muniment's, "I say, Delancey, just step down;" of Eustache Poupin shouting out "*Vous insultez le peuple — vous insultez le peuple!*" of other retorts not remarkable for refinement. The next moment he found he had himself sprung up on a chair opposite the barber and that at the sight of so prompt a display the commotion had suddenly turned to almost amused suspense. It was the first time he had asked the ear of the company, which was given on the spot. He was sure he looked very white — it was even possible they could see him tremble. He could only hope this did n't make him ridiculous when he said: "I don't think it's right of him to say that. There are others besides him. At all events I want to speak for myself: it may do some good; I can't help it. I'm not afraid; I'm very sure I'm not. I'm ready to do anything that will do any good; anything, anything — I don't care a damned rap. In such a cause I should like the idea of danger. I don't consider my bones precious in the least, compared with some other things. If one's sure one is n't afraid, and one's accused, why should n't one say so?"

It appeared to him he was talking a long time and when it was over he scarcely knew what happened. He felt himself in a moment down almost under the feet of the other men; stamped upon with intentions of applause, of familiarity; laughed over and jeered over, hustled and poked in the ribs. He felt himself also pressed to the bosom of Eustache Poupin, who apparently was sobbing, while he heard some one say "Did ye hear the little bloody beggar, as bold as a lion?" A trial of personal prowess between him and Mr. Delancey was proposed, but somehow it did n't take place, and at the end of five minutes the club-room had emptied itself, yet clearly not to be reconstituted outside in a revolutionary procession. Paul Muniment had taken hold of him and said "I'll trouble you to stay, you small desperado: I'll be blowed if I ever expected to see *you* on the stump!" Muniment remained and M. Poupin and Mr. Schinkel lingered, donning overcoats, beneath a dim surviving gasburner in the unventilated medium in which at each renewed gathering the Bloomsbury club seemed to recognise itself.

"Upon my life I believe you're game," said Muniment, looking down at him with a serious face.

"Of course you think it's swagger, 'self-loaf' as Schinkel says. But it is n't." Then Hyacinth asked: "In God's name why don't we do something?"

"Ah my child, to whom do you say it?" Eustache Poupin exclaimed, folding his arms despairingly.

"Who do you mean by 'we'?" said Muniment.

"All the lot of us. There are plenty of them ready."

"Ready for what? There's nothing to be done here."

Hyacinth stared. "Then why the deuce do you come?"

"I dare say I shan't come much more. It's a place in which you've always seen too much."

"I wonder if I've seen too much in you," Hyacinth risked, gazing at his friend.

"Don't say that — he's going to introduce us to Hoffendahl!" Schinkel exclaimed, putting away his pipe in a receptacle almost as large as a fiddle-case.

"Should you like to see the right man, Robinson, that is the real thing?" Muniment asked with the same rare grave sound.

"The real thing?" Hyacinth looked from one of his companions to the other.

"You've never seen it yet — though you think you have."

"And why have n't you shown it me before?"

"Because I had never seen you on the stump." This was more lightly said.

"Bother the stump! I was trusting you."

"Exactly so. That gave me time."

"Don't come unless your mind's made up, *mon petit*," said Poupin.

"Are you going now — and to see Hoffendahl? Is *he* the right man?" Hyacinth cried.

"Don't shout it all over the place. He wants a perfect little gentleman, and if you're not one — !" Muniment went on.

"Is it true? Are we all going?" Hyacinth eagerly went on.

"Yes, these two are in it. They're not very wise, but they're decent," said Muniment, looking at Poupin and Schinkel.

"Are *you* the real thing, Muniment?" asked Hyacinth, catching this look.

Muniment dropped his eyes on him. "Yes, you're the lamb of sacrifice he wants. It's at the other end of London. We must have a growler."

"Be calm, my child; *me voici !*" And Poupin led their young friend out.

They all walked away from the "Sun and Moon," and it was not for some five minutes that they encountered the four-wheeled cab which so deepened and dignified their purpose. After they were seated in it Hyacinth learned that the "right man" was in London but for three days, was liable to hurry away on the morrow, and was accustomed to receive visits at all kinds of queer hours. It was getting to be midnight; the drive seemed interminable to Hyacinth's impatience and curiosity. He sat next Muniment, who passed a strong arm round him, holding him all the way as if for a tacit sign of indebtedness. This gave Hyacinth pleasure till he began to wonder if it might n't represent also the instinct to make sure of him as against possible weak afterthoughts. They all ended by sitting silent as the cab jogged along murky miles, and by the time it stopped our young man had wholly lost, in the drizzling gloom, a sense of their whereabouts.

END OF VOLUME I